MW01503946

Things Left Unsaid

Discreet Special Edition

Seven Cs: ONE

G. A. Mazurke

Serena Akeroyd

Photograph: Regina Wamba

Cover Design: Chelsea Chira

Editing: Anne-Geneviève Ducharme-Audran

Proofreading: Norma's Nook

Sensitivity Reader: Chloe Stubbings

To those who leave us behind...

FOREWORD

Hey lovelies,
> Welcome to my small-town era!
> Or... more importantly...

WELCOME TO PIGEON CREEK, EST. 1813, POP. 2402

You may have visited this small town in Cole Korhonen's book—Waiting Game. You do not need to read that book to enjoy his older brother's story.

For a full list of triggers, click HERE. (Page 615)

While I'm a Brit, this has been thoroughly vetted by the resident Canadian on Team Gemma: Anne Geneviève Ducharme-Audran. So, native Saskatchewanians, I hope I've done you proud!

* * *

A few terms for non-Canadians:

Métis - People of mixed European and Indigenous ancestry. One of the three recognized Aboriginal peoples in Canada.

RCMP - Royal Canadian Mounted Police

CATSA - Canadian Air Transport Security Authority

'Z' - Be aware that the letter 'Z' is, in Canadian English, pronounced 'zed' NOT 'zee.'

RCAF - Royal Canadian Air Force

Billet families - If you don't know what that is, it's where a kid from Québec, for example, can play for a team in Winnipeg because a billet family brings him into the fold and raises him like he's one of theirs. They're trusted families and members of the hockey community and these boys can grow up in safe environments while fulfilling their goals.

* * *

The RCMP's jurisdiction covers the entirety of Canada and, in smaller towns, they have satellite detachments that cover all districts.

In 2026, Saskatchewan has announced it will introduce a Marshal Service. I'm playing fast and loose with this timeline and am starting the service in the present day of the storyline.

Zee has type 1 diabetes and during my research, I've come to believe that she's a rockstar. As are all of you guys who live your lives by the 'dots.' Thank you to Chloe Stubbings for being my sensitivity reader.

Please be aware that I'm using US spelling, however, you will see plenty of 'mums' and not 'moms' as Colton's mother is a Brit. :)

When *Things Left Unsaid* reaches 500 reviews, I'll be dropping a bonus scene in my Tea & Spoilers Room so come join me there!

www.facebook.com/groups/SerenaAkeroydsTeaAndSpoilersRoom

Much love,

Gemma

PLAYLIST

If you'd like to hear a curated soundtrack, with songs that are featured in the book, as well as songs that inspired it, then here's the link:

https://open.spotify.com/playlist/
5QdAYAzdsDc5M7oltlgRGd?si=1ab48178d70c461f&pt=
430b543f0667764645f2881b2ea43133

THINGS LEFT UNSAID *Cast*

SUSANNE "ZEE" McALLISTER

JULIETTE McALLISTER
(great-niece)

CALDER
(triplet)　　CARSON
(triplet)　　COLBY
(triplet)

WALKER
(brother DKIA)

CHRISTY "GEE" MACFARLANE
(bestie)

PARKER HENSHAW
(bestie)

RACHEL LAKER
(boss)

COLTON "COLT" KORHONEN

CLYDE
(father)

LINDSAY
(mom)

GALLAN
(brother)　　CODY
(brother)　　COLE
(brother)

MIA
(Cole's fiancée)

THEO FROBISHER
(best friend)

IDA ABELMAN
(caretaker)

Chapter 1
Zee

Pompeii MMXXLLL - Bastille, Hans Zimmer

PRESENT DAY

"I swear you're a masochist, Susanne McAllister."

My hand, seizing from pushing royal icing through a #1 tip, tightens on the piping bag. "Firstly, don't call me Susanne. You know that I hate my name. Secondly, I think I'd notice if I were into whips and chains, Tee."

"You're soooooooo funny."

"I know." I shoot my BFF a glib smile. "It's all in the wrist."

"No, that's the premature arthritis you're going to give yourself by doing this sugar-cookie shit. I mean, seriously, Zee, it's not like you even eat the cookies afterward!" she drawls, her focus on the letter in her hand so she bumps into me.

Because our apartment is tiny, she's like a foot away from me at all times while I work.

I'm used to it now, but boy, was there a learning curve when we first traded space-rich Pigeon Creek for space-poor New York City. My piping hand doesn't even falter after our collision.

"Ohhh, so leaving the cookies for you is what makes me a

7

masochist and not the winner of 'the best friend in the world' title?"

Technically, I can eat the cookies with my type 1 diabetes, but I tend not to.

Maintaining a low-carb diet makes for an easier life and I'm all about easy.

Plus, after dealing with this shit since I was four, ease is the only thing stopping me from losing my mind.

"You're definitely the best friend in the universe but I'm not privy to what goes on between you and your bedroom walls. Since, ya know, you won't tell me anything about your love life."

"I don't tell Parker either if that makes you feel any better."

Parker Henshaw's our mutual best friend. We have a weird setup—Christy 'Tee' MacFarlane and I endured the hell of school together, traversed the continent as a daring duo, stuck fast to one another through college stresses, breakups, and career lows—but we know Parker through me as I met her at work.

Technically, I'm the cream filling in our passion flakie, but we're all super close.

"How is Parker?"

I stick out my tongue as I pipe fronds onto my palm tree-shaped cookie. "You haven't spoken to her?"

"Not recently." She shrugs at my shocked expression. "She's still mad at me."

"Why you don't leave her alone is beyond me. Let her be who she wants to be—"

"She's agoraphobic! She needs help."

"She doesn't. She's perfectly fine in her safe spaces."

"She's missing out on hockey games."

"It's not like she even lives in New Jersey anymore, babe. You couldn't attend together anyway."

"Sweet Lips." She harrumphs. "It's not right for a man to be called that. It means something."

She's been pissed at Sweet Lips since he swept Parker off her feet, onto his hog, and took her to Coshocton, OH.

"Just because you're not getting any sugar, there's no need to be bitter. He makes her happy."

"I don't need sugar. I get plenty in my diet." She wafts her letter to her pen pal. "And Butch Cassidy might be deployed only God knows where, but he's with me in spirit and that's like a direct shot of glucose to the heart."

"Sounds deadly."

"He *is* a soldier."

"Thought he was a pilot."

"He is. Pilots are soldiers too."

"They're technically pilots first."

"*Whatever*. Sweet Lips isn't good enough for Parker. That 'sweetness' has nothing to do with candy and everything to do with his oral skills—"

"You don't know that."

"—oral skills he practiced on God knows how many women. I've seen S*ons of Anarchy*—"

"We watched it. Together."

"No one is good enough for you or her. It's a fact. Specifically not some Sam Crow wannabe."

"The Sinners make Sam Crow bikers look like child's play. You should see the stuff I deal with as part of their defense team." I make a motion of zipping my mouth shut when she peers at me with interest. "Anyway, whether he is or isn't good enough for her, he had to get past Rachel who, you can't deny, is utterly terrifying. She'd kill Sweet Lips if he hurt Parker. And Rex would sanction the kill."

Rex is my boss's husband as well as the leader of the New Jersey chapter of the Satan's Sinners' MC—an outlaw band of misfits.

"Murder one... *so* reassuring."

"As if she'd let herself be caught. You know she's one of the country's best criminal lawyers," I reason. "I'm almost offended on her behalf."

Rachel Laker is Lady Justice's version of a Valkyrie. Or do I mean a Fury?

Either way, I'm both proud of being her employee and—

"You're scared of her."

Yes. Yes, I am.

"Wouldn't you be? She's terrifying in a Machiavellian way."

"Parker loves her."

"Parker needs a therapist. As we've already established with the whole 'never leaving the house' thing."

"I wanted her to come to the All-Star game with me," she whines. "Was that so much to ask?"

"For an agoraphobic, *yes*. Duh. Talk about shoving her into the deep end without a life raft. Not only would she have had to come up from Ohio to watch it, but then there was the whole 'being in a crowd with twenty thousand people' disaster waiting to happen." I wiggle my hand that's cramping from working on this sugar cookie for the past twenty minutes. "Just leave her alone."

"She loves the New York Stars. Do you know how expensive those tickets were? *All-Star* tickets. On *home* turf. With Liam *freaking* Donnghal as one of the team captains!" With true Italian flair, her hands waft wide and free. "It was a travesty! Even more of a travesty that you fell asleep halfway through the game."

I grace her with an eye roll. "You should have taken your brother. Anthony loves hockey too. Knowing him, he'd have flown in for the occasion."

"Where'd be the fun in suffering through a game with him? I had a better time with you snoring next to me."

As thoroughly outraged as she'd been in February, she graces me with a sniff and then snags an unfrosted cookie from my pile. She proceeds to take a bite before I can slap her fingers.

Smirking, Tee wiggles away as I holler, "I was doing six!"

"Now you're doing five. Your hand will thank me later."

On the brink of cussing her out, though she's technically correct, my cell phone rings, announcing, "*Grand-mère*," to the apartment.

She freezes mid-bite. "The she-devil's summoning you."

Tension crawls along my shoulders. "She's not a she-devil."

The last thing I need is to manifest that into being.

10

"I'm the *sort of* Catholic. I'd know. Aren't you going to answer it?"

Both our gazes are locked on the damn thing as if it's cursed.

"This'll be the third call I've accidentally missed."

Tee hisses. "You don't piss off a demon!"

"She isn't a demon! Don't be mean to Satan's minions. You'll offend them and they'll terrorize us too." When she elbows me, I grouse, "You know I hate talking to her. She'll either anger me, upset me, *or,* worse still, guilt-trip me into coming home.

"My blood sugar has been all over the place the whole day —do I look like I'm in the mood to be agitated?"

Tee pulls a face. "I can't blame you. There's being agitated and then there's being riled up by *her.* But she's summoned you three times so you have to make the ultimate sacrifice and answer the damn phone before Bloody Mary makes an appearance and messes with your cookies."

"Gee, thanks," I snipe, but I keep my gaze locked on the cell screen until it stops flashing.

When the call disconnects, I release a soft, relieved breath, though I know I'm compounding my problems.

"What do you think she wants?" Tee whispers like *Grand-mère* could overhear from Pigeon Creek, Saskatchewan.

"I don't kn—"

The phone rings again.

Tee and I share a look.

"You're going to have to answer."

I wipe my sweaty forehead with the back of my hand but make no move to pick it up. "Yeah."

"She'll be getting angrier and angrier."

"I know."

"So, answer her!"

"I don't want to!"

"You have to!"

"I don't! I'm a grown woman!"

"A grown woman who's terrified of her grandmother!"

"Like you're not terrified of her too!"

"Well, babe, she's a piece of work. How could I not be when I'm as smart as I am?"

There's no denying that.

With another grimace, I snatch up my cell phone but I don't hit 'connect.'

Instead, I toy with the case. "It can't be that bad, can it?"

"I don't know what kind of business goes on in hell, but nothing's as bad as we imagine."

"Helpful, Tee. What would I do without your moral support?"

"I live to serve. Oh, wait, that's her. She probably gets a real kick out of sucking off Satan in her spare time." At my glare, she mumbles, "Okay, she might not be a demon but she's surely one of his lieutenants."

Wishing I could argue in *Grand-mère*'s defense when I know she'd terrify a Satan's Sinner, I swallow, close my eyes, gulp, then hit the 'connect' button.

"About damn time!"

That's *Grand-mère's* greeting.

Ninety-two going on forty-two, my *grand-mère* has been terrorizing the small town of Pigeon Creek in Saskatchewan for each and every one of her years. The only break the gen pop got was after her folks shipped her off to a boarding school in Switzerland when the family had money.

Even as a baby, she was worthy of doomsday stories—I have that on good authority from the priest who baptized her before he died.

No, she didn't have anything to do with his death.

Although...

Juliette McAllister *is* more petrifying than a sawed-off shotgun and has a worse bite than a rabid dog.

In fact, gimme the rabid dog bite over this phone conversation.

"Sorry, *Grand-mère*, did I miss your call?" I greet, keeping my voice nice and light.

"You know you did," she growls, forcing a shiver out of Tee and making her sign the cross on her chest.

12

Shoving her aside, I press my finger to my lips to hush her. "I've been very busy at work."

"If you say so." I can tell she doesn't believe me.

In her opinion, the only thing worse than a lawyer is a murderer...

Go figure.

And being a paralegal in her eyes is worse still because I'm not good enough to be a lawyer, ergo I might as well be a murderer.

Double go figure.

"Is everything okay? Are the triplets alright?"

She harrumphs. "You'd know if you ever visited the Bar 9."

"It's not so easy to get home, *Grand-mère*. You know how expensive the flights are. It's not as if we're the Korhonens and have a helicopter."

"That fool boy of theirs, the youngest, broke that damn toy. They got themselves a plane."

I can hear the jealousy in her voice—it's practically oozing from every word she utters.

"Maybe you can hitch a ride in that plane," Tee whispers in my ear, making me jolt in surprise at her proximity.

Then, I get why—she's stress-eating another damn cookie.

I flip her the bird but, to my grandmother, murmur, "Is there a reason you phoned, *Grand-mère*? I have to take a work call in five minutes."

"Liar, liar," Tee sings.

"Is someone there?" *Grand-mère* demands.

"Just Christy."

"Bah. That hussy. I'll never understand why you're friends with her."

With a smirk at Tee, I answer, "I don't know why either."

Grand-mère hums in approval. "Whether or not you can afford the trip home because of work, Susanne, I need you up here."

"Do you have the money to spare, *Grand-mère*?" That's usually the best way of getting out of this situation.

As terrifying as she is, there's little she can do long-distance with how miserly our bank accounts tend to run.

God help me if we ever strike oil.

It'd be just my luck if we did.

"I do," she retorts, tone smug. "I'll wire it over. I'll expect you at the ranch before the end of the week."

I gape at Tee, whose eyes are as wide as mine.

Horrified, I sputter, "B-But I-I need more notice than that, *Grand-mère*!"

"You never take a break as far as I know, Susanne, so that shark of a boss of yours can cut you some slack while you visit your dying grandmother."

"You're dying?! Is that why you need me to come home?" I cry, aghast.

Yet again, Tee marks the sign of the cross on her chest. "If she's finally dying, there *is* a god."

Grand-mère, on the other hand, barks out a laugh. "I'll die when I'm good and ready, Susanne, and that won't be for another decade at least."

Tee and I gulp.

My grandmother's the only person in the world whom Death is probably scared of.

Unaware of our thoughts, *Grand-mère* intones, "No, you tell that Rachel woman I'm ill and she'll spare you."

"I'll... see what I can do."

"You'll do more than 'see,' child. Safe travels."

I'm given no chance to counter that warning—there's dead air in my ear.

Tee passes me a can of soda. "I need to call my *nonna* and thank her for not being... that."

Because her offering means she checked my blood sugar on the app we use to monitor my level, I pull the tab and take a big gulp of Coke. "Is it too late to be adopted?"

"Much too late. Do you think Rachel could fabricate a reason to keep you in the city?"

"No. You know that I do most of my work from home anyway and only commute twice a month. I use work as an excuse not to go north." Tee checks the weather app on her phone and I glance at the screen. "The triplets said it's been crazy warm recently."

"I dunno. Looks like refrigerator temperatures to me. New York winters are tepid by comparison—"

"Good thing it's spring then," I drawl.

She shivers. "I don't miss Pigeon Creek's version of winter or spring."

"Me either." Collecting my piping bag, I restart my earlier task—making tiny coconuts and using a scribe to replicate the husks—because I need the stress relief. "I wonder what's going on."

"Could it be the boys?"

"Maybe."

My triplet brothers are nightmares on wheels who only obey my grandmother.

The funny thing is, of course, I used to be like them.

Until I wasn't.

Until that goddamn night when everything changed.

My personality included.

Shuddering at the memory, I jolt when Tee places a hand on my shoulder. "It won't be too horrific, Zee. It's been so long since you were home that you're building it up in your head. They'll have let the whole arson thing drop by now."

'They' being the folks of Pigeon Creek.

Anxiety coalesces into a big lump that clogs my throat.

There's no way I'll be able to stay clueless until this weekend.

Plunking the piping bag on the counter, I snag my phone and type out:

> Me: You guys know why Grand-mère wants me to come home?

> Calder: Nope

> Colby: When are you coming?

> Me: This weekend

> Carson: Huh. Weird that it lines up with us going to Saskatoon for an open-house event.

> **Me:** At the university?

Carson: Yup

Colby: Sucks we won't see you

Carson: If you'd come down last weekend, you'd have seen us win the butter tart eating contest.

> **Me:** So proud.

Carson: As you should be ;)

Calder: Let us know what she wants?

> **Me:** Will do

I tip the phone at Tee. "They're as clueless as we are."

Because I can't catch a break today, my cell buzzes. Then, spying Parker's picture illuminate the screen, I whisper, "Do you think we should start calling Parker 'Pee?'"

"PeeTeeZee. Sounds like an anti-anxiety medication."

"I could use some of that."

"Parker likes her name. It's us who don't."

Hence the abbreviations.

"Speak of the devil," Tee taunts when she connects the call.

"I'm still not talking to you," is our mutual BFF's grumble.

"Sounds like it to me."

I rub my temple. "Can we not bicker, children, please? I already have a headache."

Checking my blood sugar, I sigh when I see my level has reverted to normal. Because she's nearer the cupboard where I keep my snacks, I ask, "Hand me a granola bar?"

"Zee's *grand-mère* called," Tee informs Parker as she tosses one to me.

"What does the old witch want?" Parker's fingers clack as she types in the background. "Blood? Eye of newt? A bible bound in human skin?"

"Don't put that into the universe, please," I grouse after taking a big bite of my granola bar and continuing with my task.

16

"She wants Zee to come home."

"Why?"

Grunting when my coconut turns into a brown banana after applying too much pressure to the piping bag, I let Tee explain the situation.

"She didn't say. Just expects her there by the end of the week."

Parker whistles. "I could ask Rachel to construct an emergency?"

Anxiously, I grab the bag of powdered sugar. Scooping a couple teaspoons into a clean bowl, I tip milk and dye in next. As I stir the concoction so I can work on the sand surrounding the palm tree, I mumble, "You don't need to do that. Rachel has plenty going on without my drama."

"Maybe you'll luck out and some serial killer will need a lawyer?" Tee asks, tone hopeful.

Parker hoots. "You're sick in the head, Tee, I swear to God."

"That's why you love me. Isn't it, Parker? Huh? Huh?"

"I do when you don't try to drag me out of my house. Where I'm comfortable. Where I can wear pajama pants all day. Where I don't have to see people."

Tee sniffs but my eyes widen in horror when my screen lights up again, this time with a notification from my bank, informing me that I've been wired enough cash to buy *business class* tickets, never mind economy for the flights home.

Tee whistles. "That's a lot of zeroes."

"What is?" Parker, ever nosy, demands.

"Zee's grandma wired her over some cash to buy plane tickets." She holds out her hand to high-five me. "Hey, we could fly home together! It's been ages since we've been back."

For a reason.

My brow puckers in confusion until she drops her hand. "Where did she get all this from? She was asking me for help with a mortgage payment two months ago. No way she'd have swallowed her pride if she had this kind of cash on hand."

"Maybe the ranch had a better season than expected?"

"The ranch never has a good season anymore, Tee," I dismiss.

"What else could it be? It's not as if you have alternative income streams."

"No, we don't." My stirring reaches an agitated fever pitch.

"You've never told me why you both hate going home," Parker inserts, fingers still clacking against her keyboard.

"It's cold, Parker," Tee says with a mock shiver. "Real cold. Have you ever heard of seasonal affected disorder? You think it's bad in New York, but it's nothing compared to Pigeon Creek."

"You make it sound like you were raised in the Arctic Circle," Parker chides.

"Might as well have been. I hate the cold."

"You should have moved to Florida, then."

"Or Aruba," Tee says dreamily.

"Juilliard is in neither of those places," I point out.

Tee's scholarship was what brought her and, as a result, *me* to the States in the first place. Tee's a virtuoso. A walking oboe-wielding genius.

I'm not. I'm me.

"One day, when I have a record deal, Aruba's where I'll live," is my sister from another mister's vow.

"Okay, so Tee hates the cold but what about you, Zee? Why do you hate going home?"

I let loose a deep sigh. "Nothing's been the same since I got accused of being an arsonist and a serial killer."

For a second, silence greets my words.

Then, Parker starts chuckling.

It morphs into outright laughter.

Evolves into wheezing.

Turns into thigh-slapping, choking barks of amusement that are somehow louder than ever over the airwaves.

"Parker!" Tee reprimands as she pats me on the shoulder, but it's cold comfort.

"You're not being serious. *You*?! A-A-A serial k-killer?"

"Why would I lie about that?"

"Ms. 'Goody Two-Shoes' Zee?" She breaks down into more laughter.

18

"If you don't stop, I'm going to drive to Coshocton so I can slap some sense into you!"

"So, you're a mass murderer, Ms. 'Jaywalking should be a capital offense.' Ms. 'It's illegal to return a library book late.'" She hoots. "You're so good, it's painful, Zee. How are *you* supposed to be a psychopath? I'm not sure how you work as a paralegal for an attorney who makes it her mission to get criminals off on legal loopholes! *Zee*, ha."

"Well, the good folks of Pigeon Creek don't have as high an opinion of me as you do," I snipe, tone bitter with the pain that lingers from their accusations.

It's always stung that the people who've known me my whole life could think I was capable of something so heinous.

That one night has shaped me in ways I can't begin to unwrap. Being a Ms. Goody Two-Shoes is one example of cause and effect. That whole nightmare taught me that good people *can* go to jail unless someone speaks out for them... which is why I became a paralegal. It's also why I work for someone who screws with the law for shits and giggles.

"She can't be for real, Tee?"

My best friend of twenty-four years clears her throat. "She's not lying, Parker. The whole thing's pretty nuts. She'd lost her parents and then her brother was announced PKIA[1]. The fire was classed as her having 'an episode.'"

"You okay, honey?" Tee asks.

"Been better."

Parker's silence is all the more shocking for her amusement of before. "But this is *Zee*."

"She was only sixteen." Tee hugs me harder. "And the stables that burned down were like... You know the Ewings?"

"From *Dallas*?"

"Yeah. The Ewings hated the Barnes, right?"

"Uh-huh."

"Except, in this instance, the Barnes lost their fortune after the war and the Ewings have gazillions. The Pigeon Creek Ewings are the Korhonens and Zee's a Barnes.

"Zee was found... People spotted her hanging around outside so they thought she set it. But she didn't."

"Of course not. This is Zee we're talking about."

"I was different then. Grieving," I croak, staring blankly at the tiny sclerified cells I'd piped earlier onto the palm tree's bark. "It's why they tried to tar and feather me even though they'd known me my whole life."

"Rachel never mentioned you having a juvie record. I guess it'd have been sealed—"

"It was an accident." Tee presses herself tighter into my side. It's invasive and exactly what I need. "No one was ever arrested. They said it was some faulty wiring that caused the fire."

Nobody, aside from Tee, had ever believed that.

Colton didn't have faith in me. He'd lied to make sure I wasn't punished. That, more than anything, broke my heart.

Faulty wiring, my ass.

But who was going to believe me, the troubled girl who'd just lost her brother and was acting out? Not a single damn person. That's who. Hell, the town didn't even believe the alibi Colt gave me.

"It took a while for that report to come out," Tee continues. "Especially with the bodies and the insurance. The barn was full of horses."

Parker flinches. "Oh."

"They say my grandmother bribed the RCMP* sergeant to keep me from being arrested."

The shame of those days makes the prospect of returning home a thousand times worse.

Parker whistles. "Is that true?"

"She never told me if it was. They didn't pull me in for questioning."

Personally, I thought Colt's alibi held more weight than anything *Grand-mère* might have done...

My *grand-mère*, after all, still believes I did it.

If anything, she's more ashamed that I got *caught* hurting the Korhonens than the fact I could have committed such a horrible crime.

---

* Royal Canadian Mounted Police

"Zee, this is nuts."

"You're telling me." My spoon clatters against the bowl as I drop it. "I-I didn't do it, Parker."

"What do you think all that laughing was about? Of course, you didn't."

Tee squeezes my shoulder in reassurance, but before she can say another word, Parker croaks, "You said Korhonen. That's not a common name... Are we talking about *the* Korhonen?"

"He's the one thing Pigeon Creek did right," Tee drawls.

"My God. You grew up with Cole Korhonen?!"

"Parker, restrain yourself. Jeez. You can pepper me with questions later. For now, I can only handle one meltdown and Zee's is more urgent than your hockey-related crisis." Though Parker huffs, Tee ignores her. "Seriously, Zee, do you want me to come with you? There's enough money for two return tickets."

"Even though it's going to be the same temperature as our freezer this weekend?" I force myself to tease, trying not to jump at the offer in case she changes her mind.

"If you need me, I'll be there."

Touched despite being annoyed with her a short while ago, I pat her hand. "I'd say that the sacrifice wasn't necessary but... home isn't home anymore, is it?"

She bites her lip. "No. It stopped being that a long time ago."

Ain't that the truth.

Chapter 2
Colton

Times Like These - Foo Fighters

"**Y**ou have to be shitting me."

Pops rocks in his seat. "You think I'm in the habit of wasting words, Colton?"

I think you're in the habit of being an asshole.

"I'm not going to let this happen."

I flew in a couple hours ago from Wyoming and, immediately after, was called in to help a heifer birth a calf that was breech, and this jerk-off wants to talk about—

"You don't have a choice. The rivers are dryer than a bone. Aren't you the one caterwauling about that all the damn time?

"You want to check how much water we have to take us through the season? You think it's going to be enough for our cattle?"

"I told you we overexpanded," I snarl, slamming to my feet, hands clapping against the desk as I loom over it. "But you wouldn't listen—"

"No, I wouldn't listen. The bank wanted to invest in us. Why would I refuse free money?"

"It wasn't free! *My* grandkids will be paying off the interest, you moron."

"It's not like we can't afford it. It was only a loan, leaving me to diversify our capital elsewhere."

"Why would you take a loan when we didn't need it in the first place?" I argue, unable to understand the man's logic.

But then, I've never understood how Pops's mind works, and it's only getting worse.

What with last year when he got it into his head that my youngest brother, Callan, wasn't his kid, and then this loan—he's pulling a crazy stunt once every 180 days minimum.

"It's good business sense."

"You wouldn't know good *ranching* business if it pissed on your hand-stitched shoes, Pops. This is proof of it."

I can see the rage licking around his pupils as if his fury is a visceral entity at my back talk, but I stopped being scared of him a lifetime ago. That rage can beat at me as if it were his fists however much he wants, but we both know that in a fight, I'd be the one taking him down.

I'm not eight anymore, pretending I have bullies in the schoolyard to explain away my bruises.

"I don't know what made you think you can get away with talking to me like this, Colton," is his cool warning, "but—"

"The hot air you leak means nothing to me. I won't be marrying Susanne McAllister for water rights. *Sorry.*"

"So our herd will die!" he exclaims. "That's what you're saying. And here I thought the ranch was your everything. When the shit hits the fan, though, you're the first to jump off the sinking ship!"

"This is your mess," I snap, the urge to throttle him strong. "Why am I the one who has to rectify it?"

"You think I haven't already tried to tie that girl to me? You should see the ass on that filly." He whistles. "Almost jealous you'll be breaking her in and not me."

His words have me gritting my teeth.

I haven't seen Susanne McAllister since she was a bratty teenager in the middle of a fire so fierce the scars remain on our land.

I didn't intend on seeing her again either.

The good folks of Pigeon Creek know she was *near* the stables when they went up in flames.

Only I know that she was *inside* them.

Hell, I'm the reason she's alive—I carried her outside.

"You discussed this with the McAllisters already?"

"They're land-rich, *water-rich*, but money-poor, Colton. We, on the other hand, have plenty of everything but water."

"I can't believe Juliette McAllister agreed to this."

How bad are things at the Bar 9 if she's willing to fraternize with the enemy?

"She doesn't have a choice," he demurs, staring at his manicured nails. "They went through the same seasons we did. The bank's branch manager knows I've been trying to buy her out so he told me the bank didn't offer the Bar 9 a loan on account of their credit being shot. That's why I approached her.

"Either we join forces or she loses everything."

I don't know why because they hate us as much as we hate them, but that has me rubbing a hand over my chest, right above my heart.

There's been a McAllister in Pigeon Creek, Saskatchewan, since the early days of settlement. They've been on this land almost as long as we have.

"That's a damn disgrace."

"Might be, but it works to our advantage."

I pinch the bridge of my nose. "Why me?"

"Juliette. She said you were the only one strong enough for her Susanne."

Whatever the hell that means.

Like he senses my confusion, he grins. "Think of it as a compliment. Anyway, it's not like Cody ever stays long enough to say 'I do.' Cole's gotten himself hitched to that Mia girl, and if Callan were the same age as Susanne, he wouldn't have the balls—"

"I told you to leave Callan alone. He's eighteen years old, dammit, and he brings plenty to the table. Jesus, he's been my assistant since he was sixteen!"

"What use is a boy who won't get his hands dirty to me? I run a ranch!"

"You also run a business and his savvy is taking us places. He's still in school, for Christ's sake. Imagine what he'll do for the company once he graduates."

Before this can devolve and I give in to the urge to strangle him, I step over to the window behind his desk. This office is technically mine now, but the bastard always lays claim to it whenever he shows his face around here.

Looking at the Seven Cs' acreage always brings with it a semblance of relief.

Unlike Cody and Cole, my younger brothers, I've never felt the call to be anywhere else. Sure, city living in Saskatoon was tempting a time or two, but I got enough of that when I went there for university. A degree later, minoring in animal science and majoring in accounting, I came home. Willingly.

The plains might be bleak to some, but this is my place.

I've known that since I understood what a legacy was.

Even if two of my brothers would do anything to get away, to me, this is where my soul belongs. Callan understands that. He's the only sibling of mine who does.

But...

Marriage?

I hadn't bothered thinking that far ahead.

Mind whirring, I contemplate ways to turn this to my advantage.

As I look onto the yard, I see the ranch hands coming in for lunch, some yawning, others smoking. I can hear the horses neighing in the distance and the baying of the stock as they cross land that my ancestors staked their claim on two centuries ago.

The Seven Cs is mine.

All two hundred thousand acres of it.

Even if Pops's the idiot who puts every acre at risk with his shitty business practices.

It's a thought that makes me come to a decision.

One that'll change my life and that of a woman I haven't seen in a decade.

"I'll do it."

"Knew you'd see sense, boy."

"I never said there wouldn't be conditions."

Smug smile fading, he furrows his brow. We both know control of this situation is in my hands, and he can posture as much as he wants, but it means nothing in the end. "This isn't a negotiation."

He acts like I'm still fifteen, not thirty-two.

But there's his problem—I am thirty-two and he let me know that Juliette McAllister hand-picked me for her grand-daughter.

"As far as I can see, it is. *You* need my ass to shuffle down the aisle, and if you don't want to liquidate those assets of yours to cover the loan repayments when water shortages force us to downsize our herd, then you'd better give me what *I* want."

"You won't let the Seven Cs suffer," he jeers. "You don't have it in you."

"No, I don't. This solution of yours might be gussied-up, but there are alternatives. Expensive ones for sure, but alternatives.

"Seeing as I'm the Korhonen the McAllister matriarch chose for Susanne, you'll do as I say if you want a fast and cheap route to fixing this mess."

His chin tilts. "What do you want?"

"You. *Gone.*"

His bewildered expression is borderline comical. Or it would be if anything about this situation was funny.

"Huh?"

"You heard me. Do you want to save the Seven Cs? You get away from it. Your mismanagement is what's brought this place to its knees, then, when it was at rock bottom, you deigned to let me take over. I'm the only reason this place is flourishing.

"If you care about it as much as you claim, then you'll resign as CEO and President of the company."

"How dare you!"

He jumps to his feet much as I did earlier, but I'm not finished with him yet.

"Oh, I dare, *Pops.* Just like you dared arrange a marriage

contract without warning me. I go to Wyoming on business and come home with an engagement in the cards.

"*You* need me to help, *you* need the McAllisters' water, and that has a price tag.

"Resigning as CEO and President isn't all I want from you either. You're going to move to the house in Saskatoon and leave us the hell alone. I don't want to see you around unless *I* call you back, do you hear me?"

Ignoring his sputtering, I storm from the office, a conversation with my lawyer in my immediate future. I move past him, sticking close because if he wants to have a tantrum, I'm more than willing to brawl.

The weight on my shoulders is always heavy—he may be the head of the company, yet the bulk of the work remains mine. But after giving him that ultimatum, for the moment, the burden of being me is lighter.

It doesn't matter that I'll end up having a sociopath in my bed and as the future mother of my heir.

No sociopath could be worse than the one who calls himself my father.

If it gets him off *my* land, an arranged marriage is a price I'm willing to pay.

Chapter 3
Colt

O Children - Nick Cave & The Bad Seeds

FIFTEEN YEARS AGO

"**P**sst."

Blinking, I turn on my booted heel and attempt to locate the source of the sound.

I know who it has to be, but I can't find her—she's hiding better than usual.

The soft nickers in the stables, the scents of hay and horse and leather soothe the jagged edges of my grief. Normally, they make me feel calmer, but today, everything's different.

Tears burn my eyes like acid except I don't let them fall. I *can't.*

When my granddad passed away, my father taught me that tears are never permitted.

That's when things got worse.

Now that my uncle's dead, only God knows how Pops will escalate.

It's going to be hell.

I burrow the heels of my hands into my eyes. The urge to

scream overtakes me, but I know that'll scare the horses. I don't want to do that. I want to—

"Pssssssssst!"

Jerking at the sound, I whip my head to the side.

That's when I see the bony knees sticking out of the wad of hay in Loki's stall.

The fact that Susanne McAllister can sit so close to where my horse craps is a testament to how badly she needs a hiding place.

I found her in the stables last year. After her dad's funeral.

Our families might hate one another thanks to too many accusations of cattle rustling over the centuries, but how could I kick her out? She'd said her *grand-mère* had shouted at her so she'd run to the only place she knew Juliette McAllister wouldn't come looking—the Seven Cs.

Ever since, she visits. Always on Tuesdays and Fridays after dinner.

Ever since, I tend to check on Loki on Tuesday and Friday evenings.

Though I'll admit, I walked in here blindly today.

Stepping inside the stall, I press my forehead to Loki's and scratch my fingers under his chin.

I know what love is. I love my mum. I love my brothers. I loved Uncle Clay, but the love I feel for Loki surpasses all that.

I guess it's weird. Loving a horse this much. But I do. I can't help it. I know Cole, my brother, is the same with his Betsy.

Loki is like my brother, my child, my father, and my best friend all rolled into one.

He's in my *soul*.

There's no me without him.

Loki neighs, the warm gust of air brushing my chest as he rubs his head against mine like he knows the burning in my eyes has turned painful from holding back my tears.

That's when a grubby little hand tugs on my elbow.

Tipping my head, I see Susanne standing there, her bottom lip popped out. Not in a pout. But in shared grief.

She knows what I'm feeling.

"I'm so sorry, Colt," she warbles, her bony arms clinging to my hips.

With Loki in front and Susanne to the right, there's no denying I feel safe.

Safe enough to grieve.

Safe enough to let go.

I cry.

For Clay who died too young. For me who lost an uncle who loved a misunderstood nephew. For a future without him in it. For a childhood filled with bitter pain from a drunken father who hates his heir.

Throughout it all, Susanne hugs me and Loki's hooves tap the floor, prancing agitatedly on my behalf.

Nothing will ever be right again, but at least I have this.

Chapter 4
Zee

Runaway - AURORA

PRESENT DAY

"You can't be serious."

Grand-mère's pinkie finger gracefully points at the ceiling as she lifts the china cup to her mouth and takes a dainty sip of coffee.

The knuckles might be more gnarled than I'm used to, but it's a movement I've seen thousands of times from her.

There should be a sense of peace in this one *never-changing* act, but peace flew out the window the second she laid down the law.

I've been fine all morning, but I can already tell the stress from this conversation is messing with me. My emotions are spiking as hard as my blood sugar, which is making this tough talk a thousand times more impossible to deal with.

"*Grand-mère!*"

Her wrinkled lips purse as the cup returns to the saucer. Without a clink.

"This *has* to be a joke," I mumble, looking at the contracts in front of me. "This isn't the eighteen hundreds!"

35

I came back because I figured the triplets had gotten into mischief and they were hiding the truth from me.

I flew here with Tee because it was supposed to be a quick trip. A few days of getting scolded for being an absent grandchild then we'd return to normalcy.

This is—

"It might as well be 1820, child." Her dulcet tones are so alien that it's still jarring after a lifetime of hearing them.

She's an anachronism—a walking reminder of the times when the McAllisters had money and she was sent away to Switzerland for her education.

It's because of her that I know how to comport myself at a charity dinner while rubbing shoulders with local bigwigs.

It's why the triplets, despite their rabble-rousing tendencies, can tie the neckties they never wear into nineteen different types of knots, are able to waltz and understand which flowers mean what in a bouquet.

I always railed against the confines and constrictions she placed on us, but after the fire, I found comfort in them.

Until I jumped at the first chance I got to leave...

"We need the Korhonens' help, Susanne."

My fingers tighten around the papers in front of me. "I'm not a pawn in this game."

"You are. Just as all McAllisters are when it concerns the Bar 9."

My throat clutches. "This is my life, *Grand-mère*. You can't expect me to do this."

How can I marry Colton when he thinks I'm capable of setting fire to his stables and killing those innocent horses?

How could he marry me when he believes I'm an arsonist and a horse killer?

This has to be a joke. He'd never agree to this.

"You think I married your grandfather for love? I did it for the ranch—"

"It's always about the damn ranch! My life is in New York. Not here. And we all know how successful that marriage was. He's one of the reasons we're poor!"

"Your place is in Saskatchewan," she barks, the demure

lady act finally quivering as the queen of sulfur reasserts herself. "This foolish game you're playing in New York City is beyond a joke. It's time you came home. It's time you did your duty."

"My duty?" I jerk to my feet, the chair scraping noisily at the abrupt gesture. "I will not be bartered into—"

But I'm not the only one who stands.

That is when she hits me.

Her palm connects with my cheek and the pain ricochets down my jaw and to my neck, my skin burning from that one point of collision.

It's crazy, but I think of all the times Clyde Korhonen used his fists on Colton—how did he handle *that* when *this* hurts?!

I gape at her, staggering aside to avoid another blow. But there won't be one. She takes a seat and picks up her bone-china cup as if that didn't happen.

Except, it did.

She hit me.

And with more bite than I'd have thought possible with her current, fragile, *demure* ninety-two-year-old grandma act.

Because it *is* an act. That's how she rolls.

"You're a McAllister," she tells me, but there's a growl to the words, transforming her from society belle to cast-iron bitch. "You belong here. This is your place.

"I should never have let you leave for university. You should have stayed in Pigeon Creek. But I gave you an inch, and you took a mile. Twenty-one hundred of them. It's time for you to come home."

Her stony words have me flopping backward onto the horsehair-filled cushions of a sofa that saw better days in the fifties.

Still unable to believe she hit me, I stop shielding my cheek with my hand, but the stinging continues.

She's done many shitty things in my life, but this is the first time it's ever turned physical.

Swallowing hard, I stare at her, but she pins her gaze on the vista beyond the house.

This is *her* room.

It overlooks one of the lakes that we have on our property and lets her keep an eye on the corral too.

Even as we sit drinking coffee in china cups that were hand-painted a century ago and are arguing about purely human matters which are of no consequence to the land that's been here before the first McAllister was born and will outlive us all, a stag drifts from the forest line and lowers his head to sip from the lakeshore.

My heart stutters at the sight.

I used to adore the Bar 9. Now, my skin crawls being here.

The sensation jars me so I bow my head and take in the contracts in front of me.

Contracts, I can do.

Finding solace in the familiar legal terms that perplex so many, I begin rereading them. But my heart pounds once I realize what's on the line.

When I reach the final page of the contract, she places a piece of paper on the table beside me.

Startled, as I didn't realize she'd gotten to her feet, I pull away from her.

"Hush, child. I hit you once in your life and you react as if I'm the devil incarnate." She harrumphs. "You were hysterical."

"I wasn't but I have every right to be. You're ruining my life, *Grand-mère*."

She shoves the piece of paper at me. "Read that, Susanne."

I peer at the bank statement with dawning horror. More documents are handed to me, so I read them too—letters from our bank manager. The hand clutching the paper balls into a fist that crinkles the notes as I stare at her.

"What the hell were you thinking wasting money on airfare?"

"Clyde Korhonen paid for your ticket."

God, we're already indebted to that monster.

Blindly, I stare at the statements. "How did it get so bad?"

I guess I knew when she asked for help with the mortgage, but *this* is so much worse than I perceived.

"The price of cattle sunk. Interest waned. Everyone wants to eat vegetables and... we haven't diversified," she admits.

For a second, my indomitable grandmother looks every one of her ninety-two years. Yet, though her shoulders hunch as she moves over to the window, she does so with a grace that belies her age.

She presses her fingers to the glass like she's trying to find solace in the Bar 9—the land that reared her. "It's getting to be more than I can handle. That's why this would be so perfect. The boys are too young to take over and say what you will about that old bastard, Colton's love of the land is as strong as mine. As strong as yours used to be. He can protect the Bar 9 and modernize it."

I hear her reprimand, but I don't care.

The minute Tee and I had enough money to leave Saskatchewan behind, we did.

Tee had a scholarship for Juilliard.

I wanted away from here. Away from the Korhonens and their land and that family's poison.

And Colt.

Who broke my heart by pretending I'd ceased to exist.

Now, she wants me to become one of them!

Worse still, wants me to be *his*.

"That's why I insisted on him for you."

I choke out, "I guess I should be honored!"

"In my day, he'd have been a prize."

I need to puke.

My stomach twists and churns as I'm dragged back to that horrible night—the penultimate time I saw Colton in the flesh.

We'd gotten word that my eldest brother, Walker, was PKIA in Afghanistan.

That was why I ran to the Seven Cs.

I needed to escape.

The stables were a solace, not because of the horses but the boy who'd been my friend. Yet, as I crossed onto Korhonen land, I'd recognized those rolling clouds that represented a massive storm and had been relieved to find shelter.

My eyes close as I recall how the storm came in a few hours

too late. How the lightning made everything worse for the fire that wrought devastation on the Seven Cs.

Shuddering at the memory of the horses screaming as they burned alive, I bite off, "Walker should be here. This is his ranch. You should never have let him enlist!"

Her sigh is loaded with fatigue. This argument is ancient. One that's still filtered with grief. It might be unfair of me, but what's fair about a loss that'll haunt this family for a lifetime?

"I let you go too, didn't I? Permitted that foolishness which earned you some paltry accreditation as a paralegal.

"All you do is help criminals evade justice. Walker was fighting for our country." She pins me with a scorn-filled glare, one that's full of outrage. "His was an honorable path. Yours shames the family! But then, that's what you do best, hypocrite.

"Here's your chance to right the wrongs of the past, but you're too damn stubborn to see the opportunity I'm giving you—"

Unable to stand the sound of her voice, the same old diatribe I've heard thousands of times during phone calls I never want to take, I tune her out and focus on the bank statements in my hand.

Here is fact. No emotion. No manipulation.

Numbers don't lie, and these prove that the ranch is so far in the red, it's practically exsanguinated.

"Are you listening to me?" she yells, iron-bitch mode fully engaged because I mentioned Walker—her favorite.

And yet, when I look at her next, she's not the same *Grand-mère* I knew growing up.

Maybe I'm wrong about her act and can only discern what a childhood's indoctrination demands I see, but *Grand-mère* looks old.

It could be the stark lighting from the window...

No.

She's frailer than I'd like. Her shoulders not as straight as they once were.

Her face is more lined than the last time I was guilt-tripped into coming home for Thanksgiving too.

Her clothes sit more loosely on her frame.

Ninety-two years of grief and life and misery and stress are a burden I can tell, for the first time, she's struggling to carry.

It's a notion that amplifies the churning in my gut.

She's too old to be fighting like this. To be worrying about her land, her home—*her family's future.*

Biting my lip, I flick another glance at the contract and all the myriad concessions we earn if the Seven Cs and the Bar 9 merge... What they gain and what we retain.

I try not to think about Clyde Korhonen's stipulation that an heir be born of the marriage.

Once upon a time, I wanted nothing more than to be Colt's.

To be his wife and the mother of his children.

How bittersweet life can be.

This contract presents me with everything my teenage self dreamed of having.

But here, now, the prospect of it all has my lungs feeling like they're being compressed. My mouth is drier than the Canadian tundra. Never mind my racing heart.

I'm either going to faint or—

"I want an expiration date."

She jolts as those words explode out of me. "There's no expiration date on a union such as this. We're talking about the Bar 9!"

Good God, she won't even concede that!

"If we have a child," I whisper, feeling sick to my stomach despite knowing I have to do this, "then what does it matter? Everything goes to them in the end, no?"

Her gaze locks on mine and I can see her sag with relief. For all that she presented a stalwart facade, for all that she'd have argued and fought with me until the first spring showers next year, she didn't think I'd do it.

I don't know whether that makes me insane or not.

What I *do* know?

She'd die if I took her away from the ranch, and the bank manager's note tells me the creditors are inches from hounding us off Bar 9 land.

She's too old to be sheltering this kind of burden, even if she'd never admit it.

God help me but it's my turn to step up.

I'm her oldest surviving grandchild—who else is there to do it?

"A child of your union would inherit it all," she confirms.

"Do you think Colton would sign to agree to that?"

I don't know why I need to lock this into place but I do.

I'm acting on instincts that are centuries old, as old as those of the original McAllisters who made their way out west and staked a claim on a patch of land that they turned into the Bar 9.

"Ensuring the Korhonen legacy is the only thing that matters to him, and they're closer than they want to admit to the end because their numbers aren't sustainable. But the McAllister legacy is what matters most to us too. Ensuring his ensures ours."

"My child will inherit both ranches, then."

"Yes."

Having received the verbal confirmation I need, I nod. "I want it in writing, *Grand-mère*."

"I have it."

On shaky legs, she walks to the table holding the coffee tray so she can pass me another slip of paper, proof that this deal has been in the works for longer than I want to know.

But it isn't a piece of Korhonen paperwork she shows me.

"Colton insisted on this when he learned of the deal."

Three signatures—my kid brothers'—accepting *Grand-mère's* gift deed and promising to never contest it as she transferred ownership of the Bar 9 to the four of us. Where I inherit 55% of the company and they each inherit 15% a piece.

Even the triplets are in on this nightmare—*they lied to me*.

The betrayal cuts deep, but not as deep as the knowledge that the Bar 9's future rests on my *womb*.

Everything inside me clutches in horror at what's happening, but I still rasp, "All right. I'll sign."

Her knees buckle as she flops onto the nearest sofa, but her relief doesn't bring me much peace. Even if I *am* partially doing this for her and for the legacy I never asked to be a part of.

I scratch out a few lines that will act as an addendum

Colton will need to sign—a divorce after a baby is born and a statement that the first child of Colton Dean Korhonen born from Susanne Felicia McAllister will be the sole heir of the Seven Cs and the Bar 9.

Getting to my feet once that's signed, I throw the documents on her lap. "Confirm that a baby is enough of an expiration date, and I'll see this through to the finish line."

She snags at my hand, but I ignore her and shove past, toward the door.

"Susanne, thank you," she warbles, more of her relief sinking into her words, but that's cold comfort to me.

I don't stop walking until I'm outside where, finally, I can breathe.

Everything about the Bar 9 is massive.

Always has been.

I tend to forget that, though.

I'm used to New York. Yet as shiny and expensive as things are there, big in its own way, that's nothing to the sheer expanse of space that is McAllister land.

Two hundred and ten thousand acres—that's how much we own. Even more than the Korhonens. Manhattan itself is only fourteen thousand acres.

"How the hell are we at risk of losing it all?" I ask myself as I storm toward the lake where the stag had lapped from the shoreline earlier.

Along the way, I throw my jacket onto the ground.

Next comes my camisole.

I can see the ranch hands spying on me as they come in for lunch, but to be honest, I don't care. I hear the rumble of an engine being gunned so that means my audience is increasing, but again, I. Don't. Care.

If I'm having to marry to save this fucking piece of land, then if I want to freak out by bathing in the lake, I will.

My skirt and tights shimmy down my hips next, and I kick off the heels I only wore to avoid *Grand-mère*'s ire, uncaring that one splashes in the water.

I hear her shriek from the porch: "What are you doing, child?!"

Ignoring her, I carry on, wading into the biting cold lake in my underwear, hoping it will do the impossible—stop me from throwing up. Stop me from wanting to faint. Stop me from wondering if this is a nightmare.

But, it isn't.

This is reality.

My grand-mère sold me to the rancher next door.

The rancher who hates me and thinks me capable of the worst type of crime—equicide.

Worst still, my brothers agreed to it.

Walker wouldn't have.

He'd have fought for me.

Tears swarm my eyes when I hear the chatter at the shore-line, but I ignore the gathering crowd to swim deeper into the center of the body of water that stole my mother's life.

Because, despite that, I feel safe here.

Clyde can't get to me when I'm in the lake.

It's well known that he can't swim.

Grand-mère won't touch me either—she hates the lakes now. Has since Mom died.

"Child, come on out of there before you freeze to death!"

And it's as if a lifetime of fear has been washed away.

Uncaring if she *is* Satan's lieutenant, I holler, "Worried I won't make it to the altar in time?" I don't care that the staff will hear our business, though I know she'll loathe it.

Sounds of splashing follow my words, so I tilt upward, frowning when I see a mop of black hair bobbing in the water as a ranch hand swims toward me to *save* me.

Ha.

Too late for that!

A few feet away, his head finally breaks through the surface.

It isn't a ranch hand.

Everything inside me stills and flickers to life all at once.

My feet cease treading water as I go rigid, then my chin bobs beneath the surface and they start up again before my head goes under fully.

Him.

44

The reason I survived adolescence.

The reason I ran away.

The reason I'm coming home.

My eyes lock on a face I haven't seen in over a decade, yet it's one I'll always know—will never forget.

It's different now—older. Scars on his throat from the fire. Lines from exposure to the elements.

Beautiful, nonetheless.

As I hover there, locked in the flames of his regard, he rumbles, "Considering she brokered the deal, I think you not making it to the aisle is a definite concern, but no more so than for me, Susanne."

"What are you doing here?" I spit, jerking away from him when he grabs one of my arms.

"Same could be asked of you. Why are you in the middle of a lake in April? They only just melted. You must be fucking freezing." He slicks his hand over his drenched hair. "I know I am."

"Then get out. I never invited you in here. It's still McAllister water until you hitch your wagon to mine."

"We'll be doing more than that." His eyes narrow and the lick of distaste I see in there would've broken my foolish heart if he hadn't shattered it a long time ago. "You sign the contract yet, Susanne?"

I have no idea why I hiss the words at him, but I do anyway: "It's Zee."

"You want me to call my future wife 'Zee?'"

What I *want* is to shove it in his face how different I am. I want him to know that he was wrong not to believe in me.

All I can do is bark, "That's the only name I'll answer to."

I'm not the girl you used to know.

His nostrils flare as he sluices water from his face. "I forgot how annoying you are."

"I didn't forget how annoying *you* are."

My bottom lip trembles in misery, and when he spies that faint motion, he heaves a sigh.

Before I know it, I'm being drawn into his arms. His body against mine. Rough against soft. Hard lines against gentle curves. But it has nothing to do with 'saving' me and everything to do with *hugging* me.

My mind blanks.

"You don't have to be scared of me..." He hesitates. "Zee."

I blink at him and the only thing I can think to say is: "I want a divorce."

Chapter 5
Colton

Burn - David Kushner

"**I** *want a divorce.*"

Those aren't words a normal prospective groom would like to hear from his intended, but this isn't normal.

Nothing about this bride or groom is *normal*.

Treading water, the small yet surprisingly lithe bundle that is Susanne 'Zee' McAllister in my arms, I rasp, "Only after we have a baby."

The words are foreign to me.

A baby—I'm going to be a father at some point in the near future.

A wife—who'll divorce me the second she becomes a mother.

All with a woman I cut from my life ten years ago.

Fate has funny ideas for a good time.

"You're okay with this?" She tips her head to study me, making her hair ripple away from her features, sinking into the water and turning into amber silk, exposing the stark lines of her cheekbones.

I always knew she was pretty—she had the bone structure for it. But I never realized she was beautiful when she wasn't finding shelter behind those dirty blonde curls that shield her from the world.

There's no hiding from the fact that the last ten years look good on her.

Better than good.

She's too skinny, but I know she has to monitor her weight with her condition so I'm not worried. Her hair is about six inches longer than it was. And her moss-green eyes still skewer me like an ice pick to the skull.

When my answer isn't immediate, she prods the beast: "Why would you want to marry a killer?"

The accusation has my mouth firming.

"I've had some time to consider the prospect," I reason, my voice gruff with a thousand emotions I didn't expect to be feeling when I first reconnected with my soon-to-be wife.

I'm both *here* but also transported to the past.

To memories of an adolescence that this troubled kid helped me get through.

That night changed everything. Robbed me of Loki. Took away her friendship—

"Why the hell didn't you stanch the idea before it became a contract, then?"

For a second, I can do no more than be trapped in her gaze.

It's like she won't let me out. Won't free me.

It's as if she sees through to my very soul.

Nothing's changed there.

"You want the God's honest truth from me, Zee?" I watch those omniscient eyes of hers widen at my words. "Bearing in mind that whatever you say here will alter every single interaction we have in the future..."

Her lips purse. "I-I'd prefer you not to lie to me."

There's a push and pull between us that I didn't expect.

She's not the girl I knew. Neither is she afraid. Or cowering. So why the hell did I find her in the lake like some tragic Ophelia?

"There are a multitude of truths. I can tell you what you want to hear—that's your truth. I can tell you facts. I can tell you logic. I can tell you what my feelings are on a subject...

"See, more truths than lakes you own. The question is, which do you want to hear?"

Her throat bobs, drawing my gaze to it. Her collarbones are narrow and right in the nook, there's a small pendant. Silver. I'd say it's a saint's medallion, but if it is, she's smoothed over the figure's features with her thumb too many times for me to recognize which one.

It's new though. She didn't wear it before.

"Did you know I'm a paralegal in New York?"

"Yes. You can continue to work if telecommuting is an option—"

"Bet your damn ass I'll continue to work!" Zee grinds out, showing more of that fire I can't deny I like in her.

"Well, that's good," I soothe, hiding a smile because her knee is far too close to my frostbitten junk for me to risk it.

Which, of course, is a reminder that she's still in my arms.

I should let her go...

Unbidden, the image of her floating in the lake returns to me. Combined with hours of hearing her tell me she didn't want to live anymore once her mom had passed, I thought she was—

"Do you swear to tell the truth, the whole truth, and nothing but the truth so help you God?"

The question liberates me from the memory. "We're not in court."

"Marriage is but two defendants on opposing sides in need of an adjudicator," she dismisses.

If I'd needed a reminder we both had troubled pasts, that was it.

"You were how I finally banished my father from the Seven Cs."

She grows tense at the first mention of Pops. Water trickles as she settles her hand on my chest. It's clue enough that we need to get out—there's no warmth to be found in her skin touching mine. But, nails digging in, she demands, "He's not here?"

"What are you two doing in there? Come on out before you catch your deaths!"

I'd recognize Juliette McAllister's bark from anywhere, but neither of us reacts to it. Her because she's desperate to hear my answer. Me because I'm desperate to know why she's scared.

"Did he hurt you, Zee?"

I can feel her fear.

Lots of people are frightened of Pops in Pigeon Creek though. For different reasons. Most of them money related. But she's too beautiful for that. After the fire put a target on her back, I could easily imagine that Pops would—

She swallows. "No."

"I don't believe you."

"He didn't hurt me." Her nails dig in again, making a liar out of her. "I-I wouldn't ask you for nothing but the truth and then lie to you."

"Context is key," I mock.

"He didn't hurt me," she repeats, "but that doesn't stop me from being relieved I won't have to see him much. You say he's banished?"

"This isn't the 1700s, Zee. Business-wise, he's banished and I've had him move into the house in Saskatoon. He doesn't spend that much time here anymore anyway. He only comes back to cause havoc."

If I sound bitter, then so be it.

She, better than anyone ironically enough, understands why.

I've never liked my father, certainly never loved him. So it wasn't that I missed him during his extended absences. If anything, I resented how he always returned when a routine of sorts had settled into place.

I've been raising my kid brother for years on my own—routine matters.

She peers at me through thick lashes that draw my attention because tiny diamonds of water have collected on them. "I won't have to see him?"

Her relief sets my nerves on edge all the more. The thought that our families' dealings might have drawn her to commit the unthinkable still has me in a chokehold.

What the hell was she thinking, wading into the lake that way? This is where her mom died, dammit.

"Not if you don't want to."

"What was your deal with him?"

As nosy as ever.

That hasn't changed.

"That I'd become the new CEO and President of Seven Cs' Inc. That he'd be nothing more than a shareholder."

"And he agreed?!"

"He had no choice. Look, I know you're getting a shit payoff from this, Sus— I mean, Zee. If the promise of a divorce once you've had our child is what'll make you feel better about this situation, then you can have it.

"I'm not my father. I won't make you miserable. We don't need to live together over on the Seven Cs. We can settle here if that's what you want—"

"Would you be okay with IVF?"

My jaw clenches.

I have a healthy ego and I also own a mirror—I'm not Shrek here, for Christ's sake, but from the break in her voice, you'd think I was.

"If that'd make you feel better," I rumble.

Almost immediately, her brow puckers. "What'd make me feel better is you not believing I set fire to the stables."

"That was ten years ago."

"Ten years ago, sure. Might as well have been yesterday. Do you truly think I'd hurt the horses, Colton? Do you think I'd hurt *your* horse?"

"You were angry—"

"*That* angry? No. I was hurting. Mortified. Humiliated. All those things, sure. But to kill Loki?" Her chin juts out. "How could you want to marry a woman who you believe to be capable of that? Why would you love a child that woman bore?"

I stopped thinking about the fire ten years ago when I gave her a false alibi. I had to. Losing Loki, then my brothers losing their horses too, all because of something *I'd* triggered, it was either dissociate or go mad.

Yet, the questions sink into me like she's hitting me with an ax. I can feel my blood swirling to the depths of the lake floor.

"Put everything else aside. The reason I did it, if you think I'm vindictive enough to... Just ask yourself this: do you truly believe I could have killed Loki? Not the others. *Him*."

My mind drifts to the many times I found her in his stall.

She'd hide in the pile of hay there.

Just to be close.

Sometimes, I'd even find him with his head on her lap, both of them snoozing the quiet evening away.

And with that question, she tears off the blinders, making me see the truth. Forcing me to face reality.

"No," I growl.

She couldn't have killed Loki.

Not in a vengeful state of mind.

She loved him as much as I did.

Ergo, she didn't do it. *Couldn't* have done it.

She dips her chin, seeming to have faith in that one concession, unaware that she just triggered an earthquake that shatters the cornerstones of my belief system.

Of my life.

Because if she didn't do it, who did?

And I mean *who*—I never believed that BS about faulty wiring.

"Okay, then." That's when she wriggles out of my arms. "We need to go before *Grand-mère* throws a fit that sets off a heart attack."

I'm still floundering. Torn between the truths and lies of our shared history so it only just registers that the old bitch has forgotten her boarding-school training and is cussing up a storm.

As Zee swims over to the shore, I stick fast, waiting until I can watch her rise from the lake.

I saw her tossing off her clothes from the road and assumed the worst as I watched her wade into the water, but knowing she's safe and that my father and her grandmother's machinations haven't driven her to... *well,* I decide to enjoy the show.

Even if I am freezing my ass off.

A soft whistle sounds in the distance, drawing me away from the past and plunking me into the present.

It keeps on hitting me in the solar plexus—exactly how glorious she is.

When did little Susanne McAllister grow up to be Zee? And when did she become such a beauty?

Did that happen in New York? Away from Pigeon Creek? Or was I too hindered by the stress of life here at home to notice when we were younger? The age gap didn't help. I saw her as a traumatized kid. Not much else.

Another whistle cracks through the air. This time, its meaning registers.

"Get back to work," I snarl, the words drifting on the breeze that comes off the lake.

The order is loud and angry enough that a couple of the ranch hands jolt in surprise then, sheepishly, retreat to their original tasks despite me having nothing to do with the running of the Bar 9.

Yet.

Zee turns, and for the first time, I see the two patches on her arm.

Her insulin pump and her continuous glucose monitor.

I walk toward her, but I'm distracted by Juliette sniping, "What on earth were you thinking of, Susanne? Acting like some common hussy! What will the—"

Before she can continue her diatribe, I grate out, "I'd appreciate it if you wouldn't speak to my future wife like that."

Juliette's shoulders straighten and her eyes promise me hell.

Unfortunately for her, that's already been my home turf for decades.

"Your *future wife* or not," she scorns, "Susanne isn't the first woman whose marriage will save the Bar 9 and I'm sure she won't be the last, so I'd appreciate some decorum—"

Uncaring that it's disrespectful, I loom over her. "Screw decorum. She *will* be the last because the child that she has will also be mine and no one will *ever* force any of my descendants into an arranged marriage."

Though she bristles, her nose pointing into the air like she's smelled something bad, it shuts her the hell up.

Scooping my sheepskin jacket from the shore where I tossed it earlier, I turn to my future bride and cover her with it.

Our gazes lock as I do, and the trepidation of before is gone, so is the anger. There's some confusion lingering in those gorgeous green eyes of hers, but mostly, there's gratitude that I gave her my support.

Surprising us both, I slide my fingers across her jawline.

Her skin is like silk.

Her chin slopes into high cheekbones that are rosy red from the wind, almost as crimson as her lips. No paint stains them. She's all-natural. Her dirty blonde hair frames her face with soft bangs that are tangled from the water.

My God, she's enchanting—a water sprite.

"No one will ever force *you* to do anything again either, Zee McAllister." Gently, I chuck her under the chin as I make that vow, watching her pupils dilate as a result.

I'll give her her divorce, but as my mum found out when she finally got my father to sign on the dotted line, once a Korhonen, always a Korhonen.

Chapter 6
Zee

You've Got The Love - Florence + The Machine

PAST

"He hurt you again," I murmur, pointing to the bruise on his arm.

Colt scratches his jaw—he does that a lot since he started to get little flecks of hair growing there.

"Does it itch?" I ask, knowing he won't comment on his injury.

"A bit."

"Why do you scratch it so much?"

He rubs his chin on his arm, arms that are propped on his knees. We're leaning against the wall of Loki's stall. Some might say that it's pretty dangerous where we're sitting—right in front of him. If he stomped on us, it'd hurt. Might kill us. But this is Loki. He'd hurt himself first.

Here, we can hide so long as we keep our voices low.

When you look over the stall, all that's showing is Loki's big head and rump.

We're tucked away here.

Safe.

Together.

"It's a reminder."

"What does hair remind you of?"

I prod his chin, unsurprised that he lets me. The spiky hair is somehow soft. Not like Daddy's. His was like a wire brush. I guess it's like Walker's. They're the same age, but Walker's is a lot more blond.

"That I won't be a kid forever." He punctuates it with a bite of one of the sugar cookies I always bake for him.

I tut. "I could've told you that."

"It's a good reminder."

"Why?"

"Because it's getting full and bristly which means I'll be old enough to fight back soon."

He's talking about Clyde.

I shiver.

I hate him.

I saw him doing sex things with Mom last year and—

"I want to watch you fight him."

His grin does something to my belly. It's like when I fall off Jezebel, my palomino. But in a good way. Or maybe when I don't eat enough for breakfast and my head gets woozy.

"You think I'll be able to get my good licks in?" he asks as he hands me the Tupperware of treats.

"Of course. You're Colt." Because he shakes his head and is still smiling, I tell him something to keep him happy. *I love it when he smiles.* "Do you know why my mom called the triplets Carson, Colby, and Calder?"

His brows lift as I nibble on the cookie. "No. Why did she?"

"Because Daddy hated Clyde too. He said there was no reason that only Korhonens could have names beginning with 'C.'"

When he snorts, I let loose a giggle.

"He was a wise man."

"He was the best man," I agree, tone laced with pride.

"It's a shame he didn't give you and Walker 'C' names."

"Mom calls me mischief."

"'Mischief,'" he repeats, grinning. "I like it. I'm going to call you that too. Even if it doesn't begin with the letter 'C'. Chaos does though. Maybe that should be your nickname?"

My cheeks flush with color. "You can. If you want."

When his grin morphs into laughter, revealing his dimple, I don't bother hiding my delight.

Mom told me once that I was put on this earth to cause mischief, but I don't think I was.

I think I was put on this earth to make Colton Korhonen smile.

Chapter 7
Zee

Sun & Moon - Above & Beyond, Richard Bedford

PRESENT DAY

Settling into the cab of his truck—a truck my family wouldn't be able to afford even if we sold the damn ranch—as he drives me into town, I study him.

Unashamedly.

The boy became a man. One loaded with muscles and scars and—

"You're staring." His lips kick up to the left, revealing a dimple that has always fascinated me. "I won't bite... unless you ask me to."

My eyes flare at his teasing—also unexpected. Since I asked him if he thought I was capable of hurting Loki, he's done a one-eighty. From stern to... well, I'm not sure what this is but I don't hate it.

"I was thinking. Not staring." *Liar.*

He's more potent than 100-proof vodka in a Henley, flannel shirt, jeans, and cowboy boots. All he's missing is the hat right now and I'd—

"Looked like you were staring."

I scowl. "I wasn't."

"So, what were you thinking about?"

About how hot he is.

About how he defended me against *Grand-mère*.

How he covered me with his sheepskin coat.

How he signed the contract without reading it once I told him what I'd added.

"How we'll be married soon."

He isn't your knight in shining armor, Zee McAllister. He stopped being your safe space a long time ago.

He scrapes his fingers over his jaw. "Crazy, isn't it?"

"More than crazy." I shift my focus from him and onto the road that takes us to town. "You're so calm about it."

"I've been worrying about the situation with the water at Seven Cs for so long that knowing this'll resolve it is a massive weight off."

"Don't you care that you're going to have to marry me? I'm a stranger."

"This isn't ideal by any stretch of the imagination, but you're not a stranger."

"Of course I am. You haven't spoken to me in a decade, Colton. I'm a woman, not the girl you used to know."

"You think I'm an idiot?"

"No."

"Good. I managed to figure out you're not the same, *Zee*."

His mocking tone has me folding my arms across my chest. "How long have you known about this?"

"Two days."

"Oh."

"You asked me earlier why I didn't stop the contract. I was in Wyoming on business and when I got home, Pops presented it to me. *Fait accompli*.

"Because we're desperate for water, after he agreed to my terms, I read the contract and approached your grandmother. I told her my signature hinged on you being granted the rights of majority shareholder to the Bar 9. That was the only consolation prize I could offer you," he excuses.

My brothers' signatures weren't outright betrayals, then. Just their hands being forced by *Grand-mère.*

Like she'd done with me.

"How did you get your brothers to agree? I'm assuming they had to do the same as the triplets if our child is to become the sole beneficiary of both ranches."

"That's not how it works with the Seven Cs."

"No?"

"The eldest child of the next generation inherits everything. The other siblings only gain access to a trust fund."

"So, on your end, our child would always benefit?"

"Yes, and that's all that matters."

Who is this man?

"Two days ago, along with everyone else in this goddamn town, you thought I was an arsonist. Can we add martyr complex to the list of qualities you have now?"

"You've grown claws," he says simply, not getting angry with me or letting me rile him.

"Had to. Especially around here."

His alibi might have spared me three years in a youth correctional facility, but that didn't stop Pigeon Creek's good citizens from believing the worst.

McAllisters hate Korhonens.

A McAllister was at the scene of the Korhonen fire.

Ding! Ding! Ding!

We have ourselves a perp.

"I suppose I feel better knowing that I wasn't sabotaged," I admit begrudgingly. And that he's only had two days to collect his thoughts and measure his reaction.

"You were," he disagrees. "We both were. But I'm getting more out of this than you."

"Hardly. Our ranches are merging. The Bar 9 will finally be safe and my *grand-mère* can live out her days in her home instead of..." I pull a face. "I don't know where she'd live if she wasn't on the ranch.

"She'd rather die than go into assisted living, and I think she'd prefer that than moving in with me and Christy in New York City." My lips twist at the idea of Tee letting that happen

—talk about testing the bonds of our friendship. "I probably gave her an extra lease on life. Go me."

He sighs. "Family, huh?"

"Yeah." I study him again. "When will you be the head of your company?"

"Already am. Pops resigned from the board yesterday during an emergency meeting, and I was given the position," he says with no small amount of satisfaction. "He returned to Saskatoon last night."

His smug smile should make me want to slap him, but my memory fires to life, reminding me of the times I was permitted to see his amusement. His joy. His sorrows.

There's no denying that the boy was beautiful, but the man is so much *more*.

His hair's all over the place thanks to the impromptu swim he had this morning, but it's messy and tousled, so dark that it's almost black. Doesn't stop my fingers from itching to stroke it.

The glossy locks flop onto his forehead, where just-as-dark brows frame a face that reminds me I'm marrying the *hot* Korhonen. And all the Korhonens are handsome AF.

His mouth's firm and his jaw tells me he doesn't crack enough smiles. A man like him, out on the range as much as he is, should have wrinkles at his eyes. Crow's feet show the passage of time as well as emotions, but his face is smooth if a tad rough around the edges from exposure.

Bright blue eyes are shielded by lashes so thick I'm jealous.

I used to have the right to stare into those eyes. Once upon a time, he let me touch his chin without thinking anything of it.

"Why are you agreeing to this? Surely there was an alternative?" I rasp, fully aware that this man needs no contract to get a woman down the aisle.

He could have anyone he wanted, and instead, he's stuck with me.

Someone he already rejected ten years ago.

"I needed Pops off the ranch yesterday." His hands tighten on the wheel. "But also, Loki."

"What about him?"

That horse—I still cry some nights thinking about how he died.

I cry wondering how Colt could believe I'd do that to Loki.

I cry knowing I'll never stroke him or bury my face in his mane again.

"It was... *Everything* was a mess back then. I let grief cloud..." The steering wheel squeaks under the pressure of his grip. "I should never have thought you'd do that to him."

"Really?" I can hear the hope leaching into my voice. The long-held desperation I still feel to have him believe me.

"Really. His death is an open wound that never healed, Susanne. I mean, Zee. That you were there at all, it felt like you were punishing me. Distance and, Jesus, maturity, I know it was irrational to blame you.

"This arrangement will save both our legacies. Loki... he, we, I-I think I'd have agreed to marry Lilith herself if it meant protecting the Seven Cs—" *Charming*. "—but you're not that. You never were. And I'm the one who should be asking *you* why you're willing to marry me."

He scrubs a hand over his face as he shuffles in his seat.

Every inch of him screams discomfort.

Good.

"You know what hurt the most? I-I kissed you. I mistook the situation. I know that now. But I k-kissed you and you rejected me. I was only sixteen and you were twenty-two. You were being a good guy. But that you'd think me being rejected would trigger—" I close my eyes. "You thought I was nothing more than a no-good McAllister. You tarred and feathered me with that brush."

"I did," he agrees, his voice low and simmering with shame. "I'm sorry, Zee."

Five words.

An admission of guilt. An apology.

With my name of choice.

I don't accept his apology, just gnaw on my lip and decide to change the subject because concession and apology aside, that ache in my heart hasn't let up. I thought it would. But it's still there. Raw and weeping as if it's infected.

His opinion has changed so fast, but I don't know if I can believe it. Believe in him. And that hurts too. There was a time when I trusted him implicitly and the difference is jarring.

With Main Street in the near distance, I order, "You can drop me off on the corner."

"No. I want to talk to you first."

"But I'm supposed to meet my friend!"

That was the only reason I agreed to get in the truck with him—he was the fastest mode of transportation off the Bar 9 after *Grand-mère* declared I couldn't leave without discussing the wedding.

Colt, in full-on savior mode, swept me into his truck and took me away.

Swear to God, if I don't discuss what's going on with Tee soon, I'll lose my cool for real. I've already had to deal with one bout of hypoglycemia at the house. In front of him no less.

I need my BFF.

Stat.

"I know you are," he soothes. "And I won't keep you long. I wanted to get to know you better before you return to New York to close things up."

"Close things up?" I repeat blankly.

Get to know me better?

"You have to come back to Pigeon Creek, Zee. Whether we live at the Bar 9 or the Seven Cs, we have to minimize the gossip.

"The fact that a McAllister is marrying a Korhonen is going to trigger enough of a shitstorm but—"

"We don't have to live together!" I blurt out.

His brow furrows. For the first time, he looks angry and that's aimed at me. "I agreed we could divorce after you gave me a child, but if you think I'm going to let that kid be raised in this town and have them be gossiped about or have them trip over the bullshit that's associated with being our kid *as well as* having to deal with rumors over how our marriage worked— you're insane."

Weakly, I slump in the passenger seat.

I don't argue with him because I know he's right.

Not even death will stop the gossip in Pigeon Creek—it goes on hiatus.

Which is why I love New York City.

Anonymity FTW.

Because this is Rumorville, population 2402.

Every action comes with a consequence that will be held against you for the rest of your life.

While the prospect of motherhood terrifies the living crap out of me, he's right to be so proactive.

Right to be concerned about protecting *our* child.

God help me because as unhinged as this is, I'm grateful that he's thinking ahead.

"I can see you agree and know I'm right," he states, tone more wooden than at any other point of our conversation since we first met today.

"Yeah," is all I'm capable of mumbling. That's when I remember what he said. "You'd live at the Bar 9?"

"We have more space at the Seven Cs, but if it makes you feel better being at home—"

"No." I ignore how I can scent his aftershave—pine and a soft musk. It's oddly comforting because it's the same. My nose remembers what I'd forgotten—the first time he'd shaved. These flashes of memory make me feel like I'm waking up after contracting amnesia. "I-I can't live with *Grand-mère* so I'd prefer to move in with you." Definitely time for a change of subject. "God, this place's like a buried time capsule," I mutter, taking in the arterial street of the town.

"Some things change."

"Like what?"

"The Korhonens aren't the only ones keeping it going."

"Bull."

"We still hire seventy-five percent of the town, sure, but the Rock Eagle Casino opened twenty minutes away from here four years ago. Whoever we don't hire, or Our Lady of Sorrows, they have on staff."

My brow puckers at the mention of the nearby boarding school, but I only remark, "*Grand-mère* told me about the casino."

"She didn't approve?"

"She didn't. Her grandfather was an inveterate gambler. She also said it was on Korhonen land."

He hums. "I choose to believe that it was reserve land. We sectioned off the northwestern acreage for the Métis*."

That has me blinking. "Did you have to drug Clyde to get him to agree to that?"

"No. I blinded him with science."

I have no idea what that means and I don't have a chance to pick his brains either as he's reversing into a parking space outside Harold's Baked Goods. Which is when he turns to me and tosses me the keys.

"Put these in the glove compartment for me, would you?"

Before I can tell him to do it his damn self, he jumps out of the truck.

Water splashes as he lands in a puddle, but he doesn't grumble or grouse. Have a tantrum and stick out his boot then shout at the clouds for daring to lay rain where he was going to stand. Nah, he reminds me of the Colt I remembered by shaking his foot and closing the door.

Chill—that's Colt.

Very little riles him.

It'd be annoying if that hadn't always attracted me to him.

He's the kind of man who'll weather any storm, and for a kid raised in the chaos of loss and grief, that was something I appreciated. Then and now.

When I open the glove compartment to store the keys, a couple sheets of paper fall out.

One looks like a bill. The amount of zeroes on it makes my heart palpitate—ranching isn't cheap.

A truck pulls up beside Colt's and after he rounds the fender, he ambles over to it.

While he talks to the driver, I quickly glance at the other letter, eyes widening with every word.

---

* People of mixed European and Indigenous ancestry. One of the three recognized Aboriginal peoples in Canada

You Korhonens are all the same. You think you can hurt people and get away with it.

Well, I'm not letting you get away with ANYTHING.

Your day of reckoning is coming, Korhonen, and I can't wait to ruin your life like you ruined mine.

Chapter 8
Zee

Lion - Saint Mesa

When Larry drives off, it gives me just enough time to shove the glove compartment shut.

A gust of wind blows into the cab as he opens the door, but it doesn't blow the memory of those words away.

Your day of reckoning is coming.

What in the actual hell?

When he studies me, brow arched, I ask, "Why are we stopping here?"

"I'm going to supply my future bride with butter tarts."

I put him off with: "Don't you remember I'm a type 1 diabetic."

"Yes, but I also know you can eat Harry's pastries so long as you watch your carbs and blood sugar level."

"How do you know that?"

"Attended a class years ago," he says as he leans over to unfasten my seatbelt for me.

The chivalrous gesture takes me aback, but it shouldn't— I'm in Pigeon Creek and have rewound my life to the 1950s.

73

He barely touched me, yet wherever there was a point of contact, I can feel a tingle.

A tingle.

Though that tingle might just be the fact he took a class for diabetes management...

He had to have done that for me.

My jaw works but I mutter, "Fine."

"Though Old Harry does have a sugar-free range if you want to try some of those products instead. He went and got type 2 diabetes. He has a gluten-free range too. That might have started with Callan's diagnosis," he says dryly. "Callan probably props up the bakery more than anyone in Pigeon Creek."

Man, I forgot that's how it works here.

Everyone knows everyone's business.

Secrets are currency and information is king.

And if you can provide a service to the Korhonens, you do because they'll reward you.

As there's no reason for me not to, I jump onto the asphalt too, suddenly aware of the height difference between us.

He's over six feet five and I'm not exactly short at five-ten, but I feel like it while I'm in his shadow.

He smells better this close.

Not that I should notice.

Yet I'm reminded of what it's like to stand next to him. To feel his heat. It pipes off him as if he's his own geyser.

When I was younger, I'd hug him for warmth and he'd think nothing of hugging me in return.

All these years later, I know he treated me like a sibling whereas I looked at him with hero worship. *Adoration.* I'd loved him with all the fervor my teenage heart was capable of.

I never realized how he let me in until he locked me out in the cold.

That hurt.

It was, in fact, the worst part of my exile. If he'd believed in me, I'd have endured the town's hatred.

But he didn't.

He blamed me.

So he broke my heart.

Clearing my throat when he settles his hand at the small of my back—a respectable level, not too high or too low—those damn tingles kick in again. Never mind that the ache of his abandonment is clogging my throat.

I let him guide me to the bakery as if I need the assistance, which is further proof my sanity has taken a vacation.

Then, it all goes down the crapper when we cross the sidewalk, and a woman darts past us, almost barreling into me before righting her path at the last minute. Colt pauses, watching her go. His gaze drifts behind us, eyes narrowing.

Uncertain what the problem is, I ask, "Is something wrong?"

I recognized her from school—Bea Hollier.

I never liked her.

She used to pick on Tee something fierce until I got in her face. The town's hatred gave me a backbone ironically enough. No way in hell was I letting anyone talk smack about the one person who kept me going.

He shoots me a smile. "No, nothing's wrong."

His mask wins a solid score of eight out of ten.

It doesn't make it easier to relax around him though.

What was it about Bea that had him pausing in his tracks?

The last thing I heard about her was that she married that douche canoe—Marvin Grantley. To my mind, they'd always suited one another. Both of them had a far too high opinion of themselves.

"Do you have something going on with her?" I demand because I can't imagine what else has him so concerned.

It doesn't fit, though. He wasn't checking her out. I've seen enough guys on the prowl and his expression wasn't interested —it was worried.

"No." He settles a measured look upon me. "While I'm with you, I won't be with anyone else."

I guess that's reassuring.

"I wasn't—"

"Yeah, you were. You're thinking I'm like my dog of a

75

father. I can tell you now, Zee, I've never cheated on any of my partners."

More reassurance.

But it's not in the vein I was hoping for.

I'm still confused and annoyed, though he appeased a potential future issue that would have us being at the epicenter of a gossip-fueled whirlwind.

"If you're going to check someone out when you're with me, then you'd better be more discreet."

"I wasn't checking her out. Didn't you see the bruise on her face?" His tone is calm though I've definitely pissed him off.

He doesn't give me a chance to answer. Just urges me onward.

I notice more than he'd like because I see him flick a glance at the street as he closes the door behind us.

Was Bea bruised?

I genuinely don't remember. She was walking too damn fast for it to register.

"—you hear? The bank's foreclosing on Lydia Armstrong's house. So sad," Hilary Browne comments, sounding anything but sad. "Why, I went to visit her yesterday and she was in the middle of packing!"

"Where's she moving—" Harry, the owner of the bakery, breaks off when he sees us. "Colton! You finally decided to come and sample my new recipe?"

I almost jump at Harry's easy tone. I'd expected him to be flustered. Much as he'd have been if Clyde had walked in.

While I side-eye Colt, he grins. Not at me. But Harry. "It isn't as simple as I'd like to come to town, Harry." To Hilary, he tips his head. "Pleasure to see you, Mrs. Browne."

She preens. "And you, Colton. My daughter was telling me about the new office expansion at HQ and how you promoted her." The older woman cuts a look at Harry, making certain he heard about said office expansion as well as the promotion.

That assertion was better than putting it on pigeon-creekherald.com. It'll certainly be passed around the town sooner than its editor can update the website.

"She's one of the best at her job," is Colt's bland reply. To Harry, he asks, "How's the foot?"

Sensing the dismissal, Hilary packs her items into a tote.

My mind's still stuck on her first piece of gossip though: *Lydia Armstrong's having to move?*

Her daughter, Marcy, used to be close to Tee and me in school. But when we were sixteen, and not long after the fire, she ran away.

To this day, no one has ever heard from her.

A few tried to pin the arson on her. Using her absence as 'proof' of guilt. But it hadn't stuck.

How could it?

She didn't set fire to the stables.

Only I and the perpetrator know who did.

Hilary makes to leave but as she passes me, she hisses, "You're not welcome here, *arsonist.*"

It's not the first time someone's told me that. Hell, it's part of the reason I can count on one hand how often I've visited Pigeon Creek in the past ten years. But my teeth still grind together at the insult.

I let it go though. What choice do I have?

"Hilary," Colt barks, making both of us jump.

Like a little girl with her hand caught in the cookie jar, Hilary freezes on the doorstep. One foot outside, the other in.

Her head slowly turns to face us, sporting a placid if confused smile. "Yes, Colton?"

"I don't appreciate you hurling crude statements like that around. What happened is in the past. Not only was Susanne a child, but she didn't *do* it. I myself spoke on her behalf." His eyes narrow on the older woman. "I like it even less when people toss insults at my close friends or imply that I'm a liar."

Hilary's eyes bug, but that's nothing to mine. Or Harry's.

The baker looks as if all his gossip-boy dreams have come to life on the same day.

"I'm afraid I don't know what you mean!"

"I heard what you said." Colton's timbre shoots straight through me.

His defense is appreciated, but God if it isn't ten years too late.

"I didn't say a word!"

"I don't like liars. 'You're not welcome here, arsonist.' That was what you said. Do you still deny it?"

Hilary's throat bobs, but I can tell from the pinch of her lips she's going to stick to her lie. "I said nothing of the kind. You must be mistaken."

I release a sigh loaded with exhaustion that's a decade old. "You don't have to do this, Colton."

His nostrils flare as he pins me with a glance. "Yes. I do." To Hilary, he warns, "Poisonous words affect the speaker as much as they do the recipient.

"You'd be wise to hold your tongue. Ms. McAllister might not be able to afford a lawyer, but I can. Dealing with a lawsuit for slander can be a costly exercise."

This time, her mouth wobbles at the threat. Because that's exactly what it is—a promise, too.

She knows it and is quick to rasp, "I-I'm sorry, Ms. McAllister."

I dip my chin. That's all I'm capable of.

She stays there, hovering, her gaze darting to Colt, but he looks at me as if I'm in control of this matter.

Right.

With a huff, I mutter, "Give my best to Mr. Browne, ma'am."

She takes that as the offer of escape it is. Hilary darts away like a frightened rabbit, though not once did Colt raise his voice.

He ignores how I scowl at him and instead prods Harry with a repeated: "How's the foot?"

Harry goes with the flow like the pro he is. "They're talking about amputating it! Goddamn diabetes. Had fewer carbs than one of those keto people for the past two years and it's still winning the battle.

"Anyway, less of that doom and gloom. How do you feel about sampling some not-so-sugary sugar cookies?"

My brows lift in intrigue.

Tee was right—I *am* a masochist. The cookies I bake always use sugar because sugar alternatives, while affordable, aren't as cheap. And though I can eat them with careful carb management, Tee's the one who wolfs them down the most so why would I make her suffer their laxative effects?

Colt smiles at me. It's more genuine this time. "You ready to sample some?"

"Sounds good to me," I tell him, discreetly checking my CGM and blood sugar level on my phone.

Once I see they're normal, I input the carbs I guesstimate are in butter tarts and sugar cookies.

Honestly, I'm the world's best guesser.

Living by the dots is a never-ending balancing act.

There were times after the fire, I used to ignore the alerts. Only Tee checking on the app and not letting me get away with murder kept me in line.

She's the reason I'm alive today.

When the closed loop between my CGM and the pump is triggered, it gives me a reading on how much insulin I need so I hit okay.

Harry peers at me over his glasses. "Forgot you were a diabetic, Suzy McAllister."

"Wish I could," I say lightly.

"Long time since you've been in town." His words are polite—but after that display, he'd have to be insane to talk down to me.

Like he usually does.

"Didn't think you'd recognize me, Mr. Lippard," I mock, though I keep my expression blank.

"I never forget a face. Still, it's probably for the best you've come to visit. Your grandmother's not been doing so well and those brothers of yours are out of control.

"Why, Calder's started tagging. Colt knows—"

My brain screeches to a halt. All thoughts of the strange interlude out on the street, the stranger one in here, and Lydia Armstrong's fate fade at this news.

Disapprovingly, Colt frowns at him. "It's all handled, Harry."

"What is?" I urge. "What did Calder tag?"

"We dealt with it in-house," Colt reassures me.

I'm learning that his reassurances leave me wanting.

"Dealt with what?!"

"Calder tagged our barn," he says simply then, in my ear, whispers, "Much as I like Harry, he's the biggest gossip in town. Let's not give him fodder for the masses, hmm?"

It's too late though—Harry has some gossip.

When I look at him, I can see him calculating precisely how close the pair of us are standing. How Colt has his hand pressed against my back still. The intimacy of that gesture where his lips brushed my ear as he imparted his message. Never mind the fact Colt threatened Hilary Browne with a lawsuit *and* called me a close friend.

Because he's a top-tier gossipmonger, Harry smiles (*innocently,* HA!) when he notices me give him the side-eye.

He snags a cane and hobbles off his chair before crossing the shop with a deft spryness as he beckons us closer, singing, "Come with me!"

"If we owe you anything for the damage," I tell Colt as Harry disappears behind a beaded curtain, "then please, let me know."

Colt rolls his eyes. "As if I'm going to charge my future wife on account of my future brother-in-law acting up.

"It's fine. We painted over it and he cleaned out our barns for a month solid for free."

Though I frown, I let him guide me away from the counter with that damn hand of his at the small of my back.

When he bows his head, I study him, not wanting to think about the flecks of gray in his eyes or how his aftershave scents the air around me.

"How long's it been since you last saw your brothers?"

"A while," I confess. "We talk often though. Couple times a week. They never mentioned anything about tagging."

"Why would they? Juliette already reamed Calder a new one. Might not be a bad thing that you're coming home. Harry's right—they've been acting up."

"They're as frightened of *Grand-mère* as I am," I dismiss, though I admit I'm worried.

Tagging the Korhonen barn might not be a serious offense, but if Clyde were in charge, he'd have had the RCMP throw the book at Calder.

"Juliette's not the powerhouse she used to be."

The words hurt. A lot. I noticed that for myself though so I can't deny I know what he's talking about.

"They never listen to me, so I don't know what miracles I'm supposed to reap. Case in point our contract. They didn't warn me ahead of time." Jerks.

"Firstly, Juliette probably threatened them with pain of death if they warned you. Secondly, you don't need them to listen to you. They're the same age as Callan. I can handle them if you'll let me."

My brow furrows as I brake to a halt. "Why would you do that?"

"Because they need to do something and letting them stew is doing nothing for no one." He heaves a sigh at my confusion. "I was eighteen once. And I've steered my brothers through that age without any of them ending up in a jail cell either. Plus, there's always plenty of work to be done on ranches the size of ours."

"Then why hasn't *Grand-mère* gotten them so busy they're too exhausted to cause mischief?"

He hitches a shoulder. "They sneak off."

"How do you know all this?"

"I made it my business to know. Now, come on before Harry gets more food for the gossip mill."

Still, before he can step away, I grab his arm. "You can't humiliate everyone who calls me names. The town'll be empty—"

"They say it loud enough for me to hear, I'll do something about it. I never realized—" He shakes his head. "Naive of me to think you wouldn't bear the brunt of it in town. I'm sorry."

The simple apology—his second in twenty minutes—has me reeling.

"I know words don't help, not when it's words that are the

problem." He reaches for the hand still clinging onto his forearm. "I can't fix our past, but I can make things better."

"This is insane." I jerk free of his hold. "You believed them this morning!"

"That was before I thought you were going to kill yourself in the lake," he says simply, freezing me in place.

"I'm not suicidal."

"You were depressed when you were younger. It's half the reason I always made sure I was in the stables on Tuesdays and Fridays," he murmurs, voice low enough that Harry couldn't overhear our conversation with an ear horn.

I grow tense at the reminder. "That was then."

"That was the last time I saw you. How was I to know? The contract might have tipped you over the edge."

"I'm a lot stronger than you think."

"Oh, Zee, I know that." His gaze is soft as it settles on me. "Doesn't mean that I can't support you. Isn't that what partners are supposed to do?"

"We're not partners."

His mouth twitches into a smile. "Will be soon."

"This is too little, too late, dammit."

"Never too late. Unless you're getting soil tossed on your casket. We gotta start somewhere."

He doesn't let me reply. Just steers me deeper into the bakery, his hand settling on the small of my back again.

It's a possessive hold.

Impossible to deny that this time.

Though I don't understand his game, I don't shrug away. If I do, Harry's inquisitive eyes will track the movement.

Instead, I sample the only sugar-free sugar cookie I've ever eaten that doesn't make me dry heave. The sugar-free butter tart isn't for me though. I take half a bite then enjoy a regular one which is so *damn* good it's worth dealing with the aftermath.

It's then, while Harry explains sugar alcohols to a seemingly fascinated Colton, that it begins to register there's something more going on here. Something that the interlude with Hilary Browne disrupted.

When we're done with Harry's, he guides me to The Coffee Shop before stopping in first at the local drugstore. I stick around because, frankly, I'm curious.

First Harry, then Jocelyn who's been running The Coffee Shop for over three decades—neither of them is hesitant in his presence.

They're polite and cheerful. Kind and chatty.

It's been a long while since I've seen the town respond to Clyde's presence, but I remember it's as if a plague had drifted into Pigeon Creek.

Every store owner sees me with him. His hand on my back or shoulder. His body turned toward me.

Harry and Jocelyn are the worst gossips in town.

He's doing this for a reason, and I'm not that much of a fool that I don't figure out his game by the time we're ordering a coffee and he heads to the bathroom, for the first time leaving me alone.

That's when the shit hits the fan.

Lydia Armstrong drops off our order, snarling the standard greeting, "You're not welcome here, *arsonist*."

After the day I've had, she's so far down on my list of problems that I laugh in her face. Unfortunately for me, she takes it as a provocation and she spits, literally *spits*, in my coffee. Automatically, I snag the glass of water she brought me and toss it over her head.

Two can play that game.

I shove the mug at her, uncaring that coffee sloshes over the rim, leaving more of a mess for her to clean. "Get me another coffee."

"No."

"I'm sure Jocelyn would love to hear how you're a public health hazard."

"Who is?"

Lydia tenses at Colt's interruption, but I continue staring at her. "Get me another coffee, Lydia."

Overhearing that conversation in Harry's lets me know she can't afford to lose this job, but Lydia's obviously been swallowing crazy pills if she thinks she can spit in someone's coffee and get away with it.

Her mouth tightens. "I don't think I will."

When I jerk to my feet, my gaze cuts to Jocelyn who's making pastry like always. Our presence has garnered her attention as well as the rest of the patrons'.

"While I don't expect you to fire Lydia, Jocelyn, you should know that she thinks it's okay to spit in people's coffees."

"She did what?" Colt's hand settles on my shoulder. Not holding me in place or restricting my movement, but, together, we present a united front.

"She spat in my coffee."

He tugs on my elbow. "Let's get out of here." As we step past a frozen Lydia, he growls, "Jocelyn, the next time I'm in here, I don't want to see Lydia serving food or drink to the public."

I can't feel bad for the woman.

Maybe I should turn the other cheek, but nobody has ever turned their cheek for me inside these town limits.

A touch dumbly, Jocelyn nods.

Colt guides me out of the coffee shop. "You tell me if anything like that happens again."

It's an order.

And it's one I don't mind agreeing to.

There have to be some perks to becoming Mrs. Colton Korhonen. Still, I want to hear the words straight from his mouth:

"What purpose did dragging me down Main Street serve aside from letting you witness my humiliation?"

Chapter 9
Colton

"R eintegration. Reconnaissance. Seeding."
        It's an easy answer, even if my intention wasn't
        so simple.

Zee heaves a sigh that does nice things to her sweater.

Not that I notice.

Much.

Still, I never imagined what I'd uncover as I put my plan into action.

The town brings out the pitchforks and torches especially for her. Humiliating her was never my intention, but I can see why she's embarrassed.

Zee's gaze is contemplative as she muses, "You're getting them used to seeing me with you... while getting to know me... That conversation with Hilary shifted things though. And this interaction with Lydia will cement it.

"Everyone in Pigeon Creek will know that I'm a 'close friend' when it's common knowledge that our families hate one another.

"The problem is, of course, people *know* we're not friends. They haven't seen me around, and if I don't visit the town, only the ranch, they know when I'm here. They make sure to lock away their lighters," she reasons. Though, that *has* to hurt. No matter her nonchalance. "They know I live in New York. They know you're mega-rich and the family has properties every-where so they'll—"

"—think you're my girlfriend and that we've been dating long distance," I agree.

She grits her teeth. "You bastard."

"Why am I a bastard? Isn't it better for them to think that than for it to be about business?"

"Like you care what people think of you!"

"I care what they think of *you*," I grate out as we approach my truck.

"Bullshit. This morning, you didn't give a damn—"

"You're going to be Mrs. Korhonen, Zee. I protect what's mine."

"I'm not yours."

"Not yet. I'll be yours too. Won't that be fun?"

Amusement flickers over her expression. Hard and fast but it acts like a bucketful of water on the flames of her temper.

"You're not what I expected, Colton," she declares, eventu-ally passing judgment as I open the door to the passenger seat. "And I didn't expect much because *Grand-mère* dumped this on my lap a few hours ago. At least you haven't turned into your father."

Our gazes lock.

Hold.

"No. I'm not a monster, Zee."

"Neither am I," she whispers.

"I know."

"You didn't."

"No," I concede.

"You believed I was capable of something terrible."

"I did."

She clicks her fingers. "And it all changes like that?"

"You asked the right question."

"I should have asked it ten years ago."

"You should have. It probably would have made me see sense." It's not much, but... "I've always defended you. Today wasn't the first time."

"Whoopee," she mocks.

"Don't joke. I thought you'd killed Loki. *Betsy*. Our herd. I defended you to Cole who grieves her as much as I do Loki and told Callan you had nothing to do with it."

"You should have had faith in me. Shouldn't have just lied for my sake." Her hands flare wide. "You should have believed me, goddammit."

"I should have."

She sags. "I didn't think you'd concede as easily as you have. I asked about the fire, I don't know, to make you see how insane the idea of us getting married would be. I-I thought if you backed out, *Grand-mère* wouldn't make me go through with it. This entire thing feels... too easy."

"Both of us are being dragged into this. There's no reason to make it hell for whatever time we're together." I decide to go for broke. "I've already lived through my parent's hellish marriage. I've no desire to punish any kid we may have with that too."

My candor appears to have done something all my other reassurances haven't.

Softly, Zee nods in assent and takes a seat in the cab.

And that's that.

Because everyone in Pigeon Creek knows what my mum endured as Mrs. Clyde Korhonen.

It's a bitter pill to swallow that that's what makes her accept our mutual fate, but I'll take the win. Especially as it removes our argument from Main Street and the eyes of the town.

A five-minute ride later and I'm pulling up outside her friend's place. Christy MacFarlane's father is the elementary/middle school's principal and he's less of a fan than I'd like.

Despite a donation for a new computer lab *and* special free sessions for the kids at the 'Cole Korhonen' rink.

I guess I know why he doesn't like me now—Zee.

"Before you go, we should exchange numbers," I prompt.

"You're right."

I rattle mine off and watch her text me.

Once that's done, I order, "Wait there."

She frowns as I jump from behind the wheel and round the fender.

89

As I open her door, I hold out my hand for her to take.

She glares at it.

"I don't need any help."

I shift closer. Lean over her. Unfasten her seatbelt and move aside, hand held in the same position as before.

"You're my fiancée," is all I say. "That comes with expectations in town."

Her eyes narrow on me but she slowly slides her fingers over my palm.

As I stand in place, I wait for her to clamber down.

Her jaw works as she stares at me.

There's a big height difference between us despite her being tall.

"I'll be in touch," I inform her, amused when her lips settle into a flat line.

It's giving old schoolmarm vibes, but she's pretty enough to make it work.

Unable to stop myself, I settle my thumb on her chin. When she continues glaring at me with a defiance that'd fit if I'd said something to piss her off, I murmur, "You'll learn, Zee."

"What will I learn?"

"What it means to be a Korhonen."

Chapter 10
Colton

Leaving my words to sink in, I let her go and return to the driver's side.

It'd be too easy for her to toss other insults at me, ones that revolve around how being a Korhonen didn't keep my mum safe, or even about how I dropped her when she needed me most, but she doesn't say anything as I get behind the wheel.

She just studies me until she turns on her heel and heads for the MacFarlanes' front door.

Ordinarily, I'd have walked her to it, but I don't stick around longer than to watch her make it to the porch. The second the door opens, I reverse out of there.

On the road, I veer toward the east side of town.

Since I saw Bea on the street outside Harry's, my mind's been racing. I had to tamp it down, though, because Zee sees more than I thought she would.

I don't know why I didn't expect that. She was always an astute little thing.

Maybe it comes with the turf of her chosen career, or maybe I was more obvious than I ought to have been. Either way, she picked up on my awareness of Bea and I already have a fight on my hands with Zee—I don't need her thinking I chase anything in a fucking skirt like my pops.

Unbidden, those words from that note flicker to the forefront of my mind's eye.

You think you can hurt people and get away with it.

I meant what I said to Hilary—poisonous words hurt everyone.

Part of the reason I threatened her with a lawsuit is I suspect her of being behind the notes I've been receiving in the mail lately.

She, Lydia Armstrong, and Jessica Cardinal are all at the top of my list of suspects.

Hilary because she's a gossiping busybody. Lydia because she always believed the Korhonens were behind her daughter's disappearance. And Jessica because she's hated us ever since Pops refused to marry her sister when she got pregnant—both mother and child died during childbirth.

Sighing tiredly, I grab my cell when it buzzes. Spying my brother's name on the Caller ID, I cut the call and text:

> Me: I'll be in touch later

> Cole: Sure thing

Pigeon Creek's so small that I find my way to Bea's in less than five minutes.

As I slam the door shut, I see her standing in the window. The curtains are closed but she peeks out from the crack she made in them at the sound of my truck pulling up.

When the door opens a slither, silently, I slip inside.

"How did you get the bruise, honey?" I ask, pitching my tone softer so as not to spook her. "Has he been using you as a punching bag again?"

"N-No. I walked into a door."

Even if I hadn't been close to her since junior high, I'd know that was bullshit.

"Don't lie to me."

"I'm not."

Though I'm impatient, I lean against the door. When I fold my arms across my chest, she stares at the floor.

"Bea, I can't help you if you don't let me in."

"It's nothing. A-A dumb accident."

"If Marvin's abusing you, I need to know."

"You'll fire him," she bites off, finding some of that sass I know Marvin tries to extinguish. "That's the last thing we need. You know he won't let me get a job. If money's tight then it'll add extra pressure, and I can't cope with that right now."

My hands ball into fists.

It goes against my grain to employ an abuser, but rationally, I'm aware she's right—I only hired him for her sake.

"You know I can get you out—"

"Where would I go, Colton? I'm not like your other charity cases. They come here and you hide them. Where would you send me?"

"You're not a charity case. Neither are they. You're in a bad situation and you're snapping at me for wanting to get you out of it.

"Anyway, this isn't about charity. We've known each other for a long time. Old friends should offer help, *freely*, don't you agree?"

"I don't need help. Just leave me alone."

But that's the last thing she ought to have said to me.

She *looks* tired. Sounds tired. Her words leach it. Everything about her speaks of an exhaustion that goes bone deep. And I get that. Too well.

The need to do something rattles through me like an earthquake.

But as is so often the case in this type of situation, my hands are tied.

Nobody could ever have warned me about how frustrating it is to feel so futile. Not after enduring a childhood shadowed by abuse. The whole point of Dove Bay Sanctuary was to take action, but sometimes, action just isn't possible.

Patience—I never knew it was one of my virtues.

"If anyone tells him you were here, he'll lose his shit, Colton," she rasps when I make no comment. "I need you to go."

I grit my teeth. "You know where I am if you decide to let me in."

She turns her head aside, effectively dismissing me.

With a sigh that's as tired as her, I shift away from the door and slip out.

This whole situation is a mess, but I know there's nothing I can do to fix it. Not without her active participation. Anything I could do to help would only add pressure on a marriage that's already toxic.

Stomping over to the truck, my temper on thin ice, I don't immediately call Cole after I set off.

I love the idiot, but he can get on my last nerve like no one else. His infinite brand of cheerfulness isn't something I want to face yet.

I was headed home, but instead, I stop off at our headquarters in Pigeon County because I feel like making the pain in my ass worse.

Three annoying hours later, and twenty minutes into the ride home, my mind shifts from the corporate bullshit that comes whenever I visit HQ. Instead, I focus on what I can legally do to Marvin without direct involvement, but because my hands are tied, I decide to phone Cole.

Hopefully, he'll take away the urge I have to find my ranch hand and beat the everliving shit out of him.

"What did you do?" is my greeting.

"Colt, why do you always assume I call you with problems?"

"Because otherwise, you text."

"Ah. It's a generational flaw. That's what we do. You wouldn't understand."

"I'm barely seven years older than you, Cole. So fuck you."

"Mia does that very nicely."

"Cole!" I hear my future sister-in-law yelp.

"What? You do!"

"Don't be a jerk," I chide.

"I'm not being a jerk. I'm being truthful."

"I swear Mum dropped you on the head when you were a baby."

"It'd explain a lot."

"What do you want?"

"I don't technically want anything."

"Technically." I ponder that word for about half a second. "Get it out, Cole. You'll feel better."

"I have no sins to confess," he counters. "Just... You know."

"No, I don't."

He clears his throat.

"Just ask him," Mia whispers.

I roll my eyes. "If we could hurry this along, I'd appreciate it."

"I spoke with Callan."

"And?"

"And he said Pops left the ranch."

A smug smile creases my jaw. "He sure did. But there's nothing new there."

"No," he concedes. "Callan made it sound... different."

Oh, was it ever.

If anything, it had been a decadently different day.

The best one of my damn life.

When that realization hits, I figure I need to work on having better days because, shit, that's depressing.

"Callan barely leaves his room so how would he know?" I half-lie, fully aware that I haven't shared the news with Cole. Yet. "Not that I'm complaining about Callan living in his room. It's better than joyriding or taking drugs or playing hockey."

He scoffs at the dig. "Just because you wish I'd taken up baseball."

"'Course I do. That you never got to knock a baseball out of Rogers Centre with your Louisville Slugger is a tragic waste."

"I'm not exactly cooling my jets with the New York Stars."

"Hockey." I pshaw to piss him off.

He grunts. "Okay, before I have to fly home to smack some sense into you about why hockey is God's game of choice and how my team made it to the playoffs, tell me what made Callan think Pops leaving is different this time."

"Maybe because it's permanent," I admit.

"Permanent?"

"Yup."

Even I can hear how self-satisfied I sound.

"I'm confused."

"Doesn't take much."

"Screw. You."

"Pops wanted me to do something for him." And for the first time in thirty-two years, the balance of power shifted in my favor. "I agreed."

"If he left the ranch?"

"No. He had to make me the head of Seven Cs Inc. before retiring from the company entirely. He's only a shareholder now. *And* I tacked on an eviction notice."

"What the hell did he want?! How did you get him to agree to any of that?"

"He didn't want to be the Korhonen who broke the legacy."

"Explain."

"I warned you about the water situation last summer. He screwed us over with his mismanagement. The man knows how to manage a portfolio," I concede, "but he can't run a ranch to save his life. Our ratios are a mess. Too many steers for our water capacity. His solution was to get more water."

"Make it rain," he mocks.

"I'm sure Pops wishes he could. Instead, he and Old Bitch McAllister organized a merger." I brace myself for the shit that's about to hit the fan. "Susanne McAllister and I are getting married, Cole."

"You're *what?!*"

"The hell, Cole?" Mia shrieks in the background. "You scared the crap out of me!"

"Colt's getting married to the cow who set the fire that killed Betsy!"

With one hand on the wheel, I use the other to rub my temple. "Cole, she did not set fire to the stables."

"You can't seriously be marrying the woman who murdered Betsy!"

"Calm down, baby," Mia soothes my brother, but it's futile. There's no soothing this old hurt.

"You weren't the only one with a heart horse in the stables, Cole," I rumble, echoes of grief still lingering in my voice. "You know Loki died too."

"Then how can you hitch yourself to—"

"Because I'm telling you she had nothing to do with it."

Before, those words had been a lie.

Today, they're the truth.

I get why Zee's suspicious of my turnaround. It *is* swift. Enough to give anyone whiplash. But her question opened the floodgates of memories I'd repressed because thinking of Loki hurt too badly.

I remember how she'd hold onto him as if he were the only thing keeping her sane...

No way she'd hurt him.

Seeing her in the lake, the vulnerability in her expression, it was like a veil had been lifted off me, one that had been fogging my brain for years. Or maybe it was simply the fact that the fire *was* years ago. Time's the only thing that heals all wounds, don't they say?

"They have the water we need, Cole. Whatever dumb vendetta the Korhonens had with the McAllisters is in the past. We're about to unite and conquer to keep both ranches alive."

"It's divide and conquer."

"Not in this case."

"This is fucking insane and—"

I don't let him finish that sentence. "No, it isn't. I've never been more lucid in my life. I got Pops off the ranch. This deal forced his hand. I'm now in charge of the Seven Cs. If you think I wouldn't make a deal with the devil himself to ensure that happened, you're the one who's lost his mind."

"I can't talk to you when you're being like this."

"When I'm not listening to your pearls of wisdom? You hate the ranch. That's fine, Cole. Your future's not here. But *mine* is. I'll safeguard it when no one else in our line does because that's all it needs—one guardian—*me*.

"I'll do what has to be done. Just like always."

Disconnecting the call before we hurl insults at one another, I suck in a sharp breath and let my annoyance drain away with the exhalation.

There's no point in blaming Cole.

It's not his fault he was born third and I was born first.

99

It's not his fault that he hates the land because all it reminds him of is how we lost our mother.

It's not his fault he'd do anything to get away when I'd do anything to stay.

We're different people.

With different needs and aspirations.

Still, Marvin Grantley is good for something—a distraction.

As fate would have it, he crosses my path as I park in front of the house.

Because I leave direct staff scheduling to Theo Frobisher, my ranch manager and best friend, I follow my nose and find him over by a paddock, working with one of two fillies we're trying to gentle. One's a bolter, the other's a biter.

Theo should be managing his own ranch to the west of the Seven Cs, but he and his brothers don't get along to the point where it'd be like dumping three pissed-off cougars in a sack and expecting 'em not to kill one another. Instead, he works for me and, together with Callan, we run this place like it's a two-bit operation—not a billion-dollar company.

That's how my grandfather did it, my uncle Clay, and it's how I'll do it.

The corporate side of things, and Seven Cs Inc.'s investment portfolio, is another matter entirely—the business has exploded since Grandfather was alive—but the ranch itself is my domain.

When Theo sees me approach the corral, he ambles over, dragging his hat back and swiping a hand across his sweaty face at the same time. "You look like someone pissed in your cornflakes."

"Only you'd dare."

"Cole and Cody would too." At my grunt, his brows lift and his grin fades. "Problem?"

"Marvin's at it again."

His scowl is immediate. "That fucker."

I grab his arm when he makes to storm off. "Bea asked me not to get involved."

He grits his teeth—the sound's audible. "You. Not me. I can—"

"No. We have to honor her wishes. She's the one who gets the beating if we mess things up."

"Why does she stay with him?" he growls.

"If I had an answer to that, I'd be able to convince her to leave."

"What was it this time?"

"Black eye."

He grips his nape. "If we can't beat the shit out of him, what can we do?"

"I want you to give him the grody jobs. But don't make it look like he's being targeted," I warn. "He'll take out his frustrations on her."

The flash of fire in his eyes says it all.

But I get it.

"I'll be clever about it," he assures me, his voice like gravel as he struggles to contain his temper.

A part of me wonders why he didn't get with her when they were younger, but that's a conversation we never have.

Best buds or not, he keeps that shit close to his chest.

Because both of us are feeling murderous, I tip my chin at the filly. "How's she doing?"

"She bit me." His grin is tight. "Twice."

Snorting, I clap him on the shoulder. "It's the effect you have on women."

Though he slugs me in the arm, he comments, "Mom wants you to visit."

"Everything okay?"

"Yup. She made you some of that cake you like."

"Isn't your cousin visiting from out of town?"

He groans. "Ah, hell. You see through her better than I do. Oh, that reminds me. Gillon quit."

"Asshole. Set up some interviews?"

"On it. Everything go okay last night?"

I nod—three women had been transported to our bunkhouse under the light of the full moon. This is their safe haven. It just grates on me that it can't be Bea's too.

"More are coming in thick and fast."

"The economy nosedives so they take it out on the wife," he grinds out, ire lacing the words.

"That's why we do this."

"Some days, it doesn't feel like enough."

I wish I could argue with him, but with the lingering memory of that bruise on our friend's face, I can't.

Chapter 11
Colt
PAST

"Come here, kiddo." Lifting my arm, I tuck her into my side. "Cry it out."

She immediately burrows her nose in my ribcage. I grew used to that years ago, same with bony elbows and knees accidentally digging into me.

Susanne isn't that great with personal space.

"I hate it when you call me that. I'm chaos."

My smile is solemn. "Don't you feel like a kid today?"

Tears soak through my plaid shirt.

Guess that's my answer.

Awkwardly, I press a kiss to the crown of her head.

"I don't want to be here anymore," she garbles around a sob.

I close my eyes. "I know you don't. But you are here, and your mom wouldn't want you to join her. Not yet. She'd want you to be happy and to live a long—"

"Why? What's the point of anything? Everyone always leaves. They die. They all die."

The words cut too close to the bone.

I've felt that way many a time in my life, but that Susanne...

She's a cheeky little thing but her heart is pure gold.

That she might want to end it...

I squeeze her tighter, as if the harder I hug, the more I can

105

fight those thoughts and stop them from becoming definite actions.

"Why did she have to leave me, Colt?"

"I wish I had an answer for that, Susanne." I tip my head against the stall door. "Your mom tried to do something good and it bit her in the ass."

"I told Calder to keep his dumb dog in the house." She swipes at her cheeks. "Mom went in to save him. One second she was there, and the next she wasn't."

"I'm sorry." The words aren't enough so I press another kiss to her temple.

"What am I going to do? *Grand-mère* hates me."

"She doesn't hate you."

"She does! She's so mean to me. Even Walker said she is and *Grand-mère* treats him like Jesus has come back."

A huff of laughter escapes me. "I don't know my scripture as well as I should, but I don't think it's a good thing if He visits."

She hitches a bony shoulder. "I miss Mom. Already. She only just—"

When her words break down into sobs, a dust mote dances in the air. I track it as, woodenly, I rasp, "Of course you do."

"How am I supposed to live without her?"

"You..." I think about Uncle Clay. "You take it one day at a time."

"Will you come to the funeral?"

"You know I can't."

Susanne pulls away from me, drawing her knees to her chest and burrowing her face in them.

God, I hate it when she cries.

Over the years, I've grown used to her quirks and have adapted myself to her sense of humor, which is pretty dark when it comes to her diabetes. For a kid, anyway. Seeing her cry hurts something in my goddamn soul.

"I'll sneak in at the end of the line," I mutter, aware that if I get caught, Dad will rain hell on me for 'fraternizing' with the McAllisters.

Still, it'll only be words, not fists anymore. He stopped with that when I fought back.

Her head pops up. "You will?"

I nod. "Have you been keeping a check on your blood sugar?"

Her lips purse in mutiny.

"Susanne!" I chide. "You have to monitor it."

"I am." Her tone is beyond snooty.

"Regularly?" It kills me to say this but... "Your mom isn't around anymore to do it for you. You have to grow up when it comes to this stuff."

Her throat bobs.

But she stays quiet.

Goddammit.

"Promise me, Chaos. I don't want to lose you too."

She peers at me with wide eyes. "You don't?"

"No. So, promise me."

"I-I promise. Thank you for caring," she whispers, nestling into me again like the teddy bear she isn't.

"Of course, I care."

In the ensuing silence, I stare at Loki as she withdraws her kit from the little pack she carries with her at all times. It isn't the most hygienic place to do this, but at least she's doing it period.

When she grunts, I can tell her level isn't the greatest. Something that's confirmed when she opens a wrapper and starts snacking.

In comparison to us, Loki doesn't have a care in the world, yet he's staring at us as if he understands.

I wish he did.

"Do you think he knows how much we love him?"

A sigh drifts from my lips as I hold her close, smiling when she offers me a peanut butter cracker. "If any horse could, I think it'd be him."

Chapter 12
Zee

PRESENT THE FOLLOWING DAY

Twenty-two hours later and the most reassuring part of this entire experience is that Tee keeps turning to me and whispering, "This isn't happening."

Because I feel the same way, *floored*, it's comforting to share in the experience.

"This can't be happening," she says as she shakes my arm, acting like a human alarm clock when I fall asleep during the ride to the airport.

"This can't be happening," she mumbles as we get out of her dad's truck.

"This can't be happening," she states as we're about to head through CATSA* for screening.

Separating my liquids from my electronics, this time, I mutter, "I wish it weren't."

"This is the opposite of a fairy tale. It's *Nightmare on Elm Street!*"

"Colton doesn't look like Freddy Krueger," I counter, my mind clearly not working because that *shouldn't* have been my answer.

---
* Canadian Air Transport Security Authority

Not when she's in drama queen mode.

She shrieks, drawing the officials' attention to us.

"Tee! Keep it the hell down before we're arrested!"

"This is not an okay situation because the guy you're being forced to marry is *hot*, Susanne McAllister."

"Ma'am, is everything okay here?"

Cheeks bright red, I turn to the agent with a weak smile. "Everything's fine. My friend's worked up over nothing."

The woman's frown seems perpetual, but a glimmer of something lingers in her gaze when it stops darting between me and Tee. "Do you need help?"

"Um, no. I have this small bag of liquids—"

"I mean, *help*. Are you being forced against your will to marry someone, ma'am, with the intent of bringing them inside Canada's borders?"

Glowering at Tee, I demur, "My friend's overreacting."

"Overreacting?! If she's going to save her ranch, she has to marry the eldest son of the neighboring property! Does that sound like I'm overreacting?"

"This is outside of CATSA's purview."

Tee scowls at the agent's robotic response. "Is that all you care about? She's being forced to marry a stranger!"

"I'm not being forced," I hiss, squeezing her arm. Hard. "Shut up, would you?"

The agent narrows her eyes. "If you're in danger, I can call the RCMP—"

"No! That isn't necessary. Thank you for helping but my friend doesn't understand." Because the agent doesn't understand either, I explain, "I have water, and he has land. It's a match made in ranching heaven."

"Sounds like a plot Jane Austen would appreciate," the agent says with a distinctly *feminist* sniff.

"Exactly," Tee crows, but it's less happy and more sorrowful. She swipes a hand over her eyes. "She'll have to move back here. She's going to leave me in New York."

The agent darts another look between us then, sighing at the disgruntled line of people at our backs, invites, "If you'd like to continue with the screening process, ladies."

Relieved, I nod and forcibly turn Tee toward the counter. "Unpack your liquids. I can't believe you did that!"

"I'm sad!"

"You think I'm not? Did you figure getting us brought in for questioning would make a shit situation better?"

Tee harrumphs, but her shoulders slump.

With a couple sniffles, she unpacks her carry-on and places her things in the trays, and finally, we're good to go through the metal detectors.

The agent from earlier slips to the other side of the unit and hands me a piece of paper.

"It's for a woman's charity. If you need help—"

Doubly embarrassed, I mutter my thanks, scan the note, 'Dove Bay - Saskatoon Women's Shelter,' and stuff it into my pocket.

Collecting my things, I glare at Tee once she's through the metal detector and head to the tables where I haphazardly shove my belongings into the case.

Once Tee joins me, I grumble, "I'm grateful that you care. I love you as much as you love me, but while we're in a secured space, if you so much as mention Colton once, I swear to God, I'm leaving you and heading for the nearest bar. Now, I need chips. Stat."

I feel like a bitch for abandoning her there while she organizes her hand luggage into the packing cases she relies on, but I need a minute to myself.

Yes, my situation is shitty.

Yes, it's dire.

But it's not criminal.

Needing chips wasn't a lie so I head to Relay.

It's times like these that I wish I could gorge myself on junk.

I can enjoy fast food in moderation so long as I balance it with insulin, but sometimes, I just want to drown in carbs. I've spent a lifetime watching Tee eat her feelings with ice cream and candy without worrying about her blood sugar, and today, I'm jealous.

Because I need some of that, I snag two bags of All-dressed

chips and head to the line, making mental calculations about how to combat the influx of carbs.

That's when someone grabs my arm.

Startled, I turn, half-expecting to see a CATSA agent, but it's not.

Neither is it Tee.

I can literally feel the blood drain from my face when I set eyes on Clyde Korhonen.

For the first time in years.

I can't speak, can't breathe.

Fear has me in an immediate chokehold.

Unbidden, the bags of chips tumble to the floor.

"It's been a long time since we last met, Susanne."

I don't answer.

I can't.

"How many years has it been?"

Oh, God.

Not enough.

Yet it also feels like yesterday since I saw him in the—

"You've grown up very nicely."

There's a lag between 'very' and 'nicely.'

A lag that he uses to look me up and down.

He's...

My mind blanks.

That voice... his tone...

He's flirting with me.

Trying to charm *me*.

My skin feels clammy and tacky and it's hard to swallow.

I'm going to be sick.

Finally, though his ego must weigh more than he does, he picks up on the fact that I'm not talking back.

He frowns at me.

Somehow, that's worse.

It feels as if there's a band around my ribs and it's constricting my lungs.

Inwardly pleading with any deity that'll listen for Tee to burst into the store, I manage to choke out, "What are you doing here?"

It sounds more like, 'What doin' 'ere?'

Inside, I'm wailing.

I'm going to faint—I know it.

"I'm leaving for Vancouver," he chirps, apparently relieved that I can talk. "But when I heard through the grapevine you were returning to the States today, I had to delay my flight and stick around until I got to see you."

My eyes widen.

He *orchestrated* this?

"W-Why?"

And how did he know about my travel dates?

Grand-mère.

Goddammit.

"By now, I'm sure you're aware of the deal my son brokered with me." His smile is pure sleaze. "That's proof of my dedication to the future of the Seven Cs *and* the Bar 9. I hope you see that."

"Why do you care if I do or don't?"

Leaning forward, he lifts a hand.

It takes everything in my power not to projectile vomit all over him when his finger strokes the line of my jaw.

"I'm aware that you get very little capital out of this deal, Susanne."

"The ranch's debts are covered—"

"The Bar 9's safe, but what about for yourself? Every girl needs some spending money, doesn't she?" He chuckles. It's oily and nauseating. "I can make that happen."

His thumb presses into the small indent on my chin and that vaguest pressure triggers another memory, but this one is so deeply entrenched that it yanks me out of this terrified stasis.

Retreating a couple steps feels like I've run a marathon. I know I'm panting as hard as if I made it to the finish line.

He stares at me in confusion but seems to shrug past it. "I want you to be my eyes and ears in Pigeon Creek, Susanne. My son's never managed the ranch on his own before. As someone who understands the importance of a legacy, you'll also comprehend that I'm worried about the Seven Cs being in his hands. It'd ease my heart to know the ins and outs of... say, the daily management.

"I had an attack last year. Arrhythmia." He pats his chest. "The old ticker's not what it was."

Good.

"You're asking me to spy on Colton," I mumble, making sure I understand what he's after when he tends to couch everything in four or five layers of BS. "Is that right?"

The irony here is that he'd believe whatever 'intelligence' I shared with him when half the reason my life turned out the way it did is because no one ever trusted my word.

When coming up against him, I knew whatever I had to say would be dismissed.

But this man is evil. To the core. Yet his position outranks mine so I'm the one who's easiest to ignore.

"Spying's such a harsh word." He tsks. "I'm keeping an eye on a ranch that's been a part of my family for two centuries."

"There you are!"

I jump.

It's humiliating, but I do.

At least three inches in the freakin' air.

And when I come down, I nearly knock over a stand of postcards showcasing Saskatoon's delights.

Tee clings to me until I gain solid footing.

"Jeez, how are you supposed to live on the range again without me there to prop you up?"

It's a soggy joke, an attempt to put things right between us, but my eyes prick with tears that the confrontation with Clyde only exacerbate. "I'm going to miss you so much."

Unaware that we're not alone, she hurls her arms around me. "I'm going to miss you too."

In the center of the store, like the crazy people we are, we hug.

I can feel her tears on my cheek mingling with my own.

We've never been apart for longer than two weeks—it feels like I'm asking to have my right arm cut off for funsies.

"Excuse me," someone snaps.

We pull apart and Tee, ever the tigress, barks, "What? You

afraid of two women hugging or something? Get your damn magazine. It's so much more important than genuine human interaction—"

"Tee, cool it. We *are* in the way."

She huffs but tugs me with her, which is when I remember Clyde.

Only, he's not there.

I peer around the store, trying to find him, but he's nowhere to be seen. He isn't outside the store either.

Confused but relieved, I faze that confrontation out. Tee's jabbering on about how she got delayed when this cute guy flirted with her outside the screening area. Even though I keep up with the conversation as I return the chips I dropped to the shelf because eating my feelings is no longer an option, my thoughts are racing a mile a minute.

A glance at the flight board tells me the time...

I reach for my phone and head for my contacts.

My thumb hovers over his name.

It's obvious that Clyde wouldn't want me to share that conversation with anyone. Tee included—his disappearing act tells me that much. But... Colt?

My loyalty lies with my family.

I can't say that after our marriage Colton will be that.

This is a transaction.

And yet, my loyalty will never stand with Clyde so Colt needs to be my first port of call.

Something that's backed up when I see he sent me a message earlier.

Colton: Tell me when you land? Safe flight.

He hasn't changed.

Even as a teenager, he was a nurturer. That was part of the reason I kept on coming around. I always felt safe with him. Which is why it killed something in me, something fragile, when he cut me loose like I meant dick to him.

> Me: I'm through security. Will be boarding soon. But when I get there and have a chance, we need to talk.

I start to tuck my phone into my pocket but before I can, I get an alert.

> Colton: Everything okay?

> Me: Sure. Just need to tell you something.

> Colton: You're a cereal killer.

Despite the anxiety that still has me in a chokehold, my lips quirk. The joke, considering our past, could fall flat, but I know he's trying to lighten the situation.

I can't fault him for that.

Nurturer.

Protector.

I always wanted him to shield me from the boogeyman...

Who knew we'd end up sharing the same one?

> Me: If I am, it's the low-carb option. No one would kill for muesli.

> Colton: The Germans might.

> Colton: Let me know you arrived safely.

There it is again.

> Me: Sure.

This time, I tuck my phone away for real.

Trying not to feel something for the man who cares about whether I land or not when my grandmother or brothers didn't ask me to keep them informed...

Chapter 13
Zee

I t's eleven PM before I get the chance to call him. Hardly late for the city that never sleeps but hella late at ten PM for a rancher.

> **Me: You okay for me to call?**

> **Colton: Sure.**

He picks up almost immediately. "Hey."

"I'm sorry about the time," I excuse.

"It's fine. What's going on?"

The meeting with Clyde's had me in its grip all day—screwing with my blood sugar as well as messing with my head.

A part of the reason it's taken me so long to call him is that I've been second-guessing myself.

Telling him about Clyde's request is akin to trusting him, and I already promised myself I'd never be such a fool again.

I've filmed six videos because the only thing that soothes me is baking and decorating my cookies. The panic kicked in when he texted me after I told him I'd arrived, saying I could phone him any time.

"I know you're there. I can hear you breathing."

Though he sounds amused, I stutter, "S-Sorry. I-I'm struggling to get my thoughts together."

Your day of reckoning is coming.

I've no idea why that horrible letter pops into my head. Talk about bad timing.

The note feels like it's more suited to his father. But if it isn't, is the facade Colt showed me a lie?

Should I trust him?

Is the man so different from the boy I knew?

"You breaking off the deal?"

Huh.

Of course, that's where his mind went.

"No."

He clears his throat. "I'm relieved to hear that."

"I didn't mean to make you think—" Hesitating, I rub my tired eyes. "I don't like your father."

"Join the club."

"No. I mean it. I hate him. Have for a long time." Since I was a child. Never mind how he ruined my life.

"To be honest, I figured that out from our conversations," he says calmly, and he's not talking about our recent ones. "Trust me when I say, *proudly*, I'm nothing like him."

"This isn't about you. It isn't about our deal."

"What's it about then?"

"He was waiting for me. At the airport," I whisper.

Silence is my only answer.

Until: "Did he hurt you?"

There's a zip of emotion that threads through the words— rage.

I've listened to this man talk like every word he uttered was from God's lips to my ears. I shouldn't be reassured by his anger but I am.

"Of course not. We were in a secured area. He'd have been a fool to hurt me."

"He was in a secured area?" he repeats, his confusion obvious. "Wait a minute, he wasn't waiting for you in the parking lot?"

"No. Past security. Said he was flying out to Vancouver. He orchestrated the meeting between us."

"That asshole," he barks, and the insult is infinitely more reassuring.

He didn't know Clyde intended on sabotaging me today.

So *Grand-mère* did tell him.

Probably over a conversation where they celebrated the 'merger.'

"What did he want? Did he try to bribe you?"

There are moments in life where everything can hinge upon the decision one makes in that second...

I can literally feel the air throbbing with the importance of this occasion.

A relationship forged.

Ties mended.

An olive branch extended.

Or not.

Clinging onto the faith I had in the boy I once knew...

"Yeah."

He grinds his teeth. Audibly. "What did he offer you?"

"Cash. I don't think he realizes I'll be working. Says I need spending money—"

"The bastard lives in the Middle Ages." He sighs. "Sorry for cursing."

"New York's my home. I hear worse on the regular."

Still, that slight bit of levity does what it did earlier—encourages my anxiety to trickle away.

The release from its crushing weight comes with great relief.

"Still, I shouldn't be cursing so soon. What will my future bride think of me?"

I bite the inside of my cheek at his teasing. "That you're human? I think I'd prefer that. Pigeon Creek can't decide whether the Korhonens are demigods or demons."

He snickers. "Demons, maybe. Fitting considering that's who Cole used to play for."

The New Jersey Blue Demons, to be precise. I've lived with Tee for too long not to know that.

"That didn't help matters, I'm sure," is my prim retort. "Anyway, I wanted to tell you about your father."

"I appreciate it. You didn't have to say anything..."

I can sense he's taken aback that I did.

"I know." I pause. "I-I didn't accept his offer."

"Zee," he interrupts before I can continue. "I know you didn't."

"O-Okay."

I hate that his approval still matters to me.

I can hear him drumming his fingers. Fingers that belong to a man who'll be my husband soon enough.

Before the year's out—that's all the contract stipulated—but neither of us can afford to wait.

"I guess I should go," I mutter. "We need some rest."

"Yeah, we do." Another pause, but from him this time. "Look, I think I'm speaking for both of us when I say we want our relationship to be low-key."

I huff. "Definitely."

"How about we get married in Saskatoon?"

Any future wife of his would come under public scrutiny. But I'm *me*. My baggage is legendary in our corner of the world so it makes sense...

"You'd want that?" I ask warily.

"I don't care where so long as it isn't the church in town."

He knows I'd probably get stoned by the locals when we left said church as man and wife.

I shouldn't be offended. Not when he's giving me an option that doesn't involve pebbles and rocks. But once upon a time, I used to dream about marrying him in that tiny church...

Instead, he's offering to marry me as if I'm a secret he wants to keep under lock and key.

"Great idea," I rasp, the words burning my tongue like acid.

"Good. I'll make the arrangements. When do you think you can get your things squared away?"

"I spoke with my boss earlier. She's fine with me moving. Says our in-person meetings can be online."

"That's awesome news."

Because he sounds genuine, I cut him some slack as my fingers toy with the weave of the blanket covering my knees, one that *Grand-mère* crocheted for me. "Yeah, it is. She also gave me some time off. A week. Guess I know what I'll be doing."

Seven days to wrap up my life in the city and to return to Pigeon Creek...

It shouldn't be as daunting as it is, not when this marriage solves a lot of problems, but my mom didn't raise no fool. Green flags or red flags, this is the opposite of a healthy relationship.

"I'll be in touch with a moving company about transporting your belongings here," he murmurs, breaking into the whirlpool of thoughts that's been threatening to drown me all day.

"I appreciate that."

I'd been wondering how I was going to pay for the expense.

But then I forgot how much of a gentleman he is.

"Just let me know the number of rooms you need to be packed."

"I will, for sure."

"The company will box up—"

"No, it's fine. Tee has time on her hands through the day and she promised to help me."

"I thought she'd refuse. Everyone knows how close you are."

Not even Tee knows how close *we* used to be.

"She's as happy as we are about our current situation," is all I say. "But she's a friend and she helps where she can."

Another hum.

"I'll book flights for myself this—"

"Why?"

"To meet you in New York."

"You don't have to do that."

"Sure I do."

"It's a waste of money."

"I'm not going to let you do this on your own." That shouldn't make me want to cry, but it does. "I'll fly down on Wednesday and be with you Thursday morning. We'll head for a license once we're in Saskatoon. Zee?"

"Yes?"

"It'll be okay."

"I-I guess."

"I couldn't prevent what happened with my father at the airport but I'll be on my guard from now on. I know he scares you even if you deny it. I'll protect you from him. I promise."

Staring blindly at the crocheted flower pattern covering my knees, I whisper, "I believe you."

A satisfied grunt sounds in my ear. "We're starting this off strong by having each other's backs. I'll see you on Thursday but keep in touch, okay?"

"I will."

"Zee?"

"Yes."

"You can trust me with your ranch. I'm not Clyde—"

"I know you're not, and I know I can." An annoyed laugh escapes me. "Your father tried to tell me that you weren't used to managing a ranch. Even when you were seventeen, you knew the Seven Cs better than he did."

"Thank you."

"There's no need to thank me. It's the truth. The Bar 9 will be in safe hands with you. Hell, the triplets will be too." *It's just me I'm worried about.*

Before he can comment, I cut the line.

Once the silence of my room is all I can hear, I rub my eyes.

That entire conversation was unexpected and yet, when I climb into bed a few minutes later, the burden of my upcoming marriage is lighter than it was.

Just like last night, I press a hand to my stomach once the light's off.

I could be pregnant soon.

By next summer soon.

And Colton Korhonen and I could be divorced by the following Thanksgiving.

"No way I'm going to sleep thinking stuff like that," I grumble as I give myself permission to do something I never permitted in the past... "Colton Korhonen images," I ask Siri.

His face pops up almost immediately. Though his younger brother, Cole, populates a good chunk of the search results, there's plenty for me to see of my future husband.

Blowing up one of the shots, I stroke my thumb down his cheek.

He's a handsome man, make no mistake. Like the best whiskies, he's gotten better with age.

But his eyes...

I recognize something in them that I know is in mine.

The past is more than memories for us. Wistful wisps of times gone by, old laughs, and happy occasions that cover up the sadder ones.

No, ours come with chains.

Pain.

Grief.

Loss.

I'm reminded of the fact he doesn't smile much from picture after picture of him staring somberly into the camera.

I can see it in my mind's eye, though.

Lost to our mutual histories, I fall asleep.

Staring into eyes that don't see me back.

It's the first time I share a pillow with Colton Korhonen, and it's nothing like how my teenage self hoped it'd be.

Chapter 14
Colton

"**W**hat the hell kind of game do you think you're playing?" I growl, hours after my call with Zee because it's taken this damn long for him to answer.

"Is that any way for a son to greet his father?"

"Leave her alone, Pops."

"She told you."

"Of course she did."

"Damn," he mutters.

Irritation flares inside me, hot and wild in its fury. "How dare you ask my fiancée to spy on me?"

"Like that, is it? Told you she was a tasty piece of ass."

Fuse well and truly lit, I snarl, "Don't contact her. Don't try to see her. Don't talk to her—"

"She's going to be my daughter-in-law! Of course, I'm going to see her. At Christmas and—"

"No. You're not welcome at the ranch anymore."

"What?!"

"If you think I'm going to trust you anywhere near her after the last time you turned my girlfriend into one of your mistresses, you're an idiot. Back off, Pops. I'll make you regret it if you try anything else."

"You can't throw me out of my own home."

"Watch me. I'm having Mrs. Abelman pack up your stuff. She'll be shipping it to Saskatoon within the next few weeks.

"This is my ranch.

"*Mine.*

"I can do whatever the hell I want with it and invite whoever the hell I want onto it. You're no longer welcome."

"You little shit—"

"I learned it from the best."

Not letting him make a rebuttal, I disconnect the call and text her:

Me: He won't be a problem anymore.

The trouble with Pops is that I know he can't let shit go. Can't help himself.

This won't be the last we hear of him, but what I did tonight, I'll do again.

If this marriage is going to be anything more than two one-time friends-cum-strangers being 'donors' for a child that neither knew they were going to share until a few days ago, then she has to know I'll keep her safe.

That's the least I can offer her.

Text Chat
THE FOLLOWING DAY

Calder: You not talking to us now?

Carson: Don't blame her

Colby: We were jerk-offs

Calder: But you know how Grand-mère is, Zee. She went all Rabid Wolves on our asses

Colby: She's not answering :(

Calder: We suck

Carson: Harder than Holly from Advanced Calculus.

Calder: LMFAO

Colby: We got Dysons for mouths?

Zee: Guys, if this is your way of making it up to me for BETRAYING me, it's not working

Colby: We owe you like a trillion

Carson: But with the exchange rate how it is, can we owe you in CAD and not USD?

Colby: Why would she need USD when she's coming home?

Carson: So, a trillion CAD

Zee: You owe me ten trillion. USD.

Calder: Ouch

Zee: What's this bull I hear about you tagging, Calder?

Calder: GTG

Zee: Carson, glue his phone to his hand

Carson: I have literal permission to superglue you to your phone, Calder. You know I'm not afraid to do it

Calder: FML

Calder: I hate the Korhonens

Calder: I hate Grand-mère for making you marry one of them

Calder: And there was no way in hell you set fire to the stables. It was only right that I take a stand.

Zee: What was the tag?

Calder: The Bar 9 logo, of course.

Zee: As much as I appreciate you defending my honor, Colton's not like a regular Korhonen

Zee: AND, in the future, using our logo as a tag is pretty much a signature. As well as an admission of guilt.

Calder: If Colton's anything like Callan, I'll need to headbutt him immediately

Zee: No headbutting

Calder: :(

Zee: Colby, I thought you were keeping an eye on Calder.

Colby: Hey, I'm eighteen too and I'm not my brother's keeper

Zee: I'm twenty-six, live in another country, and I'm still your keeper. The perks of being the eldest.

Colby: *sobs*

Carson: Is this how it's going to be when you're home?

Zee: No. I'll be at the Seven Cs

Colby: You'll be LIVING there?!

Zee: Colton gave me the choice. I didn't feel like living with Grand-mère again so behind enemy lines I go

Colby: :O :O :O

Calder: o.O

Carson: :%

Zee: Have I figured out a way to shut you all up?

Zee: How did the open-house event go?

Carson: Calder sprained his wrist.

Zee: FFS

Colby: Carson got into a fight

Calder: Colby fell asleep on a city bus lol. We had to chase it down because we got off without him.

Zee: The only reason you three are still alive is because you're always together, I swear.

Zee: Nightmares. That's what you are.

Calder: Awwwww, we wuv you too, sis

Zee: Yeah, yeah

Carson: You gonna start being the responsible sibling?

Zee: Lol, nope.

Zee: Colt says he'll handle you. That was all it took to get me to agree to the marriage ;)

Calder: You're okay with this?

Zee: Not particularly, but we do what we have to, don't we?

Colby: I guess. Grand-mère looks brighter since you signed the agreement

Calder: We were in a lot of debt, huh?

Zee: We were. She didn't tell you?

Colby: No. Still thinks we're kids.

Carson: When are you getting married?

Zee: Next week in Saskatoon

Carson: We don't get to be there?

Calder: *pouts*

Colby: SHE DOESN'T WANT US THERE

Zee: You can attend my wedding when it matters.

Zee: I'll let you be my ring bearers and everything

Colby: SHE LOVES US AGAIN

Carson: I dunno. We're not five. Ring bearers, Zee?

Zee: Shuddup. Of course, I love you, but that doesn't mean I don't have my own ways of punishing you.

Carson: Now I FEEL the love.

Zee: So you should.

Zee: I also love Grand-mère but I don't want to see her for a while. That means you have to come to the Seven Cs if you want to hang out with me

Colby: You'll only get Calder over there if you tell him he can tag something lol

Calder: Sir, yes, sir

Zee: No tagging allowed, hellions

Carson: Hey, do you think this marriage BS is why the old man was here two weeks ago? You know, when Colby backed into that fancy car of his?

Zee: OMG. You did what?!

Calder: *snickers* Colby was overzealous with the clutch. Busted up Clyde's Porsche.

Carson: The best part was Colby 'accidentally' forgetting how a stick shift worked. Clyde had to get into our truck and drive it himself because Colby just kept on ramming into it over and over.

Calder: And over and over :P

Colby: I should have won an Academy Award for best actor

Carson: We didn't tell Clyde that we've been driving on the ranch since we were nine LMAO

Zee: You're going to be the death of me, I swear to God

Zee: So, you didn't know about the arranged marriage thing?

Colby: Dude, no

Calder: Fuck, Zee. You think I'd have let her get away with this BS if I knew her game?

Zee: Okay, so you don't owe me trillions then

Zee: See you soon? (Though I don't know why I want to!!!!!!!!!)

Calder: For realz

Carson: Hey, we got your back, sis

Colby: But if you could loan us a couple hundred bucks to fix our quarter panel, you'd be the best sister in the world.

Zee: You have some freakin' nerve, kid.

Zee sends $400

Zee: I can't afford more.

Colby: Can confirm we have the best sister

Carson: 100%

Calder: Legit

Chapter 15
Zee

"Someone tells me we're losing you to Canada." An arm hooks around my neck. "Is that true, Ms. Suzy?"

"Don't call me that, Link." I groan.

"Ignore him," Lily, his Old Lady, says with a tut. "He's been pouting ever since I told him in Canada, they think they live above a crack den."

"I thought it was a joke."

I cough. "I mean... ha, ha, ha?"

Lily pats Link's cheek. "To be fair, you help create the crack den vibe down here, baby."

"Sugar tits, you wound me." He slams a hand to his heart. "I'm a man trying to make an honest buck—"

"Since when is anything we do honest?" Nyx rumbles.

Once upon a time, when I first met Nyx, the now-VP, and Link, the Road Captain of the Satan's Sinners' MC, I'd almost crapped my pants, but I've gotten used to how terrifying they both are.

Rachel calls it 'immersive therapy.'

I call it 'adapt or die.'

"Hi, Nyx!" I chirp. "Everything okay with Giulia and the baby?"

"She's due any day and she's making my life hell." He scrubs a hand over his face. "And Samael thinks it's funny to piss in the garden since this asshole—" He slaps the back of Link's head. "—got drunk after a game and used Giulia's rose bushes as a toilet."

I cough. "I'm sure it's a phase."

He points a finger at Link. "It had better be."

Link tries and fails to hide his grin. "What's in Canada that you can't get here, Suzy?"

"I hate it when you call me that. My name's ZEE, Link. And there's my ranch."

"A ranch?" Link frowns. "Rachel never mentioned a ranch."

"My family's owned one for years."

Lily blinks. "You're a farmer?"

"No. I'm a rancher." I crinkle my nose. "Not that *I've* ever ranched, but I'm the daughter of one. On my mom's side. It's time to go home, I guess. The non-crack den awaits."

Link snickers. "You're lucky you're not a guy. That's all I'm saying."

I wink. "I'd best go in and see Rachel. I have some stuff to finalize before I leave."

"You're still working for her?" Nyx questions.

"Yep. Just changing my location."

As we make our farewells, the three of them take off out of Rachel's front yard and cross the patch of land that leads to the Sinners' clubhouse.

Yes, I work for Rachel Laker. But she works for an MC and a myriad other consortiums with dubious legal ties.

And no, my *grand-mère* will never, ever, *ever* learn that because I already get grief about being lower on the career ladder than a murderer. If she knew I work for actual murderers then—

"She's here!" Parker yells from the staircase, rushing down the final steps so fast I thought she was falling, but she lands like a pro gymnast and immediately tugs me into a hug. "I expect daily messages—"

"I'm going home, not to the other side of the world, Parker."

"My baby's growing up."

"I didn't even know you were here," I mumble, squeezing her tightly because I thought she was still in Ohio.

From her position by a coat rack where she's shoving her daughter into a raincoat, Rachel snorts. "Leave her alone, Parker. She has more sense than you anyway. She'll be fine."

Parker pouts. "And she calls herself my friend."

"It's because I love you that I can give you crap." Rachel, ignoring Sommer's wriggling, arches a brow at me. "It'll be strange you not popping by for visits."

"I know."

"You sure there's nothing I can do? Want me to reach out to some attorneys in Canada?"

"It's fine. Honestly."

Rachel shakes her head. "I didn't think arranged marriages happened outside of the mob and for religious purposes."

"Business. That's all it is."

Parker and Rachel share a look.

"If he hurts you," Rachel growls, "then you tell me and I'll send Rex to deal with it."

"Who's taking my name in vain, little swimmer?" Rex, the President of the MC, demands as he swoops in to grab Sommer and tosses her up and down, making her chortle in delight.

"I'm telling Zee that if she finds herself in a sticky situation, you'll sort out her new husband for her."

Rex settles his attention on me. "Without a shadow of a doubt. I know you wanted to keep the reason for your departure a secret from the rest of the MC, but you're one of us—" *Grand-mère would love to hear that.* "—and we protect our own. You get me?"

My lips twitch into a smile. "I get you, Rex. Thank you."

"She didn't want a farewell party. That's why she didn't want anyone to know," Parker inserts.

"I'm not leaving. Not really."

"I think you need to look up the definition of that verb," Rachel derides, her tone as cool as ever.

I spent the first two years of my position with her thinking she detested me.

Now, I can't decide if she likes me.

I *do* know that she didn't want to lose me. Enough that she's given me a stipend to set up a proper home office at the ranch and she doesn't have a problem with me telecommuting.

I guess that means I do something right.

Rex kisses Rachel on the cheek. "I'll see you later."

"You'll be okay taking her to the pool?"

"I think I can handle it," he drawls before he whispers something in her ear that has her blushing.

"Would you like some coffee?" Parker asks, rolling her eyes at their antics.

"I have some work stuff to finalize with Rachel."

"Boring." Parker boos. "You'd better come and see me in my office before you leave. No sneaking out like a big, sneaky sneak."

Rex chuckles. "Original, Parker."

"You don't appreciate that I refuse to swear around your offspring, Rex."

"Come on through, Zee," Rachel directs as the other two start bickering.

I almost appreciate Rachel's MO—the second I'm through the door to her office, it's all work and there's comfort in that.

I didn't want to make a fuss about leaving and I sure as hell didn't want to attend what the Sinners consider a party. Farewell or otherwise.

The calm of Rachel's office is found in the highly stressful work we both undertake on her clients' behalves.

Three hours later, we've finished and have discussed how things will be once I'm in Canada.

"I appreciate you being so flexible, Rachel. I didn't want to stop working for you."

"And I didn't want to lose you. You're a damn good paralegal.

"I know your grandmother gives you a hard time about your chosen career, but you can tell her from me that it'd be a shame for you to quit." She pulls open a drawer in her desk. "Here's a 'goodbye' gift from me."

My mouth rounds when the case reveals a Mont Blanc fountain pen. "Rachel!"

"You're right about it not being a true farewell, but I have no idea when I'm going to see you again—" Her words cut off with a sniffle.

A sniffle.

Rachel is crying?

I sit there in perplexed silence as my boss cries (while pretending she isn't) and continues, "You deserve this, and I hope you know how much I appreciate you."

I clear my throat. "Rachel?"

"Yes, Zee?"

"Would you be okay with a hug?"

She sniffles again, and my day gets weirder when she nods, rounds the desk, and opens up her arms to me.

As I hug my boss a non-farewell farewell, as lovely as it is, it acts like another death knell on my stateside era.

The US might be a crack den in the eyes of Canada, but I've loved my time here.

It gave me shelter when I needed it. Provided me with anonymity when I craved it.

And offered me a future when I was stuck in the past.

Whatever my grandmother says, these bikers might be murderers, but they're also good people.

I'll go to my grave believing that.

Chapter 16
Colton

"**Y**ou're insane."

Shifting my focus from the Hanjie logic puzzle in front of me, I cut my youngest brother a look. "Figured you'd get it more than anyone. That weed farm I uncovered is huge. Power of attorney or not, I've already set men on the Bar 9 and—"

"Stop thinking like the mindless bourgeoisie, Colton."

Ah, the ultimate insult.

I take a deep sip of my coffee. "I knew reading Marx would make you spout crap like that."

It's going to be one of those goddamn days.

"Of course, you're going to set men on guarding that weed farm. We can't let asswipes from the city think they can get away with growing pot on our ranches." He sniffs like I'm a moron.

If so, I'm the moron who did a scan of the Bar 9 and discovered an audaciously large plot of land being used to cultivate weed.

That alone was enough to tell me how disorganized and understaffed the McAllister ranch is.

The hiring process is going to be a nightmare.

"—as happy as I am about this development, you're going to make him worse."

Confused about the topic shift, I demand, "Who? Pops?"

"Yes, *him*. You cut him out, but he's like Hydra. Another head will spawn."

"That's what I'm insane for?"

"Yes." His expression turns knowing. "Still, at least you're heading the company and not just the ranch. We can shift some of the herd to market." He forks up a piece of bacon. "We probably need to sell a quarter even with access to the McAllister's water rights."

"I was thinking a third." I snag a couple spoonfuls of scrambled eggs when Mrs. Abelman dumps the bowl on the table.

What she offers in rudeness, she makes up for in cooking.

And love.

You'd never think to look at her dour expression, but she's singlehandedly kept us from falling apart since the divorce.

"We'd only have to buy them back when we get our situation regulated," Callan points out.

"I'd prefer to keep the herd numbers low."

"Why?"

"Chickens."

"Chickens?"

"They cluck."

"I have an IQ of 159, Colton. I know what a chicken is."

"Such modesty," I remark. "Chickens are more sustainable than cows."

Callan hoots. "You want to turn us into a chicken farm?"

"No," I grumble as I snag three slices of toast from the stack Mrs. Abelman drops in front of me. "But that land over on the border with the Frobishers—it'd be a good place to start. Even if we can only supply the town, it's something. Proactive."

Callan frowns at me. "There won't be enough money in it. Not on a small scale."

"Doesn't need to be. Not everything's about profits." I wag my fork at him. "Sometimes, you have to preserve the land as well as your soul.

"I'm going to implement a ton of measures that Pops wouldn't sign off on to help prevent wildfires and we're going back to breeding horses. That'll fund some of my 'quirky' ideas."

"Oh." His eyes brighten with excitement as he sits taller in his seat. "Really?"

"Yeah. Proof that I *am* insane. Cole's going to give me nothing but shit for wanting to restart the breeding program."

It'll be worth it though.

"He's still grieving," Callan says calmly.

Calmly because he was on the brink of turning nine when the fire happened.

The aftermath is nothing but a distant memory for him after the trauma he experienced in his childhood. All the same, it triggered an inherent need to secure the ranch.

We have more closed-circuit cameras than North Korea.

"Betsy was his heart horse," Mrs. Abelman interrupts as she seats herself at the table. "You can't be restarting that breeding program without telling him. I'm not going to be the one who picks up the pieces when he has a meltdown."

"Mia'll do that. The perks of being an engaged man, Mrs. Abelman."

"You say that and watch him get his anger issues out with those damn pucks in the vestibule again!"

I grimace. "That window cost ten grand to replace."

"Be double that now," Callan inserts. "Best to tell him outside. Away from expensive stained-glass windows."

"He's never here anyway."

"So you intend for him to just show up and see the stables?" Mrs. Abelman demands, tutting as she pours herself some coffee. "Colton, your mum raised you better than that."

"I have enough shit on my plate without thinking about Cole's feelings."

"He's your brother," she chides. "For good or ill."

"Mostly ill," Callan comments, making me chuckle. "What time's your flight?"

I check the clock on the wall. "I need to be on my way in two hours."

Mrs. Abelman nods. "Your mother called."

Unsurprisingly, Callan braces himself for disappointment.

147

"When's she coming?"

"Next week. Said she put her resignation in as soon as you told her."

I flick a look at Callan who's evidently relieved by the news.

Who can blame him?

Eighteen years old and he barely knows his mother because his father's an asshole.

Pops didn't *want* us.

He sued for custody to spite Mum—the only parent who genuinely loves us.

Ever since I told my kid brother I was bringing Mum home, he's been warily excited—waiting for the disappointment of her not coming when I know nothing would stop her from being here.

He'll learn.

"Chickens," Mrs. Abelman says out of the blue. "I'd like some of those. Your father'd never let me have a coop. Said he got sick of being woken up by roosters when he was a boy."

Pops had weird ideas.

Who has a ranch and doesn't have a coop for eggs?

Clyde Korhonen, genius extraordinaire, that's who.

"You can have your own personal one, Mrs. Abelman," Callan inserts cheerfully. "Can't she, Colt?"

"Definitely."

It's the least I can do for the woman who's been half-mom to us all.

She tries to hide her pleased smile but mostly fails.

It's... *odd*.

Mrs. Abelman doesn't do smiles.

She's dour and quiet. Scuttles around like a mouse but has a bark as bad as her bite. I'm sure that's how she survived here as long as she did with Pops hanging around.

Cole calls her Poltergeist Abelman for a reason.

"I'll arrange the coop when I'm home," I inform her.

"With the McAllister girl."

Her tone's not disapproving, but...

"Yes."

148

Her lips purse. "Never thought she'd agree to live here."

"I gave her the option of living at the Bar 9."

Primly, she sips her coffee. "You were willing to move?"

"It was the least I could offer."

She clucks her tongue. "We did raise you right. Faith in you restored.

"She probably jumped at the chance of not having to live with Juliette. That woman would turn a nun to Satanism."

Callan snorts. "Just think, Colt, she's going to be your grandmother-in-law."

I toss my napkin at him, satisfied when it gets him right in the face.

"No fighting at the table," Mrs. Abelman orders. "Where shall I put her? And your father's things now that they're out of his suite?" A menial task she'd insisted on taking because she's a control freak about her domain. "What about your mother? Should she still stay in the guest quarters?"

The multitude of questions has me rubbing my chin.

The house is split up into wings. Head, guest, and sons, with staff accommodations off the kitchen. The head shares one wing with his wife, the guest beds number in the half-dozen, and the sons all share a wing because the Korhonens rarely breed girls.

The last one died in the forties—killed in a shell factory when ammo she was making for the troops exploded in her face.

"Send Pops's shit to the house in Saskatoon—"

"You're kicking him out *for real*?" Callan sputters, eyes wide with delight like the time I told him we were going to Disneyland when he was nine.

"Sure am," I retort, unsettled when I take note of his relief at the news.

This time, Mrs. Abelman smiles fully.

It's disturbing.

"I'll get on that today. The sooner I don't have to see his face again, the better."

I warn, "He might bounce back in this direction. You know he won't like us evicting him from the house."

149

"Can we change the locks?" Callan queries. "I could buy those electronic ones. With a code."

I think about how Zee sounded on the phone after he tried to hijack her at the airport...

"Good thinking. But don't you have some exams to study for? Deal with them first."

"I could ace them in my sleep."

"Don't be precocious." To Mrs. Abelman, as I butter some toast, I direct, "Keep Mum in the guest wing. She was happy there last summer." When we'd been hoping God would evict Pops from the world permanently after his first bout with arrhythmia. "As for my stuff, if you could move it into Pops's room, please, Mrs. Abelman, and make sure Mum's old suite is ready so Zee can unpack in there when her things arrive.

"The changes are going to be..."

"Rough?" Mrs. Abelman nods. "We'll get through it. Just like we always do."

The 'together' part of the sentence goes unspoken.

"Two came in last night," she informs us both.

"Everything go okay?"

Callan, like always when this topic arises, clams up.

He certainly doesn't disapprove of what we do behind the scenes here at Seven Cs, but it unnerves him.

The pain men can put women through, women they vowed to cherish, is something I don't think he'll ever fully be able to accept.

The funny thing is, he's the one who remembers how Pops beat on Mum the least but our guests affect him hardest.

I say that but it's not like Cody or Cole know what goes on here.

They'd have to stick around for more than five minutes to look beneath the surface, and that's more than either of them are capable of.

"I settled them in the bunkhouse as planned. It's getting too full," she warns.

"There's an empty house by the gas station that we can use if need be. The tenants moved out last month."

It's not like we can refuse someone sanctuary because we don't have the space.

"There are no scheduled drops, are there?" Callan asks, anxiety riddling the words.

"No. But emergencies happen." She pats his shoulder, fully aware of how sensitive he is in these situations.

He might be eighteen in the eyes of the law, but he's still a kid. A kid from a broken home with a fucked-up parental unit.

Callan's fork clatters on his dish. "There won't be the anonymity of the bunkhouse in a rental."

I glance at him, making sure to present a calm facade. "I'll look into having another bunkhouse built."

His sigh of relief tells me that was the right answer. "Did you hear about the Linnox place?"

"What about it?"

"It's no longer for sale. They're closer to us than the McAllisters. It could be important for logistics."

"Can you find out who the buyer is?"

"I heard in town it's someone famous."

My brows lift at Mrs. Abelman's words. "Since when do you listen to the rumor mill?"

"That old fool, Harold, sometimes knows more than the *Herald* does." Her disapproval is a tad hypocritical, seeing as she's using him as her source. Not that I point that out.

"Ugh. Famous?" Callan whines. "Are we going to have an influencer breeding alpacas next door?"

I grin at the thought. "It might shake things up in town."

"Things need shaking," Mrs. Abelman says dourly.

Callan pulls a face.

With a pointed nod at Callan's breakfast, and only once he's started eating again, she asks, "Are you going to tell Susanne?"

"About the famous person?"

Mrs. Abelman pins me in a glower. "No, Colton. About Dove Bay."

"The fewer people know the better."

She nods her understanding.

Our operation is sensitive. Its success lies in secrecy—only a handful of people know about it. Us, Theo, and the two trusted ranch hands who work in that quadrant—Darrel and Buck who've both been with us for two decades.

Building another bunkhouse will eat into that anonymity, but Callan's right about the rental and we've been needing to expand for a while now so it's time to bite the bullet.

"She's bound to notice. Plus, is it any way to start a relationship with that kind of secret?

"'Oh, once or twice a month, *darling*," Callan mocks, "a truck drops off women at our bunkhouse who've been psychologically and physically abused by the monsters they married. We're not people trafficking, I promise.'"

I think about how she picked up on my barely-there interaction with Bea that day in town...

"We'll deal with that if and when it comes to it," is all I say.

And if she's anything like the girl I used to know, I have a feeling it'll be sooner rather than later, but it's still tomorrow's problem.

Today, I have a flight to catch.

If she doesn't notice, then she won't be here long enough for Dove Bay to be an issue.

I refuse to ponder how that makes me feel. Because if I truly thought about it, I'd upend this table, inadvertently scaring the shit out of my brother and Mrs. Abelman, and that's never on my to-do list.

Chapter 17
Colt
PAST

The One That Got Away - Katy Perry

"Chaos? What are you doing here?" For a second, my brain reacts to her presence like I'm the one who forgot it's Tuesday.

But that's impossible. It's Thursday and I'm only here and not in class because I caught Callan's cold this past weekend and today's the first day the fever broke.

"You can't be here. Not out in the open. What if Pops sees—"

She whips around before I can finish chiding her, and when she does, words fail me anyway.

Her face is ravaged with grief.

I've seen her through the deaths of both her parents, but that's nothing compared to this.

A heavy sigh escapes me and I open my arms.

Walker.

It has to be.

She runs to me like I'm the only solace she has left in the world, and I brace myself for impact. Her arms immediately tunnel around my waist. Her insulin pump digs into me but I'm mostly relieved because the last time she lost someone, we almost lost *her*. Even though I got her to promise to take care of herself, it didn't stop her from ending up in the hospital.

"He's g-gone," she sobs, her whole body heaving in her misery.

I close my eyes, her grief triggering tears when I stopped crying years ago. I hold her tighter, wishing that hugging her this hard could keep her together, could stop her from falling apart.

Ever since I've known her, she's been fragile. First her dad's heart attack, then her mom drowning...

One of the reasons I've always made sure that I was here on Fridays, even during university, wasn't only for my brothers—but for her. It's also why I attended a diabetes management class in Saskatoon, so I could understand the ins and outs of what she deals with on the regular.

A part of me has always expected to hear that she tried to kill herself by just not keeping a check on her blood sugar.

The thought has me holding onto her harder because I don't know if this one small girl can withstand another loss.

"H-He's gone," she repeats, but this time, it's a wail. Her fists clutch at my jacket, clinging and tearing, yanking on it as if she's fighting Death himself.

I hold her as the storm ravages her. What else can I do?

I can't bring Walker back.

Can't do anything at all, aside from be here.

I rub my cheek against the crown of her head, but her face tilts, and our eyes lock as her mouth seeks mine.

For a moment, I don't know what the hell is happening. One second, she was wailing, and the next, she's kissing me.

I attempt to dislodge her from my embrace, but her arms curve around my shoulders. "Please, Colton. Please. Hold me. Kiss me."

"No, Susanne. No!" I bark when her arms cling to me and won't let go.

The second 'no' has her jolting. Mouth round, she covers it

with trembling fingers, then she gasps. "But I love you. Don't you love me too?"

"Not like that," I appease, but there's no letting her down gently.

One second, she's standing there, gaping at me in horror, and the next she's running off, along the corridor toward the side entrance at the office.

I make to go after her, wanting to ease her mortification, but then I falter.

Rubbing my temple, I retreat a step.

It hurts, though.

She's going to need me to get through Walker's—

"Fuck. Why did she have to do that?"

I'm twenty-two, for Christ's sake. She's still a girl. Only sixteen.

I take another step, but guilt laces that movement too.

I'm almost relieved when Callan shrieks, "Colllllllt, I did it!"

Twisting on my heel, I find Loki staring at me.

I know it's transference but I swear he looks like he disapproves.

I tweak his ear before running my knuckles down his muzzle. "*She* kissed *me*, Loki."

His head jostles as he steps away from me, settling deeper in his stall.

I swear to Christ that's the only time he's ever done that.

"COLT! What do I do when it's in the lasso?"

Callan's screech has me retreating another step.

To Loki, I promise, "I'll make it up to her," before I jog back to my brother.

I don't know that that'll be the last time I see Loki alive.

Hell, I don't even remember why I went in there.

I just race toward Callan, growling, "I told you not to practice while I was in the stables."

157

Chapter 18
Zee

PRESENT DAY

"A t least he's cute."

"You changed your mind," I grumble. "You nearly bit my head off when I said he didn't look like Freddy Krueger."

"Yes, and being the optimistic person that I am, I realize how lucky you are to be trapped into marriage with a man who looks like Colton and *not* Freddy." Her stare is both pointed and chiding. "It's called 'glass half full,' Zee. You should try it sometime."

Wryly, I nod. "If you say so, Tee."

Tee sniffs, but Parker asks, "How cute?" before she can gripe at me.

"You didn't google him?"

Watching us pack, Parker shrugs. "Wanted to see for myself."

Humming as she folds up the last of my clothes, Tee declares, "He's a nine."

Parker whistles. "A nine?!"

"I'm knocking a point off because he's forcing my best friend to marry him."

"It isn't forced if she signed a contract," is Parker's input.

"Plus, she's packing of her own free will. I don't see a gun pointing at her head."

"We're Canadian. We don't do guns."

I cough. "Ranchers do guns."

"Shotguns. Not handguns and pistols. We're polite," Tee insists.

Parker props her chin on her fist. "If you love Canada so much, why don't you freakin' live there?"

"It's better to pine. You appreciate it more."

"I don't. I like it here plenty." I plunk another box by the door. "This officially sucks. Even if my honeymoon isn't on Elm Street."

"According to Tee, the perk is you get a cute husband so no complaining," Parker says helpfully.

"I don't want a cute husband."

"She gets a baby out of it too," Tee tacks on.

Parker grimaces.

I point a finger at her expression. "That's exactly how I feel about this."

"She asked him if he'd agree to IVF." Tee folds one of my sweaters. "Honestly, Zee, the one perk is literally that he's fuckable and you don't want to fuck him."

"I don't know him!"

"You didn't know that guy from *Russu* three weeks ago."

"I didn't have sex with him either. We went for a Reuben," I admit sheepishly.

"You told me you screwed him. Three orgasms, you said."

"That wasn't a lie." I wiggle my hand at her. "You know I did a better job than he would have."

"She has a point. They're so drunk, they make two-pump chumps look like they have stamina when they get out of a club."

"How would you know, Parker?" Tee derides. "You haven't been to a club in decades."

"I haven't been an adult for decades!"

"The last time you went to a club was when you were *in utero*."

Parker mutters, "Screw you."

"Screw you back!" Tee pouts. "I'm going to come and move in with you. It'll stop me from being lonely."

"When I'm in Jersey, I live with Rachel and her motley crew. It's already a full house."

"I'm little. I'll fit into a shoebox."

"If only that were true." Parker's smirk slowly fades. "You're going to have to find another roommate, aren't you?"

"Yeah." Tee rubs her hand over her forehead. "No 'glass half full' optimism takes away how much that blows."

"Why don't you go with Zee? It's not like your music career is thriving."

"That was mean, Parker!"

"Mean but true," she counters unapologetically. "She's cutting herself up about losing you when the simple answer is to go with you. She loves Canada. If I hear her tell me about how Timmies is better over the border one more time or how Walmart isn't for insane people up there, I'm going to scream. As far as I can tell, the winters are the only thing she hates."

Tee points a finger at her. "You need to get laid. You're crabby."

She sniffs. "Sweet Lips had to go home. I wanted to stick around to help Rachel with the transition of Zee moving away. I miss him."

"It's always about sex with you, Tee," I complain. "Sex doesn't heal all the world's ailments."

"If Mother Earth got it on more, I'm sure that global warming would be a thing of the past. It's the friction between her thighs. Nothing more."

Pausing in her work—ordering Rachel's groceries for the week—Parker snickers. "When's Colt coming?"

Tee elbows me in the side. "In an hour. It's their wedding night tomorrow."

"Oooooo-oooooh," Parker teases. "If there's a wedding party then I expect to be invited over Zoom!"

My cheeks turn pink. "You two are horrible."

Tee cackles. "You love us."

"I shouldn't, but I do." If I sound grumpy, so be it.

Tee tugs on my arm and links ours together. "At least there's one perk to Parker's weird lifestyle choices—"

"Hey!"

"What's that?"

"We're used to Zoom parties! We can still hang out. Long distance."

I curl an arm around her shoulder. "You're the best."

"Don't I know it. Underappreciated too."

Parker blows a raspberry so Tee flips her the bird.

Packing more of my stuff away, I stiffen when the doorbell rings.

The whole room falls silent. Until...

"Is that him?" Parker whispers.

"If it is, he's early."

Tee quickly checks her phone and the doorbell camera she installed last month when there were some B&Es in our building.

"It is," she whisper-shouts. "THIS IS NOT A DRILL."

I gulp.

Straighten.

I can't help but feel as if I'm about to face a firing squad.

"What am I supposed to say to him?"

"Hello. Then bring him over here and introduce us. I'll be the judge on whether he's a nine or not."

"Parker, I'm telling you he is," Tee argues.

"Shut up, you two. He'll hear!"

"I heard," he calls through the door. "I appreciate the assessment."

Damn him for sounding amused.

Tee cackles again, and Parker lets out a chuckle.

My cheeks feel like they're on fire as I walk over to the door. Prisoners on their way to the hangman are probably more enthusiastic than I am.

Everything has already changed but this is it.

I can't walk back from this.

My life's about to shift on its axis and there's no return.

Swallowing, I unlock the gazillion locks on the door and finally open it.

He's there.

And Tee's right—though I never like to tell her when she is —he's definitely a nine with a point knocked off for marriage contracts.

"Hello," I greet uncertainly, stepping aside so that he can join us in our shoebox apartment.

"Hey." He glances around the place, absorbing the details in a nanosecond before beaming a smile at Tee and Parker.

That smile...

The rare one that's never captured on camera.

It's bad that it makes my heart hurt, isn't it?

Heading for the computer, he looms over the screen. "I'm Colt. I hear you want to vet me."

"I'm Parker. I know a lawyer and a lot of bad people who'll gladly murder someone if I ask them to—"

"Parker!"

Tee hoots.

Colt's smile deepens. "I'm glad that Zee has someone looking out for her."

"She does," Parker warns. "But Tee was right. You're a nine. She also tells me you're going to have a baby with our girl?"

"You told them everything?"

"They're my best friends," I mutter awkwardly, spying a pair of panties that, of course, are in his line of sight. Snagging them, flustered, I shove them in my pocket. "I'd go nuts if I didn't loop them in."

"Plus, babies are kind of hard to hide." Leaning against the kitchen counter, Tee eyes him. "So, Mr. Korhonen, you've come to whisk my sister away."

"I have," he intones, not glumly like he's getting a raw deal but as if he knows how important the words are to her. "And it's Colton. Or Colt."

Tee sniffs. "When will the movers show up?"

He checks his phone. "On their last update, they said they were a half-hour's drive away. So, they're due any time. Are you mostly done packing?"

"These are the last ones." I point to two boxes. "I need to seal them."

"Is this everything?" he asks.

The collection of items I've gathered during my years in New York City is meager.

"It's not like I'm rich or have an abundant amount of space on my hands," I bite off, aware I sound defensive.

"Take a chill pill, Zee," Parker advises.

Tee slings her arm around my shoulder. "What you don't know, Parker, is this is a rags to riches kinda story. The Korhonen house is fancy as fuck. Think *Downton Abbey* but on the prairie."

Colt laughs. "That's one way of describing it. Badly." But he winks at Parker and, of course, totally charms her.

She even blushes.

My girl who splits her time being a VP's Old Lady in Coshocton and living with an MC Prez and his First Lady in West Orange... She. Blushes.

When the buzzer sounds, Colt warns, "That's probably the movers."

"Crap," I mumble as I scurry around, collecting stray trinkets and dumping them into the two open boxes.

Colt deals with the moving company and leaves me with the task of making sure I haven't forgotten anything too big for the suitcases I'll be traveling with.

Ninety minutes later, my room is empty and the apartment is bare of my belongings.

Sinking onto the sofa, tears prick my eyes at the bareness of the space.

Until Tee hurls herself at my side and starts sobbing.

Her exuberance calms me. It's as if she gives me permission not to be a McAllister and to feel things like a normal person.

I hug her, holding her tight, both of us rocking as the reality hits—tonight, I won't be sleeping here.

Tonight, I'll be in a hotel in Saskatoon.

Tonight, this will stop being my home.

I can't deny I thought he'd hurry us along. But he doesn't.

Of course not.

He's still as kind as he used to be... before it all went wrong.

Colt stands there, talking quietly with Parker about God knows what, and leaves us alone in our misery.

Eventually, Tee's all cried out but she's still sniffling as she wails, "Who's going to wait up for me when I get in from a gig?"

"You can always call me," I tell her, gently stroking a hand over her hair. "That won't stop. You can call me whenever you want."

Tee's bottom lip wobbles but she nods. "And who's going to make sure your blood sugar's all right?"

My laughter is croaky. "I can manage."

I haven't had many major incidents since I was a teenager. Day to day, I've gotten good with the balancing act as a type 1. As good as you can get when experiencing an adrenaline high in the afternoon can make your blood sugar bottom out at 2AM.

"And if she can't, I will," Colton assures her, stepping toward us and invading the conversation.

I don't mind though. Not when his smile is kind and his gaze is gentle as he studies Tee and me.

"You'll check her monitor?" Tee demands.

Colton nods. "Gladly."

"You'll get alerts at 5AM," she cautions.

"I'm awake then," he soothes. "I got this."

She sniffles. "It's my job."

I kiss her cheek. "Technically, it's mine."

"You need a blood-sugar keeper, Susanne McAllister."

"Ouch. Full name?"

We share a look—one that speaks of the many occasions she's force-fed me snacks and how she carries sugar gels in her purse for me. Sometimes, she's who realizes that I'm acting loopy or more confused than usual...

This transition is going to be difficult for both of us.

"Who will make you laugh when you get all sad?" is what she says, though.

"You will. Because I'll call you and you can cheer me up long distance?" I squeeze her tighter. "And you can do the same with me. I'm moving, not dying. I'll always be on the other end of a phone."

"Dying is not allowed."

"We have to go catch our flight?" I whisper, shooting Colt a look.

"Yeah." But he doesn't push or press. "I arranged every-thing regarding the ceremony. We need to get the paperwork sorted in Saskatoon." As I kiss Tee's cheek, he continues, "I'm sorry you couldn't fly back for the ceremony, Christy. If you've changed your mind, I can—"

She swipes at her cheeks and then grants him a great honor. "You can call me Tee. My asshole boss won't grant me PTO on such short notice." Her bottom lip wobbles. "I hate that I can't be there, Zee."

He leaves us to our second sobfest as she sputters apologies for not being able to afford time off from work but gives me twenty minutes to get ready for the airport.

Once I'm showered and dressed in a simple pencil skirt and silk shirt that I combine with leather boots and a warm winter coat, I retreat to the living room and find them laughing with one another.

That he got Tee to relax is something I need to be thankful for.

As bitter as we both are about this situation, I can tell she likes him.

I'm not sure if that makes things better or worse.

It physically hurts to hug her goodbye and to wave farewell to Parker. Hurts more to grab my carry-on while Colt sorts out my luggage and to eventually leave the apartment and hear her turn the six locks behind us.

It's especially rough when she starts crying again.

Wishing I could ease her suffering, I press my hand to the door.

"You'll see her soon," Colt rumbles, his voice kind.

How soon? Not tonight. Not tomorrow night either.

Summer?

The holidays?

God.

"Are you okay?"

His question breaks into my thoughts.

The elevator doors open and he waits for me to step inside before joining me.

I'm not sure if this chivalry is going to wear on my last nerve or ultimately charm me.

Either way, it's a problem for another time.

"It's the end of an era," I finally say.

"That always hurts."

"Yes." The doors close behind us. "Thank you for being kind to her. I know she's... dramatic. It's her creative soul. She feels too much."

"She's a musician, isn't she?"

"Among other things. She's damn good, though. Just can't catch a break here."

"Sometimes, it's not what you know but who."

I tip up my chin. "Very true."

He checks his cell phone. "Tee doesn't know we used to be friends, does she?"

"No."

"Why?"

Because you were my secret.

Not a dirty one. A happy one.

I wanted to keep him to myself. I didn't want to share him. Selfish, but true.

"Does it matter?"

"I suppose not."

The elevator doors open and, outside, there's a car idling—ours.

You're not in Kansas anymore, Doro-zee.

The driver handles my suitcases and Colt deals with him, presenting me with the opportunity of contemplating the man who'll be my husband.

On the way out the door, Parker sent me a thumbs-up while Colt's back was turned...

I didn't need her approval to know that he's a catch.

But it's ten years too late for my silly girlish fantasies to come true.

167

Right?

Chapter 19
Colton

Hotel - Montell Fish

"**D**id Callan know you were going to get married here?"

The question has me studying her.

She looks beautiful.

When I saw her yesterday morning, I was reminded of *how* beautiful. Not when she gussied up for the ceremony, but hair a mess, leggings on, a slouchy sweater hiding most of her shape while she was packing her stuff...

A part of me wasn't sure if I'd made it up, but no.

She's gorgeous.

Both technically mine and technically not.

I raise my wine glass to my mouth and drink.

Deeply.

It's going to be a short night as well as a long one. Which is only fitting considering how interminable yesterday felt—after heading for our license in the afternoon for today's ceremony, making it to our appointment just in time, we both spent the rest of the day in the suite.

It was boring.

And strange.

I missed slumming it with her in Loki's stall where conversation flowed easily between us.

This suite might cost a regular guest two thousand bucks a night, but as I'd stared at the ceiling from the comfort of my fancy bed in a fancier room in the fanciest suite of the hotel my family owns, that was what I craved—those simple times.

Since that day in the lake, everything's shifted. And not just because of a contract, either.

Part of me's been wondering why I was so quick to tar and feather her like she accused. Another part's been thinking of how much that night impacted our lives and veered us off course.

When she clears her throat in a silent prompt, I remember what she asked me. Callan. The wedding. Saskatoon. "He knew."

"Why didn't he want to attend?"

"Not because of the past," I assure her. "Callan never leaves the ranch if he can help it. I've no idea where in the world Cody is, and as for Cole, once he gets over himself, he'll be pissed he missed the ceremony."

His attitude is why I stayed in a hotel on Wednesday night and not at his apartment.

Her mouth tightens.

Maybe it's the wine, or maybe it's the wedding band constricting my finger, but my tongue's loose as I ask, "What happened that night?"

"You want to start married life lost in the past?" she mocks, not even pretending to misunderstand which night I'm talking about as she carefully scoops some of France's finest onto a cracker.

It's funny how quickly I've adapted to seeing her check her level and her grazing—she never skips a meal. Never goes anywhere without a purse that has her kit in it, emergency snacks too.

The first thing I had her do when we made it to the hotel room was share her apps with me so that I can also monitor her.

I knew she didn't like it.

"Colt?" she prompts at my extended silence.

"I'd prefer to start it without any lies between us," I clarify, finger running along the rim of the glass, making the crystal sing. "Why were you there? Did Marcy Armstrong have anything to do with it? Is that why you never said a word about what you saw that night? Do you know where she ran away to?"

"I don't want to talk about this." She pats her napkin to the corners of her mouth. "I think I'll head to bed."

"You'll tell me eventually," I inform her as she gets to her feet.

"Why would I do that?"

"You will." I smile at her. *Blandly*.

"If I told you, you wouldn't believe me."

I can feel her bitterness but I'm unsure if she's hiding behind it.

"I believed you about Loki."

"That's different."

"Why?"

Her hand tightens on the dining chair. "Firstly, it took you ten years to be open to hearing that question, never mind answering it. Secondly—" Her fingers clench. Hard. "—I don't want to start things off on the wrong foot."

"Can the truth do that?"

She hitches a shoulder. "It shouldn't, but it usually does."

"Do you think it's wise to have this between us?"

"What does it matter? We won't be married long."

I swirl the red wine in my wine glass. "Long enough. IVF doesn't always take."

"I don't want to talk about this."

I get to my feet and stride over to her side. Her head tips back at my approach.

"Tomorrow, then," I rumble, not willing to let this go.

Her jaw works. "Fine."

"Sleep well." *Mrs. Korhonen*. "I'll knock on your door when it's time to wake up."

"You don't have to do that. I can set my alarm—"

173

"I'll wake you," I state, gaze locked on hers as, purposely, I press a kiss to her forehead.

A breath catches in her throat as we're both transported back a decade.

To the last time I did that.

I could be mistaken, but I'm sure her lips quiver before she firms them and, frowning, heads to the door that leads to her bedroom.

As it closes behind her, I dip my hand into my pocket and release the marriage certificate from its confines.

God only knows why I didn't store it in my luggage. But I'm glad I didn't now.

Mrs. Susanne Felicia McAllister-Korhonen.

She didn't expect a wedding band. Never mind an engagement ring.

It was satisfying to slide first one onto her finger and then the other. Even more so to hand her the ring I intended on wearing too.

I could tell she wanted to argue, but only our witnesses and the marriage commissioner's presence stopped her. Then, after the ceremony, her brain kicked in—it'd look odd in town if she, in particular, didn't wear both.

It seems each of us is sensible.

I'm not sure I like that.

She didn't used to be.

She was emotional and quick to cry and faster to laugh. Now, she's wooden.

It hurts something in me to see that.

Never mind *knowing* that I'm part of the reason for the change in her.

Carefully, I fold the certificate up and return it to my pocket, then I set the alarm on my phone and handle the messages on there.

Thanks to ignoring it today, I have a bunch of missed calls. Everything's urgent so I deal with emails, enough that ninety minutes pass in the blink of an eye.

With a sigh, I glance at her bedroom door then head for a shower.

Once I've stripped off, I pack the suit I wore for my wedding ceremony into my garment bag.

It was a simple affair—neither of us expected much more, but that didn't mean I couldn't make it special.

I doubt I'll be doing this again even if she does after we divorce.

So, I tried.

I think it worked—I saw her tuck the small posy of flowers I had delivered to Marc Robard's club into her purse. And she keeps on rubbing her thumb over her rings.

Marc is my personal attorney. The reason I asked him to be a witness was to access the orangery in his club that's famous in Saskatoon for its domed, stained-glass roof that lets in even the most meager of wintry light.

Surrounded by orange trees, in the sticky warmth of a silent conservatory, we said our vows to the marriage commissioner.

Whether I asked for this or not, it's a day I won't forget in a hurry.

For a second, my hand hovers over the faucet as my mind drifts further.

I think about those intense, dewy green eyes of hers. The simple skirt and shirt she wore—business casual but more relaxed in their cut. I think about the elegant heels that arched her feet, making her ass stick out.

She looked gorgeous, but this isn't just any woman I'm talking about.

This is my wife.

I didn't think those two words would resonate as deeply as they are, not when I didn't get a chance to pick her. Not when there's a definite expiration date on our marriage. But there you go. My brain belongs in the Dark Ages.

I guess it helps that she has bite but is soft enough to show her emotions in front of me, like when she left her apartment and Tee behind.

She straightened her shoulders as we took our vows—no weeping, only solid resolve.

She's brave and bravery comes with strength. I've dealt with enough shit in my life to appreciate her courage.

But no matter what promise she got out of me, Zee and I both know the truth—if she has my baby, she's going nowhere.

I barely know her anymore, but I know *that*.

And that seals my decision for me.

I flick on the cold water.

It's going to be a long night.

Chapter 20
Zee

Lifestyles of the Rich & Famous - Good Charlotte

The sound of the shower coming on in the neighboring bathroom has my pruney fingers freezing on the final button of my pajama top.

Colton's naked.

And less than twelve feet away from me.

This isn't the time for my mind to go *there*, but hell if I can stop it when the spot where his lips touched earlier is still tingling.

Even after I soaked in the massive tub for nearly two hours.

Honestly, I feel like a teenager again.

A forehead kiss should not set off a giddy state in a woman my age.

But this is Colton.

My teen crush and living fantasy.

And out there, it was like time reversed itself and I felt how I did *then*.

I can't stop alternating between brushing a hand over

179

where he kissed me and staring at my wedding and engagement rings.

Unknowingly, Tee comes to my rescue and I snatch my cell when it buzzes. "Everything okay?"

"I'm not the one who's sharing a suite with my new husband."

She has to be down if she didn't hear the desperation in my voice.

Not that I'm desperate.

Nope.

No, sirree.

I'm not sixteen anymore. My crush on Colt ended then. Right?

Annoyed because my answer is less definitive than I'd like, I grouse, "Why are you whispering?"

"In case he's there."

I roll my eyes. "Demanding his husbandly rights?"

"Is he?"

Her squeak has me double-rolling my eyes. "Of course not."

But... would I say no if he did?

I think about the intensity of his regard at the ceremony. The calluses on his large palm as it cupped mine. Though I've never been short, I've always felt tiny in stature around him and today was no different.

"He's hot."

He is.

Jesus, I don't think I'd SAY NO IF HE CAME TO MY BEDROOM DOOR.

What the hell is wrong with me? Nothing's changed. Not really.

"He... is attractive."

"I forgot how hot."

Me too.

"Spending two days in a hotel with him must be awkward."

"I'm part of Canada's ruling classes now, Tee," I mock. "We're in a suite *and* it's The Manchester."

"Ohh, the lifestyles of the rich and the famous."

I hear her jeer and smile. "It's like being in an apartment."

"Fancy. Thank you for the videos by the way."

"Just keeping you in the loop."

"And making me jealous."

"Yeah. Sure. You'd switch places with me."

"Hey, I wanna be rich too."

"Just without the husband."

"True dat, girlfriend. I'm so pissed I couldn't go to the wedding."

In all honesty, I was glad she couldn't make it.

Today was like a Pap smear—important but something to endure and definitely a task to handle alone.

"It was impersonal but pretty."

And he tried. I have to give him that.

I even pressed two of the wildflowers from the bouquet he bought for me between the pages of *Persuasion*—a favorite of mine.

"Explain."

"He took us to this club where there was a kind of greenhouse?"

"Bleugh."

"No, not that type of greenhouse. There was no fertilizer, Tee," I snipe. "Like an... orangery? It was ornamental. All glass. But Victorian. Very pretty. It was unexpected. I didn't even know men's clubs still existed."

"Me neither. Who were your witnesses?"

"Strangers."

At least, for me. I think the guy was Colt's attorney, and all I know about the wife is that she channeled Cruella de Vil. Complete with the fascination for animal prints—Tee would have hated her.

"Jacobie's such a jackass for not giving me time off. I should have pretended to be sick."

"Like you'd keep up that subterfuge."

She huffs. "Where's the husband?"

"Showering."

As soon as I whisper the words, I regret them.

"Lord above. I bet he looks sexier wet. I envy men."

"Why?"

181

"They get to see themselves naked."

I huff through a laugh. "Your logic, Tee, I swear."

"Plus, it's awkward using a showerhead."

"Tee!"

"What? It's true. Tell me it's not."

"You put it between your thighs, Tee, and direct the spray. You're doing it wrong if you think that's complicated."

"Lot easier to have a pole in front of you that you stroke a few times."

"Only in your brain. At least we don't have clean-up duty afterward."

"True. Never trust a man's sock."

"Thank God I was out of the house before the triplets hit puberty."

"Ewww. Three times as many socks. They get hard and crusty—"

"I don't need to know this!"

She sniffs. "Knowledge is power. As you're so invested in the IVF route, avoid Colton's socks for the foreseeable future."

The thought has something inside me squirming.

My gaze drifts to the wall we share.

Something changed today. I heard him shower this morning and it didn't trigger *this* in me.

Is it the rings on my fingers?

The vows we spoke?

They were meaningless, surely, but that he could be rubbing one off makes my body temperature surge.

Tee distracts me yet again by mumbling, "I bet Butch Cassidy knows how to direct a showerhead."

Butch Cassidy?

My brain takes a couple seconds to get with the program.

Her pen pal.

Right.

"Considering the government puts him in charge of tech that's worth billions of dollars, I'd hope he can ride a showerhead."

"Wonder what Colt's skills are..."

"Shut up."

"You're thinking about it, aren't you?" I can *hear* her smirk.

"No, I'm not."

"Sure you are. You have eyes and a libido." Her smug tone's irritating enough to make my teeth itch. "You brought up IVF..."

"He doesn't want me."

"Men will fuck anything—"

"Gee, thanks!"

"You know what I mean."

"What's the game plan here?"

"No game plan. Just a genuine concern for your vagina. Pretty sure you have cobwebs in them there hills—"

"My vagina cobwebs are my own business, thank you very much!" I heave a sigh when she snorts. "I'll talk to you tomorrow when I get to the ranch."

"Hey... I miss you. It's not the same without you."

I bite my lip. "I know. I miss you too. Even if you do give me nothing but crap."

"It's my job to keep you on your toes. *And* to remind you that you rock. Also that you don't have to be a good girl all the time. Hint hint."

"Shut up."

"I mean it. Hop on that cowboy, cowgirl."

"Tee!"

"Go for a ride. You'll save a horse."

"CHRISTY!"

"Jump in the saddle—"

"I'm hanging up."

"Safe travels, hmm?"

"Bye, babe."

"Night, Zee. Don't be a stranger."

She says that in a rush as she hangs up so I send her a message.

Me: Never. You're stuck with me for life.

Tee: I'll provide the super glue.

Me: :*

183

Homesickness is a new feeling for me. But it makes my mind veer away from Colton... until the shower switches off.

And I think about saddles.

And the fact that I *am* a cowgirl.

And he's a cowboy.

And—

The water comes back on?

The hell?

Unable to stop myself, I head for the mini fridge.

If ever there was a night for cracking open the mini bar, it's this one. I don't care if a thing of peanuts costs forty bucks. I'll owe Colton if he brings the charge up.

Not that I think he will.

Has he ever had to check an itemized bill in his life?

Well, outside of the ranch.

Ranchers nickel and dime like it's a college course.

With the jar in hand, I twist it. Trying not to think about him twisting—

"Stop it, Zee. You're turning into Tee. Do. Not. Be. A. Pervert."

Still, the harder I twist, the less it wants to open and the more my hand gets sweaty and the lid refuses to budge.

I tap my foot on the floor.

Stare at the connecting wall.

He's my husband—there has to be perks to these rings I'm wearing, and gaining an official jar opener is one of them.

"He'll be naked."

The whispered words sound overly loud in the room.

"There might be a towel if he comes straight from the shower," I concede.

Comes.

I stare at the jar.

Clear my throat.

Hunger surges, but it's twofold.

One for the peanuts. The other for something I shouldn't want.

Except, I'd be lying.

I've wanted to see Colton naked for a helluva long time.

This is just an old habit dying hard.

Yeah, that's all it is.

That, of course, is when I hear a low noise.

My mouth rounds as I turn to face the wall that joins his bathroom to my bedroom.

"Was that what I think it is?!" I rasp, stepping closer.

Tee's corruption is complete because I press my ear to the wall. When that gives me nothing, I rush to my bathroom, grab the tumbler, hold that to the wall instead, and—

"Oh. My. God," I whisper under my breath as I hear rhythmic grunts that can only mean he's stroking himself.

Eyes wide, lips gaping, heat flushing through my body, I stare at nothing as I listen to the sounds of his pleasure, all the while wondering what fantasy he's using to get himself off.

It doesn't matter that a decade separates us. I'm sixteen again. Full of hormones I don't know what to do with and an incessant desire to feel Colton's stubble between my thighs.

When he comes with a groan, the corresponding desire in me takes away my hunger for peanuts.

Mouth like cotton, I gulp as I back off from the shared wall, dropping the peanuts on the nightstand and nearly smashing the fragile tumbler as it falls to the carpeted floor.

Flopping onto the bed, I can no more stop myself from sliding my hand below the waistband of my *Beavis and Butthead* pj's than I can stop my lungs from transporting oxygen around my body.

My very overheated body.

"God..."

Chapter 21
Colton

Cities - Toby Mai, Two Feet

THE NEXT DAY

"Y ou sure you don't want to go to the Bar 9?"

She peers at me over her shades. "Why would I want to do that?"

"Because it's home?"

"The Bar 9 hasn't been home for nearly twelve years."

"You left eight years ago."

"Mom died twelve years ago."

"I'm sorry. I didn't think..."

"Not your family, not your grief." Her tone's light enough that I know she's not trying to be insulting. Even if I *am* insulted. "*Grand-mère* will call me when she'd like me to visit. As for the boys..." Her shoulder hitches. "They'll come over soon enough."

I shift focus onto the controls of the private plane that I'm piloting home. While she doesn't exactly appear nervous, I get the sense this is her first trip in a light aircraft.

When I was going through the preflight checks, she kept

jumping every time I adjusted a dial or scrawled a notation on my clipboard.

"I guess you want to talk about the fire," she says on a rush.

My hands tighten around the controls. I didn't expect her to bring this up and I didn't want to push it... "What happened that night?"

"If I say any of this, it can't be retracted."

"I don't want you to retract it. I want to know. Hell, I need to know. I wouldn't have asked otherwise. It's all I've been thinking about—who killed Loki?"

"Think about the worst things that have happened to your family."

"To make me depressed?"

"No. Think about it. Think about who's behind most of those 'worst things' and then throw the blame on that one person for this too."

Stiffening, I demand, "*Pops?* What the—"

The plane jerks as my grip tightens on the control yoke.

Startled, she jolts. "Believe me or don't."

Suddenly, I regret her bringing this up. Because if we're going to make it home, I need to not lose my shit.

Grinding my teeth, I bite off, "This is why you're scared of him?"

Her lips kick up at the corner in the most pathetic excuse for a smile. Jesus, it hurts my heart to see it. "I wish that were all he'd done to make me scared of him."

"Why didn't you say anything?"

"He's Clyde Korhonen. I'm me. Who'd have believed me over him? And don't say you. You didn't believe me then. Only forced proximity opened you up to the possibility of doubting what you knew, to listening to that question, never mind answering it.

"I watched him set fire to a newspaper and drop it onto a bunch of hay. God, the smoke was so bad, so quickly. I can still feel the pinch in my lungs." She shudders. "I knew I couldn't leave the stables until he'd gone—"

"Why not?"

"Because if he saw me, a witness to his crime, what do you

think he'd have done to me?" Her gaze is knowing. "I'd have ended up amid the pile of horse bones, that's what—"

"No. He's not—"

"Not what? A killer? I saw him set fire to the stables and he didn't open a single stall door." Her jaw works. "Sounds like a killer to me—"

"But—"

"No. No buts. If you want to hear this, then shut up and let me tell you what happened."

"Fine."

"As soon as he got out of there, I tried to open the stall door, but Loki was freaking out. All the horses were. It was so thick of smoke in there and he must have been choking already. He reared up and hit me. I'm lucky he didn't clip me on the head, but I fell down. It took me so long to just regain consciousness. Every time I tried to stand, I nearly passed out from the pain and I'd already inhaled so much smoke too." She gulps. "I was pretty sure that I was going to die in there, that's how bad things were."

"Fuck, Zee."

"By the time I was able to get to my feet, Loki had passed out." Her mouth trembles. "I'm pretty sure he was gone. When I ran my hand over his muzzle, he didn't react. I'll never forgive myself for failing him. It's part of the reason why I can't force myself to shut out those sounds he made. I can still hear him, but I deserve to suffer—"

"God, no—"

"*Yes.*" Her fingers rub her temple. "I only stopped having nightmares about them a few years ago."

I know what she means. The sounds. The smells. Then, how the roof caved in, the rush of oxygen-stealing heat, trapping our herd inside—

"I didn't want to die too," she rasps. "But it was too late. I left the stall but the last thing I remember is hacking up my lungs. The strain must have been too much. The next thing I knew, I was outside and you were..."

Walking away.

Self-hatred is an old friend of mine, and it rears its ugly

head. Especially as I remember finding her in the stables—in the middle of the aisle. Splayed out.

I'd thought she was dead.

The memory of how that shattered my heart has me rasping, "I'm so fucking sorry, Zee."

"Do you believe me?"

There's little I couldn't imagine my father doing to get what he wants. But why he'd want the horses dead is something that doesn't compute.

"Unequivocally."

Her throat bobs as she swallows but she lowers her head and starts reading something on her phone.

I let her.

Mind racing, memories flickering to life, I'm torn back to that night.

"Colton? How long until we're at the ranch?"

Dragged from my thoughts, I check our position, well aware that I need to refocus on my current task before I screw this up too. "Twenty minutes."

"Thank you," she says softly.

How she can even stand to be in the cockpit with me is a miracle in itself.

As we approach a pocket of turbulence, I want to reach for her hand but I have less right to do that than I did before this conversation. "It'll be bumpy for the next few minutes."

"O-Okay."

The turbulence is nothing I haven't dealt with in the past, but it's almost worth it because while my hands are busy piloting the plane, one of hers settles on my knee. I glance down at it in surprise, but I'm almost relieved when she squeezes it in a death crush.

It might hurt, but after letting her down for so damn long, that I can be her safe space is something I don't deserve but equally *need*.

Guilt—the fire always engendered it in me because I believed I was partially to blame. Now, I'm well aware of what I damaged and what I lost.

Something that I might never be able to find again.

An hour later, she practically falls into my arms while scuttling out of the passenger seat once we've landed.

The weight of her has changed—she's no longer a kid. All big eyes and bony shoulders. She's a woman now.

My inner caveman wants to tag a 'mine' on that but this, I remind myself for the tenth time since I said 'I do,' isn't the Dark Ages.

She owes me nothing but her disdain.

And I can admire her, but it needs to be from a distance.

"Yo, boss, everything good up there?"

"Yeah, it's handling like a dream," I confirm, turning to Jerry, the mechanic I hired to look after the plane and to repair the helicopter Callan busted last year. Whatever the little shit did to it, Jerry has yet to fix.

"Glad to hear it," he chirps as he heads off to take care of the post-flight checks. "Ma'am," he aims at Zee, curiosity oozing from that one greeting.

He might be an outsider, but Pigeon Creek's gossip train works fast.

She nods at him, and, disappointed to have no more fodder for the masses, he grabs our suitcases from the plane and dumps them on the ground.

A pickup truck pulls up shortly after and I leave the bags to Albert, who packs them in the box.

That's when I notice Callan.

About twenty yards away, he's idling on an ATV. His curious gaze takes everything in, making me wonder, as always, what he sees.

A part of me wouldn't be surprised if he saw security blueprints.

"Callan's here."

"I guess I should be grateful he isn't armed with a torch and a pitchfork."

"Callan isn't like that."

Nervously, she whispers, "You swear you don't think I did it anymore?"

I can't stop myself from cupping her cheek. "I swear."

"I want to believe you so bad, but I'm used to everyone here hating me," she whispers, head tilting ever-so-faintly into my palm.

Jesus.

"Even your brothers?"

"No. Not them. But *Grand-mère...* She resents that I got caught."

"Never liked her."

"There isn't much to like. *But,* she raised us, made sure we were fed and safe and clothed. She did her best when faced with raising four kids in her seventies after losing her daughter and a beloved grandson. It might not be what I'd want for my child, but we're still standing."

"I want more for *our* child than that, don't you? To be still standing?"

"Definitely."

"Then that's something we can both work toward, hmm?"

Her smile is tremulous but it feels good to bask in its warmth—meager or not.

If I could hit rewind...

No. There's no use in thinking that.

She flicks a look at Callan and visibly braces herself again. "I guess you'd better introduce me to him."

"You'll be fine. He's a good man."

Together, we amble toward my brother. My hand finds its way to the small of her back.

Naturally.

Of its own volition.

"Figured we'd see you at the house," I greet when Callan studies Zee and she stands there awkwardly.

"I wanted to meet your wife in her natural habitat."

Zee's brows lift but I snort. "You're a weirdo, Callan." To her, I state, "Ignore him when he comes out with crap like that. The little shit thinks he's Pigeon Creek's resident anthropologist."

"I am here, you know." He holds out his hand. "I'm Callan."

"I'm Zee." She shakes his hand. "Pleasure to meet you, Callan."

He hums. "Might not be. You could hate me."

"I doubt that. Takes a lot of energy to hate anyone."

"Some people deserve it though, wouldn't you say?"

Her fingers find their way onto her elbows again, and I can tell she thinks that's aimed at her. "They do."

"Colt said you're frightened of Pops."

I huff. "Callan!"

"What? Did you or didn't you say he scared her?"

"It's fine. He does. There's no point in denying it."

"Callan, why didn't you bring a truck?"

"I'd have to ride with you if I did."

"At least you're honest," Zee teases, and for the first time since we left her apartment, hell, since before I entered her damn home, she relaxes.

Typical.

Callan's nose crinkles at the bridge. "Sorry. I didn't know if you were going to be a bitch or not. Cole hates you so it was a fifty-fifty shot whether he was right to."

"Wow, you're not honest. You're brutal." She doesn't appear offended though. "It's fine. He can hate me so long as he leaves me alone."

"Cole never comes home. He stays in New York City. This place has bad vibes for him."

"I think Pigeon Creek has a lot of bad vibes for many people," she says softly.

"It does for me too," Callan shares, "but I'd never leave the ranch."

Her fingers pinch her elbows. I only notice because they turn white from the pressure. "You're lucky to love your home." To me, she says, "I do need to get my office ready."

"That's fine. I arranged for them to transport your things here ASAP. They should arrive tomorrow night. Until then, you can make your suite your own."

Her smile's rueful. "Ah, yes. My suite."

"Mrs. Abelman had it painted," Callan relays. "It still stinks."

"We can open the windows, air it. It'll be fine." Her gaze turns inquiring. "Does Mrs. Abelman hate me too?"

"No. No enemies within the house," I assure her. "And Callan wasn't lying. Cole rarely comes home."

"Lies. He visited twice this past year," she retorts.

"Ah, the gossip train." I roll my eyes. "Pops told everyone he had a heart attack and dragged us home for a bedside vigil. As for the last time, he was introducing us to his girlfriend. Both are extraneous circumstances, as I'm sure you'll agree."

"So formal," she mocks, but she does concede with a regal nod.

That word suits her—regal.

I point to an SUV. "Our ride." To Callan, I ask, "Did you finish your chores?"

"Yes, *Dad*," he mocks. "What do you think I am? An idiot?" He doesn't let me answer, just starts the motor and revs the engine before taking off.

Once we're in the SUV, she hesitates. "He's..."

"Annoying?"

She graces me with a soft grin. "Sensible."

"Yeah. You got that about right. Kid was born sensible. Doubt he'd ever jaywalk. Pops can't understand why he's not a pain in the ass like the rest of his spawn."

"You might all be ornery, but you're not him."

Considering her accusation, I'll take that for the compliment it is.

But the mere mention of him has me eager to get to the bottom of why he'd set fire to the stables, otherwise it'll eat me alive.

Silence reigns until we make it to the homestead. I reckon she's thinking about the shit she needs to do to establish herself here. As for me, I'm trying to figure out who to approach to reconcile Pops's behavior that night.

What I do know—I'll be making sure Seven Cs Inc. is disentangled from his companies ASAP.

If he's capable of *this*, then God only knows what he might have done with the family's billions.

Though I get out and open her door when we arrive at the big house, I wait for her to alight before I guide her to the porch.

That's when I warn her: "I'm going to pick you up."

"From where?" she asks, confused.

"Here." I point to the door. "If you think I'm telling our kid that I didn't do this, you're mistaken."

Before she can so much as blink, I swoop in and pick her up, holding her high against my chest.

Letting loose a shriek, her hands slipping around my neck to cling to my nape, she snaps, "That wasn't much of a warning."

Carrying her over the threshold, I drawl, "I'll be sure to give you two weeks' notice in the future."

Chapter 22
Zee

Colt might not see it, but he's very much like his brother. Even if Callan is so brutally honest, it's painful. A trait the older sibling doesn't share.

Colt's quiet and watchful. Humorous when he's relaxed but stoic. Ever the responsible adult. Callan's still a kid, but I learn he's unafraid to speak his mind when he feels safe.

I guess I should be honored considering I've known him ninety minutes and since I came into the kitchen, he hasn't shut up once.

Tee has a similar MO so the white noise is comforting. This certainly isn't my home, but Callan's chatter makes me feel less alone on new turf.

"Coffee?"

"Please," I say with a smile to the housekeeper, though nerves have me toying with my wedding band and engagement ring.

Colt carrying me over the threshold has only made this worse... in a good way?

Man, I don't know.

It was a blip of normality in a field of bizarre chaos, which highlighted one truth—this kid that neither of us expected to have before last week, especially with one another, both of us are committing to them.

Mrs. Abelman's grunt distracts me as she places a china cup alongside a matching dish of sugar complete with a silver milk jug in front of me.

It's oddly...

Huh.

Of course.

British.

Just like Callan and Colt's mother.

As I doctor my coffee with milk, I smile. "You should probably know that I'm type 1 diabetic."

"I know for the future," is her stiff reply, but the sugar pot is swept away as if by magic and plunked between Colt and Callan, who add four sugars a piece to theirs.

Ida Abelman's an odd duck.

Cold and stark, she fits in with the Korhonens.

I get the sense Callan feels doubly 'safe' because she's around. While she isn't effusive, she pats him on the shoulder and speaks to him like he's still a child, though she doesn't stop him from cursing if he drops an F-bomb here and there.

For obvious reasons, her tone's maternal.

Everyone knows about the custody agreement Clyde battered over his ex's head.

Literally.

We all saw the bruises.

Like cowards, we let it go on as well.

Some community we are.

"I'll do my research, of course, but how can I accommodate your dietary restrictions?"

"I tend to eat low carb, but that's it."

"We can talk later about routines you want to integrate and—"

My brows lift. "Routines?"

"You're the lady of *Seven Cs Abbey*," Colt teases, his lips twitching though he doesn't bother looking up from his phone.

"The chatelaine," Callan corrects.

"The what now?"

"Chatelaine, Colt." Callan jabs a finger at him. "It doesn't take an IQ of—"

"I only have a master's degree, Callan. I'm too dumb to talk to you."

The corners of Ida's mouth flicker.

Slightly.

"Less infighting, you two." She takes a dainty sip of coffee. "Callan, we know your IQ is high. We knew it before you were tested. Stop bringing it up."

Callan's sigh is long-suffering. "I don't bring it up."

"Objection," Colt rumbles.

I cough out a laugh.

Ida smiles. "Sustained."

"This explains so much, you guys." Callan pouts. "It's why I don't fit in with people."

"That's because you prefer computers and horses to humans, Callan. Don't whitewash the last eighteen years and pretend otherwise."

Ida's tone is so droll, I outright grin. "What's your IQ, Callan?"

"159." His gaze turns earnest. "It's why real people don't like me."

Because I thought he'd be cocky and he isn't, more distressed, I tut. "I'm sure that's not true."

"He has a habit of calling people idiots." Colt's brow furrows at something he's reading on his cell. "That doesn't help."

I hide my smile behind my coffee cup. "What do you mean by 'real people?'"

"Not online ones."

"Oh, you mean most of your friends are online?"

"Yeah. Do you know what a chatelaine is?" Callan inquires. "I won't call you an idiot if you don't."

I riffle through my memory. "They're the women who ran estates, I think. They wore a chain around their waists that held the keys to the doors of their homes."

Thankful I'm not an idiot, Callan beams with pleasure. "Correct!"

"Ten points to Zee," Colt mocks, but he winks at me.

It's more charming than I'd like to admit.

This whole *thing* is.

His ease with his kid brother. How Ida sits with us at the table and chides Callan for calling a ranch hand a moron earlier.

It feels like family.

Man, it's been a long time since I had a glimmer of *this*.

Grand-mère tried. I'll give her that. But Mom and Dad were keystones. The triplets never got to experience it in the same way Walker and I did.

This is also comforting.

It lets me sit back in my chair and relax more than I thought I'd be able to in enemy territory.

"As I was saying before Callan interrupted with his version of *Jeopardy*. We can talk later about routines you want to integrate."

"Which routines in particular, Ida?"

"When you'd like to pick out menus—"

"Menus?" I interrupt in confusion as Callan heads out to use the bathroom.

"We can agree on them a week in advance."

I shake my head. "*Grand-mère* used to be this formal before she turned eighty. I truly don't miss those days. You do what you need to do, Ida. I won't be here for long so it's not fair for you to change your routines for me."

"That's quite defeatist," Ida remarks.

Awkwardly, I cast a look at Colt.

He's still staring at his phone.

Just when I think he won't say a word, he rumbles, "This might be business, Zee..." His gaze finally lifts. Our eyes lock. "But you must treat this like your home. This is where our child will be raised whether we're together or not—even if it's only part of the time. If nothing else, make yourself comfortable here."

Before I can sputter a response, he stands. The movement is pure grace. Years of horseback riding are evident in his elegant posture. His strength.

"I need to change clothes and visit HQ," he informs the room at large and nobody in particular.

I watch him go.

Unsure why I feel like I disappointed him but knowing I have, I wish with every foolish part of my being that I was back in his arms and he was carrying me upstairs to make me his for real.

God, my stupidity knows no bounds.

Just like always, he's pushing me away... and it's all my fault.

Chapter 23
Zee

Callan shows me to my room.

Along the way, he informs me, "I was going to dislike you on purpose."

Amused by his candor, I state, "How's that going?"

"You had to be nice. I didn't expect that."

"Do you naturally expect people to be awful?"

"Yup." He shrugs when I wince. "Just in my experience. I'm glad you're nice. Colt doesn't deserve a bitch."

"Maybe I am."

"Nah. You have kind eyes."

"I do?"

He nods. "It's why I couldn't be mean to you from the start. Plus, you look like this filly Colt's gentling—"

"That sounds like less of a compliment."

"She has a great pedigree but she's terrified. Of everything. You can whistle under your breath and she'll bolt."

"That's where we differ, then. I'm not a bolter."

"Isn't that what you did when you headed to New York?"

Though that question leaves me floundering because he's not wrong, I don't have a chance to answer as we stop outside a door.

Instead of leaving me the first chance he gets as I expected,

Callan steps inside and settles on the edge of my bed. "This used to be my mum's suite."

I glance around the elegant space, aware that my entire apartment could fit inside this *one* room.

Hell, maybe my neighbor's too.

Despite his presence, I raise my arms and twirl in a circle. "One thing you don't get used to in a city—the lack of space."

He glowers at the comforter. At least, I think that's the target of his ire. "I traveled when I was real small. I remember how crowded it was. Just sharing oxygen with so many people felt arduous."

My lips curve. "You don't strike me as a natural rancher, Callan."

"Very perceptive of you," he demurs. "I'm not. I hate it. But I love the land and seeing as the internet's a thing, I can help Colt out in other ways. He loves being on the range, I don't, so it makes sense for me to help him run things behind the scenes."

"You're only eighteen though."

"I could run this place blindfolded by the time I hit sixteen. I warned Colt that Father was mismanaging it. He tried to stop him but what can you do when the head of the company is so short-sighted, not even glasses can help him see?"

I drop my purse onto the bed as I read between the lines. "You aren't going to university?"

"If I bother with it, I'll attend online."

"You should experience city living," I reason, seeking the keys to the locks on my suitcases from the inner pocket of my purse. "Even if it only makes you appreciate the ranch more."

His brow puckers. "Why would I do that? That's illogical."

"Humans *are* illogical," I assure him as I move over to an antique vanity beside which my bags have been stacked. "You never heard of that saying, 'The grass is greener on the other side?'"

Which is pretty apt for my current state of mind... Unable to credit that this is my room, my hand smoothes over the walnut vanity. I'm in Lindsay Korhonen's suite with furniture that's worth a fortune, on Seven Cs' turf without being shown off the land with a shotgun up my ass.

In the words of Christy 'Tee' MacFarlane, 'Shit be crazy sometimes.'

I turn to face my new brother-in-law.

A Korhonen.

Crazier still.

"I like it here," he dismisses.

"Maybe you'd like it out there better. You won't know if you don't try it."

His frown deepens. "Do you want to get rid of me?"

"Why would I need to?" I chuckle at his suspicious squint. "I'm telling you what I'd tell my teenage brothers if they opened up their ears long enough to listen to me."

His expression turns curious. "They're in my class."

"I'm sure, at some point or another, you've called them idiots."

He grimaces. "Maybe."

Smirking, I grab my carry-on and lay it on the ground. "As I suspected."

"It's not because they're McAllisters. They're just dumb."

I only hum as I set my drawing pad to the side on the hunt for the pajamas I intend on wearing for the rest of the day.

Hey, I see no reason why my routine has to change because I had to marry my family's archnemesis.

Huh.

I guess I need to book time in the kitchen now?

That'll be awkward.

The kitchen's plenty big, but the idea of being in a communal area and having to maybe talk to people who are strangers while I frost cookies is horrifying to me.

Sure, I have to get to know them better at some point, but when I'm kinda aching to dive into something creative to take my mind off things, that kills the buzz in its tracks.

"Did you like New York?"

Absentmindedly, I stack my things onto the dresser.

"Sure. I'd have preferred it if I had your budget though." I shoot him a grin. "I doubt you'd have to live in a tiny apartment with a roommate in a less-than-grand neighborhood."

"No. I guess I wouldn't. I think I'd be more alone down there than I am here."

"You can be surrounded by people and still be lonely." Softly, I ask, "*Are* you lonely, Callan?"

His gaze cuts to mine. I can see his hackles rising—normal in a kid his age with a question like that. To be honest, I'm not sure why I even asked. It's hardly my place, but his capacity for brutal honesty makes me think of Tee and, in turn, tells me he'd prefer to deal with that than BS.

Before he can snipe at me, I murmur, "I think I'll be lonely here."

That defuses the tension.

"If you are, we could... hang out. Do you play video games?"

"It's been a while," I demur, not telling him that Tee and I play a few times a week. "That'd be nice. Thank you for the offer. The same goes in return."

He smiles back.

And that's how I inadvertently made a friend out of my brother-in-law in the first three hours of knowing him *and* pissed off my husband too.

Text Chat

Tee: The apartment is empty

Zee: Hello to you too

Tee: No 'hellos' when you abandoned me

Tee: *sniffles* It's a good thing that I love you enough to forgive you for leaving me in Gotham City. All on my own. When Batman is refusing to answer my calls.

Zee: Honey, how about we swap places, huh?

Tee: I'm starting to think Parker was right

Zee: Don't tell her that whatever you do

Zee: About what?

Tee: Returning to Pigeon Creek

Zee: Babe, I love you but it's been three days.

Tee: Yeah, but New York sucks without you.

Zee: Awww <3

Tee: *sobs*

Tee: And it's lonely here

Tee: I can't yell at you from across the room to turn down that godawful trash you listen to

Tee: I prefer the trash to silence :O

Zee: *faints*

Zee: I get it though

Tee: We were very interdependent.

Zee: You mean codependent

Tee: I mean both

Tee: So it sucks that you're not here anymore :(

Zee: You need to give it some time before you leave everything behind

Tee: You didn't!

Zee: My circumstances were different. ARE different. Jesus Christ, this is a week-old problem

Tee: Yeah, and it's a crappy one.

Zee: Plus, we wouldn't be living together if you came home either

Tee: No, but I could see you

Zee: Let's video call

Tee: Nah, I'm sitting in the dark

Zee: Why?

Tee: Because I either move to Pigeon Creek or turn into a vampire

Zee: If you were going to turn into a vampire, why didn't you invite one over before the shit hit the fan?

Zee: Vampires have generational wealth. They're great at sex, like to bite, have mates, AND he'd be able to buy the ranch!

Tee: Damn, you're right. I was slow on the uptake there

Zee: Lol

Zee: I miss you too, you know?

Tee: Don't or I'll start bawling

Zee: Love you, Tee

Tee: Love you, Zee *SOBS*

Text Chat
A WEEK LATER

Parker: I'm shooketh

Zee: About?

Parker: Tee told me Colt carried you over the threshold, Zee

Tee: Why are you shooketh? He gives off that vibe

Zee: Have you visited Parker yet, Tee?

Parker: She hasn't

Parker: She's trying out agoraphobia too. It's all the rage in the city. Liam Donnghal's made it trendy.

Tee: Yeah, yeah

Zee: You haven't left the apartment?!

Parker: No. She hasn't

Zee: What about work?

Tee: I decided to call in sick. Jackass Jacobie can't say no to that.

Parker: He can eventually lol. Doctor's note, anyone?

Tee: Like you can tattle on me, Miss 'I haven't entered a public space since Labor Day three years ago.'

Parker: I've been out

Tee: When?

Zee: Where?

Zee: And riding from Ohio to Jersey doesn't count...

Parker: Two months ago

Zee: *groans*

Zee: How am I the one in an arranged marriage I didn't ask for and I'm coping the best?

Parker: It's because you're our sun

Zee: I am?

Parker: Yup. The center of our universe, Zee.

Tee: I know you're joking, but I think she was and I didn't realize it.

Zee: Fuck a duck, Tee, you need to chill out! I got on your nerves a lot

Tee: I miss that *sobs*

Parker: Wow, our girl's having some kind of episode, huh? You're awesome, Zee, but the center of my universe? Sheesh.

Parker: Do you want me to send one of the girls over, Tee?

Zee: Not Giulia! She'll get mad at her.

Parker: True. Being a mom hasn't increased her patience levels. If anything, she's more impatient with everyone else and only patient with the demon child. Who knew she'd be worse than ever when she's pregnant? Lol.

Tee: It's awful you call a baby that

Parker: Not read much scripture for a sort of Catholic, have you? Samael is a demon's name.

Tee: They named their kid after a demon?! I thought they misspelled SamUel

Parker: They ride for the Satan's Sinners' MC, babe. Do you think they were going to church to get him baptized?

Zee: LOL

Tee: I'd have paid to watch that

Zee: Definite pay-per-view content.

Zee: ROFL

Parker: ;) Think we got our girl smiling?

Zee: I think we did

Tee: Didn't. *pouts* And yes, I know I'm acting like I'm five! But I didn't expect this to be so bad. It's as if my right tit has gone missing.

Parker: Not your right hand?

Zee: Had to be her boob

Zee: SMH

Tee: Excuse me. Both serve a purpose. Even if one of mine is bigger than the other.

Zee: It's not that bad.

Tee: Sure thang, Ms. Perfect B-cups

215

Tee: How did I get curves and no tits? It's not fair

Parker: We have her talking about herself. I think she's feeling better

Zee: *snorts*

Parker: Lemme guess… You tried to fill the void. Literally. And hooked up with someone last night? You know you get maudlin when you do that, Tee.

Tee: Men suck.

Tee: He said, and wait for it, that because I was fat, he figured I'd have good food in for breakfast.

Zee: WHAT?!

Parker: OMG, what the hell?!

Tee: THANK YOU

Tee: He quoted some baseballer and he stands behind it wholeheartedly.

Parker: The baseballer sounds like a jerk.

Zee: Agreed.

Tee: It didn't put me and my wonky boobs in a good mood, I can tell you.

Parker: Did you at least get an orgasm out of it?

Tee: Meh. I wanted to feel a connection.

Parker: Were you two having sex and I didn't realize it?

Zee: No, we weren't lol. Tee's being melodramatic.

Parker: I dunno if you can talk about melodrama, Zee. You looked like you were gonna pass out when Colt showed up.

Parker: Here I was, half expecting Quasimodo to walk through the door, and instead he could be featured on GQ.

Parker: IN A STETSON.

Parker: He was giving aftershave ad model

Tee: He was LMAO

Zee: Shut up

Zee: You'd have been petrified too

Parker: I mean, no? He seemed charming. But not like in that creepy way, you know? Genuine. Yeah, that's the word

Parker: How are things up there?

Zee: Odd

Tee: Why? Is that Ida cow being mean to you?

Zee: Ha. No.

Parker: Firstly, who's Ida, and why is she a cow?

Zee: She's the Korhonen's housekeeper and she isn't a cow

Tee: You drive over someone's toe once and they hate you forever!

Parker: Jeez, I wonder why

Tee: Zee was in the car with me

Zee: Yeah, but I wasn't driving

Tee: You were distracting me

Zee: I can't argue

Parker: Can't or won't?

Zee: I plead the Fifth lol

Parker: Wrong country, haha

Zee: :p

Tee: I'd broken up with Percy Manvers, hadn't I?

Parker: I didn't know people called their kids Percy still lol

Zee: Harry Potter can be blamed for a lot of bad names

Parker: Who'd name a kid after Percy Weasley though?

Tee: Someone who's a seer. He lived up to the name

Parker: You know since this whole marriage thing happened, you two are a lot more interesting than you used to be

Tee: So kind of you to say!

Zee: Yay?

Parker: Honestly, you're full of surprises

Zee: You know things are bad, Tee, when we're entertaining the woman who splits her time between the house of an MC Prez and his First Lady and her Old Man's.

Tee: Don't blame me!

Tee: You're the one who started it o.O

Chapter 24
Colton

All My Life - Foo Fighters

A FEW DAYS LATER

"Where's your head at, son?"

I peer at Mum over my teacup, then, staring into the muddy liquid, I hide a grimace.

There's an unspoken rule among my brothers and me—we never tell her how godawful her Earl Grey is.

And since she moved in, I'm drinking gallons of the stuff.

"Just work. The usual."

"I know you too well for that."

My lips kick up at the side. "What am I thinking about then?"

"That wife of yours. The one who spends most of her time in her bedroom."

I frown at her. "Where else would she be?"

"I never imagined she'd be locked up in there for days on end."

"Why is it a problem?"

Her eyes narrow. "It isn't for you?"

"I want her to be comfortable, and if her room makes her comfortable, then I see no issue."

"She spends a lot of time with Callan." Mum clears her throat. "I heard them yesterday. They were playing a video game."

"They do that a lot. I never imagined they'd get along but I'm grateful. You know Callan doesn't like many people."

"He finds it hard to be around idiots," she corrects. "Peculiar though your wife might be, she's not a moron."

"No, she's not. But you might be looking at one." I plunk my teacup on its matching saucer then set both on the coffee table. That done, I rest my elbows on my knees and rub my eyes once I've bowed my shoulders. "I've been a real idiot, Mum."

"Not possible."

If only. "You know what the town thinks of her."

"I do and I know it makes things awkward. The small-town nonsense is ridiculous. They don't like your father. I've no idea why they were so quick to vilify Susanne when you vouched for her."

"I'm not him."

"True. People don't fear you. You've always been too popular for that.

"I'm not sure how Clyde and I made you. I was a geek and he was *Clyde*. Somehow, we produced the most popular boys in school. I swear I don't know where you came from."

"Maybe the stork brought us?"

"Maybe," she says, amused. "So, what is it? Why are you an idiot?"

"I..." I sigh. "I vouched for her and gave her an alibi but I thought she started the fire."

"Why would you think that?"

"I saw her in the stables."

"I never did understand what a McAllister was doing in there."

"You didn't think she was behind the fire?"

Mum sips at her tea. "You don't want to know what I think."

"What's that supposed to mean?"

"It means I have a habit of blaming genocide, the razing of the rainforests, and the rising sea levels on your father. It's a failing of mine. *But* that's neither here nor there. Continue with the story, son. You look like the burden'll make your spine buckle soon."

I scratch my jaw. "She was there to see me."

"You? But—"

Her aghast expression has me huffing. "We were friends."

"Friends?"

I nod, wondering why I've only just recognized how badly I missed her all these years.

The fact she's here, but barely present, makes the absence of her friendship even starker. Like pouring fresh salt in a wound that healed badly.

"So, she was meeting you?"

"She was."

"But why would you think she started the fire if you were friends?"

"She tried to kiss me."

Mum drums her fingers on her armrest. "Hell hath no fury like a woman scorned."

At least she didn't accuse me of taking advantage of Zee.

"That's why I blamed her."

"Why didn't you tell the Mounties?"

"She was already messed up as a kid. I didn't want to add a juvie charge to it. She didn't do it, of course."

"How do you know?"

"I should have had faith in her but I didn't. It wasn't faulty wiring, Mum."

Our gazes catch.

She releases a breath. "Clyde—the original sinner."

Her lack of surprise sums up my father well.

Mum stays silent for what feels like endless moments, then she decides to blow my mind by changing the subject: "Callan knows about that DNA test Clyde did last year."

"What?!"

"I heard him tell Zee. He said he only wished he weren't Clyde's son... She's becoming quite the confidante of his."

Primly, she takes another sip. "You have feelings for her, of course."

I run my thumb along my bottom lip. "Perhaps."

"No 'perhaps' about it. It's why you spend half the time hiding behind your phone whenever she's grabbing coffee in the kitchen." She sniffs. "I'll tell you something, son. If you want her, you need to keep ahold of her. *But* there's no keeping ahold of something that doesn't want to be here... You need to give her a reason to stay *if* that's what you think is best for you."

"I didn't think you liked her," I admit.

"I barely know the girl. Still, it's a mother's lot to think that no one is good enough for her son, but I can see she has a kind heart thanks to her dealings with Callan." She pats my hand. "The way she stays in her room doesn't bode well though, Colt. You need to make a decision. Nip this in the bud before it can sprout stinging nettles, hmm?"

"I guess."

She fusses with her teacup. "Ida said Clyde came around yesterday."

"What?" I snap, the news blindsiding me.

"She told him to leave because you weren't above calling the cops on him."

"That worked?"

Mum purses her lips. "Apparently."

Concerned he might have frightened her, I demand, "Did you see him? Did he threaten you?"

"No. I was taking Hellie for a ride." *Thank God.* "Ida found him in your office."

My brows lift though I know what he was looking for... Something Mrs. Abelman found when she was packing his stuff and which is now in the new safe in my bedroom. Something which has kickstarted an investigation that, I hope, will ruin him for good.

"Ida wasn't sure whether to tell you or not."

When I think of the promise I made Zee *and* Callan, never mind the unspoken one I gave my mother once I asked her to return home, the fuse on my temper explodes.

Grabbing my cell, I hit dial on his name in my contacts, but much like the other times I've called him since the day he confronted Zee at the airport, he doesn't pick up.

Having to rely on texts, I type:

> Me: You go anywhere near the Seven Cs and you'll learn what happens when you break the protective order I've obtained against you, but only after you come face-to-face with Grandad's DP-12.

> Me: You're not welcome here.

When the ticks show 'read,' I ring him again but the coward still doesn't answer.

"Who are you trying to call?"

"Who do you think? He isn't picking up."

> Me: Callan, after school, can you order those new locks you want to install on the doors?

Though he's in class, *of course* he replies:

> Callan: Sure.

> Callan: Everything okay?

I cut Mum a look. "Did Ida tell Callan about Pops showing up?"

"Of course not," she scoffs.

Relieved, I type:

> Me: Everything's fine. But with Mum here and now Zee, I like the idea of securing the place better.

> Callan: It's that rock you put on her finger, isn't it? She has no idea how much it cost btw.

> Me: Let's keep it that way

> Callan: I tried to tell her it was a Brazilian Alexandrite, but she wasn't interested

225

Callan: Somehow, this arranged marriage saw you hitching your wagon with someone who doesn't care about your wealth.

Me: I know

Callan: Funny how some stuff can work out for the best...

I ignore that leading statement.

Me: Aren't you in class?

Callan: It's boring.

Callan: I'll order the new locks. They'll be here tomorrow.

Me: Perfect. See you later

I shoot Mum a look. "We're getting new locks."

"Good idea. Your father's your father," she warns. "He'll test your limits, so don't let him get the better of you."

"What's that supposed to mean?"

"It means that you shouldn't let him make you lose your cool. He didn't hurt anyone. Nobody apart from Ida saw him yesterday, and Lord knows she isn't scared of him. In the grand scheme of things, no harm was done."

"Only by luck."

"Of course, but it *was* lucky and it's an opportunity to fix a hole in our security."

"I didn't think he'd come around," I admit, snagging my teacup.

"Ida must have missed something when she was packing his belongings," she says with a shrug. "He's devious when crossed though, Colton. You know that better than I do. It's not a bad thing we're getting those new locks."

When she busses my temple and makes to leave, I murmur, "Where are you going?"

"I told Callan we'd go pick up some of that ice cream he likes from Saskatoon so I'll be collecting him from school."

I hide a smile behind my teacup. "Drive safely."

"Will do, son." She squeezes my shoulder. "You deserve to be happy, Colton. Maybe she isn't that for you. Maybe she is. But this ranch won't keep you warm in bed at night. It won't give you children that'll fill your heart. It won't give you comfort when the world is knocking at your door, demanding entry.

"She's close and accessible. Don't settle for her because you had a... strange relationship when you were younger. Equally, make her yours if that's what you decide is right for you. Just be happy, son. For me."

With those parting words, she leaves me to my thoughts.

But I soon realize that my problem stems from not knowing what happiness is.

Contentment, yes. Happiness, no.

Could the Zee-shaped hole in my life be the reason for that?

Or was I just born this way?

Chapter 25
Zee

"**H**ey, do you have a minute?"

Twirling on my office chair to face the door, I find my husband standing there.

It's still very surreal. Not only to think about Colton Korhonen being *that*—my husband—but how I'm here in this house.

What doesn't help?

The fact he's leaning against the doorjamb in a plaid shirt and jeans that do things to those thighs of his which should be beyond my attention.

It also doesn't help that Parker and Tee have been driving me crazy about how hot he is and telling me to be a proper cowgirl and to jump on his—

"Zee?"

I clear my throat when I realize I was sitting there.

Staring at him.

He knows it too.

His smile's...

Pained?

Ugh.

"What did you want?"

His gaze drops to my jersey. At least, I think it does.

He couldn't possibly be checking out my—

229

"Since when are you a hockey fan? You hated it when you were younger."

I need to not be disappointed that he wasn't checking me out.

Why would I be disappointed?

Colt and I mean nothing to one another.

Absolutely *nada*.

"I do hate it," I grouse, thoroughly annoyed by my so-called friends and the stupid fantasies they're triggering in my stupid, stupid, stupid brain. "But Tee loves it. She couldn't get Parker to attend the All-Star game in New York so she dragged me along for the ride."

He smirks. "Lemme guess... you fell asleep?"

I kind of hate that he still knows me well while also loving it.

It's complicated.

"I might have. But the night was a good one—"

"You had a nice dream, huh?"

I squint at his mockery. "Tee bought me this jersey as a memento."

"Not going to lie. It pisses me off that you're wearing another man's name."

If anything could have me gawking at him, it's that.

"Huh?"

That shouldn't be hot.

Shouldn't be.

But it is.

And my brain is dumber than I thought!

His shoulder hitches. "I'm surprised too. Anyway, I have some papers for you to look over. If you want to come to my office?"

Still gawking at him, I watch him leave my room, unsure how I feel about his admission.

Mostly because I kind of liked hearing that.

And I shouldn't. Should I? This has to be forced proximity—

"You coming or not?"

His holler has me jerking to my feet and scurrying after him.

I need to catch up because I have no idea where his office is located in the house.

His gaze is locked on his damn phone when he hears my footsteps. A quick glance at me has him heading down the stairs. Honestly, it's a wonder he isn't tripping up, down, left, and right with how often he's glued to his cell.

"What do you need me to sign?"

"This and that."

"Helpful."

His eyes twinkle as he looks at me. "Don't I know it. I also figured it was time you knew where some of the rooms were. Mrs. Abelman told me you refused her offer of a guided tour."

"Why do you call her Mrs. Abelman?"

"That's her name."

"I call her Ida."

"I can't call her that. She's Mrs. Abelman to me. Has Callan shown you around the place at least?"

"To his favorite den so we can play games." As I step onto the first floor, I murmur, "I thought you might have given me the tour."

"Why would I do that? I'm not going to force my presence on you when you don't want it, Zee," he dismisses, making me feel bad, but then he thought I killed his horse…

Bad is relative.

I don't answer because I have no idea how to, so, in silence, we meander along a hall that I didn't know was here and he guides me into an office.

Much like the rest of the house, it's massive.

Bigger than my bedroom, even.

It's also not to Colton's style.

I might not have spoken to the man in a decade, but this is too dark and dour for his taste. The walls are paneled in a rich redwood and his desk matches. There are no pictures, only paintings of landscapes. The desk itself has a large screen on it and a keyboard.

It's surprisingly neat.

Very boring.

And so shadow-filled that the overhead light doesn't make a dent in the inherent gloom.

Though the room doesn't suit him, he's at ease in it. Which tells me he's been using Clyde's office as his own for a long time, longer than he's been sleeping in Clyde's suite.

The family politics shouldn't interest me but they do.

It's complicated, okay?!

Speaking of family—there's a large picture on a bookcase shelf. Something tells me that Colt put it there, not Clyde. While there are no other trinkets that are related to the man having sons, Colt's not in-frame so I figure he took it.

Wearing a back-to-front cap, Cole's grinning at the camera, his arms slung around a uniformed Cody and a miniature Callan who's more scowl than anything else.

It does a great job of highlighting each brother's unique personality.

Cole's always been exuberant—he made every teacher's life hell, so much so they were glad when he got billeted in another province—Callan's brooding but at peace because he's with his brothers, and Cody looks like the world is resting on his shoulders. It's a trait he shares with Colt, but it's different. How couldn't it be when he's in active service?

Then, right beside it, I squint at a piece of cardboard that's in a frame. Bending down to get a better look at it, I realize it's a baseball card—Honus Wagner. Whoever the hell he is. Still, must be important if it's next to the picture of the boys.

Colt slouches in his desk chair, waving a hand for me to take a seat opposite him. "Get it out. You'll feel better for it."

"Who took the picture?"

"Me."

That sums him up entirely.

Always watching. Shielding.

The parent.

That's what happens, no?

The parent takes the picture. Well, the mom. But it's not like Lindsay was permitted to be around after the divorce. And it has to be a while ago. Callan's more kid than preteen.

I tip the frame at him. "It's a good composition."

"That's all Cody. He's the photographer of the family."

"Why aren't you in the shot then?"

"Didn't want to be."

Humming, I drift over to the desk. "Why haven't you changed this room?"

He blinks. "I didn't think either of those questions were what you were going to ask."

"You mean you don't know everything? Shock, horror!"

His sheepish grin is half-shielded by his hand as he scratches his jaw.

I forgot how much I missed that nervous tick of his.

It always made me want to smooth my fingers over his stubble.

That's when I see the two coffee cups on the desk and I *know* one is for me because it's the color of mud—just enough milk to take off the bitterness.

I also know it'll have no sugar in it.

When I reach for it, he nods ever-so-slightly as I take it, murmuring, "It's always been Pops's room. Why would I change it?"

"It's not anymore though, is it?"

The coffee is prepared perfectly.

He's always seen too much.

"No. But it doesn't bother me."

"How can't it?" Pulling a face, I glance around the space. "It's so depressing. And how do you see what you're doing without ten lights on?"

"Is that you asking me to turn on ten lights?"

"Yeah, if you want me to sign something."

"Quite a few somethings." He taps the desk. "Nothing major. Just the transfer of ownership from Juliette to you and the triplets."

I stagger back, hard enough for the coffee in my hand to spill. "Nothing major?"

"Was that you entering a whole other octave?"

"Y-You... You're s-serious?" I sputter, deciding that it'll be safer all round if I return the coffee to the coaster on the desk.

"Sure am. There are also power-of-attorney forms."

"On whose behalf?"

"Mine so that I can act for you in matters regarding the Bar 9." His chair creaks as he rocks it. "It's fine if you don't want to sign that over to me yet though. I know it's a big ask."

"You think I'd sign myself over to you but not the Bar 9?"

"You didn't sign yourself over to me."

"Sure I did. You figure the Bar 9 means more to me than my safety? If *Grand-mère* had tried to get me to marry your father, I'd have run away faster than you could say 'Zee.' But, you're you. I know you wouldn't do anything to hurt me. Or the Bar 9. Unlike your father."

"Wish I could say otherwise, but he'd take advantage of the situation for sure."

"You, on the other hand, want our child to have a legacy, don't you?"

It's getting easier to say those words without triggering a panic attack.

Our. Child.

At his nod, I step toward the desk and take a seat opposite him. His phone, forever in his hand, receives a few taps, and a welter of light floods the desk.

"Better?"

"Much."

He leaves me in silence to read the agreements and myriad papers that are unsurprisingly simple because this isn't necessarily a merger here. Colton will be acting as a guardian of sorts until *our child* can inherit.

Head bowed over the documents, I hold out my hand. In silence, he places a pen on my palm. I know it's accidental, but his fingers drag over the tender skin there, and how I contain a shiver is a miracle worthy of canonization.

That slight contact has the tiny hairs at my nape standing to attention. It rushes along my spine, spurring every nerve ending into wakefulness.

And that's *nothing* to the party taking place in my panties.

With a shuddery breath, I force myself to focus.

Legalese. Addendums. Codicils.

They're a language I can hide in.

A language I shouldn't need to hide in because Colton's only a temporary husband.

So why is my body not obeying my brain?

When I'm done, the task that should've taken ten minutes having tripled in time because of my drifting focus, a slip of paper slides onto the desk in front of me. But it's different. The paper's yellowed and there are a bunch of crinkles marring the sheet.

"Your uncle's will?" I sputter.

His hum is an invitation to read the contents.

As I do, my eyes grow wider with every clause.

"Where did you find this?"

"I didn't. Mrs. Abelman did when she was packing up Pops's stuff."

"You mean he kept this?!"

Nodding, he rubs his thumb over his top lip.

"I knew the man was arrogant, but this is proof he's an imbecile."

"Clay left him nothing but a parcel of land outside Estevan. Eight years ago, they discovered an oil field on it. They reckon there are twenty million barrels of oil to extract. That document's proof he owns it—not me."

Flabber truly gasted, I mumble, "So, he never had any rights to run the ranch?"

"No. It always irked me that Uncle Clay picked him over me. He used to tell me that I'd be the next person who'd protect the Seven Cs.

"When Pops took control, I didn't think to question it. I just figured Uncle Clay changed his mind as it's only tradition that sees the eldest son of the next generation inherit everything.

"Prior to the oil being discovered, Pops would only have had his trust fund to get by. They meter out the dividends annually. Recipients don't receive a bulk sum."

"And if you have fancy taste…"

"Like Pops does," he continues, "then it's not enough and will run out fast. I know for a fact he'd have been in debt. It's how he works. When I took over the ranch, he owed our creditors millions despite having the liquidity to cover the loans."

"Why are you showing me this?" I ask, tone soft.

"There's your motive. *That* is why he set fire to the stables. It's why he didn't let the horses loose. Franny was a blood bay with a sire who'd won gold at the Kentucky Derby. She won the King's Plate the previous year and we were starting her on the US circuit for the upcoming season. Alone, her insurance payout would have given him the funds to establish himself."

Bewildered, I just gape at him.

"He falsified Uncle Clay's will—I have a copy of that too. But because he's useless at ranching, we were operating near bank-ruptcy that season and had no working capital. So, to save the Seven Cs from ruin, he set fire to the stables, banked the millions from the insurance, and coasted along like the best of con artists."

Feeling sick, I ball my hands into fists that I press into my lap. It's either that or tear the will apart.

"I hate him," I intone, the words seething with my wrath.

"No more than I do," is his grim retort.

"What are you going to do?"

"That's the bitch of it. Though I've set an investigation into motion, I have no proof that he *did* set fire to the stables. Only an eyewitness…"

The sensation of nausea swirling around my insides inten-sifies. "You want me to file a report?"

"That's down to you," he assures me, his voice calm, as if he can read my panic.

My mind drifts to the many times that people blamed *me* for the fire.

And that same old fear metastasizes inside me.

"No one would believe me," I rasp.

"I do."

I jerk to my feet. "You're you and even you didn't believe me without the Loki connection. Everyone in town hates me."

"More than they hate him?"

"No. They're scared of him. All the more reason to keep things simple and blame me." My hands are trembling as I cup my elbows. "Y-You know the authorities would never take my side over his. I-I want to b-but—"

He gets to his feet too. Warily, I watch him approach me. As his hands settle on my shoulders, he urges me to lean on him.

For a second, I hover there.

I want to collapse into him, needing him to prop me up when I'm most vulnerable, but this isn't ten years ago.

Then, one of those large paws of his settles at the center of my back.

The heat of it whispers through me, like smoke getting into all the cracks, warming me from the inside out.

He encourages me to rest against him, and because I'm a weak, weak, weak woman, I do.

Gingerly, he curves his arms around me, and as the scent of him permeates the air, I sag in his hold.

God, he feels good.

So strong and stalwart.

As if he could take the burden of the world off my back and would carry it for me.

But that's wishful thinking, isn't it?

I'm just his temporary wife—

"It's fine, Zee. I'll have to figure something else out."

When his chin settles on the crown of my head, I nearly choke because I'm surrounded by him at all angles. That's when the realization hits: I haven't felt this safe since the last time he held me this way.

The day that changed both our lives—forever.

Tears prick my eyes at how wonderful the sensation is.

To be under this man's protection, temporarily or not, is a glorious thing—all the more so because I know what it's like to have it and to exist without it.

Then, he shifts, not to end the hug but to tuck my chin in his grasp and tilt my head so he can look at me. "I'm not going to make you do anything you don't want to do."

Still trembling, I study him. "What's your goal, Colt?"

"To make the bastard pay."

Though my lips part at his answer, when his head bows, I'm prepared for the fallout.

The air around us has shifted—turned. Grown charged.

His mouth hovers so close to mine.

Is he going to kiss me?

His jaw tightens and he moves again, higher this time. When he brushes my forehead with a soft peck, I stiffen and, like a fool, cup his jaw and unite our mouths, half expecting him to pull away.

But he doesn't.

He kisses me back.

He. Kisses. Me. Back.

My inner teenager is squealing in delight, but the adult Zee knows that this is a kiss beyond compare.

He tastes like coffee and the sugar cookies Ida bakes for him.

Before I can have a meltdown, against my stomach, I feel him harden.

The way he explores me has my heart pounding and my lungs burning, but it's worth it. So worth it. His tongue tangles with mine. Fast at first, until he slows it down and I realize I was the one rushing it.

My skin feels tight. I want to crawl *out* of my clothes and *onto* him, but I don't. Can't. Not when his hands cup my chin like mine hold his.

Neither of us is letting go. We're staying put and there's nowhere else I'd rather be than here until the end of time.

But, of course, life doesn't work that way.

Eventually, he edges away.

My lips tingle with the ferocity of that kiss, the hunger, and the fire, and I drop my forehead against his chest.

I can feel his heartbeat pounding. Experience the rush of his lungs as he brings his breathing under control.

He doesn't push me aside.

If anything, he encourages me to lean on him.

And for the first time, I get the feeling that he'd let me do that forever.

Not just until I have his baby.
But I was wrong before...
Am I now?

Chapter 26
Colton

"**W**hat?"

I narrow my eyes at the kid in front of me as he throws himself in the seat opposite the desk in the Bar 9's ranch office.

Hell, what am I talking about?

This 'kid' is as much of a man as Callan is—the one who needs to shift perspectives here is me.

"Is that any way to start a conversation with your new brother-in-law?"

Calder McAllister sniffs. "Isn't a real marriage."

"The law disagrees."

Today's kiss does too.

Jesus Christ, I can still feel the lingering aftereffects of it and it's been a whole three hours since she left my office in a daze.

"I don't. I know my sister. She'll get pregnant and then she'll fuck off back to New York." His declaration hits me on the raw. He knows her better than I do now. Is he right? "She hates it here," he continues, "because of *your* family—"

I can't argue with that so I hold up a hand to stall his words. "I didn't ask you to come to the office because of her."

"Then why am I here?"

"Over in the east quadrant of your land, by the highway, there are three ponds that are pretty much in a row."

His mouth tightens. "Mom said they were our ponds. One for each of us."

That he shared that memory with me has me pausing before, softly, asking, "There's a copse of trees up there. You know where I mean?"

"Near the watchtower?" At my nod, he demands, "What about it?"

I bridge my hands on top of my abs. "There's a weed farm."

His eyes bug. "A what farm?"

"Marijuana," I clarify, rocking in a chair that I don't think has been sat in for a decade. This whole office makes mine look modern. "You got anything to do with it?"

"I tagged your barn. That doesn't make me a drug dealer."

"If you're not lying to me, the fact that you don't know about it tells me you three haven't been pulling your weight around here." Though, admittedly, the emotional attachment to the ponds might be why they've avoided the area. "That'll have to change—"

"You can't boss me around!"

"Sure I can. Won't just be me either. Theo Frobisher will be taking on the duties of ranch manager at the Bar 9, so you can expect to be bossed around by him too. And what he says, Calder, goes or I'll hear about it."

"I'm so fucking scared," he snipes, jumping to his feet, his attitude of before shifting into a more normal adolescent pout.

This I can handle.

This I'm used to.

Callan might like to think he's mature, but he's still only eighteen years old.

"You should be. You think I won't toss you in one of your many lakes if you don't start acting like this is *your* legacy? Won't be one with a mineral spring either."

"I'm not scared of water."

"All the more reason to do it then."

"You gonna waterboard me or something?"

"What?! This isn't Guantanamo Bay! Jesus, Calder."

"Then what's with the threats, dude."

"I like to call them incentives."

"Pay us, that'd be an incentive," he grouses. "Otherwise, it's child labor—"

Because that's exactly what Callan would say, making me wonder why the hell he and my youngest brother don't get along, I chuckle. "You're not a five-year-old. Anyway, it's your ranch—"

"Look, we don't want cash. Our truck's busted and the mechanic won't fix it without us paying upfront. We owe him too much."

"So, you'll work for your truck?" I query as he sinks into the chair again.

"Yeah, and none of us have to get wet. How were you going to shove us into the lake anyway?"

"Barrels."

"That's worse! Does my sister know you belong in the Spanish Inquisition's hit squad?"

"I'm sure she thinks the worst of me as it is." I arch a brow at him. "Theo will be implementing a schedule—"

"Yeah, yeah. How long until you'll pay the garage bill?"

"I won't be paying dick. You'll be earning your own wage so you can pay for it yourself. There are three of you so it shouldn't take long."

"Takes a genius to work that out." Folding his arms across his chest, he huffs. "Can't you just pay—"

"No. I'd hate to be accused of using child labor," I mock. "Do the work. Prove yourself—"

"It's our ranch."

At his deepening scowl, I sigh. "Look, the contracts and arrangements aside, if you want to work on the ranch in management, then I'm not going to stop you, but you'll have to prove yourself.

"This place is so deep in the red, your bill with Jim in town probably looks cheap. I'm not taking your legacy away from you. I'm protecting it so that there's something left for future generations to have—including you and your brothers. You understand me?"

Calder's gaze turns pensive. "I understand you. We have nothing to do with that weed farm."

I grunt. "Good to know."

"I mean it. I'd never do anything to risk the land. Not when this is *Mamie's* home. Anyway, if I got my ass hauled off to jail, the shock'd kill her. I know she's an old bitch, but she's fragile and I love her. I wouldn't jeopardize—"

Again, I hold up a hand. "I believe you."

He sags in his seat. "Good. What are you doing about it, then?"

Not sure what it says about me that he already expects me to have a plan in place.

Of course, he'd be right.

"I put men in the watchtower nearby. We're going to make sure whoever's growing it knows they don't have free rein over our turf."

Calder's jaw tightens. "Damn straight."

I peer at the clock on my phone. "In fact, I need to get out there—"

"You're going?"

"Of course." I study him. "First rule of ranch management. Don't ask your men to do anything you wouldn't do yourself."

"Can't see Clyde living by that rule," he snipes.

"Clyde didn't teach me to run a ranch," is my simple retort. "My uncle did.

"Keep your noses clean and stop with the tagging or I'll be taking the cleanup out of your wages. I know you hit up the Frobishers' truck the other day. At least this time, you didn't sign the Bar 9."

His grin's sheepish. "They're assholes."

"Yeah, I agree. Theo isn't though. He's good people so don't give him any shit, you hear?"

"I hear."

With that being said, I get to my feet and round the desk. Before he can stand, I clap him on the shoulder. "We're family, Calder. No matter the circumstances. Your land and mine will be tied together forever. Let's make your ancestors roll in their graves at a McAllister working with a Korhonen, hmm?"

A loud snort escapes him. "I like the sound of that, Colt."

"Good." I pat his arm. "Spread the word with the other two. I don't like having to repeat myself."

Before he can sass me anymore, I head on out, jump into my truck, lower the window as the radio blares, and get my ass over to the weed farm.

Technically, the rotation of manpower shouldn't have started until Zee signed over the power of attorney to me, but there was no way in hell I wasn't monitoring that situation.

It's a beautiful day to stare at the clouds while waiting for some stoner hippie to collect his crop of weed.

I make it to the watchtower and take over for Darrel who, yawning, finishes his shift.

Then, it's me, my thoughts, and I.

Knowing that the sound of a car on this barren stretch of the highway will give away the 'cultivators,' I close my eyes and take in some sun.

It's not often I get the chance to sit and be. Which makes Calder's belief that I'd leave this kind of chore for someone on my staff all the more hilarious—why the hell wouldn't I want this task?

The hours pass swiftly. Mostly because the one thing on my mind is the one thing I don't want to chase away—my new wife.

Aside from this morning when *she* kissed *me,* Mum had a point when she said that Zee has barely left her bedroom. In fact, she's channeling Callan two years ago when he was hooked on camgirl sites and I could barely get him into the kitchen unless I offered him new games, ice cream, *and* led him out of there like a donkey with a carrot in front of its nose.

Not that I think they're doing the same thing.

But Calder's words come back to haunt me in the sleepy somnolence of the afternoon.

Did our kiss change anything? Has it—

A crankshaft sounds in the distance, making my eyes pop open.

The rumble of a motorbike along with the louder motor of another vehicle has me descending the watchtower, heading to my truck, and picking up the shotgun I stored in there before I drove over to the Bar 9.

Shoving some extra cartridges into my pocket, I load the shotgun and then storm over to the farm on foot.

I timed it pretty damn well—the dead stretches of highway updated me faster than radar.

Moving to the front of the farm, off the patch of land where their tires have previously drawn rivets into the soil, I wait for the vehicles—a Harley and a white van—to come to a stop.

The cut and patch have me cursing.

My fervent hope for a stoner hippie drifts away on the wind because this is clearly the endeavor of an MC.

And they're not like the ones we work with in the US who transport victims to the Canadian border. No, it's the goddamn Rabid Wolves.

I remember them from when I was attending university.

They held up a series of gas stations and killed some of the attendants.

At least I know what I'm dealing with...

"This is my fucking land." I punctuate the declaration by shooting the ground a few feet away from the bike. "You want to explain to me why weed is being cultivated on it? In fact, no. I don't give a shit. You get off my property and we can forget any of this ever happened."

The biker just tucks a cigarette between his lips and flicks a lighter. "You think you and your shotgun are enough to—"

Taking aim, I shoot out his front tire.

"Fuck, man! I didn't sign up for this shit!" the van driver yelps.

"You didn't sign up for dick," the biker growls, standing straight as he climbs off his bike. "Look what you did to my—"

I don't let him finish the sentence.

Shifting to the side so I'm not facing straight on, I shoot out the engine next.

"You fucker!" the guy curses as I reload.

"You're going to get off my property, asshole, and you're not coming back."

He drags out a handgun from his cut as I cock the shotgun

and aim at him. "You can shoot me, but I can shoot you too. And double-aught buckshot will fuck you up faster than anything you have in that peashooter."

"This is no peashooter. It's a—"

"Do I look like I give a fuck? You can get off my land *now* or I'll shoot to kill. So be smart, use that peanut you have for a brain, and get. Off. My. Land."

I can feel the veins in my forehead and throat bulge as I yell the warning at him.

It's the guy in the van who screams, "Come on, Vinnie. It's not worth it! Get in. Please. Fuck, I don't want to die for some weed."

"You'll regret this," Vinnie snarls as he backs off, running around the van's fender. I shoot at his feet as he jumps into the passenger side. "You're fucking crazy, man!"

As the driver reverses, Vinnie's eyes are locked on mine. It's only when they pull away, wheels smoking as they turn hard and fast onto the road, that I shoot again. The rear window shatters, and the van jerks to the left before, brakes shrieking and engine groaning, they fly down the highway.

"That was so cool!"

Jolting, I see the triplets. "What are you doing here? You're lucky I didn't shoot you!"

"Oh, my God, I thought that asshole was gonna piss his pants," Carson crows and mimics, "'Use that peanut you have for a brain and get. Off. My. Land.' *BOOM*."

Colby presses, "Please tell me you're going to teach us how to use a shotgun."

That clears the adrenaline from my brain. "You mean you don't know how to already?"

In tandem, their cheeks flush, but it's Carson who mumbles, "No one would teach us."

I scrape a hand over my head, but they don't give me the chance to answer because Calder's cocking his arms like I did the shotgun and shouting, "This is my fucking land. *BOOM*."

Carson jumps on his shoulders. "So cool."

Colby dives in front of Calder. "'Shotgun pellets will fuck

you up faster than anything you have in that peashooter.' *BANG*."

As they burst out laughing, their adrenaline buzzing as high as mine, I shake my head.

No way in hell did I expect I'd come face-to-face with the weed farmers today, but more than that, I could never have anticipated *this*.

If ever there was proof these little shits need corralling, I have it.

Still, I call the cops first and report the weed farm and the day's events, then I drawl, "Right, you three. I have to deal with the RCMP, and then we'll return to the homestead and I'll teach you how to fire a shotgun."

Their whoops and cheers have me chuckling at their antics as they leap around like I told them they'd won the lottery.

Still, as an impromptu bonding session, I guess it worked...

Text Chat
SEVEN DAYS LATER

Irreplaceable - Beyoncé

Tee: I left the apartment

Tee: But only because the orchestra threatened to fire me

Zee: I haven't left the ranch yet lol so you're doing better than me

Tee: o.O

Tee: Really?!

Zee: Yeah, I've been busy with work and settling in, you know?

Tee: Haven't you gone to visit your grandmother yet?

Zee: No, and she hasn't called me either.

Tee: Damn, I know she's a bitch but that's cold

Zee: Gratitude never was easy for her lol

Tee: What about the triplets?

Zee: No sign of them. BUT that might have something to do with Colt. I get the feeling he's keeping them busy with work on the ranch.

Zee: We've been texting. They haven't bitched about it to me though.

Tee: Not like them.

Zee: Think they're scared of Colt

Zee: Which is interesting

Tee: Why?

Zee: Because he's not scary

Tee: Some guys don't have to be scary to keep people in line

Tee: He's like a sheepdog

Zee: You did not compare my husband to a sheepdog, Christy MacFarlane!

Tee: OMG. Did you just 'my husband' him?!

Zee: What? No!

Tee: YOU DID

Tee: You said, 'My husband!'

Tee: YOU DID

Tee sends image

Zee
You did not compare my
husband to a sheepdog, Christy
MacFarlane!

        Tee
        OMG. Did you just 'my
        husband' him?!

Zee
What? No!

              Tee
              YOU DID

        You said, 'My husband!'

              YOU DID

Tee: Look, I've screenshot it for posterity

Zee: Fuck, I did!

Zee: But in my defense, you compared him to a German shepherd

Tee: I was thinking more of a Border collie

Zee: THAT'S WORSE!

Tee: How is that worse?! Border collies are one of the best breeds! They're intelligent and capable. They're fit and can get a hundred-strong herd of sheep in line by running around 'em in circles. If I were a dog, I think that'd be sexy as all get out

Tee: Plus, they're pretty

Zee: Colt's not pretty

Tee: You looking at the same man as me?

253

Zee: Calling him pretty's like calling him a Border collie!

Zee: Don't try to walk it back

Tee: I. Walk. Back. Nothing

Tee: You know I'm right.

Zee: Pfft

Zee: So, I need to tell you something.

Tee: You've decided to come home?

Zee: No.

Tee: You think Tim Horton's is better in the US than in Canada?

Zee: NO. I haven't even had a Timmies yet. It has nothing to do with the States or Canada. Jesus H. Christ. You'd try the patience of a saint.

Tee: What is it then?

Zee: I kissed him.

Tee: Who?

Zee: What do you mean who? WHO do you think?

Tee: Colton?!

Tee: YOU KISSED COLTON?

Zee: Yes.

Tee: WHEN?

Tee: Wait, no. Was it good? Tell me that first.

Zee: It was about a week ago.

Tee: YOU KEPT IT FROM ME

Zee: I knew you'd overreact!

Zee: It was just a little kiss

Tee: Was there tongue?

Zee: Maybe

Tee: Then it wasn't a little kiss. OMG. How good was it? On a scale of 'stick a finger in me now' and 'go brush your teeth.'

Zee: That's not a measure!

Tee: It's my idea of a measure. TELL ME OR I'LL GET A FLIGHT RIGHT THIS SECOND AND DRAG THE ANSWER OUT OF YOU

Zee: Sheesh

Zee: It was, um, 'stick a finger in me now' good

Tee: :O

Tee: :O

Tee: :O

Tee: I. Am. Deceased.

Tee: Did you let him?

Zee: Stick a finger in? No.

Tee: Why not?

Zee: Because, I don't know, it wasn't the right time

Tee: When would be the right time?

Zee: When we weren't in his office, for one.

Tee: Desk sex is hot.

Tee: Who am I kidding? The man's hot all round if he's that good at kissing.

Tee: Plus, he leaves you alone to work, doesn't pester you, AND he herded your brothers out of the way.

Tee: Though, you could visit them yourself.

Zee: That'd involve leaving the ranch lol. I'm not brave enough for that yet.

Tee: Brave enough to kiss him though…

Zee: I'm going to regret telling you this, aren't I?

Tee: Very likely.

Tee: You're getting along well with Callan still?

Zee: He's very empathetic. I think he's the only reason I'm not freaking out about the transition, TBH

Tee: Great. I'm being replaced by an eighteen-year-old Korhonen. Traitor.

Zee: *sings You're Irreplaceable*

Tee: You can't work around me with Beyoncé

Tee: Anyway, she's throwing her bae out of the house in that video. That's not a compliment.

Zee: ;)

Zee: You feeling better?

Tee: I'm sorry I've been such a big baby about this, but I was obviously lacking a Callan and a Colt in my life

Zee: *snorts*

Zee: Everyone needs a Callan

Zee: He has a stash of junk food in his room. I told him that his future girlfriend would always come to him for sugar when she gets her period. His blush was so cute.

Tee: Wonder why he's not dating someone. If he looks anything like his older brothers, that is.

Zee: There aren't many pictures in the house, but I've seen one in Colton's office. They all share the same genes for sure lol.

Tee: Who's the best-looking one?

Zee: Don't make me answer that

Tee: Is it so bad that you find the guy you're married to attractive?

Zee: We're having IVF. I don't need to be attracted to him.

Tee: *double snorts*

Zee: We are!

Tee: Yeah, okay. I'll believe that when it happens. What with him eyeing you up and down like you're a donut that needs to be stuffed with Korhonen jam.

Zee: EW

Tee: The analogy works! He can stick his finger in and make the hole bigger and everything :P

Zee: I'm not a donut and I hope his cum isn't red!

Tee: Okay, you're a donut that he wants to frost?

Zee: TEE!

Tee: :P

Tee: How about you're his Pigeon Creek Cream Donut he wants to fill?

Zee: I'm going to kill you.

Tee: Deny it!

Zee: Of course I do. We barely talk.

Tee: You just kiss

Zee: We kissed ONCE

Tee: If you say so

Zee: He's busy. I'm busy. We lead separate lives. The only real change for me is that I'm living here and I hang out with Callan instead of frosting cookies with you griping at me about your lack of a sex life.

Tee: They were the best times, weren't they?

Zee: :* They were <3

Tee: What were you doing in his office?

Zee: Whose office?

Tee: Colt's office. You said that you were in his office. That's where there's a picture of Cody?

Zee: Oh, yeah. It was nothing. He needed me to sign a few things.

Tee: Like what? An NDA? Postnup... Is that a thing? He didn't make you sign a prenup, did he?

Zee: No, he didn't.

Zee: They were regarding the Bar 9. Transfer of ownership from Grand-mère to me.

Tee: WOW

Zee: Yeah. Heady stuff. Then things like power of attorney to give him the ability to pay off debts etc.

Zee: It's odd now that you mention it

Tee: What is?

Zee: I DIDN'T sign a prenup.

Zee: I was too busy freaking out about everything else that I didn't realize.

Tee: Oh, I realized. I didn't say anything. I thought you didn't want to talk about it.

Zee: Since when do I keep secrets from you?

Tee: You kept this quiet.

Tee: SEVEN whole days. Is this what our relationship has come to?

Zee: Who's the drama? YOU'RE the drama, Tee. I just didn't want to make a big deal out of it

Tee: No, because clearly, it means nothing. If you ever have IVF, I'll pay for it myself.

Zee: Shut up

Tee: You shut up

Tee: You know I'm right

Tee: Why get him to stick a finger in when he could stick his dick in AND make a baby for free?

Zee: And you think you're romantic.

Tee: I'm a pragmatist.

Tee: Plus, IVF doesn't come with orgasms. If he's that good at kissing that you kept it on the down low for a week, imagine how good he is at the sex

Zee: 'The' sex?

Tee: Oh, yeah. When it's good, it deserves a definite article

Zee: I'm already regretting telling you this

Tee: You shouldn't. Me and Colt are working on seducing you.

Zee: FML

Tee: So, why do you think he did that?

Zee: Did what?

Tee: Keep up! Didn't make you sign a prenup?

Zee: Oh. He has an odd way of viewing the world.

Tee: Meaning?

Zee: He's very unlike his father

Tee: That's a hop, skip, and a jump away from your initial reaction to him

Zee: Yes.

Zee: He's very disarming in that sense

Tee: Explain. And no vague answers. Cold, hard facts are what I'll accept.

Zee: Bitch

Tee: You know it :P

Zee: I don't know this for certain, obviously, but I imagine that he thinks if I do take him for half of everything, then it won't matter because it'll all go to the child we have together in the end.

Tee: Huh

Tee: Evidence?

Zee: This isn't a court of law!

Zee: But it's like when he told me why I had to return here. So that our child wouldn't deal with gossip and rumors in school about the circumstances of their parents' marriage

Tee: It's quite sweet he considered that. I mean, it's hopeless because people will speculate anyway

Tee: You should give him a plant

Zee: A plant?! Why?

Tee: It's his birthday in a few months, isn't it?

Zee: How do you know that?

Tee: I know a lot of things that you're not privy to.

Zee: Since when?

Tee: Since you abandoned me!

Tee: I activated full stalker mode

Zee: For lil 'ole me? I'm honored

Tee: Hush.

Zee: What did you find?

Tee: What I didn't find is fascinating. Not a whisper of your wedding has been in the press

Zee: Must be sweeping it under the radar

Tee: It'd need an industrial-sized brush

Zee: *shrugs*

Zee: What else?

Tee: He donates about three million a year to various horse charities in the province

Zee: :/ I guess we know why that is

Tee: Yeah. I cringed and sighed in delight at the same time. Honestly, it's unnerving how perfect this guy is.

261

Zee: Back that statement up

Tee: Yes, your honor.

Tee: He donates a further three million to various charities, with the bulk split between a couple women's shelters.

Zee: Also makes sense

Tee: Uh-huh

Tee: In university, he had a steady girlfriend. She visited the ranch once and they broke up shortly after

Zee: How on earth do you know that?

Tee: Stalked her profile too.

Zee: Jesus wept!

Tee: Oh, He cried about SOMEthing.

Tee: There's this shot of them with his brothers and Clyde's in the picture too. He's oozing slime. Wanna bet that breakup had something to do with Daddy Dearest?

Zee: *pukes*

Tee: Agreed

Tee: That was his last 'official' girlfriend

Tee: I think he has/had a side piece in Saskatoon though

Zee: Proof?

Tee: Jealous, Mrs. Korhonen?

Zee: PROOF?!

Tee: She'd take pictures of them every couple months. Nothing overt. You wouldn't think they were dating. But they stand too close together to be friends and whoever they're with, it's not the same crowd so it's not like he's hanging with a group of university buds

Zee: When was the last time she posted a picture of them?

Tee: Before Thanksgiving so I think that might be over too?

Zee: Good

Tee: My, my, is that you turning green, Zee?

Zee: What else did you learn?

Tee: Aside from his birthday, lol?

Zee: What else?

Tee: Whenever the Foo Fighters play in Canada, he attends at least one concert. Two years ago, he went to three

Tee: And he subscribes to this Japanese logic puzzle magazine.

Zee: I'm impressed

Tee: He's a grunge-loving, logic puzzle-annihilating, horse-obsessed, potential model, Zee. I think without the billions, he'd be a catch, babe. So, I don't know what to tell you aside from jump on that cowboy and ride him hard and wet

Zee: TEE!

Tee: Trust me. You haven't dated that much recently. You don't know what the dating pool looks like out there. You got this guy (who's KIND) to marry you without having to sell a kidney!

Tee: I'm almost jealous lol

Tee: Okay, I AM jealous. He gets to live with you and I don't. *pouts*

Zee: *snorts*

Tee: You need him to fuck you, Zee

Zee: Why would I need that, lol?

Tee: Because I need to know if he lives up to the promise of being good in the sack. There has to be a defect. He's too perfect to be real. And for my self-esteem, I need to know this information

Zee: What if he IS great in bed?

Tee: Then I'll die an old maid because I can't deal with these lackluster lays anymore. Honestly, is it so hard to rub the clitoris and not pick at it like you're scooping a jellybean from a jar?

Zee: That's some imagery

Tee: Look, it's only sisterly love that's stopping me from asking if I can have a go when you're done with him

Zee: This is you restraining yourself, huh?

Tee: Yes.

Tee: So, do me proud, cowgirl.

Chapter 27
Colton

Please, Please, Please, Let Me Get What I Want -
The Smiths

What with selling a third of our herd and distributing the rest onto Bar 9 land, speaking with engineers to have the Seven Cs tap into the Bar 9 water sources, and getting a team of men to break ground on a new bunkhouse for Dove Bay, you'd reckon I wouldn't have time to think about my new wife...

You'd be wrong.

It's been four weeks since we married and if we're still in the 'gentling' phase of our relationship, I'm nowhere close to getting near Zee. Not even after that kiss.

One kiss—is that enough to sustain a man for a lifetime?

She didn't rush off after it, but ever since, she's been jumpy around me.

As far as I know, she leaves her room for food and to play games with Callan.

And it's driving me crazy.

More than that, Calder's belief that she'll pick up and run is messing with my head.

Fear of loss is what I'm writing it off as. But it's insane because I have nothing to fear when I never had her in the first place.

Leaning on the gate that looks onto one of our larger pastures, I watch a ranch hand we're interviewing prove his mettle on horseback.

Theo's putting the guy through his paces so I'm only monitoring the process while also keeping the interviewees' skill sets in mind for other projects—the Bar 9 and the chicken farm I haven't gotten started on yet.

"Shoveling out chicken shit's all these morons look capable of," I grumble to myself as I preside over job interview number twenty.

"First sign of madness is talking to yourself."

I squint at Callan. "What are you doing out here?"

"Just finished walking Harriet around the paddock. How did her vet appointment go?"

Harriet's one of his favorite stock horses—and she's on the brink of 'too old' to be carrying her foal. It's only because of Callan's security system that we realized how Fen, my stallion, even got to her—I love him but he's no gentleman like his sire.

"She's doing fine. Took her booster vaccinations like a pro."

"She shouldn't have had to."

There's no arguing with that. "We fixed the issue in the pens." His harrumph tells me it's not good enough. "What do you want me to do, Callan? Put a chastity belt on her? She went into heat early and we weren't prepared for it. We will be from now on."

His sniff is loaded with disdain. "I should have been here for the vet's visit."

"School's important and I made sure I was with her."

He grunts. "You got a clue who to hire?"

"So far, they're useless."

I'm out here monitoring because we take our hiring process seriously.

They only get through the 'door' after a criminal record

check. It's why it's taken weeks to get to this point after Gillon quit.

With eight domestic violence survivors on my land, I'm not about to invite the wolves that are their ex-husbands into the fold. There's little those psychos won't do to get their exes back.

"Do you think there's a reason Father hasn't come around?" he asks abruptly.

"He's been in Vancouver since he left here," I half-lie, grateful he doesn't know Pops broke into the house.

His jaw clenches. "Oh."

Understanding the source of his fear, I sling an arm around his shoulders. "When have I ever let him hurt you?"

Goddamn never, that's when.

"I hope he doesn't come back here."

"I think that's unlikely. I'll head him off though. Get him a room at the Pigeon Inn."

As intended, that has a gust of laughter escaping my baby bro. "Can you imagine him there? 'Where's the butler?'" he derides. "And where are the silk sheets? NO ROOM SERVICE? What is this place? A hovel?!"

Snickering, I cuff him upside the head. "Sounds like fun to me."

"Oh, to be a fly on the wall." His eyes light up. "I bet I could convince Eloise to plant a camera in the room they'd assign him—"

"Eloise?"

"Eloise Grant. You know her—the cheerleader I tutor in biology. Her parents own the inn. She owes me."

"I created a monster," I tease, but he's smiling and that's all I could ask for. With a final squeeze, I let go of him. "You okay?"

It's not like him to come out here so I figure the situation with Pops has been worrying him more than I reckoned.

"Yeah."

"What's with the 'Father' shit, anyway?"

"Pops is something you call a nice man. He's not nice. He doesn't deserve to have an affectionate name."

269

"Traditions are hard to break. I figure that's why we carry them on," I concede.

"Yeah, well, I'm breaking this one."

Because that's a healthy boundary he wants to implement, I don't question it, just ask, "How you coping with Mum being around?"

"I'm sick of tea."

"She does drink a lot of it."

"I saw something in the kitchen the other night." At my questioning glance, he murmurs, "Mrs. Abelman was holding her hand."

"Mum's hand?"

He nods.

"Huh. They've always been friends. I think that's the only reason she didn't have a breakdown when she had to leave us. She knew Mrs. Abelman would protect us like we were her own." My glance turns knowing. "How's that feel?"

"How's what feel?"

"Getting a decade's worth of love showered on you?"

His cheeks blaze with color and it has nothing to do with the wind. "It's kinda nice."

"You have so much female attention, Callan, it's a wonder you're not hanging out with Theo and me on the range more to breathe in the testosterone," I tease.

"Jerk."

I wink.

"I like her."

"Who? Mum?"

"I didn't mean her."

"Who did you mean?"

"Zee."

I nod. "You'd know better than me." If I sound bitter, so be it. It's my own damn fault.

"We're going to play a game tonight. You could hang with us. I have three controllers."

"Why do you have three controllers? Until Zee came along, you only ever played by yourself."

"What if I need to charge both of them?"

"First world problems. I don't think Zee would like it if I hung out with you guys. Not yet, anyway. I know she's still getting used to living here. I don't want to push her."

"Push her? Colton, you could be in Nunavut for how much distance you keep putting between you.

"Yesterday, she was staring at you throughout breakfast and you didn't notice. You were too busy with your damn logic puzzles."

"They were particularly challenging yesterday. Wait. She was?"

"Uh-huh. It was the first time she came to eat with us too." He shuffles from one foot to the other. "She's pretty."

Great—he has a crush on her.

"Callan," I warn.

"What?! I'm just saying. I have eyes. I use them, unlike some brothers I know."

I clear my throat. "Are you still going on those camgirl sites?"

"Maybe. Don't tell Zee though!"

"Oh, yeah, Callan, I'm going to tell the wife I barely speak to that my kid brother has a crush on her and is obsessed with camgirl sites!"

He gapes at me. "I do *not* have a crush on her."

"Sounds like it to me."

"I do not! She's my..." He shifts from one foot to the other. "...friend."

The coil of tension that had been tightening inside me releases with that information.

"Your... friend?"

"I'm quite likable. Just not with people my age."

"That's because you tell them they're idiots."

"People don't seem to mind it when they're older."

"They think you're being facetious," I drawl, amused. Though I swiftly narrow my eyes at him. "You haven't called her an idiot, have you?"

"No." He huffs as if I insulted him. "She's not dumb. Not like her asshole brothers. I can't wait until I don't have to see them at school anymore."

271

"Forgot you hated them."

The hilarious part, of course, is that Calder's as much of a little shit as Callan is.

The more time I spend with the triplets, the more I realize that these two are too alike for their own good.

"Zee has great taste. She doesn't particularly like them either. Just puts up with them. Though she *does* love them. It's kinda how we feel about Cole."

I yank on his tuque again. "I should invite them over here."

"What?! God, no. You can't invite them to my home. They're horrendous. They burp and fart and talk about pussies all day. They're so boring—"

"They sound like teenage boys to me." *You included, but you just watch pussies all day.* "They're not bullying you, are they?"

"No."

"You lying to me?"

"I'd tell you."

I'm not so sure if he would but, in this instance, I believe him.

"If I invite them in the name of family unity, I won't expect you to leave your room," I attempt to appease.

"Aren't I family?" he blusters.

"You're the one who doesn't want me to invite them! They're her kid brothers, Callan."

"You paid their debts. I saw the bank transfer. Isn't that enough?"

"Sparing them from penury isn't an olive branch."

He snorts. "You clearly haven't been poor before."

"And you have?"

"No. Anyway, *Grand-mère*—"

"Grand-who now?" I sputter.

"—doesn't seem like the kind of person who'd appreciate you butting in. You're probably expected to foot the bills and to cover her taxes and that's the extent of your duty until she either dies or you get Zee pregnant. Which will never happen if you don't woo her."

"Woo her?" I repeat.

"Yeah." He burrows his nose so far beneath his scarf that he's mostly eyes. "You know, like, to make her fall in love with you."

"Who said I want her to fall in love with me?"

That has him popping out of his scarf like a mole waiting to be whacked.

If we continue this conversation, I'll be doing the whacking.

"Why wouldn't you want that? She's awesome."

I groan. "Callan, I don't want to have this conversation with you!"

"Which brother would you prefer to hear this from? I mean, you have three to choose between and one of them is going to pull your head out of your ass whether you like it or not. I'm a good listener—"

"Since when?"

"You can tell me what the problem is between you two."

"There's no problem."

"Liar. I've seen you in town, Colt. You can charm both sexes from twenty feet away. Yet you barely speak to your wife. The woman you're supposed to have a child with."

"If I needed a therapist, I'd hire one."

"You're too stoic for a therapist. You have undiagnosed CPTSD—"

"Since when?"

"Since I read up on it to see if you had it."

"I don't have it."

"You do. But see? This proves my point." He squints at me. "Father messed you up, and don't pretend that you didn't see him hit Mum because you'd be the liar.

"So, what's the problem? It can't be that you don't find Zee attractive. She's beautiful."

She is.

I've no idea why I admit this to him, but I do. "I can't ever expect her to love me. I don't deserve it."

"Shut up. Why would you think that?"

"I have too much to make up to her."

"Like what?"

"It doesn't matter."

273

"Sure it does."

"I let her down," is my simple retort.

"You have to try. You're a great man, Colt. If anyone can figure out how to right a wrong, it's you."

Laughing, I draw him in for a noogie. "Your opinion matters more to me, kiddo."

Though he yelps and fights to get out of my hold, he argues, "That's not how it's supposed to be."

"What do you mean?" I watch as he straightens his tuque, folding it over his forehead.

"She's your wife, Colt. Her opinion of you is supposed to matter."

"We're not like a regular husband and wife though."

His disgusted glower tells me how little I'm impressing him. I swear he should patent that expression.

"No reason you can't be. I think she'd be good for you."

"Since when are you a romantic?"

He scowls. "I'm not."

"Sounds like it to me," I mutter as he hunches his shoulders and slouches over to the house.

It's a habit to watch him until he's inside. I'll never forget that time he was twelve and almost got run over by a pickup truck because he was watching his feet more than his surroundings.

Scratching my chin, I turn my attention to the pasture.

I already know Theo won't hire this guy seeing as he can barely stay in his saddle. Imbecile's trying for a job on a ranch and he looks like he has motion sickness.

"Next," I holler at Theo, impatient with how he's coddling the idiot.

Then, because Callan's contagious, I glower at nothing.

I don't need my little brother to set me up with my wife.

I *know* she's awesome and beautiful—

Jesus, I hate it when he's right.

Chapter 28
Zee

We Didn't Start The Fire - Fall Out Boy

"You finished?"

Turning my head so I can see Callan in the doorway, I nod. "Gimme five."

"Sure thing."

He steps into my bedroom, meandering over to the window where he looks onto the ranch.

In the time I've been here, I've grown used to Callan hanging out with me. Not only do I not mind because I'm used to Tee hovering while I work, but I like the kid.

Sure, his candor is borderline offensive, but he's kind. And he always seems to know when I'm having a bad day.

It's uncanny.

Today, however, it appears that he's the one in a mood.

Once I've finished the email I was working on—a deep dive into a complaint against the strip club in West Orange that the Satan's Sinners own—I twist in my chair and stretch a kink in my spine.

"You look pensive."

"I heard your alert earlier," he comments.

"Sorry. I know it's annoying. Tee set it to a crying baby because she knows that'll make me react fastest."

"I know Colt has apps on his phone that monitor your blood sugar. Can I be included on the account?"

"You don't need to—"

"I'll feel better."

"The alerts can sound in the early hours," I protest.

"It'll make me feel better," he asserts.

"Colt and Tee are on the account."

"I'd still appreciate being included."

"The weight of the world isn't yours to bear, Callan."

His gaze is measured and so like his brother's that I have to shake my head. Whichever girl hooks this one is in for a ride.

"Fine," I mumble as I add him to the apps.

"Colt says Father is staying in Vancouver," he rasps—ah, the reason for his mood. "Clyde could bounce around Canada for a while, thinking that time will make Colt change his mind. *Then*, he'll come back."

Ah, the mega-rich—they seriously live in a different stratosphere.

"And the prospect bothers you?" I ask, joining him at the window.

In the distance, I see Colt standing by a pasture, the fence propping him up as he watches two guys inside the corral. There's one on a gorgeous pinto Mustang who's figuring out how to use a lasso, another yelling instructions.

From a conversation I heard at breakfast, I know they're in the middle of dozens of job interviews to cover the severe staff shortages afflicting both ranches.

Even from over here, I can tell this guy's not about to be hired.

"I don't want him to come back here. *Ever*."

"I've never been to Vancouver," I muse out loud because I don't blame him for never wanting to see his father again.

"Ask Colt. He'll take you. You should go on a honeymoon."

"Why would we do that?"

"Duh. Because you're married. That's what married people do."

This matchmaking schtick of his is new. Especially as he knows the ins and outs of the contract that binds Colt and me together—I learned *that* over a game of *Titanfall*.

Narrowing my eyes, I ask him a question that's a mirror of the one he asked me the day I moved in: "You want to get rid of me or something, Callan?"

"Huh?"

I poke him with my finger. "You want me to seduce your brother so I can become pregnant sooner and we can divorce?"

He gapes at me. "Why would you divorce when you're having a baby together?"

Okay, so that's not his goal, then.

"What's with the matchmaking?"

"Colt deserves to be happy," is his immediate retort. "What the hell were you talking about?"

Turning away from him, I stare at the yard.

Naturally, my gaze goes where it shouldn't.

Him.

Always freakin' him.

It's pissing me off how I can always find him out there. Whenever I stand up from my desk, I manage to see him some-where. He's like Where's Waldo?

Now that we're married, he owns the largest ranch in North America. Four-hundred thousand acres are his to roam, and yet, whenever I look outside, he's goddamn there.

"Zee!"

"What?"

He grabs my arm. "You can't leave when you have his baby."

"Part of the contract was that he wanted an heir."

"Don't make it seem like he was behind the verbiage. My father wrote it. As did your grandmother. Don't tar Colt with the same brush, not when you signed identical agreements."

That has me squirming.

I hate it when he's right.

Which he is.

A lot.

"But I don't understand. What's this about leaving when you have his child?"

Ah—did he only read the initial contract and not the amended one?

It'd make sense that Colt would keep that on the DL, considering what I know of Callan's childhood.

Shit, why didn't I think of that before I opened my mouth?

"Do you know how hard it was for me to sign that damn thing?"

"As hard as it was for him!" he growls. "Do you know what Colt's life's been like? Do you? The one thing he deserved was to have a choice about who he'd spend the rest of his days with, but Pops, I mean, Father can't even give him that!

"Do you know he practically raised me? He had four years of independence when he went to Saskatoon. Four years out of thirty-two of blood, sweat, and tears, Zee. And do you know how he spent most of those four years?" He barks out a laugh. "Studying his ass off. No parties for Colt. No fun. That wasn't allowed. He had to get back here, you see. To us. Because Cody was only sixteen when Mum left and he knew what Pops would do when he wasn't around.

"He drove up every weekend. It's the only reason he studied in Saskatoon. My brother might not have my IQ, but he has the brains to be a Harvard alumnus. Instead, he went to a tiny university in an off-the-wall city in Canada so that he could drive home as often as he was able.

"You think Father's a dick now? That's nothing to what he was like when he was drinking. Mum left us with him and as much as that hurt, Zee, to be left with a monster, we all knew what would have happened if she'd stayed."

He's breathing heavily by this point, and my voice is soft as I inquire, "What would have happened, Callan?"

"He'd have killed her. She'd have been a statistic. And knowing Colt's luck, he'd have been the one to find her.

"Father didn't want us. He doesn't like us. But he made sure that he gained custody to hurt her. Just because he could." His nostrils flare. "Ever since, Colt's been like both my parents.

So bet your damn ass I want him to be happy and I don't want him to have to raise another kid on his own when you two are freakin' perfect for one another!"

What?! "Perfect for one another?"

"Yes! And neither of you see it! I'm surrounded by idiots!" he snarls, then he stuns the hell out of me—his hand pounds into the wall.

Once.

Twice.

I grab his shoulder when the drywall gains a crevice I'll have to cover with a picture frame. "Callan, you will stop that right this second."

He twists around to glower at me, but his fist immediately drops. "I'm so tired of idiots," he screams, then he shoves his back into the wall he damaged and he slides to the floor, hands shifting to cover his face.

The bloodied knuckles of one are like an exclamation mark as I study him, uncertain what to do next.

He's not crying as far as I can tell because he's digging the butts of his palms into his eyes.

I crouch beside him. "Callan, you have to understand that when I signed the agreement, I had no way of knowing if Colt was like your father or not.

"*Grand-mère* didn't provide me with a character reference. She gave me very few options," I tack on bitterly. "But if, *when* I get pregnant and we divorce, I won't leave my baby behind. I-I'm not your mom."

My words have him gradually moving his hands from his face.

"You swear?"

"I swear. I-I never thought I'd have kids like this but..." I hitch a shoulder. "Colt's a good man. There's no reason we couldn't make shared custody work."

"If you know he's a good man, then why don't you want to be with him?"

Frustrated, I surge to my feet.

A part of me wants to slam my fist into the wall too, goddammit, but I don't.

281

I'm the adult here, after all.

Scoffing at the notion, I return to the window where, of course, I find the man of the hour.

Why does he always seem as if he's brooding?

He's standing there, leaning on a damn newel post. But he looks like Emily Brontë's Heathcliff—a long-suffering hero who needs a hug.

And maybe a blowjob.

My cheeks flush at the thought.

Since Tee found out about that kiss, I've been hyperaware of all things *him*. Honestly, she's part of the reason I've been avoiding Colton. According to her, we're a hop, skip, and a jump away from sex. The body might be willing, but the mind isn't.

So I have trust issues—could anyone blame me?

"Why don't you want to be with my brother?"

"Because he's a stranger," I sputter.

"And? People fall in love with strangers all the time."

"It's barely been a month, Callan!" I stomp my foot because he's exasperating the living shit out of me, but before I can lay into him about consent and choices and free freaking will, I happen to see Colt straighten up.

At first, I think it's because he's radar and he heard my ever-so-loud stomp.

But it isn't me.

Of course, it isn't.

His gaze locks on something in the distance, though. I know because his scowl is like thunder. It practically booms into being around him.

Curious, I peer in that direction. Whatever took the man from brooding to outright furious does more than prick at my inquisitive nature.

That's when I see what turned my stoic husband into a wrathful alpha.

As much as the ranch hand disgusts me with how he's whipping his horse, it's the way Colt lopes over there, moving behind the rider and the bucking Camargue that draws my attention. With one hand settling gently on the gelding's hind, he snags the bastard by the back of his jacket and drags him off the saddle.

God, if I wasn't already tied up in knots for the not-so-strange stranger I'm married to, I am now.

Gravity has the guy plunking on the ground. Colt's quick to tap the horse's rear. The creature tosses his head before he gallops off.

Even with the distance, I can see the red stripe where the bastard managed to break skin. But at least the gelding's out of harm's way.

Colt grabs the ranch hand by his collar, hauling him up with it.

The punch he doles out to the bastard has me biting my lip. It shouldn't be hot but this punishment is deserved and my inner Neanderthal appreciates the primal display.

The thought almost has me face-palming.

I'm cringing at my brain which Tee has corrupted.

"Colt can't stand it when they mistreat the horses," Callan mumbles, making me jump because I didn't realize he'd joined me at the window. Still, he's a welcome distraction from my embarrassing inner monologue. "You don't have to be scared—"

I need to nip that in the bud. "I'm not."

Ten years might be missing from my 'Colt' encyclopedia, but I know him well regardless.

"It's the only time he gets mad," he assures me, though I don't need the reassurance. "Grantley's on his last warning too."

"Grantley?"

"Marvin Grantley. He's a piece of work." Callan hisses as blood explodes from the guy's nose in an impressive arc when Colt's fist collides with it. That's when he drops Grantley like a sack of potatoes.

Even from this distance, I can sense the control it takes for Colt to leave Grantley alone.

But he does.

That's freaking hotter.

I'm not going to loop Tee in on today's development. She'll

be asking for a play-by-play, and that's not only dangerous for her imagination but for mine too.

Hugging my arms to my chest, I cup my elbows. "Why was he on his last warning?"

"He's usually late. Aggressive with the animals. Things like that."

"I'm surprised you're in the know about the particulars."

He sniffs. "Just because I don't go out on the property much doesn't mean I don't pull my weight in other ways."

"I wasn't accusing you. I didn't think staff minutiae would interest you."

His grunt is the only answer I get. Still, after that meltdown, it's better than silence.

A couple ranch hands approach when Grantley staggers upright and takes a swing at Colt, but he sidesteps him, kicks his leg out, and down Grantley goes again.

Callan whistles when Colt, still seething with anger, turns his back on the asshole and strides over to another horse that's been tethered to a nearby post. He jumps on saddleless and takes off in the direction the Camargue went, leaving his men to deal with Grantley.

If there's one thing that's my catnip, it's *that*.

No saddle. Just pure command of the beast. And what command. He maneuvers the nineteen-hand Percheron X like he was born in that position.

Having been raised to ride as soon as I could walk, I know the feeling, though I'll admit I haven't jumped back on the saddle yet.

Neither have I gone home to the Bar 9 *or* frosted any sugar cookies.

My time here's been strange.

The days have passed quickly. The hours drain fast when you call your best friend at three and don't stop talking until nine. Then, there's work to be done and video games to play with Callan.

I guess I've been hiding out here and I didn't even realize it.

And Colt let me.

He hasn't pushed me.

He's left me alone to come to terms with my new reality.

Watching him ride off, I know part of that is because he's a busy man. Taking over the Bar 9 as well as tutoring the triplets have cut further into his time. There are only so many hours in a day, after all.

But I can't stop wondering if he's put me in the same pigeonhole as that filly Callan mentioned the day I arrived...

Is Colton gentling me and I didn't realize it?

If so, I can't help but think that it might be working.

Text Chat

Cole: Heard you gave Marvin Grantley a pounding

Colton: Callan, what have I told you about gossiping?

Callan: I was sharing news. Not gossiping.

Cody: I always hated that asshole. What did he do?

Cody: Also, I see how it is, CALLAN. Why didn't you tell me too?

Callan: Cole called. You didn't.

Cole: Because I'm the better brother

Cody: Whoa, that's a pretty cocky statement coming from a big baby.

Cole: Next time we're both at the ranch, I'll show you how big of a baby I am.

Colton: I don't think that's as much of a threat as you want it to be lol.

Cole: Oh, it's a threat. This big baby can punch.

Cody: I'm shaking in my CF-18.

Cole: Ahh, so it was you who wrote in the sky, 'Cody sucks ass'?

Colton: How is it Callan is the youngest but you two bicker the most?

Callan: I'm the smartest.

Cole: If you tell us your IQ again, Cody's not the only one I'll smack when I get home

Callan: Gratuitous violence is a sign of idiocy

Colton: Cole, don't threaten Callan.

Colton: Callan, watch your mouth.

Cody: What did Grantley do?

Colton: Was cruel to a horse.

Cody: That motherfucker

Cole: Thought he'd have jumped at the chance to report you to the cops

Colton: You didn't see the state of Jupiter

Cole: He hurt him?

Colton: Yes.

Cole: Why is he still employed by us?

Colton: We've had this discussion. Bea. But Grantley's been suspended.

Cody: Why Theo didn't marry her is beyond me. He was all up in her business

Colton: Some mysteries are above my pay grade to solve.

Chapter 29
Colton

Later, when I get back to the house to finally ice my knuckles, I find a pile of letters waiting on the hall stand and the kitchen empty.

With a frown, I check my phone for the time and see that I'm not late for dinner.

Dismissing it because the house is currently on crack—Mum keeps taking Callan to McDonald's and the arcade in the vain hope that'll rewind ten years of her absence—I head for the freezer.

After snagging a bag of frozen peas, I grab a beer from the fridge, where I see there are aluminum foil-wrapped baking trays containing my dinner, and then head for the table.

That's where I see two candlesticks right in the middle with slightly burned wicks.

Though I arch a brow at the sight, I sit, dump the peas on my knuckles, and, because no one's at home and I'm a thirty-goddamn-two-year-old man, I pop the cap on the side of the table.

Then, I drink.

"God, that hit the spot," I mutter to no one, sighing as I work my neck from side to side to crack it.

That's when I riffle through the mail.

Spotting the too-familiar handwriting on the front of one envelope, I pause when I notice there are two of them.

The top letter's addressed to me.

The other is to Zee.

That bitch.

It's one thing to send it to me, but it's another to get Zee involved in this BS.

You're so high and mighty, but you're nothing more than a murderer.

You think I don't know you're laughing at the town now that you've moved into their fancy house?

I should make you pay.

Make YOU hurt.

Maybe I will.

Maybe words will become action soon.

It all depends on what your new husband will say.

Because they only care about money, maybe I'll be seeing you sooner than you think.

My eyes widen in horror.

Normally, it's this crazy bitch telling me I'm scum or that I don't deserve to live because I committed the crime of being born a Korhonen.

This is an active threat against Zee.

And it means that one of my household staff is a fucking gossip.

Quickly, I tug open the other letter.

You're going to pay, Korhonen.

Your family's gotten away with murder for too long.

If you don't want me to go to the cops, then you'll transfer twenty-thousand dollars to this account.

I have proof you're a murderer.

I'm not afraid of you.

Then, there's a bank account listed.

"What's that?"

Spying my wife in the doorway, hesitating like she still doesn't know if she's allowed to share oxygen with me, I murmur, "If you want a beer, there's a six-pack in the fridge."

I try not to watch her, but it's an immediate fail.

She draws me like iron to a magnet.

Whatever room she's in, I track her.

The hunter in me can't help himself.

Focus shifting from these dumb letters onto something worthy of my attention, I watch as she gingerly treads over to the refrigerator.

After the day I've had, I rub my jaw and decide to tear off the Band-Aid for both of us. "Let me guess—you saw what happened out in the yard?"

Her head whips to the side, hair flying with the movement. "I did."

Is she scared of me? That's all I need.

Exhausted by the prospect, I sigh. "I'm not going to—"

"He deserved worse," she growls before I can get the word 'apologize' out. "You should have whipped him. See how much he likes *that* kind of treatment." For the first time since that kiss, she stops walking on eggshells around me and it's a damn fine sight to behold. "You did fire him?"

"I wish it were as easy as that. He's suspended."

The bottle in her hand clatters against the marble coun-

293

tertop when she almost drops it. "You can't let him be around the animals!"

"I know." I resettle the peas on my knuckles when I make a fist and accidentally dislodge the bag.

She scowls but takes a seat at the table. "So, why didn't you cut him loose?"

"You remember Bea Hollier?"

"She's Grantley's wife."

"Callan told you?"

"No, *Grand-mère* did a while ago."

"You saw the bruises on her that day we went into town. He beats her. Hospitalized her a couple times." My thumb scrapes at the label on the perspiring bottle of beer. "She won't leave him."

"Are you... close with her?"

My brows lift at her hesitation. "Can't I spare an enemy from an abusive husband?"

"No." She grimaces. "I mean, yes. Of course."

God, she's pretty.

Does she know that?

I don't think she did when she was a kid. She was all gangly limbs and bruises from tripping. Massive eyes that saw too much—they swallowed up her whole face.

Not anymore.

"I know you were in the same class."

"Theo Frobisher used to date her."

Deep in contemplation, she takes a sip of beer. "Why didn't he marry her if he wanted her?"

My gaze locks on her mouth. "Is anything in life ever that easy?"

"The Holliers and the Frobishers have never liked one another."

"The Frobishers hate everyone." I tip my bottle at her. "They would get along with your *grand-mère*. But they have a distinct dislike of the Holliers."

"Wasn't it because Bea's granddad shot Old Man Frobisher in the ass?"

"Nearly made him a eunuch, which would have ended the

line."

"God, we waste so much time thinking about our lineage. We're no better than breeders fretting about pedigree!"

"Wish I could say otherwise."

"So, I'm guessing there's a correlation between Marvin being a piece of scum, Bea, and you not being able to fire him?"

"Who's the first person he's going to take his frustration out on? Tonight, he'll be nursing his injuries." I rub my temple where an ache is gathering. "He won't be able to do much more than groan and moan at her. Two days suspension, without pay, will hopefully make him simmer down rather than have him using her as a punching bag."

"Do you ever get tired of having the weight of the world on your back, Colton?"

As I'm about to drink some beer, my hand freezes on its upward trajectory. "I don't."

"Seems to me like you do." She hitches a shoulder. Her oversized sweater trickles over one arm, revealing creamy flesh that I want to— "Just an observation."

"From someone who's seen more of my brother than me since you moved in."

"That's probably why I noticed. You're very alike." She tips her head at the letter in front of me. "What's that?"

"Mail."

Of the *black* variation.

The bitch of it is, I'll end up forking over the 20k.

Not because I'm scared about the 'truth coming out.' The only thing I've killed in my life is game. But keeping Zee safe is a priority *and* I know the blackmailer needs the cash.

Can't stop being everyone's goddamn father. That's my problem.

Changing the subject, I mutter, "Where's Callan?"

The pucker of her brow furrows deeper as she stares at me in silence. Eventually, though, after I wait her out, she answers, "Your mother took him to McDonalds again."

I chuckle into my bottle. "I wonder if she orders Happy Meals for him."

Zee's lips twitch. "She's not that bad. They're going to the movies. That's why Ida went with them." Her soft smile flattens and she follows that up by clearing her throat. "I came down after they left and..." She points to the candles. "I think, okay, no, I *know* Callan is setting us up."

"Ah."

It's all I can think to say.

"There were dishes set for two and music playing... You should probably talk to him."

"You've spoken to my brother, Zee. Why do you think he'd listen to me?"

With a sigh, she taps her nails on the table. "True."

I study her.

This woman who sleeps next door to me, who's technically mine but also isn't.

This woman creeps about the house like a ghost because this isn't her home.

This woman sometimes cries out my dead horse's name in her sleep.

This woman gave me the best kiss of my life.

This woman is fucking killing me.

"Penny for them?"

The only thing I can think to say to her is, "You cried during your sleep last night."

She stiffens like I shot her.

But she doesn't deny it.

Zee takes a deep gulp of beer. "I used to get nightmares all the time after... that night. They went away. But they started up again. Recently."

Fucking A.

The suffering my father knowingly put this woman through will be the death of me.

"Maybe Callan got it right."

"What do you mean?"

My jaw works. "Not calling Pops 'Pops.' That's a label you give to someone who cares about his children, but the only thing that matters to Clyde is Clyde."

"Oh."

"*Oh.* I'm sorry, Zee."

"For?"

"Everything. That you have to live here, that you have to be with people you don't know. That you're sleeping in the room beside a stranger—"

"You're not a stranger. And I *could* be at the Bar 9. You gave me that option. I never expected you to. And after getting to know Callan, I can't imagine how he'd cope with you moving, so it's more impactful of an offer than I first recognized."

"He'd have been fine with Mrs. Abelman. But you're right. He has attachment issues. Also Clyde's fault."

Her brow lifts. "You're downgrading him to his first name?"

I nod. "That man's been no father to me. I always called him that because of the younger kids."

"How bad..." She bites back the words.

"Go on. Ask," I say calmly.

"How bad were things when you were younger? I saw some of it, but what Callan shares... it makes me think you hid more from me."

"I did. Things were pretty damn bad." When I drain my bottle dry, I retrieve another beer. "Want anything?"

"No. I'm good."

Grunting, I return to the table and flip the cap on the edge again. "Pretty much from the start, he and Mum disagreed on how to raise me. He worried she was making me too soft."

Her mouth rounds before she flattens her lips. "What an asshole."

"He is. It got worse when I was scared about the monster under my bed." I chuckle at nothing. "That earned me my first whooping."

"I hate that man."

"You and me both. But it was only the beginning. Anything that set him off about me not being a perfect alpha male at age four, I needed to learn a lesson. I swiftly realized nothing I did would please him."

"Why?"

"Because he's a crappy rancher. He doesn't understand the land. Not like Uncle Clay did. I take after him. We listen, *watch*, and react." I tap my nose. "But Clyde's jealous. He thinks it's a language when, really, it's just taking note and being proactive. I made suggestions for anti-wildfire measures last year and he said it was a waste of money." I shake my head. "Dumb fuck."

"So he beat you because *he* didn't measure up?"

"I'm pretty sure, yeah. In part, at least. I remember Uncle Clayton was teaching me about foraging crops one day. Alfalfa is a natural species here—"

She smirks. "Rancher's daughter, Colt. I know that."

"You might have forgotten. Anyway, he was talking about starting a breeding program, wanting to integrate legumes like sainfoin and meadow bromegrass into our land.

"He got me researching the different species, learning what the pros and cons of each variety were. Pretty soon, I could talk about it like an eight-year-old pro. The importance of it made sense to me.

"Clyde clipped me once for being boring because it was all I could talk about." My smile is bittersweet. "That time with Clayton as the land's guardian is why our herd is as hardy as it is."

"Why did Clayton let your father treat you that way?"

"I don't know."

We share a look. Hers disturbed, mine fatigued.

"How did Lindsay even fall for him? Bleugh."

"She was new to Canada. New to the province. New to everything. He charmed her, and then afterward, she learned he was a bastard. He's relatively handsome and, don't forget, we're rich. I'm not saying Mum's a gold-digger, but she was raised in a poor area of the UK. Coming to Canada was something she'd dreamed of."

"Why Canada?"

"My grandmother fell in love with a Canadian during the war. She was set to cross the Atlantic and then he was killed in action. They were married and everything, but she didn't dare make the move without him."

"What was his name?"

A smile twists my lips. "Ralph. Grandma told Mum a lot of

stories, ones Ralph shared with her. That's why she came here. To see the place her mother always regretted not visiting."

"That's sad."

"It must have seemed like a rags-to-riches story. She came over with nothing and then married into one of the richest families in the province. How was she to know that everything comes with a price?"

That has her pulling a face. "I'm sorry she had to go through that. I'm sorry *you* did too."

"It's fine."

"No. It isn't."

"Why didn't you want to live at the Bar 9?"

"Because the temptation to smother my grandmother was too strong?"

Snorting out a laugh, I retort, "She'd have fought you like a bear in a trap."

"Don't I know it."

"You're not the murdering kind."

"The town doesn't believe that."

"No," I agree, rubbing my eyes. "That why you haven't left the ranch?"

"What's there to leave for?"

"Amazon deliveries?"

She grins but hides it behind her beer. "The ranch hands bring the mail."

"There is that."

Zee releases a sigh. "Does this place have any happy memories for you?"

"The house, the ranch, or the town?"

"The house."

I hum. "Plenty. Bad ones, sure. But I grew up with my brothers. I'd do anything for them. *Did* anything for them. I wanted them to be safe in a way that I never was so I took a lot of pleasure in seeing them grow up normally."

She blinks. "You're a very good man, Colton."

"Hardly." That *she* thinks that matters.

More than she'll ever know.

"Not many would..." She plays with her earring. The

fidgeting is new—that's why I notice it. "The bulk of my memories from home are good ones."

"Then why don't—"

"Because the two people who made them good aren't there anymore," she admits, her voice raw with grief.

"I'm sorry, Zee," I rasp, leaning forward so that I can snag her hand in mine. "It's not fair. How my douche of a father can still walk this Earth but your parents, good people, have both passed away."

Her chin butts her chest, but she doesn't free her hand. "The prospect of living there, full-time, without them was more than I could stand.

"Plus, I know my grandmother. She'd never give me any peace. At least here, I can do what I want. I knew before we married you'd never pressure me into anything."

"You know you can use a truck whenever you want, right?"

"Callan said as much." She bites her lip. "Thank you."

"For?"

Zee hesitates at first then murmurs, "You've been very generous. With everything. I couldn't have... expected that."

"We're married."

"Yes, but you've still been kind. I'm not saying this because you're a Korhonen, either. You've welcomed me into your home. You've offered me the use of a truck. Staff clean my bathroom and Ida makes dinner." She huffs out a laugh. "It's more than I expected and more than I deserve too."

I squeeze her hand but before I release it, I press my lips to her knuckles. When she squirms on her seat, I do it again, rumbling the words against her skin: "Don't tell Mrs. Abelman that. She has her schedule to abide by."

She swallows.

Hard.

My gaze locks on hers as I run the tip of my nose along the seam where her pointer and middle fingers meet.

"She's pretty terrifying," she croaks out, but she doesn't pull away. "I thought the rumors were creative lies."

With a wink, I relinquish my hold on her hand. "I made up most of the rumors but they were founded in the truth."

Her smile hits me on the raw. Mostly because it's genuine. Honest. A shared moment of humor.

What catches me like a fist to the solar plexus is when her thumb comes out and swipes over the place I just kissed.

Not to wipe away my kiss.

But to hold it in place.

Text Chat

Carson: Feel like being the best big sis in the world and taking us into Pigeon Creek, Zee?

Zee: You have a truck.

Colby: We HAD a truck

Zee: What did you do to it?

Calder: Technically, Colby and I did nothing.

Colby: We're the innocent, injured parties.

Zee: Why don't I believe you?

Carson: Because you're a wise woman

Carson: Who doesn't believe slanderous lies.

Zee: Don't lay it on too thick, Carson lol. What happened?

Calder: Carson decided to use deodorant on our serpentine belt

Zee: You're using English words but it's not the same language as mine.

Zee: Huh?

Calder: Our serpentine belt was squeaking.

Colby: Carson saw a video online that said if you rub deodorant on it, the squeak will stop.

Zee: O.o

Colby: That is an accurate representation of our faces, Zee.

Colby: Especially as we only just got it back. Dumbass decided to do his magic trick that same night!

Carson: Long story short, we don't have a truck anymore.

Colby: And we learned a hard lesson that not every hack on the internet works lol

Calder: No. No 'lol,' Colby. This isn't funny. We have to catch the bus again for school.

Carson: Ugh

Zee: Want me to ask Colton to have a look at it?

Colby: Nah. Don't waste his time.

Zee: I'm sure it wouldn't be the highlight of his day, lol, but he's kind and appears to be good with his hands

Calder: Ewwww

Zee: Calder! I didn't mean in that way.

Carson: Damn, sis. Need me to talk to him? Mano a mano?

Zee: NO! And that doesn't mean what you think it does.

Zee: I've seen him fixing a tractor is all I was saying. Jeez, you guys.

Colby: You could do that and we could thank him, but you could also take us into Pigeon Creek…

> Zee: When I say I'd prefer to stick pins in my eyes…

Colby: No fun

> Zee: Which part of being treated like Quasimodo would make you think I want to spend any time in town?

Carson: But we're your STRANDED baby brothers

> Zee: And?

Calder: Heartless woman.

> Zee: In this, definitely. I'll tell Colt to come over and help you guys out.

Calder: No!

> Zee: Why not?

Calder: He'd learn that we broke it twice.

> Zee: Huh?

Calder: Colt's already bailed it out of the garage after we paid to have it fixed.

Colby: And he was big on being responsible the last time.

> Zee: Clearly, he was asking for too much.

> Zee: You're enjoying hanging out with him?

Colby: Sometimes. He teaches us how to do stuff.

> Zee: Like?

Colby: He taught us how to shoot.

Calder: That was cool as shit

Carson: Is shit cool?

Calder: When it's not fresh from the source, yup.

Zee: *shudders*

Zee: What else?

Colby: Taught us how to fix a fence post properly. That was boring but we'd been doing it wrong.

Carson: Colby didn't listen though, so Colt had to teach us how to wrangle forty head of cattle back to where they were supposed to be.

Calder: So, please don't tell him about the serpentine belt, sis? He already thinks we're morons and we're trying to impress him.

Zee: Why?

Calder: We want a raise.

Carson: And it's not looking good, what with him bailing us out already with the truck once this month.

Zee: No, I can see your problem.

Carson: So, can you?

Zee: Can I... what?

Carson: Give us a ride into town.

Zee: Nope. You'll have to save up to get it fixed. This is obviously a teaching moment and I'm not interfering lol.

Calder: What do we do in the meantime? This is so unfair. Carson's the idiot! But we're all getting punished.

Zee: I'm sure there's some girl whose good nature you can abuse who'll give you a ride

Calder: Ouch!

Carson: A stunning indictment of our characters

Zee: Am I wrong?

Colby: Tracy would give us a ride if you called her, Carson

Carson: NO WAY. She's clingier than a jellyfish and her sting is twice as hard.

Zee: There you go. Call Tracy

Carson: Didn't you read what I said?

Zee: You're speaking that language again. The one I don't use...

Colby: Who's going to tell Colt?

Calder: I will. Carson almost shot him and you caught him in the lasso. That means he owes me a favor.

Zee: Your logic is terrifying.

Calder: ^^

Chapter 30
Zee

THE FOLLOWING DAY

"Hello. Susanne McAllister speaking."

"Isn't that Susanne Korhonen?"

When Clyde's voice registers, I shudder with distaste.

I thought it'd be a work call. Instead, it's *him*.

"It wasn't specified in the contract that I change my last name." There, that sounded calm enough.

His low chuckle rattles in my ear, prompting me to shift the call onto speaker. It's too creepy hearing it up close and personal.

"I see that you're the type of woman that needs to be hemmed in." Um, nope. "You McAllisters always were rowdy."

"Is there a reason for this call, Clyde?"

"Can't a father-in-law check up on the newest addition to his family?"

If he were any other man, then sure.

"What would you like to know?" I inquire, tone polite. Distant. Better to dissociate than to panic.

"I wondered if you'd had a chance to consider my proposition."

It takes me too long to figure out what that proposition was.

Then, I remember Colt saying he'd brought this up with him and I realize his audaciousness knows no bounds.

"I'm not interested."

"I told you that I'll make it worth your while."

"Not only would I make a terrible spy, I have no desire to. I don't know why you're approaching me—"

"It's a father's right to know what's going on with his children."

"I agree—if they're under the age of sixteen. But all your boys are old enough to be fathers themselves," I say dryly. "The argument isn't as strong when you take that into consideration."

"I think you're not taking my suggestion seriously."

"*I* think that *you* aren't listening. To me. Or to Colt."

"No, Susanne. *You're* not listening. I've tried to ask you nicely. Politely. Keep this friendly. But you've gone behind my back and discussed this with my son. This is no longer a suggestion—"

"You think you can make me spy on them?" I laugh. "You and my grandmother forced me into marrying a man I barely know. Any power over me you two had faded the day I said 'I do.' I'm done dancing like a puppet on a string."

"You forget how badly the town dislikes you, Susanne." The truth of that slips through me like poison. "A few words spoken to the right ears and you might find—"

"You can say whatever you want to them. You can do whatever you want," I snarl. "You can't and won't hold anything against me to force me into complying.

"You picked the wrong bride if that's what you wanted. I might have seen the wisdom in Colt and me getting hitched, but if you think I'll let you dictate my every move, then you're the fool."

"You'll regret making an enemy out of me."

"You always were my enemy," is my flat retort. "You're the one who believed otherwise."

And with that, I end the call.

That's also when I realize my heart is racing, sweat's beading at my temples, and my stomach's churning as if I ate the hottest ghost pepper in the universe a few minutes ago.

When my monitor sounds an alert, distracting me from calling Colt, I snag a juice box and chug that. Immediately, I feel better, but what surprises me is Colt rings me first.

"Are you eating something?"

I don't want to feel this warm and cozy inside at his care but I do.

I'm such a sucker.

"I had some juice."

> Callan: You checked your monitor?

I roll my eyes.

> Tee: Don't make me fly up there and force-feed you.

I grin then copy and paste the same message to both of them:

> Me: On the case. :)

"Good. Everything okay?"

I swallow. "Why do you ask?"

"You're working. You don't tend to have lows during work hours. After is another matter entirely."

He's right.

Ugh, I shouldn't love that he knows that.

"Your father's been on the phone."

Silence greets me. Then... "What did he want?"

That rumble.

Oh, boy.

"The same as before. But he upped the stakes. Threatened me—"

"He did what?"

His anger is reassuringly swift and acts like a warm hug. Relief has me sagging into my desk chair.

I hate how easy it is to fall into old habits with him. But Colt hasn't changed. He's quieter, and oddly stoic for such a young guy, but his inherent sense of honor and decency are as strong as ever.

It's more attractive than that pretty face of his.

And honestly, he's so pretty it's a crime.

"Tried to blackmail me into compliance. Said he'd spread gossip in town." Checking my blood sugar, I snag a granola bar. "He might."

"Let him. Leave this with me—"

"No! You don't have to do anything."

"He needs to be dealt with."

"Don't make me regret sharing this with you."

A soft growl sounds in my ear. In comparison to Clyde's, it sends shivers down my spine. "If he contacts you again, you'll tell me immediately."

"Of course. I was going to call you but you rang first."

"You were?"

"Yes."

"I could kill him for triggering that alert."

"Hormones," I say lightly then bite into the bar.

"Were you stressed before?"

"No." Work rarely stresses me out. "I overreacted."

"You didn't. He's an asshole. If he threatens you—"

"You'll be the first to know."

"I don't like having my hands tied," he warns.

A smile dances on my lips. "I already knew that wasn't your kink." I can't regret saying those words, not when he sputters in my ear. Grinning at finally getting the upper hand, I murmur, "I'll speak to you later."

And that's the second Korhonen I hang up on in less than ten minutes.

This time, however, my smile curves into a grin.

My heart's stopped pounding and the unease in my core has shifted into something else.

A mental picture of Colt tied to my headboard forms of its own volition.

Yum.

Chapter 31
Colton

LATER THAT DAY...

"How's the construction on that new bunkhouse—"

Before I can finish the question, Theo rasps, "Bea's in the hospital."

No way in hell did I expect that to be his answer. Gaping at the stretch of land ahead of me, I try not to lose my shit. "Marvin?"

"Who else?" is his bitter retort.

His hatred for the man echoes along the line. Marvin is clearly suicidal with how he keeps pushing us. But that's the problem. He gets to hold his wife hostage all while knowing we won't touch him for Bea's sake.

First Clyde, now Marvin.

I could strangle someone and Marvin's closer.

But that would diminish Theo's satisfaction so I'll back off. Begrudgingly.

"Is she all right?" I ask, gaze darting to Fen who's rolling around on his back ten feet away. His satisfied grunts and whinnies would ordinarily make me smile, but Marvin destroyed any chance of that.

Looks like the suspension backfired on us.

"The asshole did a real number on her. I'm here with her at

the hospital. How do you feel about setting her up somewhere?"

"Ecstatic. I've been waiting years for this. Is she being discharged today? How soon do I need to set everything up?"

"She'll be here for a week. Minimum. Plenty of time for me to convince her to leave that son of a bitch."

"Okay, we can make arrangements by then." I rub my eyes. "This means we can get that asshole off my ranch permanently. End his contract with us."

"Consider it done."

Hearing the satisfaction oozing from his tone, I rumble, "Whatever you do to him, don't get caught or let it go too far. The last thing Bea or I need is for you to be sent up over this."

"And I thought we were friends."

"If you go to jail, you know none of your brothers will bail you out. It'll be me and I'll say I told you so—"

"All right, all right. I won't kill him."

"Good. Give Bea my love and tell her I'll be in to see her later."

"She doesn't want any visitors."

I pause. Ponder the tightness to his tone. "You included?"

"Yeah."

"That's how bad she looks?"

"He treated her face like a punching bag."

"Tell me she's pressing charges."

"Going to work on that too."

"You acting on her behalf here or just hoping she'll listen?"

"Hoping."

Fuck. "I'm here if you need me." He has the Korhonen purse strings at his beck and call—that's pretty much all I can do for him.

"Thanks, Colt. Talk later."

"Text me updates."

"Will do."

Grabbing the shirt I discarded earlier, I swipe it over my face.

Dropping the plaid again, I toss my cell on top, then get back to work fixing this fence. This time, each hit acts as a release of pressure, and considering I'm close to blowing my lid, this thankless chore comes in handy.

The rhythmic blows of hammer against wood vibrate along the airwaves. I feel each thud in my shoulder—the one I busted when I fell off Fen during a barrel race when I was twenty-five —but it's a simple job and sometimes, I like the simple jobs.

Even before Zee, my life was complicated.

Now, the responsibility of both the Seven Cs and the Bar 9 starts and ends with me. I love it, but there's no denying it's a lot of work so these types of mindless chores are a great escape. Take this morning, I went to HQ at six AM and I'm here now to clear my head.

My cell buzzes, drawing my attention.

> Theo: You'll never guess who arrived at the ER DOA—Lydia Armstrong. Hit-and-run.

When I tap connect on his name, he answers immediately.

"You serious, Theo?"

"Not something to lie about," he mutters. "The RCMP is here."

"Not surprising with a hit-and-run. Where?"

"On the corner of Main Street and Pigeon Drive."

"There'll be witnesses, surely?"

"I guess."

"Is it Reilly on duty?"

"Yup. Want me to put him on the line?"

"Please."

As I shrug into my shirt and grab my tools, I hear Theo's short conversation with the sergeant.

"Colton?"

"Yeah. Terry, what's going on?"

"Lydia's dead." There's an awkward silence that hangs heavily between us. I don't push it, mostly because I know he wants to ask me something and is building up the courage to—

"Have you heard from your father?"

"What? No." I hesitate. "Last I heard he was in Vancouver. But I know Susanne just got off the phone with him."

"Did he mention his whereabouts?"

"No. She'd have told me if he said he was in town." His hum doesn't sound disbelieving, but it still has me asking, "Why?"

"The EMTs are saying Lydia was muttering his name before she passed."

My brows lift. "You know there's no love lost between Clyde and me, Terry. Hence the protective order. He hasn't been to the ranch."

"*The ranch.* Doesn't mean he's not in Pigeon Creek."

"No."

"Not looking good, Colton."

"No, it isn't," I agree, perplexed by this turn of events. "I'll update you if I hear anything."

"Appreciate that."

I rub my chin. "Let me know if you make any arrests. Something like this won't go down well in the court of public opinion if the matter isn't dealt with swiftly."

"Agreed. Will you feel the same way if Clyde *was* behind the wheel?"

"Damn straight." Still, I rub the bridge of my nose. "I should probably let you know that Lydia Armstrong was sending me poison pen letters—for the past six months or so."

"What kind of poison pen letters?"

"If you come to the ranch, I'll give them to you. You can see for yourself."

"How did you know it was her?"

"Theo Frobisher caught her hanging around our mailbox on a day when I received a letter. I asked Callan to check our security footage and he confirmed she delivered them. A mastermind she was not."

"Always was a troubled woman," he remarks. "Even before Marcy went missing. She's had a problem with the Korhonens ever since, hasn't she?"

I think it's smart not to mention that the RCMP failed to find Marcy in the first place.

"Yes. I don't know why either. None of us dated her."

"I heard about that confrontation with Lydia at The Coffee Shop...?"

My brows lift. "Did Lydia approach you about it?"

"No, but she wouldn't, would she? Not if she's been sending you letters."

"She spat in Zee's coffee. Zee didn't appreciate that—"

"Quite right."

"And upended a glass of water over her. I told Jocelyn that she was a public health hazard."

"Jocelyn fired her."

"Yeah. Does Doug know about Lydia yet?"

"No. I'm not looking forward to telling him either. First his girl, now his wife. Not sure the man can take being kicked around much more."

"If there's anything the family can do, extend the offer of help to him from us. Funerals aren't cheap."

"I'll thank you on his behalf and tell him not to be a stubborn fool if he doesn't accept the helping hand."

"Give him my condolences."

"Will do." He clears his throat. "Hate to have to do this, Colton, but where were you between the hours of twelve and one?"

I scratch my jaw. "Out on the land. East quadrant. Over on the border between us and the Linnox place."

"Anyone with you?"

"No."

He clears his throat. Again. "Might have to call you to the detachment, Colton. Get a statement."

Two words float through my mind—*probable cause*.

I keep my tone light. "Whatever you need, Terry."

What was I saying about my life being complicated?

"I'll be back at the detachment in ninety minutes."

It isn't couched as a demand, but I know what he's saying.

"I'll be there."

Chapter 32
Colton

"Appreciate you coming into town, Colt."

I shake hands with Terry and take a seat.

While he's recording the conversation, that we're one-on-one tells me he's keeping this informal.

Wise man.

"Also appreciate you not lawyering up."

"I have nothing to hide. Whatever you need, I'll help with." I shove a paper bag at him. "These are the letters Lydia Armstrong sent me."

"Let the record show that Colton Korhonen has passed me a paper bag with..." He pauses to count them. "...twelve letters. When did this start, Colt?"

"That's not all of them. The first ones I received I thought were a joke so I tossed them out. Looking back, I think it's when Lydia first learned she'd have to move. So, last November?"

Terry scans the letters, his brows lifting higher the more he reads. "She got nasty."

"Fast. That's why I hung onto them."

"She thinks you're a murderer."

"I assume she meant Marcy."

"Earlier, you said you never dated Marcy Armstrong?"

"No. She was a lot younger than me."

"I notice they're handwritten." He eyes me over the letter.

321

"Would you be able to provide us with the footage of Lydia dropping off the letters?"

"Yes."

I'll have to figure out how for myself. No way I want Callan involved in this mess. I didn't like him knowing about the letters, and this situation is only going to keep on deteriorating.

As he scans the notes, he grunts. "We have no idea what happened to Marcy. Her calling you a murderer—"

"Look, I didn't know Marcy. At all. You remember back then. I was in university and trying to keep Callan from falling apart after Mum left."

Terry pulls a face. "I remember. The EMTs came—"

"Exactly." The word is harsh. "We managed to hush that up. Let's not bring it to light again. But he was my priority. Not sleeping with some barely legal kid.

"I don't mean to sound facetious, Terry, but I'm a Korhonen. What the name doesn't pick up, the wallet does."

"A full wallet and a handsome face don't preclude someone from being a murderer."

"No, but who else is missing or murdered in Pigeon Creek?"

"Why didn't you report the letters to us?"

I shrug. "What would I have said?"

"That you were being harassed?"

"And what would you have done?"

"Not a lot, but it'd be on the record."

"Next time, I'll know what to do."

"She blackmailed you."

"She needed the cash."

"You paid the demand?"

"After she threatened my wife? Bet your ass I did."

"You're not joking, are you? Wait—I heard the McAllister girl was living with you, but you're married?"

"It's a recent thing," I demur.

Terry gapes at me but he reverts to the topic at hand. "If we look into her financials, we'll find a transaction from you." He stops the recording. "What the hell were you thinking? It looks like you paid her off!"

I lean forward. "I have nothing to hide. No skeletons in my closet. My father, on the other hand, has plenty. His is the name she was repeating when she died. Look at him, not me."

"This is probable cause!" Terry argues, spreading the letters over the table.

The words I didn't need to hear. "Wasn't it a car accident?"

"It could have been premeditated. If we throw in that little contretemps with Susanne too..."

"Lydia spit in her coffee!"

"Colton, people have been killed for less! You need to get yourself a lawyer."

I study him. "Am I under arrest?"

"No. But only by the skin of your teeth and because I know you're not a flight risk. What the hell were you thinking?" he repeats.

"I was thinking that she was threatening my wife. *And* I was feeling bad."

"About?"

"Getting her fired from The Coffee Shop," I admit. "She was a bitch, but she didn't deserve to be homeless."

He sets the recording back on. "Where were you at twelve-thirty today?"

"Out on the range. East quadrant, by the Linnox place."

"Would your new security system have picked up on your location?"

I'm going to have to discuss this with Callan. Damn. "Perhaps. I'll check."

"Can I come to the ranch and speak with your staff?"

"Of course."

"Maybe someone saw you."

"It's a possibility. Ask Theo. He'll tell you who was working in the same quadrant or thereabouts."

"Do you own a beat-up red pickup truck? Could be a Japanese make. One was seen driving through town shortly after the accident."

"I drive a late-model Chevy, Terry." *But that description rings a bell.*

"Does your wife—"

"No. She doesn't have a vehicle, and if she did, most of our garage is stocked with Chevrolets or Fords."

"That concludes the interview with Colton Korhonen." The recording switches off again. "You've made my job a lot harder, Colton. In the future, please don't be kind to your blackmailers."

Calmly, because I see no need to worry, I inform him, "I didn't do this, Terry."

"It's a good thing I know you and believe that," he grumbles, getting to his feet. "If I ask you to return to the detachment, bring. A. Lawyer. Understood?"

I sigh at his about-face. "I understand."

Once he guides me out of the small interview room, we shake hands and I take my leave, fully aware I shot myself in the foot by paying Lydia off. I don't regret it, though. Not if it kept Zee safe from that psycho.

When my phone rings, my day gets worse.

As one of my ranch hands murmurs in my ear about finding a mysterious *red* pick-up truck on the Seven Cs, I know exactly what's coming my way. Still, I have to make arrangements before I'm detained for the next twenty-four hours. All being well, I'll be out tomorrow and they won't have grounds to arrest me.

Zee's busy on another call, so I loop her in with a text message. Not ideal, but I'm running out of time. Neither Mrs. Abelman nor Mum pick up either. So I drop a voicemail with them and email Theo to apprise him of my whereabouts.

That done, I call Juliette who answers immediately. "Colton?"

"The triplets' truck mowed down Lydia Armstrong." I keep my voice low. "Do you know where they are?"

"School. They weren't behind the wheel, Colton."

"I'm not suggesting they were. *But* it's their truck and it was found on my land. Once the cops check the license plate, they'll know who owns it. It's likely the triplets will be brought in for questioning. I'm volunteering the car's location to the RCMP so I'll make legal arrangements for them now before I'm detained."

Sniffing, she thanks me by declaring, "That bitch couldn't even die in peace. Always had her nose into everything."

Leaning against my truck, I frown at the ground. There's something in her tone... "Did you get any letters from her recently?"

Silence hums on the line. "Perhaps. Did you?"

I scrape a hand over my jaw. "Did she ask for money?"

"Maybe."

Fuck.

More probable cause—this time, for the triplets.

Digging my fingers into my eyes, I mutter, "Don't say a word about that to anyone else."

"You think I'm an idiot? Make sure my grandsons are home tonight."

With that, she disconnects the call.

No one can say she doesn't have a way with words.

Grunting, I call Marc Robard's office and make arrangements for him to come to Pigeon Creek to help me out and for him to send three other attorneys for the triplets.

That done, I turn on my heel and head back into the station.

Terry's there, hovering at the front desk as he flirts with the receptionist. When he looks up, he arches a brow. "Colton?"

Chapter 33
Colton

Elastic Heart - Sia

Three hours into my detainment, the door to the interview room opens.

Being a Korhonen afforded me the gold-star treatment so I was never tossed in the cells, and most of the officers have been in and out of the interview room with coffee and water.

Is it fair? No. But everyone at the station has someone in their family on my payroll.

I'll take it seeing as this is a waste of time more than anything else.

I glance at Marc Robard when I spot him behind Terry. "What's going on?"

"Your alibi checks out," Marc states. "You're being released."

Terry folds his arms across his chest. "I guess you're the reason my detachment's been overrun by sharks?"

My lips twitch into a smile. "The triplets okay?"

"They're at the Bar 9 and one of my men is scarred from getting an earful from Juliette McAllister."

Nodding my understanding as I'm released pending further investigation, it's only when I step outside that I ask Marc, "Why am I being released early? What alibi?"

"Susanne informed the RCMP that she came to visit you for lunch. Brought you sandwiches which you ate together.

"She has more bite than you'd think. Terry mentioned you'd never said a word about sharing a meal, and she told him that you're too much of a gentleman to kiss and tell."

My brows lift at the statement and what she implied, but the cocktail of emotions that news stirs in me is both complex and simple. Simple because she's the only reason my ass won't be moldering away in that interview room for another twenty-one hours, complex because she perjured herself on my behalf.

Another man, one who'd also perjured himself and falsified an alibi for their now-wife, might think this was a case of balances being redressed. But though years may separate us, I know her well enough to discern this has nothing to do with scores being settled...

"What about the triplets?"

"They were in school at the time of the car accident. Several witnesses saw them in the lunchroom." He clears his throat. "Apparently, they were in the middle of some sort of skit? Most of the faculty as well as the student body can vouch for their whereabouts."

My brows lift. "Skit?"

"Involved a Sia song and nude leotards. I didn't ask."

"Sounds elaborate."

"Indeed. Contact me immediately if they bring you in for questioning again."

"Will do."

Thanking him, we shake hands and part ways beside my truck. I jump behind the wheel and take off for home.

When I make it to the homestead, Zee's sitting on the steps that lead to the veranda. The sight of my truck has her rushing over to me. I don't even get the chance to apply the handbrake

—she's dragging the door open and demanding, "Are you okay? What's going on?"

"Everything's fine," I attempt to soothe. "You didn't need to lie for me."

Finger prostrate, she jabs me in the arm. "Bet your ass I did! I've already been tried by the court of Pigeon Creek. I'm not about to let you go through that when you're innocent! I was so scared, Colton. So scared. For you. For Callan."

Her mentioning Callan is the reason I alight from the truck and draw her into my arms, pressing my lips to her forehead as I hold her close.

"Thank you." I sigh. "Callan wouldn't have taken it well if—"

"No. He'd have freaked the hell out," she mutters, hands settling at my waist as she clings to me in turn. "Much as I did when I read your text message. I was in a conference call with 'do not disturb' mode on or I'd have reacted faster. Are they insane? Why would you kill Lydia Armstrong?!"

"The truck was found in the—" The sound of a whinny has me jerking both of us around on the hunt for it. When I see Fen out of his stall, I grit my teeth. "That Harry goddamn Houdini horse! How the hell did he get out this time?"

"Huh?" She peers over my arm when Fen approaches us, calm as can be, nuzzling into our shoulders before nickering proudly. "Oh!"

"How did you get out?" I grumble, rubbing my hand over the bridge of his nose before gently flicking the tip. His nostrils flutter. "Please tell me you didn't impregnate another mare."

Zee clears her throat. "He makes a habit of getting loose?"

"He's the reason one of our older mares, Harriet, is pregnant... I retired her from the breeding stock three years ago. You're an asshole, Fen."

"Don't call him that!" she chides.

"I'll call him worse if he's going to be a daddy again." Because Fen's like a puppy, I expect him to wander off until I can give him attention—I've spoiled him. "Look, Zee, I didn't hurt Lydia—"

"*Duh.*"

"You didn't have to lie on my behalf. I was only being questioned. It was routine—"

"I wasn't going to let them treat you like a criminal!" she grinds out, fire in her eyes. "This way, they won't. They'll leave you alone."

Her strident belief in me, a belief that's tempered by concern for my family, has guilt riddling through me like worms in a rotten apple.

I didn't have the same faith in her.

I should have.

I failed her but she showed up for me.

Squeezing her shoulder, I rumble, "Thank you."

"You don't have to thank me," she says with a sniff. "You told him about Clyde calling me."

It's a statement, not a question.

"He asked you about it?"

"He did. How that sergeant's kept his job is insanity. The fire passed without any arrests when it was arson, Marcy went missing on his watch, and now this! His main suspects are you and the triplets when she died mumbling Clyde's goddamn name."

"You don't have to be scared—"

Her chin firms and a militant gleam quenches the fire. "I'm not scared anymore. I'm furious. I'm pissed off at our detachment's incompetence. I'm sick of this, do you hear me?"

I hide a smile. "I hear you."

"Good. You will *not* be going to prison for a crime you didn't commit. Understood?"

More amusement filters through me. "Yes, ma'am."

"Right, now we have that settled, I've got some work to do. You need to sort out Fen. I'll see you at dinner."

My brows lift at that news, but she steps back and away. I can no more stop myself from snagging a hold of her hand and returning her to my embrace than I can stop the sun from chasing the moon.

It's too easy to press my lips to hers.

To cup her cheeks.

To tilt her head.

It's too easy to imbue my kiss with my thanks but also my desire.

This woman is a fighter. If I hadn't known that before today, I know it now.

Her defense of me, the lengths she'll go to to shield not only me but my brother sends bolts of desire through my veins, decimating me for this woman who I call 'wife' but who is so. Much. More. To. Me.

Her mouth opens, letting me in. Her arms wrap around my waist—our hunger is mutual in its ferocity.

And relief and want and need coalesce inside me because we're in this together.

This.

Tongues tangling, lips seeking, breath mingling—this kiss has her arching into me, her hips chasing the brand of my dick. My hands settle on her shoulders because this is more than about sex.

This is *life.*

My lips brush her ear but though there are a thousand words I want to spill, I can't seem to say any of them.

She sighs. "I need to work." Her fingertips dig into my chest as she pulls away, but how she lingers tells me it's the last thing she wants.

With our gazes locked on one another, she rubs her kiss-sore lips with her knuckles and retreats a pace.

She fought for me.

The notion takes over my brain.

"Watch where you're going," I rumble as her hip nearly bumps into the truck.

Her throat bobs. "My eyes are where they need to be."

A soft growl escapes me. "More fighting talk, Zee?"

It's a taunt but she lifts her chin, turns and strides off toward the main house. "Maybe I'm just waiting for you to catch up."

"I'm plenty caught up," I holler at her.

"Says the man stroking his horse and not his wife," she retorts, lifting her hand over her head and flipping me the bird.

My knuckles freeze mid-rub of Fen's muzzle and I let out a

bark of laughter. When she glances at me over her shoulder, her grin in place, we lock eyes, the sizzle of need arcing between us like a lightning bolt until Fen nickers, dragging my attention from the only place it wants to be.

I don't even get the chance to track her path into the house —she's already gone.

Goddamn, her kisses are becoming a craving of mine. I want nothing more than to chase her down, show her exactly how caught up I am, but I don't.

Can't.

My goddamn responsibilities will be the death of me.

"What do you want, mischief?" I ask Fen when he butts my arm.

At his nicker, I shake my head, close the truck door, then grab my phone.

Scraping a hand over my jaw, my attention split a thousand ways, duty and responsibilities bearing down... all I can focus on is my wife.

Are we finally on the same page?

I can only fucking hope so.

Switching to my texts, I contact Callan and keep it light.

> Me: Wanna explain to me how Fen escaped from his stall?

> Callan: WHAT?!

> Me: I put him there myself before I had to leave for town.

> Callan: Dammit. I'll figure it out. I'm almost home.

> Me: Lydia Armstrong was killed today.

> Callan: I know. It's all the school's been gossiping about since the triplets were escorted off school grounds by the RCMP.

> Me: Their truck was found on our land. I was brought in for questioning too. I'm home now.

> Callan: Everything okay?

> Me: Of course. Might not be here when you get back. But will see you at dinner.

> Callan: Gotcha

That done and the situation downplayed, I head for the nearest tack room on the homestead, suit Fen up with a harness, and make my way across Seven Cs' turf and onto the Bar 9.

It'd have been easier to drive there, but I'm a cowboy—why would I drive when I can ride?

The journey's a chance to decompress too.

I wasn't worried. I didn't mow down Lydia Armstrong. But that doesn't mean having Zee's alibi won't make my life a hell of a lot easier.

Much like their sibling, the triplets are waiting for me at the border of our land.

Calder, ever outspoken, yells, "We didn't do it. And if we did, we'd never have dumped the truck on your land. We like you."

My lips curve at his declaration, but we're far away enough from one another that I can erase my smile before I reach him.

As I jump from Fen's back, Carson mutters, "He's so fucking cool and he doesn't even know it."

"Who rides without a saddle?" Colby agrees with a hiss.

Barely withholding the urge to laugh, I turn to them, demanding, "What happened?"

"Nothing! We didn't even know the truck was ready to drive. If we did, I wouldn't have had to deal with Ten-Hand Tracy today," Carson grumbles.

Calder continues, "Didn't you hear what I said? If we'd done it, we wouldn't have dumped it on your land."

His sullen tone has me rolling my eyes. "I appreciate the vote of confidence, guys. Thank God you were up to mischief when Lydia was killed."

Colby smirks. "It was a full choreographed routine."

"I'll bet," I counter. "I was told it was memorable."

"Lucky that it was today," Carson admits. "Yesterday, we snuck out to practice."

My jaw works at that news. "Clyde targeted you. Do you know why?"

Calder bites off, "We didn't do it."

"I'm not saying you did, dammit. I'm saying the opposite."

Colby clears his throat. "We didn't like Mrs. Armstrong."

"Why not?"

"She was a bitch to Zee. Not that Zee'd ever say anything. You think spitting in Zee's coffee was the first time she caused our sister trouble?"

"Don't know how Clyde would have known we hated her guts though."

"Watch your backs," I order. "Tell me if you see Clyde hanging around—here or in town."

I rub Fen's muzzle when he nudges my shoulder as Carson asks, "You still coming over to teach us how to lasso tomorrow?"

"'Course I am."

That they're hellions is to be expected. Juliette might have been a hard ass with Walker and Zee, but these three have gotten away with...

My mind skips over the word.

Even if they didn't have an alibi, I believe them when they say they wouldn't have dumped the truck on my land.

As for the accident, Colby has a weird sense of justice and the others are equally as outraged by Lydia's apparent mistreatment of their sister.

Mistreatment that, I realize, they believe kept their sister away from them.

Still, I snag Carson around the neck and haul him into my side so I can scratch my knuckles on his head.

As he yells, "Get off, man," I ignore him and drawl, "No more pranks. Not for another couple months."

"Even if it saved our asses from a vehicular manslaughter charge?" Colby exclaims as I jump onto Fen's back.

"Even if." Under my breath, I mumble, "Little shits," before Fen and I take off for home.

Text Chat

Callan: COLTON WAS ARRESTED

Cole: WHAT?!

Cody: Excuse me?

Colton: Don't exaggerate, Callan. I wasn't arrested. They detained me for questioning. We talked about this over dinner.

Callan: Yes, where you tried to downplay everything, but I overheard Mum and Mrs. Abelman talking!! You lied!

Colton: I did not lie!

Cody: Holy shit. Spill!!

Colton: Lydia Armstrong was killed in a hit-and-run today

Cody: Poor Lucifer.

Colton: She was definitely a piece of work.

Callan: Those dumbass brothers of Zee's were brought in for questioning too. Their truck was used in the hit-and-run.

Colton: I don't understand why you don't like them. Especially Calder. You have similar senses of humor.

Callan: :O

Callan: Do you realize how offensive that is?

Colton: Just saying... two peas in a pod never get along well.

Callan: :O

Cody: Have we finally figured out a way to shut him up?

Cole: Seems like. Go, Colt!

Cole: Why were you called in if the McAllister triplets' truck was the vehicle that killed her?

Colton: The truck was dumped on the Seven Cs.

Cole: Jesus

Colton: Yes

Cody: Why did they let you go early?

Colton: My alibi checked out

Cody: Your alibi?

Callan: He was with Zee at the time of the accident.

Cody: Good thing you got married then, huh?

Colton: Marriage comes with perks

Colton: I gtg. I have a feeling Callan will keep you updated

Callan: That's me. Better than the Herald.

Colton: Then get investigating into how Fen broke out of the stables, hmm?

Callan: Jeez. I told you I'm on it!

Text Chat

Zee: Can you ask Rachel to send over what she has on the Valentini-West case, please? She isn't picking up my calls and I know she has issues with our cloud.

Parker: Will do. She's having a slow day so it might not be today. Sommer started puking last night.

Zee: Oh! I hope she's okay

Parker: I'm learning kids do this stuff.

Parker: They leak. A lot.

Parker: Hey, you have that fun coming to you in the future

Zee: Gee, thanks

Parker: At least you'll have Rachel to advise you.

Zee: You're right!

Parker: Tee said that your mother-in-law moved in recently

Zee: Yeah

Parker: How's it going with her?

Zee: Fine. She's nice :) Mostly, she hangs out with Ida and Callan though. You can tell she's making up for lost time

Parker: Ohh. Tee told me that your father-in-law got the kids in the divorce but's like the worst dad alive?

Zee: He sucks

Zee: Sorry if I've been quiet. It's been crazy around here. This woman died in a hit-and-run and Colt got brought in for questioning.

Parker: This small town of yours isn't as boring as I thought it would be.

Parker: Arson and vehicular manslaughter... it's all go.

Zee: It's no NYC, but it's interesting.

Zee: The vehicle used in the accident was abandoned on our ranch.

Parker: YOUR ranch, huh?

Zee: Shut up. I could have been talking about the Bar 9.

Parker: You weren't though, were you?

Zee: ANYWAY

Zee: The only reason Colt wasn't arrested was because we were having lunch together at the time.

Parker: He doesn't seem the type.

Zee: To hit someone and run?

Zee: Of course not. He's innocent.

Zee: Callan's had a bit of a meltdown too

Parker: What kind of meltdown? Is he okay?

Zee: He built a security system for the ranch but there was no footage of the truck being dumped. We tried to tell him that it's impossible to secure four hundred thousand acres, but Callan didn't take that well.

Zee: He's barely been sleeping or eating as he brainstorms a solution.

Parker: Shit. It's always the innocent who suffer the most in these cases.

Zee: Ugh, so true. There's no solution either. You can't install cameras in the middle of nowhere. There's no point. Wind could knock them over or cattle would ram into the posts. He's just going to have to learn to deal with the holes in his security. :/

Zee: As it stands, he's come up with an army of drones that monitor the land, lol.

Parker: Hello, dictatorship.

Zee: *cackles*

Zee: My blood sugar's been all over the place too. I don't know what Tee did when she set my alerts as a crying baby but I can't change it. It's annoying as hell.

Parker: Precisely why she did it. Are you okay?

Zee: Just stressed.

Parker: Unlike you. You didn't even get stressed when Nyx was arrested on a murder charge!

Zee: I'm wired for those situations :P

Parker: Cool and calm under pressure more like lol.

343

Zee: Speaking of... when was the last time you heard from Tee?

Parker: Today lol. Why?

Zee: She's not talking to me outside of making sure I'm eating something.

Parker: Why not?

Zee: Because I told her I was Colt's alibi and I won't give her the details.

Parker: o.O

Zee: And she had another shitty hookup the other night lol

Parker: She's taking your leaving weird. I mean, she's always been an oddball, but she's stranger without you around.

Zee: *snorts*

Parker: I think it's the genius in her

Zee: Maybe. Colt said after he met her that she reminded him of Callan

Parker: He's smart?

Zee: Has an IQ of 159

Parker: That means dick. IQ tests inherently have more holes in them than a net

Zee: Perhaps, but he can back his shit up.

Parker: Oh?

Zee: Someone from MIT came to talk to him lol... Something about a free ride. They don't do that for just anyone, Pee. Not when the kid sucks at sports too.

Parker: NO! I like my name! I'm not Pee!

Zee: :P

Zee: How's Tee doing?

Parker: You noticed we're both more worried about her than we are about either of us? Ya know, the girlies with agoraphobia and an arranged marriage?

Zee: She's alone in the Big Apple. We're not.

Parker: She could come to me if she needed to.

Zee: Not the same as having someone across the apartment lol

Parker: True. It's a shame I'd prefer to hit myself over the head with a hammer than live in the city

Zee: Wow

Parker: *shudders* I hate it there

Zee: How's Sweet Lips?

Parker: Missing me. He's coming to Rachel's tomorrow. Can't wait to see him.

Zee: I'll expect you to go quiet then. :P

Parker: Never let it be said that you're not a wise woman.

Zee: Do me a favor? Text Tee and tell her I had sex with him.

Parker: Two mins

Zee: Lol. I have an incoming call. Speak later <3

Chapter 34
Colton

THREE DAYS LATER

"Jim at Ravenly & Daughters said you brought in a truck bearing the description of the vehicle recently discovered on your property. You know, the one Lydia Armstrong was mowed down in?"

Though I admit I've been waiting for this second interview since I was released from custody, I'm calm as I answer Terry's question. "I wasn't behind the wheel."

"See, it's looking less like vehicular manslaughter and more like first-degree murder, Colton," the sergeant muses, his gaze flickering between me and Marc Robard.

"I had no reason to kill her."

"Those poison pen letters say otherwise. Plus, there were prints on the steering wheel—"

I snort. "Where else would they be? But I can tell you who they don't belong to—me. As the forensics proved or you'd have arrested me by now."

His eyes narrow. "Know what *was* in there?" When I don't answer, he drawls, "One of Lydia's little love notes to y'all, and when I say y'all, I mean it. Juliette, this time—"

"Make up your mind, Terry. Who's behind this? Me or Juliette? Anyway, you can't seriously think Juliette McAllister is a murderer. She hasn't driven a truck in the last thirty-five years!"

"She was seen in town that same day." Terry drums his fingers on the table. "As were the triplets, though their alibi is solid. You, of course, were with your wife. Weren't you?"

There's a flicker in his expression that tells me he doesn't believe Zee and that, more than anything, riles up my temper.

I'm so goddamn sick of people not having faith in her word.

Sure, she lied this time, but hell, whenever she's spoken the truth, the folks of Pigeon Creek never believed her anyway.

"Where are you taking this interview, sergeant?" Marc intones, seemingly bored by Terry's weak interrogation skills. "My client is a busy man and you've brought him into the RCMP detachment for *questioning*.

"No arrest has been made, ergo this is a waste of his time. As you said, his wife provided Mr. Korhonen with an alibi. He was not behind the wheel on the day of the road accident which the forensics attests to—"

"Mr. *Korhonen*," Terry bites back, "failed to disclose that he was aware the McAllister triplets owned the truck dumped on *his* land. Did you take it to Ravenly & Daughters, Colton?"

"You do not have to answer that," Marc slots in before I can answer.

Terry sneers as he slaps a sheet of paper on the table.

As Marc reads it, I murmur, "The truck was in need of repair. I didn't know that it was ready to be driven. As far as I was aware, the serpentine belt was still screwed. One of the triplets used deodorant on it to stop it from squeaking."

"Why hide that from us?"

"I wasn't hiding anything."

"If that's all, sergeant, I don't believe Mr. Korhonen can further your inquiries—"

"I'll be the one who decides that," Terry snaps, glaring at him before it softens into a scowl. When he shuts off the recording, Marc makes to protest but I stall him. "If you have any information on which triplet did this, Colton, you should share it with me now."

"They're innocent. Just like I am."

Talk about pissing in the wind.

"Evidence says otherwise."

"There's no evidence. It was their truck. That's it. I don't even want to know what kind of DNA is in that cab," I mutter. "We all have alibis. And if you ask around, I bet Juliette does too because everyone takes notice of where that ticking time bomb is."

"She was also being blackmailed by Lydia. That's more probable cause. Maybe this was a family affair?"

I keep my expression blank. "Wonder who else she'd set her sights on. You should look for more of her victims before you accuse innocent folks of mowing her down—"

"Innocent folks who were seen using that truck!"

"I never got behind the wheel. I was only there as their tow and to put a payment down," I bite off.

"This is getting us nowhere, gentlemen," Marc interrupts. "Sergeant, you have no grounds for arrest. You're merely wasting my client's time."

My lips twitch at Terry's disgusted look. "You're the one who told me to bring a lawyer."

"I didn't mean to get an asshole," he grumbles.

"I'll take that as a compliment," is Marc's retort. "Are we done here?"

Terry sniffs. "We are."

"In the future, I'd appreciate it if you deal directly with me. Here's my card."

When we're out of the station, Marc pulls me aside as we walk to our vehicles. "While the forensics show your DNA wasn't in the cab, an unidentified sample was found on the wheel."

"Must be Clyde."

"Who's Juliette?"

"The McAllister matriarch. Her prints would be in the cab because the triplets ferry her around in it when they're not in school. Anyway, Juliette's not the type to run someone over. She's more likely to shoot someone in the face with a shotgun."

Marc grunts. "Unless an eyewitness comes forward, they can't put you behind the wheel."

"Seeing as I didn't do it, we're fine and dandy."

"I'm not saying you did. Just saying that if an eyewitness puts you in the cab—"

"I. Didn't. Do. It."

"Fine." He pinches my shoulder. "Hopefully, the next time we talk, it won't be to visit the station."

My lips twist. "We live in hope."

As we part ways, I jump into the cab and start for home.

On a hunch, I call Juliette. "Why were you in town the day Lydia was killed?"

"Is it a crime to pick up some butter tarts for the boys?"

Relief swarms me. "You were with Harry?"

"Yes. Unfortunately. And I stopped in at The Coffee Shop too." She sniffs. "Am I being interrogated for a reason?"

"I was just hauled in for questioning again."

"That you're harassing me tells me you were allowed to leave."

"Only because I have an alibi," I grind out. "Did you see anything that day? If you were on Main Street, you might have noticed—"

"I wouldn't worry, Colton. Reilly is a moron. He's wasting valuable time looking in the wrong direction. Anyone with eyes can see you've been targeted." She huffs. "I never did like him or that father of his. His grandfather was just as much of an idiot too. At least the inspector's from Montreal. Reilly's corrupt as all get out."

"He knows you were being blackmailed."

"I'm sure he does. But what he doesn't know, boy, is however many others that bitch was skimming cash from."

"What made you pay her?"

"Can't control many things but I wanted to control that."

"Reilly said he found a letter in the truck."

"Damn, that means the triplets knew..." She sighs, sounding every one of her years.

"What did she have on you?"

"That's McAllister business," she growls. "Now, if you think I'm going to waste more oxygen on this conversation, you're wrong. These are minutes I'll never get back, I'll have you know."

And with that, she cuts the call.

Shaking my head as I continue the drive home, I can't stop myself from grinning.

She might be the wicked witch of Pigeon Creek, but there's no denying the impressiveness of her bark.

Text Chat

Colt: You knew your grandmother was being blackmailed?

Carson: Knew someone was trying to lol. They clearly had a death wish.

Colby: Fuck, wait a minute…

Colby: You saying that was Lydia?!

Carson: o.O

Colt: Never mind

Colt: What were they holding over her head?

Calder: Something about our mom.

Colt: Was it true?

Calder: We barely knew her but I doubt it.

Colt: I'm sorry, boys.

Calder: Life's shit and then you die.

Colby: Like Lydia discovered…

Colby: Too soon?

Carson: Don't worry, Colt, I clipped him on the back of the head.

Colt: *thumbs-up*

Text Chat

Colby: Did you get hauled in for questioning again?

Zee: No. But the sergeant came to the Seven Cs to discuss Colton's alibi

Calder: Why? Isn't it cut and dry?

Zee: Nothing is with me lol.

Carson: I hate this town sometimes.

Zee: Me too.

Carson: I'm sorry you had to come back, Zee

Zee: Hey, it's not your fault

Colby: We could have tried harder around the ranch. The things Colt's been teaching us, we should have learned a long time ago.

Zee: I'm curious why you didn't. Walker was dragged into lessons when he was a brat

Calder: She kind of gave up when we ran away from every lesson.

Calder: Maybe the ranch wouldn't be as in the red if we'd tried though. *shrugs* I think Carson's right. We do owe you an apology.

Carson: If this BS has proven anything, it's that the no-good McAllisters will always be the ones who get blamed.

Zee: Don't say that. Look, everything'll be fine. I'll make sure of it.

Calder: Did they really not believe the alibi you gave Colt?

Zee: They did when I detailed everything from what he was wearing to the sandwich we ate lol.

Zee: Hey, aren't you supposed to be in class?

Colby: We won't tell anyone if you don't

Chapter 35
Zee

Anchor - Novo Amor

"I was thinking about inviting your family over for a BBQ soon."

My eyes widen as they dart from the apps on my phone where I check in with my blood sugar. I had to change my pump site today and already got the tube caught on a goddamn doorhandle. Some days, I get so sick of this shit I want to scream. Still, that's not Colt's fault.

Tiredly, I mutter, "Um. Why?"

"You've had to put up with mine. In close quarters. Figured I should do the same in return."

"*Thanks.*"

His grin is hidden by the morning's newspaper, but I saw it. He thinks he's so clever.

"Heard you were teaching the triplets how to shoot."

He snorts. "Nearly got a butt full of lead for my pains."

"They're not naturals?"

"No. They're not." The paper rattles. "Do you mind?"

"What? Whipping them into shape? No. If anything, thank you," I say honestly. "By the looks of the Bar 9, they need it."

"They're good kids."

"Callan wouldn't agree."

"Because they're too alike."

"Oooooofff, don't tell him that."

He winks at me. "Already have."

I'm grateful he takes up residence behind the paper again because I'm squirming in my seat.

Ever since I found out that he's been taking care of my brothers, without a single word of encouragement from me, without any expectation, even going so far as to provide them with a defense attorney we'd never have been able to afford before our marriage, the tingle in my dingle (as Tee has horrifically started calling it) is getting worse.

Squirming in my seat at the prospect of watching 'Daddy Colt' in action (another Tee-ism), I eat some oatmeal and make a couple of notes on my to-do list as I drink the coffee he made for me when I came down for breakfast.

It's a disturbingly domestic scene, but it's happening more and more often.

Since the news spread that Colton was with me on the day Lydia died, Callan, Lindsay, and Ida think we're hiding our relationship from them. That means, for whatever reason they can come up with, most of them atrociously weak, the table's absent of anyone's presence apart from my own and Colton's.

For whatever reason, neither of us has yet to skip a meal since I gave him an alibi.

And for whatever reason, I'm enjoying his company.

It's like the old days but better—there's no reason to be frightened of running into Clyde or to pretend I don't exist. Nor do I have to return to the Bar 9.

A part of me doesn't want to trust in this new normal but it's Colt. And old me, whether he betrayed her or not, does.

It's like my lungs taking in air or my heart beating.

I can't stop the process even if I want to.

"A BBQ would do them good. With their truck impounded, they're looking stir-crazy for outside contact."

"I think they're having a hard time at school."

"None of this makes any sense. We all have alibis but we're still the prime suspects. I'm beginning to think your grandma is right. Reilly *is* an idiot. *Or,* he's just corrupt."

"You talked to her?"

"Had the pleasure, yes."

That tingling dingle is turning into an outright vibration.

"You sure you want them to eat here?"

The top corner of the paper flops down as he peers over it. "Any reason why they shouldn't?"

"Wasn't messing around when I said Callan doesn't like the triplets."

"Callan doesn't like a lot of people." His frown makes an appearance as he tosses the paper on the table. I can see he has it open where the Sudoku puzzle is. Has he been hiding behind the paper as he solves it? I shouldn't find that endearing but I do. "The triplets aren't that bad, Zee."

"No, but they're..."

When my words wane, he prompts, "What? Teenaged kids with a lot of hormones?"

I purse my lips. "The spitting image of Dad." It's probably why it's always been easier to text them than to video call.

Unlike Colt, who's great at being the older sibling, I suck at it.

His frown lessens. "Oh."

"Dad was very artistic," I muse as my spoon drifts through the bowl of oatmeal.

"I remember he had a class in town."

"Yes. If *Grand-mère* hadn't been his mother-in-law, he'd have gone into art full-time. He had the soul of a creator, but you're not allowed one of those if you marry into the McAllister family."

"Or the Korhonens," he remarks as he doodles beside the Sudoku puzzle.

"His kids didn't even inherit his last name," I whisper.

It never registered how tiring it was to talk with people who don't understand the burden of a legacy. That's one thing we both share. Yet I never imagined it'd be our common ground in the here and now.

"Mom told me that she loved his artist's heart but as soon as they married, *Grand-mère* laid down the law and made him learn how to run the ranch.

"H-He was an orphan, you know?"

"I do."

Of course, he does. Everyone knows everyone's business here—*duh*.

"I think he was happy to be a part of a family. Enough that he let go of his dream for it. It must have been that, otherwise, why would he put up with *Grand-mère*?"

"He was a good man."

"The best kind. The boys are like that too. In their own way."

"So what's the problem?"

"I don't want Callan's safe space to be invaded by people he's not friends with. Or for him to feel unwelcome in his own home like Dad was."

Colt pins me in place with a grateful smile. "Thank you for that."

"After everything with Lydia and him finding out about you being detained, he's not in the best of headspaces." I hitch a shoulder. "They don't get along."

"They're family. Whether they like it or not."

"Yeah, but—"

"It'd be a BBQ in the yard," he reiterates in a calm tone.

"So, they'd be on his turf but not *in* it." I eat some oatmeal. "That's not a half-bad idea."

"I'm capable of them sometimes."

His teasing tone has me blushing.

"I'll talk to Mrs. Abelman," he continues, "and get it set up."

"Thank you."

"You don't have to thank me. I should have done it sooner. I promised I'd take them under my wing and I've fallen short."

"Hardly."

"If you'd seen them with a lasso last week, you'd disagree.

I'm pretty sure they're getting worse." He rubs his chin. "That reminds me. Cole's birthday is in a few weeks. It could be a double celebration. I know he intended on coming up but he hasn't mentioned it."

"Maybe because I'm here?" I ask, hating the necessity of the words but not wanting him to be blindsided.

Just because he believes me doesn't mean Cole does.

"I'll make him come," is his simple retort.

My cheeks flush. "You can't make him do anything he doesn't want to do."

His gaze settles on mine. It riles me while soothing something raw and ragged in my soul. "Sure I can."

Before I have a chance to reply, his cell buzzes. He snags it, lips pursing as he scans the screen.

"Problem?" I ask, oddly annoyed that he might have to leave soon.

"No more than usual." He flashes me a look. "Feel like coming on a ride with me?"

The offer is unexpected but, I can't deny, appreciated.

I don't think he purposely withheld the use of their horses from me, but I felt the lack of permission to go horseback riding, nevertheless.

A truck was one thing. The run of the house another. But their horses? That was a whole other level of trust.

At least, it felt like that to me.

"I-I have work."

It's a lie. I'm so far ahead with Rachel's caseload that I'm hoping a Sinner will commit a heinous crime to keep me busy.

He shrugs. "It'll only take a short while."

It's dumb how nervous such a simple request makes me. "I-It's been years since I've ridden."

"It's like riding a bike. You don't forget."

Much as his humor often does—disarms me—I snort. "Will you put me on a pony so that I don't have as far to fall?"

The grin sharpens. Wicked amusement flickers in his eyes. "I'll save you before you fall."

Why do I believe him?

"Okay." Giddiness sparkles inside me but I tamp it down as

I judge my choice of clothes. "Looks as if I'm inadvertently dressed for a morning on the range."

This time, the emotion in his gaze has nothing to do with humor.

In fact, it steals the air from my lungs.

Whoa.

Where did that come from?

The room is warm. Not overly so but pleasant. Until that look. The heat in his eyes triggers a visceral response in me. My mouth dries up and my palms feel clammy. I know I'm flushing—

His cell rings again.

Shattering the moment.

It relieves me that he's as annoyed as I am because when he answers the call, he snarls, "Theo, this had better be—" Silence. "Oh." He rubs his forehead. "Shit."

And with those two words, I know that our horseback-riding date is canceled.

The depth of my disappointment is a sharp wrench in my plans to live here, go through IVF, and then leave.

Colton heaves a sigh but he disconnects the call without another word. "I'm sorry, Zee. Rain check?"

"Sure."

His eyes collide with mine again. "Later. At two? You can finish your work?"

Surprised by the concession and hating the anticipation that immediately sizzles through my veins, I nod.

Eagerly.

Ugh.

Tee would either be ashamed or proud of me—I'm not sure which is worse.

His grin is quicksilver fast, though, and it makes up for my bobbing head.

At least we're both excited.

Colton gets to his feet and tucks his cell in his pocket. "I'll be back by one. We can eat lunch. Together." He coughs. "If you want."

"I'd like that," is my prim response.

"Have a good morning."

"You too."

As he leaves the room, he pauses behind me.

My heart stutters as he rests a hand on my shoulder then presses a kiss to my cheek.

The simple contact has me immediately turning my head so I can capture his lips with mine.

A startled grunt escapes him as I lift my arms, curving them around his neck as I tug him into me while I twist in my seat. One of his hands settles on my thigh. The heat of it sends electric shocks through my nerve endings, which doesn't sound pleasant but God, it's everything.

Especially because his fingers are so big and they're ridiculously close to the inseam at my crotch.

As his tongue explores my mouth, I fight back. Needing more. Needing everything. Our conversation shouldn't have riled me up, but it did. Daddy Colt is hot as hell and I've no problem with hellfire.

A soft whimper breaks free of my vocal cords when he finally retreats, breathing hard and heavy as he pushes his forehead into mine.

"Rain check," he rumbles.

Ugh.

My nostrils flare. "Lunch."

It's a promise.

His eyes widen then he smoothes his thumb over my kiss-sore lips. "No pressure, Zee."

I clear my throat. "Go. Now. Before I climb you like a tree."

I feel his amusement when he kisses my cheek again. "Lunch."

That's *his* promise.

I hear his cowboy boots clipping against the parquet flooring, and as the door closes with a soft snick, I press the back of my hand to my forehead.

Then, I freeze.

And I have no idea why I do it, none whatsoever, but I stand.

Darting over to the window, I watch him stride over to the

stables that they consider 'private'—where they house their personal stock and where the pregnant mares reside during foaling season.

It's a short walk, only five minutes from the front door, unlike the regular barn that's a click away.

I keep my focus locked on him as he heads inside, then a few minutes later, he brings out his ride.

The Houdini horse. Who, according to Callan, Loki sired.

Funny how Loki was a good boy but his son, Fenrir, or Fen for short, is the mischievous one.

That's when my phone buzzes. Rather than answer, I snag my AirPods from my other pocket, pop them in, and hit connect.

"You'll never guess what Phill did across the hall," is Tee's greeting.

"He thinks you're cute so... he tried to ask you out."

Her harrumph tells me I'm spot on. But I'm too distracted to gloat because I start drooling when Colton mounts Fen.

His butt in those jeans—my god.

This definitely isn't the first time I've seen him ride but it might as well be for all the punch it packs to my ovaries.

"What are you ogling? Or should that be who? Have you finally decided your husband can stop the tingle in your—"

"Stop calling my clitoris a dingle! I'm just admiring his skill bareback."

"That had better be a euphemism for something else," she grouses, making me smile.

"Are you going to go out with Phill?"

"He stinks."

"He doesn't."

"He does!"

"It's only motor oil. I love a man who can get down and dirty with anything mechanical." Just like my husband. "Plus, free engine checks for the win—"

"Neither of us owns a car."

"That's not the point! The point is if you *did* have one, he could be relied upon to keep the hunk of junk roadworthy."

"But he stinks. And your lack of disagreement says you know I'm right."

"He does smell like the shop," I concede.

"His nails are black."

I grunt.

"How am I supposed to let him go to town on my pussy if he has filthy hands?"

"Did you forget that he has a mouth for a reason?"

"He gets oil all over his face too."

I laugh but it morphs into a sigh over Colt's prowess on horseback.

"What are you doing?" she demands.

"Spying on my husband."

"Oooh, you 'my husband'ed him again. What's he doing?"

"Riding a horse."

"You're such a cowgirl."

"Since when is that a crime?"

"Since your idea of porn is watching a man ride—"

"Without a saddle, Tee. Without. A. Saddle. Remember?"

"Oooooh. That changes things. Man, I bet he has the best thighs." She clucks her tongue. "Don't worry. You don't need to 'my husband' him."

"You watch too many rom-coms."

"No such thing. You don't watch enough. If you did, you'd see this whole arranged marriage as an opportunity."

"An opportunity?!"

"Yeah! You're married to a hot, wealthy rancher who wants you to have his baby.

"Honey, in a dating real-estate market where men who don't wash their hands or face want to date you, Colton is a Catch."

"Capital 'C'?"

"You know it. What's he wearing?"

My cheeks flush. "You did not ask me that!"

"I'm setting a scene!"

"What do you think he's wearing? Short shorts? He's a rancher!"

The bickering helps calm me as is often the way with us.

"A sexy one." She whistles. "I've decided that you should marry him for real."

"We're already married."

"I read this book yesterday and the sex, Zee, the *sex*. If Colton's capable of that, then you need to keep him."

"Colt is not a character in a book!"

"He could be. You know he's good in the sack. He's too kind not to be. Any dude who'd agree to IVF when you're fine as all get-out is too generous not to have a similar mindset between the sheets."

"You can't attribute—"

"The hero was called Colt. I can attribute whatever I want to him."

"Gah! You're so annoying. Why do I miss you?"

She snickers. "I think you're selfish."

"Excuse me?"

"You're not on video so I can't share in the show."

The sharp bite of jealousy startles me.

It fizzles in me like I downed three cans of Pigeonberry energy drink back-to-back.

A soft chuckle sounds in my ear. "Ooooooh. Feeling possessive, are we?"

I grunt. "Despite how long I've been here, I've only just started opening up to him."

"That's usually when men fall short," she disregards. "If he's withstood a couple conversations with you, no wonder you're eyeing him differently.

"I wondered why you hadn't been posting any videos. You've been all loved up in Pigeon Creek. Honestly, that could be the title of your real-life Hallmark movie—"

Aghast, I blurt out, "That is *not* why I haven't been posting videos!"

She clucks her tongue. "Shame. I know you said that lunch date was second base only but I lived in hope.

"Honestly, if I have another shitty date, I'm going to rethink my sexuality. Maybe that's why we get along so well. I have a secret crush on you and I didn't know it."

"You can't say stuff like that."

"Sure I can. The girl in the coffee shop is hot. She looks like she knows what a clitoris is too."

"She has one."

"EXACTLY MY POINT."

Though I huff, I murmur, "Is this your bi-awakening moment?"

I can hear the smirk in her voice. "I'm not too old for experimentation."

"Only you'd figure out your sexuality because you're tired of the male species."

"What can I say? We're not all gifted a Colton."

I huff. "You've changed your tune."

"I'm lonely." She sniffs. Not sniffles. It's taken a while, but we've gotten there. "What else am I supposed to do apart from work, read, watch TV, talk to you, and find someone who can make me feel good about myself?"

"Go to the gym. That does the same thing as a guy."

"Now I know you've been spending time with your grandmother."

"Actually, I haven't."

"You haven't spoken to Colton, or the she-devil, or your mother-in-law, or the triplets. You haven't visited my folks either. So, what the hell have you been doing apart from hanging out with my nemesis?"

"Callan is not your nemesis," I mumble, craning my neck to keep Colt in my field of vision.

"He is. He's stealing you from me."

"Technically, the guy you're setting me up with did that," I point out. "Callan's making me feel more at home."

"What's he doing?"

"Callan? He's in school—"

"Not *him*," she hisses. "Colton!"

"He's riding out of sight. Behind the house."

"Follow him!"

"How?"

"Keep him in view!"

"Why?!"

"Because I have to live vicariously through you! Duh! Ugh, you're so slow on these things sometimes."

"Work. *Work* is what I've been doing."

"Boring."

"How's the orchestra?"

"I hate it. Hate everyone. Hate New York."

"Apart from the girl at the coffee shop."

"Apart from her."

Though I *am* traipsing through the house on the hunt for Colt, stalking him via the windows, I muse, "You're not joking, are you?"

"About my sexuality?"

The trouble with knowing someone as long as you've known yourself is that you sense when there's a joke beneath the truth and the truth beneath a joke.

"Yeah."

She clears her throat. "No."

"Why didn't you tell me sooner?" I tut. "This isn't something that happens overnight. You must have been feeling this way forever."

"I didn't want you to freak out. Think I was in love with you or something. I mean, I love you. But I'm not in love with you."

"I'm not that self-centered that I think the world revolves around me, babe."

"No, I know. I am, though," she teases, sounding more like herself. "I dated some chicks behind your back—"

"We weren't dating so you weren't technically—"

"I think I'm holding out for Butch Cassidy." My snort triggers a second sniff. "Where's Colt?"

"Jesus, you're worse than the FBI!" I harrumph as I make it upstairs, finally getting to the den where I know I'll be able to see in which direction he headed. "Gotcha! He's already a blip in the distance though."

That's when I notice...

"Huh."

"What?"

"A bunkhouse."

"So?"

"I didn't realize it was there before."

"Doesn't sound like you've noticed much around that place. If that were me, I'd know every inch of that land already."

"You're nosy."

"I'm curious."

"Same difference." I squint into the distance, and then, annoyed with myself for being dumb, I open the camera app on my phone. Zooming as much as I can, I say, "It's occupied. There's smoke coming out of the chimney. But why's it over in that quadrant?"

"Are you asking me?"

"No. I know you don't have a clue."

"Why wouldn't it be in that quadrant?"

"It's too far out. There are no stables nearby. No trucks, either." Toying with the St. Christopher's medallion Tee's nonna gave me before we left for New York, I murmur, "Plus, no cattle are grazing anywhere so I reckon it must be in fallow."

"The trucks wouldn't be there at this time of the day, though, would they?"

"Maybe not." I purse my lips. "Also, why's Colt even going to the bunkhouse? Ranch hands come to the owner, not vice versa."

"Sounds elitist."

"It's not not."

"Not not not not, huh?"

"You're in one of those moods."

"Gee, ya think. Okay, so what's he doing?"

"What else could he be doing, Tee? He's on a horse! Riding to a bunkhouse! I'm not a spy. I don't know why he's heading that way."

"To a super-secret bunkhouse."

"Shut up." I clear my throat. "We're going riding later."

"Ooohhhh. Another euphemism, I hope?"

"Have you been drinking original Coke again? You only get like this after you drink pop," I grumble so I can hide from the fact my nose is smushed up against the window as I squint to see what Colton's doing.

"I had one ice cream soda."

"Ugh. I'm so jealous." I might love the taste, but it does *not* agree with me.

"Unlike you."

"Today feels like a day for sugar."

"Why? You're not sad."

"No, I need to eat my feelings."

She falls silent before whisper-screaming, "Meaning you have feelings?!"

"I'm not an alien!"

"Are these feelings for a certain cute cowboy?"

"Don't call him that."

God, Colt's not cute. He's *everything*.

"Which part? Cute or a cowboy?"

"Ugh. Both." My cheeks blaze with heat. "Clearly, I'm about to get my period or something. You know I'm always horny then."

The sound of someone clearing their throat rumbles behind me.

I freeze.

Turn back to find—

"Oh, shit." I blink at one of Colt's brothers—Cody. "Um. Hello?"

A soft smirk curves his lips. "Hello."

"Who is that? Does he know he has a sexy voice?"

Ignoring her, I swallow the urge to be buried beneath this very spot forevermore and stick out my hand. "I'm Zee."

"Zee, I'm Cody."

As we shake hands, I stare at the crutch in his free one but spy no other visible sign of injury. "Are you okay?"

"What's wrong with him?" Tee asks.

"Yeah. I heard your voice, though, and didn't recognize it." He angles his head to the side. "You've grown up since the last time we saw one another."

"God, he sounds so hot. Is he?"

Wanting to die, I gulp. "I need to end this call, Cody—"

"Noooooo."

"I'll talk to you later," I snap at my so-called BFF. Then, I disconnect the call and smile at him. "Sorry. My friend was distracting me."

"Yes. Apparently."

You did not talk about being horny in front of your brother-in-law...

"Um, could you at least lie to me and tell me you didn't overhear the last part of our conversation?"

His lips roll inward. "Sure."

Oh, he's lying. But badly.

I gust out my cheeks. "So..."

"So... You're horny and find my brother attractive."

"God, you're as bad as my friend!" I sputter, mortified.

He chuckles. "Sorry. I couldn't resist." The chuckle dies as he coughs and clears his face of all expression. "Hello, sister-in-law. I'm your brother-in-law. Squadron Leader Cody Korhonen reporting for duty."

"I'd stand to attention but I'm not allowed to pop my heels for another two weeks."

Wincing, I mutter, "Do you want something to drink? I know this is more your house than mine, but I have no idea where Ida's lair is."

"She has quarters just off the kitchen, but seeing as Mum's home, she's probably with her in the solarium." His head tips to the side. "Thought you'd have known that already."

"I haven't done much exploring."

"But you live in this house."

"Yes, but it's not mine to be nosing around, is it?"

Though his brow lifts, he states, "I'd love a coffee. No one answered their phone when my cab pulled up outside."

A part of me wants to blanch over how much that taxi ride must have cost from the airport, but then, these guys are all loaded so why bother worrying about their bank accounts?

"Can you manage to get back down the stairs?"

"Sure. I'm slow. Feel free to go ahead."

I know it's an invitation, but I don't take it.

That'd be plain rude.

"So, um, Callan's told me a lot about you."

"Callan talks too much," he grumbles, but he's obviously

uncomfortable because it takes him a while to bluster out the words as we make it onto the first level.

"You should have stayed on this floor," I mutter worriedly. "I know the boys have a wing on this level—"

"I heard a voice I didn't recognize. Considering everything that's going on in town, I had to check things out."

It's with relief that we make it to the ground floor. It seems dumb to guide him into the kitchen when he knows its location better than I do, but guide him I do.

When he plunks his ass at the kitchen table, right where I'd been sitting twenty minutes ago, he releases a pained sigh. "God, it's good to be off my feet."

Inwardly cringing on his behalf, I scurry to fix him a coffee.

Plunking the cup and creamer in front of him, I watch as he takes a deep sip before, staring me square in the face, he asks, "So, did you burn down our stables?"

Chapter 36
Colt

I'm God - Clams Casino, Imogen Heap

I'll be back in a few days to replace the unit.
Just be careful with it until then.
Colt

O nce I finish writing the note, I stick it on the
refrigerator for the occupants of the new bunkhouse
to see.

Having temporarily fixed the finicky waste disposal, I head
out and jump astride Fen's back after giving him an apple from
the fruit bowl on the kitchen table.

As I do, I spy two of the occupants peeping through the
folds of the drapes like I'm the Zodiac Killer reincarnate.

With a sigh, I set off for home.

The task took a lot less time than I figured so if Zee's still
game, we can ride before lunch.

The silence of the prairie, land that my forefathers roamed and ranched and laid claim to, lets me admit something to myself that I probably wouldn't admit anywhere else—I want to see her on a horse.

I know which one too—Jas. Short for Jasmine. Callan named her when he was twelve. She's a Camarillo. Pure white. No pink skin or undertones. Nothing gray about her coat.

Zee'll look like some kind of faerie princess astride her.

The strange image plants itself behind my eyes, so I shutter them to better appreciate it as Fen plods back to the homestead, treading a path he could take with his own eyes shut.

When we make it there, I stable him and toss him another apple from the bag we leave hanging on a pillar.

Once he's satisfied, I leave him and retreat to the house.

That's when I hear laughter.

To be honest, I've heard more laughter in the past month than I've heard in years.

Now that Mum's back, the atmosphere is lighter all round. *But* I'm used to hearing Callan and Zee laugh too.

It's a nice thing to come home to.

Nicer than I could have imagined.

Feeling like a numbnut, I toss my hat on the stand in the hall then stride over to the source of the noise—the kitchen.

Which is when I hear Cody's voice.

I rush in, absorb the rare sight of him at the kitchen table, and grin. "You dickhead. You never told me you were coming home!"

Cody chuckles but he doesn't get up, instead wiggles a crutch at me. "It was unexpected."

Zee clears her throat. "He's been in a car crash."

I gape at him. "Tell me you're kidding? You spend God knows how many hours in a cockpit but you get injured in a car?!"

"Don't sound disappointed." He slugs me in the arm as I take a seat next to him. "Broken tibia-fibula. Nightmare. Had surgery and everything. Two more weeks with the crutch then I'm done."

"Jesus. You're an asshole for not telling us sooner," I snap, but a soft thud sounds in front of me—a mug of coffee. I flick a glance at Zee. "Thanks, Zee."

Her smile's shy as she turns to the counter where I see she has all the fixings for sandwiches.

My brow lifts. "Have you got my wife making sandwiches for you?"

"*Your wife,*" he mouths.

I scowl at him.

"Oh, I don't mind," Zee reassures us both.

He smirks.

"As far as I can tell, your hands aren't broken."

"I was getting to know *your wife.*"

My scowl darkens.

His smirk deepens.

A dish is settled on the table in front of Cody. But her hand lands on my shoulder and she asks, "Would you like a sandwich too?"

I peer at her. "Do you mind?"

Her lips twist. "If you want something fancy, then you can rely on Ida..."

"He's the one who introduced me to peanut butter and fluff, Zee," Cody half-croons, urging another frown out of me.

Not the words. Just the tone.

He elbows me when I don't reply so I clear my throat. "Sounds great." I flick a look at her, watching as she puts together another sandwich. "When did you get in?"

"Saskatoon? This morning. The ranch, two hours ago."

"You should have told me. I'd have flown you here."

"Thought I'd spare you the backseat driving," he counters.

"So gracious of you," I mock. "How long are you here for?"

Taking a bite, he shrugs. "Dunno."

"You don't have to ride a desk? Or can you stay home as you recuperate?"

"I can stay home."

Frowning at him when he doesn't open up, I start to ask him what the hell's going on, but Zee places the dish in front of me before I get the chance.

I don't think about what I'm doing. I snag a hold of her wrist—that's the second I feel her racing pulse.

I stroke the soft, velvety skin with my thumb and feel it stutter then kick back into high gear. "Do you still want to go riding?"

Her long lashes shield those gorgeous green eyes of hers.

God, she's beautiful.

Zee flicks a look at Cody. "Um, are you sure? Don't you want to—"

"Hang out with him?" I scoff. "No."

"*Thanks*, bro."

Ignoring him, I stare at her. "How about in an hour?"

"U-Um, yeah. Sounds good. I-I'll... I don't have any boots."

"Just wear sneakers. I won't tell anyone if you don't, and Cody can keep bigger secrets than that." I wink at her. "We'll get you some the next time we're in town. I have to head that way in the next couple days. Want to come with me?"

Her cheeks flush. "Sounds good. Okay. I'll be down shortly." A whisper of vulnerability appears in her eyes. "You'll wait for me?"

I smile at her. "I promise."

She nods again, gives a small wave to Cody, then heads out of the kitchen.

Yes, I watch her go.

I only live like a monk; I'm not one.

Cody whistles. "You have it bad, brother dearest."

There's no point in lying. I shove him in the side, hard enough he almost falls off his chair. "What's with the flirting, asswipe?"

"I was being nice!" he grumbles, settling himself on his seat before punching me in the shoulder. "Also, *OW*. That hurt, dick."

"You were flirting. 'He's the one who introduced me to peanut butter and fluff, Zee,'" I mock.

"Firstly, that sounds nothing like me. Secondly, you have it worse than I thought if you can get jealous over the most asinine sandwich in the world." He takes a big bite. "Callan was right."

"He often is, the little shit. But about what?"

"This being a business arrangement but you'd be good for each other."

"And you figure that how? At least Callan's hung out with her!"

"I did too," he defends. "You're both so fucking nice, it's sickening. Both packed with guilt for shit you didn't do and overcompensating when you've nothing to compensate for. Hero complexes—"

"Says the goddamn soldier," I deride with a huff.

"So I'm perfectly placed to make the diagnosis," he states smugly. "You're both sweeter than this fluff. Honestly, it's puke-inducing. Callan was right about that too. Why are you pussyfooting around her? That's what I don't understand. You're obviously not screwing—"

"Don't talk about my wife like that."

His grin is slow. "'My wife' again, huh? Mr. Possessive."

I grit my teeth. "It's the only thing I'm allowed in this relationship."

He cups his ear. "Say that louder for the people in the back."

"You heard me."

"So, you want more?"

I narrow my eyes at him.

"I mean, she is beautiful. Who knew the McAllisters made girls so pretty, huh? Maybe if our ancestors had fucked, we wouldn't have been at each other's throats for centuries. Why steal a dozen steers when you could marry the enemy?"

"She's not the enemy."

"Naw, she's 'your wife,'" he mocks, including the finger quotes and everything.

I scowl at him and start eating.

"You both like each other, so why haven't you made your move?"

"Because this isn't *Sweet Home Alabama*."

"Sweet Home Pigeon Creek doesn't have the same ring to it."

"No. It doesn't," I agree. "We're in this for one reason only."

"So what's with the puppy-dog eyes as you ask her to go riding with you?"

Trust him to call me on my bullshit. "Why did you come home again?"

"And the invitation to go into town? Sounds like a date to me."

My scowl darkens. "Condoms."

"Huh?"

"Condoms. Mum and Clyde should have used them more often."

His smirk is unrepentant. "Are you dating your wife, Colt?"

"Why are you home?"

"Because I initiated the release process." He coughs. "A few months ago."

"What?!"

"It was time."

Gaping at him, I sputter, "Time?!"

"Yeah. I'm getting old and I don't want to ride a desk."

"You wouldn't quit. Not unless you were pushed."

"Another hospital stay sealed the deal," he admits dryly. "Spent so much time in a hospital room that if I never see another, it'll be too soon."

"So, it wasn't a car crash."

Not a question.

His gaze is amused. "Not unless the car was worth three hundred million dollars."

"You crashed it?"

"Excuse me. I've never crashed a plane. Some fuckwit over the Baltics decided to steer into me."

"The Baltics, huh?"

He arches a brow at me. "Hotbed of tension."

"War's brewing?"

"Isn't it always."

"You don't want to be involved this time?"

"Probably makes me a coward, but no."

"How are you a coward? All those medals you have weren't given to you because of your ugly face."

He pulls said face.

"Nor was it because you're a Korhonen. The name means dick in the CAF*."

He plops his sandwich on his plate. "True dat."

I watch as he rubs the back of his neck. "I thought you had to go through a bunch of interviews—"

"I did."

"And you didn't think to tell us about being injured?"

"What was the point in worrying you?"

"You're an asshole, do you know that? I have a father who sneezes and wants me at his bedside, but you crash a plane—"

"—I didn't crash the damn plane—"

"—and I don't get a notice from the RCAF†." Anger ripples through me. "Family automatically gets notified."

"Pops visited."

My mouth tightens. "And didn't tell us."

"Asked him not to."

"He listened?"

"He listens to me."

God, he's such an asshole.

I know where Cody gets it from.

Rubbing the bridge of my nose as I seek patience, I ask, "You okay?"

Cody and I used to be close, but too many deployments messed with that. Once upon a time, I missed him like I'd miss my right arm, but then Callan grew up and became *Callan.* You don't replace that type of closeness, but someone can rise in your esteem and stake a place in your soul.

That was Callan.

Even if he *is* a little shit who has no problem gossiping about his brothers.

"Been better."

"You want to talk about it, let me know?"

"'Course."

"I mean it."

His gaze is measured as he settles it upon me. "I do too."

---

* Canadian Armed Forces
† Royal Canadian Air Force

"Good."

"I had a job offer."

"Leaving as soon as you get here. Sounds about right," I mutter, oddly annoyed with him.

Is it a crime that I miss my brothers?

This time, he shoves me. "It's in town."

"Can't see you packing bags at the General Store."

"I did that when I was a teenager and those were the best-packed bags in the entirety of Canada."

"You always did think a lot of yourself."

Chuckling, Cody finally answers with the truth. "The job's with this new branch of cops they're starting in the province. Marshals. I know some people who know some people and they got me an interview."

"I never heard anything about this from the mayor." Though granted, I'd heard about it in last year's throne speech.

"Diddums," he mocks. "Anyway, this is above the mayor's pay grade. You're looking at Pigeon Creek's new marshal." Then, he amends, "Once I complete basic training."

"What about the RCMP?"

"We'll stand shoulder to shoulder."

"I'm sure Terry Reilly will love that."

"Sucks to be him. Anyway, I can make my ranks up myself. Wondered if you could help me with that."

I rub my cheek as I think about the town's occupants. "What numbers are you talking about? What's your juris-diction?"

"Twenty. And it'll be covering Louisville and Grangetown and the twenty-mile perimeter around the three towns."

"What about the Marguerite Lake community?"

He grins at me. "Yup."

I hide a smile. "Let me guess, those on high don't want the tribe on board but you're going to shove that shit on its head?"

"Oh, yeah. They hired me because of my name. Let's face it. *I* was given the job for a reason. If Cole had retired this season, they'd probably have approached *him*."

I hoot at the idea of my hockey-boi brother being the local marshal. "Let's be thankful for small mercies."

"We have a large Métis population in this area, but they're never represented and this marshal service is a concern. The First Nations' councils are gathering about it because they know they're the ones who will be shafted.

"I was going to do a recruitment drive in Marguerite Lake. You still get along well with the chief, don't you?"

I nod. "Gabriel hasn't spoken to me in a while though."

"Why not?"

"Theo dated his sister."

"Not your fault," he points out. "Plus, Theo's Métis."

"His mom is." I shrug. "But Gabriel said I should have warned him. I probably should've but Theo's good people. If you or Cole had been sniffing around her heels, I would have."

"Thanks, bro."

"You know it's true."

"You're no monk," he complains, bringing me full circle to my earlier thoughts.

"No," I concur. "I'm not."

His expression is knowing enough that he's lucky he's using a crutch. Still, he doesn't have a death wish. "You willing to speak to Gabriel for me?"

"Sure, but it might not work in your favor."

"I think it will. He has to know what your reaching out would mean. It'll be a relief, I figure. The powers that be don't know how close our ties are with the Métis."

I hum. "True. They would if they *looked*. We're descended from them thanks to our great-grandma, and our workers are eighty percent from the reserve."

"That's higher than during Uncle Clayton's guardianship."

"Clyde's a racist asshole. He cut the numbers and that's one of the reasons we suffered for a long time. No one knows the land in this area better than the Métis. It took me a while to get them to trust me again, but they did and slowly, I've brought them in.

"Gabriel only ascended to chief during the last election so he knows I've been working hard on that front."

"If you only have them out on the range, does that appear discriminatory?"

I snort. "Who said that I only have them out on the range?"

"You don't?"

"Of course not. Who do you think was behind the expansion at HQ? With Clyde off the scene, I'll be promoting more on a corporate level too. Laura Goulet and Katherena Villeneuve were my first picks for CFO and VP—that was before I became the head of the company."

His brows lift. "Wow. You're so woke, bro."

"It's not woke. They're the best women for the job." I tap my nose. "I'm very secure in my masculinity."

"Speaking of... this wife of yours. What are you going to do with her?"

I scowl at the change of subject. "Shut it."

"No, seriously. I've seen the way you look at her and I've also seen how she looks at you." This time, his ever-moving brows waggle. "You've always had a thing for her, haven't you?"

"Not consciously." I drawl the half-truth, tossing the rest of my sandwich on the plate.

"Lies," he jeers, but his eyes are twinkling.

Twinkling.

"Is this how you're going to be now that you're no longer a serving officer in the Air Force?"

He mockingly salutes. "Amazing how freeing it feels not to kill people for a living, bro."

"Yeah? Let's not switch out that burden for the one where you're into matchmaking. I have enough of that with Callan!"

Cody chuckles. "Callan? Not Mum?"

"Nah. She's been quiet about this. But she's letting Callan get away with murder, so she's going along for the ride."

"Is she okay?"

"I think so. She seems to be."

"How's she getting along with Zee?"

"As far as I can tell, they don't talk. Not because they hate one another, but because—"

"Ships that pass in the night?"

The words sink into me.

He's right.

Zee doesn't bother getting to know Mum because this is still temporary in her mind.

Mum isn't bothering to open up to Zee because I'll be divorced longer than I'll be married.

I rub my forehead, trying not to feel like I've been sucker punched.

"It's not a crime to want your wife, Colt," Cody murmurs, his voice soft and free from ridicule. "It's a good thing, in fact."

"I failed her."

He shrugs. "That's what the Korhonen charm is for. You can make it up to her." His smile is bright. "And I get front-row seats for the charm offensive. Talk about brilliant timing."

"Dick," I grumble, but I lean over and muss his hair.

Though he punches my shoulder to get me to stop, he reasons, "Why shouldn't she want you? You're a good man. The best. Fair and kind. Generous. And you don't have a face only Mum would love. Why shouldn't *you* get the woman you want, *if* you want her that is...?"

Chapter 37
Zee

Something in the Orange - Zach Bryan

"*Why shouldn't you get the woman you want, if you want her that is...?*"

The words travel over to me as I step down the stairs.

That's Cody talking.

"She doesn't want me."

Who doesn't?

"You're blind," Cody scoffs. "Of course she does."

"I'm not blind. She barely talks to me. We only just started eating together for breakfast. And I'm not talking about sex. I'm talking this. Life. *Here.*"

That's when my heart stops beating double-time.

They're discussing *me.*

I know that eavesdroppers never hear good of themselves, but I take a seat on the step anyway and crane my neck to hear as much as I can.

Especially as Cody was very quick to believe me when I denied that I set fire to the stables. Those all-seeing eyes of his

391

merely shifted from alert to lazy as he schmoozed me into making a sandwich for him.

"Like I said. She needs a charm offensive."

I have to hide my snort.

If Colt got any more charming, my panties would combust.

"What kind of charm offensive, though?" Colt inquires.

"Going riding together is a good way to start. Which horse are you giving her?"

"Jasmine."

Cody whistles. "Man, she'll look pretty as a picture on her."

"Right? Like a faerie queen."

He sounds... *dreamy*.

Not like dreamy hot. But *dreamy,* as if he's lost to his imaginings.

Cody grumbles, "You and your fantasy books."

"Screw you. Like you didn't devour Tolkien too."

My lips twitch as Cody retorts, "Yeah, thanks to you. You're the one who read them to me and Cole before bed. But I'm not putting my Arwen on a horse, am I? Bet the next thing you do is give her a quiver of arrows and a bow!"

"Arwen was half-elven. You need to read the trilogy again—"

"Why are we eavesdropping on my brothers?"

I jerk forward, nearly toppling off the step until Callan saves me, shoving a hand over my mouth to soften my yell. He's so smooth it's criminal for a geeky eighteen-year-old.

I relax though, watching as he settles on the step beside me once he lets go and has assured himself I'm safe.

"They're talking about me," I whisper.

"What's Cody doing here?"

"Got into some kind of accident."

Callan rolls his eyes. "Dumbass."

Because the insult is a throwaway—panic flickers in his eyes —I tut. "I thought I told you to quit it with the attitude around me. You can be yourself."

He huffs.

"You can," I assure him. "I won't judge you for it. You're allowed to be scared for your brother."

His nod is all the answer I know I'll get out of him.

When I tune into the conversation in the kitchen, they're still talking about Arwen and Jasmine.

"Jasmine's pure white," Callan explains. "A Camarillo." He tugs on my hair. "Your coloring'll fit." Then, his gaze turns disapproving. "Not that your sweater and jeans will."

"I'm not the most beautiful last-gen High Elf Middle-earth has ever seen."

Callan grumbles, "Trust you to have read the books."

"You haven't?"

"I'm not into that stuff. I like steampunk. Duh. You should know that already."

"I did but I figured Colt would have read it to you as a bedtime story."

He hunches his shoulders. "He started to but it gave me nightmares."

I pat his hunched shoulder. "You might enjoy them now. Though I'm not getting dressed up in a big white gown to cosplay Arwen!"

The teasing eases his discomfort. "You could at least wear a white sweater."

"I have one but it's not warm enough for the weather." I nudge him with my elbow and lift my finger to my mouth when the brothers stop bitching about *The Lord of the Rings*.

"Less of the Tolkien," Cody grouses. "It's not like I'm about to have more time on my hands to do a deep dive. And more importantly, what are you going to do about her?"

"Sounds ominous," Callan whispers.

"No, he's on the same offensive as you are." I shoot him a knowing look, watching him flush at the jig being up, though he still goes for broke.

"I'm not on any offensive."

"Matchmaking wasn't on your to-do list?"

Before he can answer, Colt does. "Not much I can do. I gave her time to settle in here. She has to figure out she's not a McAllister anymore. She's a Korhonen."

"*That* sounds ominous," I mumble.

Callan shakes his head. "Comes with perks."

"Doubtful. For you, yes. Not for me."

"That's probably what he means. Colt's always said you never burned down the stables. It's time he makes sure everyone's on the same page."

"Is that why you never asked me if I did it? Because Colt told you it wasn't me?"

"Of course."

I knew he had faith in Colt, but the extent of it still makes my heart skip a beat. Because when Callan had learned this news, Colt hadn't believed me to be innocent.

I'd been like him once upon a time.

From Colt's lips to my ears—I'd have believed it if he told me the sky was purple and grass was orange.

They'd been more complicated times, yet oddly simple too.

Now, things are simple, yet oddly complicated.

"Heard about Bea Grantley."

"Who from?"

"Bast Frobisher." That's Theo's brother and, if memory serves, he and Cody were tight in school. "Says you fired Marvin Grantley and that she's moved into one of our properties in town."

"That's Theo's doing," is all Colt says.

"Right."

"No, it is. He had to convince her to leave Grantley while she was in the hospital. Didn't realize you and Bast were still friendly."

"Of course. We always kept in touch." Cody sighs. "Callan told me about Lydia Armstrong blackmailing you."

My ears prick.

"We should stop eavesdropping—"

I ignore Callan and grab his arm to keep him sitting.

"Callan brought that up with you?"

"They arrested you! Of course, he did."

"How many times? I wasn't arrested."

"Called in for questioning, then."

"If you're going to be the new marshal, you should be aware of the difference."

Cody derides, "Stop being an ass. What's this about poison pen letters?"

"Callan told you about that too?"

"Yeah, after Zee received one. That was the first and only blackmail note."

I gape at Callan. "You knew I received one when I didn't?"

He shrugs. "I always check the mail first. You know about them?"

"*Clearly.* Just not that I was getting them too. What blackmail note?"

"Callan was worried, Colt, and I don't blame him," Cody rumbles.

"There's no need to be."

"They must have had probable cause—"

"Maybe they did. But I have an alibi. Zee."

"You weren't behind the wheel, were you?" Cody asks in an aside.

"No! Jesus H. Christ, Cody. What do you take me for?"

"A man who'll do anything to protect the people he cares about." Before Colt can say a word, Cody continues, "Did you pay the blackmail note?"

"Of course I did. She was threatening Zee. And as much of a bitch as Lydia was, the Armstrongs were on the brink of losing everything—"

"Fuck, Colt! You weren't her daddy. Who pays off a blackmailer because they feel sorry for them?"

Callan crows, "Daddy Colt, that's who."

Have he and Tee been talking behind my back or something?

Still, as insane as Colt is and as much as I understand my brothers-in-law's disbelief, it's such a *him* thing to do.

"Anyway, the Armstrongs have already lost their daughter, Cody. If the cash helped them out then—"

"You're crazy."

"Have you lost a daughter?"

"No."

"Do you know if your daughter is dead or alive?"

"No, but—"

"No. No buts."

"How did you know it was Lydia?"

He grunts. "Theo happened to mention one day that he saw Lydia up here, hanging around our mailbox."

"That was dumb on her part."

Colton snorts. "I never said she was eligible for Mensa, Cody, just that she was grief-stricken. Why do you think I wasn't worried once I paid her off? I knew it'd pan out when their house was secured."

"I'm not sure who's crazier. You or Lydia Armstrong."

"She's dead. The dead don't blackmail."

"You're lucky they didn't detain you again."

"Clyde did it and Reilly's sitting on his hands."

"You think he's corrupt?"

"I don't 'think.' I know."

The sound of a chair shifting backward has both Callan and me jerking to our feet.

Loudly, I mutter, "Callan, I told you I hate playing first-person shooter games!"

He picks up on my lead and then winks at me like this is some great subterfuge. *This kid, I swear.* "You just haven't played the right one."

"Now Cody's home, you can play with him."

"He always wins," he grumbles as we trudge, extra noisily, down the steps.

On the final landing, that's when I see Colt standing there, looking up at me, a soft grin curving his lips.

Above me, there's a picture window that lets in the sun at certain times of the day. It's uncanny how he stands in the center of the puddle of light that shines through the glass.

It makes him look like he's wearing a halo.

At my prolonged stare, his smile only deepens.

But it's the gleam in his eyes that seals my fate.

Because this man *owns* me.

And for the first time, I feel as if I might own him back...

Chapter 38
Colt

Wicked Game - Chris Isaak

Her first step into our private stables takes us longer than a first step ought to.

"It's all right," I assure her. "You're allowed inside."

Her harrumph is reassuringly impatient. "Do you know how many times I've sneaked inside the Korhonen stables?"

"I can hazard a guess if you give me some time to work it out—"

"It's weird being allowed to enter. It's like the devil passing through church gates."

"That's extreme, isn't it?"

"Not if you'd asked our great-grandaddies."

She's not wrong...

The tension between our families lessened with the passing of that generation. Ranching in the modern world became hard enough without neighbors cattle rustling and sabotaging one another for shits and giggles.

In one hand, I have a bag of snacks she could need after

exercising, so with my free one, I slide it beside hers and tangle our fingers. "Come on. You're invited in."

As I cross the threshold, I gently urge her alongside me.

The scents of the stables immediately welcome me, but it's Callan's stock horse, Leviathan, butting my shoulder that makes me smile.

Turning to her, I run my hand along her nose. There's a tug on my arm, from Zee this time, and suddenly, she's standing beside me.

"Leviathan," she exclaims.

"How did you know?"

"Callan described her. Chestnut, but she looks like she's been dipped in paint from the forelegs on."

I scratch behind Levi's ears. "That's not a bad description. Cole says she's like salt water meeting fresh."

"She's beautiful." Her fingers hover as if she's afraid to bridge the gap while her other hand trembles in mine.

But Levi's an old pro—she's had to be with Callan as an owner.

The kid can ride like he was born in the saddle, but on her back is the only time he's ever rowdy. Little heathen. I was always tempted to put him in the junior rodeo but I know he hates crowds.

Levi's muzzle seeks out Zee's hand, demanding her due—adoration.

"Fuck," she whispers.

A frown puckers my brow as realization strikes. "Wait a minute. You haven't ridden since the fire, have you?"

Her mouth trembles. "I couldn't. Not after... Then Jez passed when I was seventeen and I never wanted to..."

"I'm so goddamn sorry for not trusting you, Zee." It's the only thing I can think to say and it's not enough. It'll never be enough.

All these years, she's borne the blame and she couldn't bring herself to fucking ride.

The urge to strangle my father has never been as strong as it is right now. But it's no worse than what I want to do to myself.

My lack of faith—

"It's okay."

"It's not."

Levi knows that's bullshit too because she pushes Zee with her head. A happy chuckle drifts from her, one that urges a smile out of me.

"Didn't your *grand-mère* make you?"

"You know she didn't rely on me for help around the ranch. Said I was a liability."

"I never understood that."

Her fingers drift over Levi's muzzle. "I've never seen Callan ride her." *Change of subject—right.*

"He gets up early and takes her out onto the property."

She quirks a brow. "How early?"

"Four AM."

"Seriously?"

"It's the only thing he does that's normal on the ranch," I say dryly. "It started after Mum left. He didn't like to be in the house without me there so he'd follow me around. He was so cute back then."

"He had separation anxiety."

"Something like that."

She peeps a look at me, for the first time taking her eyes off Levi. "It must have been hard. You were only young yourself. I was selfish back then. I didn't realize how much pressure there was on you, didn't realize how much pressure *I* added onto you—"

"You didn't add any pressure."

"I did. I was in the stables when I shouldn't have been. And I was needy." Her nose crinkles. "We spent a lot of time together when you probably had other stuff to do."

"I never thought of it that way. I liked your company. It was a sea of normalcy in a world of chaos," I tell her, my tone calm. "That's really how you earned your nickname. You were the only person who ever knew what was going on with me. I couldn't tell my brothers. They depended on me too much. I had to be the strong one. I didn't need to be that with you. I needed to be me."

"Honestly?"

Our gazes clash. "100%."

Her lips curve. It's infinitesimal, but I notice it. "Why?"

"Loki, probably. I came to him to escape and you saw me with him so you picked up on stuff by association.

"I didn't know you could share a heart horse until I saw you with him. Do you want to know what one of my biggest regrets has always been?"

"Aside from the obvious?" she rasps.

"Uh-huh. It's that I didn't get to see you ride him. You never did. I think that's a damn shame."

"I didn't need to. I enjoyed being with him."

"I know. But I'd still have liked to see you ride him." I clear my throat. "Speaking of, do you want to meet your mount?"

She gives Levi a final rub to her ears before she takes a step back and glances around. "I don't know why I'm surprised the stables look this way."

There's barely any wood here. It's mostly concrete with steel joists.

"Callan insisted."

"I bet all the tack is labeled, right?"

"Yeah." I grin. "Most of the food and supplements are too. We have a multitude of printouts for every horse, every day, every week. He enjoys it though.

"God only knows what he'll be like when we build a horse barn for the breeding program."

She tugs on my hand. "You're restarting it?"

"I was always going to but I wanted to wait until Clyde died," I admit. "Now, I don't need to."

"Why?"

"Why wait?" My jaw works. "I never liked him around the horses."

"He was... cruel?"

"He was. I swear the first time I hit him was built-up rage from the last time I saw him on Jude—his Irish X. I wanted to kill him. I settled on beating the shit out of him."

"No one ever dared say anything to the SPCA, I'm guessing."

"No. You know what he's like. Had everyone under his

402

bootheel. Plus, he had the RCMP officers so far up his ass, they were his resident butt plugs. It was a relief when the old inspector retired and Burbanks got shipped in from Saskatoon."

"It's good news about the marshal office, isn't it?"

"You overheard that?"

"Cody told me."

"Yeah, it's good news." I gently guide her down the pristine aisle. "Out with the old, in with the new. And Cody runs a tight ship so there'll be less corruption around the county too. Exactly what we need."

"Agreed. How much of the stables is wood?"

"As little as possible. Everything's concrete or metal. It's as fireproofed as we can make it."

She exhales. "Good."

"Did Cody ask you about the fire?"

"You know him well."

"Of course I do. Did he?"

Zee tugs on her necklace and rubs her thumb over the medallion. "Yes."

He must have believed her or he wouldn't have asked her to make a sandwich.

"He's always been a good judge of character. Did he ask who..."

"No. I gather he assumes it was faulty wiring like the reports said but he wanted to check."

"Too protective for his own good."

"Maybe. Maybe not."

I bring her to a standstill beside Jasmine's stall, watching the horse carefully—she's known to be bitchy with strangers.

"Hey, beautiful girl," Zee breathes, the adoration in her tone exactly what Jas needs to hear.

It's also what *I* needed to hear.

Memories flicker, blurring the past and the present.

How many times I heard her talk to him...

God, I miss Loki.

"God, I miss him," she rasps.

"Me too."

"Thank you." Tears collect in her eyes. "For trusting me with her."

I just swipe at one as it trickles down her cheek.

Jas neighs, nudging Zee's shoulder in a silent demand for attention. I dip into the bag I brought with me and transfer a carrot over to her.

She takes it with a smile and offers it to Jas, who whickers before accepting the donation.

As she's chomping, Zee continues stroking her, gentling Jas to her scent, her presence.

"Jas is strongheaded," I warn. "Likes to do her own thing, but she's a solid ride. Fast. We can use Frank today if you want to take it easy seeing as it's your first ride in a while."

"No. It's fine. Like you say, easier than riding a bike."

I smirk at Jas who nudges my shoulder, not content with one human's attention today. "Might have exaggerated."

"You? *Never.*" Amusement leaches into the words. "Where's the tack room?"

Twenty minutes later, I watch as she croons and murmurs to Jas as she gently stretches her hind and forelegs, encouraging her to do the same with her neck as she holds a carrot out of reach to each side. Jas might not be happy about being 'teased,' but I am—Zee remembers more than she lets on. I still have to prompt some ranch hands to do this and it always pisses me off.

Takes less than five minutes to stretch a horse out but they begrudge it. Assholes.

When Jas's limbered up to Zee's satisfaction, she saddles her and attaches a bag that I stuff with the snacks I brought along. I still keep an eye on Zee, mostly to make sure she goes through all the safety checks, but she does.

After being raised with horses your whole life, when you *love* them, you don't forget the monotonous routine that's the precursor to the fun stuff. I cut Callan a lot of slack over the years, but never with the horses. Many life lessons are instilled from caring for these noble beasts.

Once Jas's ready, I leave them to continue their acquaintance while I greet Fen, who welcomes me with an impatient neigh.

I rub my knuckles along the bridge of his nose and chide, "As if I'd forget you, bud." I pass him a carrot which he devours as I prepare him for the ride.

When I'm done, I guide him out of his stall and then head for Jas's.

Finding Zee with her face pressed against the mare's, forehead to forehead, has something inside me tightening.

It reminds me of the past but also tells me that, for however long Zee's around, Jas'll be her ride.

Neither prospect saddens me.

"Zee?" I prompt.

She hums as she grabs the reins. Gently tugging on them, she leads Jas out of the stall and joins me in the aisle.

That's when she slips her foot into the stirrup and kicks her leg up and over.

"The joys of being under six feet," I tease, knowing that with Fen's height—nineteen hands—and my own, there's no way I'm getting out of the stables *elegantly* if I mount him inside.

"There have to be some perks," she agrees, her hips rocking from side to side as she finds her seat.

I don't move from my spot, not wanting to rush her.

It might have been a decade since she was on horseback but her posture's still there—she'll ache like hell tomorrow though.

"Did you check your monitor?"

"Yes, Daddy."

My brows lift. *Well.*

She peeps at me, her cheeks flushed. Clearly, that did something for her too.

Both of us ignore the buzz that lit between us and she walks Jas forward, hands relaxed at the reins.

I follow her outside, watching the sway of her slim hips. There, I bound onto Fen's back, and together, we trot onto the small, graveled path that'll lead to one of the hundreds of gates on the property.

Neither of us says a word.

I keep an eye on her, making sure she's okay, maintaining a slow pace that'd have Fen chomping at the bit if we used one, but Jas keeps him in line for me—Fen has the hots for her and tends to let her have her head.

I know how he goddamn feels.

Zee's a balanced rider. Quiet and gentle with the bit and reins, constantly leaning over Jas's neck to praise her and smooth a hand over her mane. It doesn't take long for Jas to get used to Zee's much lighter weight, either. Or the saddle.

I've never been light and I stopped using a saddle with Jas years ago, but she doesn't appear to be affected by the difference.

When we make it onto the open prairie, she drops the reins. Jas stops immediately but with a soft click of the tongue and a gentle nudge of Zee's knee, she continues onward while her rider raises her arms and opens them to the world.

It's like a stretch and a homecoming all at the same time.

I stay silent, but I watch her. More than I do the path ahead. I trust Fen to guide me safely, for one. Mostly though, she's more interesting than anything Pigeon Creek, hell, *Canada* has to offer.

The sun glints off her dirty blonde hair, making her pale peach skin gleam gold. When she turns to look at me, her mossy green eyes glitter in the light beneath the hat I plopped on her head before we left the house.

She's not Arwen—she's more. Everything.

I stare at her and the years blur again.

I rarely got to see her on Jez because she'd sneak in and sneak out of the stables, using a worn path between our properties to ride onto the Seven Cs.

But here she is.

My past.

My present.

My future.

Fen neighs his displeasure when my knees dig into his sides, and though I automatically correct my seat, it's like something life-changing occurred.

Something that has me reeling.

There's always been this blank space in my life.

And it's shaped like her.

"Did Callan uncover how Fen got loose?"

"No. But we're changing where we put him out to pasture."

My answer was unintentionally brisk because my mind isn't on the ranch or that hit-and-run or anything other than—

"What are you thinking?"

I'm jerked back to myself with the question. It's curious, not concerned.

So I look at her and I admit, "That there are no words to describe how much I missed you."

Chapter 39
Zee

His statement might as well make the hard-packed soil beneath Jas's hooves quake.

But it also settles a decade-old hurt that's been like a tear in my soul.

How easily I was forgotten.

How easily he blamed me.

How easily he moved on.

I tug on Jas's reins to bring her to a halt, not wanting to think about how she gently stops as if she's an extension of me.

Maybe it's because I'm on horseback, grounded in a way that I haven't been in years that I ask, "Why should I forgive you?"

Another time, another place, I'd never have said that.

But Jas gives me strength.

This conversation, and the one he had with Cody, as well as what our kisses, plural, represent provide me with fuel.

"You shouldn't," is his answer, but he leans over and his hand snags ahold of mine.

His fingers are callused. Rough from hard work. He's no backseat manager like his father, content to sit in his office and let others run the ranch.

I've seen him with the horses out front, breaking the older

foals in. I've seen him head onto the range with his staff. My window gives me too good a view of him at work.

Colton Korhonen plays at nothing.

That means *this* isn't a play either.

I slide my fingers through his, knotting them together, squeezing his knuckles. That's when hope starts to form like a slowly building storm that's gaining ground, steadily building into a tornado—I can't help but feel I'll be blown away if I don't hunker down with him.

His voice is low, gritty, as he rumbles, "I can't give you the world, Zee, but I can give you the Seven Cs. This place has my heart until and *if* you're willing to safekeep it."

My chin butts my chest. "You don't love me."

A soft bark of laughter escapes him. It isn't loaded with humor, more a release of tension. "I think I've always loved you. Just like you've always loved me. But girls are smarter than boys. You figured it out sooner than I did."

"That was ten years ago," I dismiss, though he's right.

"Yeah. Ten years ago when you were jailbait. I saw you as a kid. Because you were. You were to be protected and shielded. Now, I feel the same—" There's no denying the sharp ache in my chest is disappointment. "—but *different*. It's an evolution I didn't anticipate and that'd probably have never developed if my sperm donor hadn't forced us to be together."

Fen, working on his own agenda, steps closer to Jas. I could think it's a move on Colt's part, but there's no mistaking the designs the Percheron X has on the white Camarillo who deigns to accept the attention.

Just like I do.

When Colt's other hand cups my cheek, I could pull back.

But I don't.

When his thumb smoothes along my jawline, I could nudge Jas into a jog.

But I don't.

No, I tilt my head to the side so his large, warm, callused palm can touch more of my face.

"Don't go," he rasps. "Stay."

My eyes flutter to a close. "I wasn't going anywhere."

"Sure you were. One round of IVF or ten, you were going to leave. Whether it was to the Bar 9 or to be the first McAllister to live in Pigeon Creek proper in two hundred years, you were going to go."

"Not New York?"

"No. A part of me used to worry... but you wouldn't deny me or the child a relationship."

"You know that but didn't know I couldn't hurt Loki?"

There's a slight pressure on my jaw as tension whispers through him. "I'll never forgive myself for thinking the worst of you, and I'll spend every day that you let me helping you work up the courage to go to the cops about Clyde."

"Cody'll be the head of the marshals soon."

"Would you tell him?"

"M-Maybe."

His thumb pinches my chin. "Good girl."

He takes control of Jas's reins. I'm not sure if she's my wingwoman or a traitor but she remains steady as I find him taking up a whole lot of my personal space, which is some feat on a horse.

He moves ever nearer.

Looms over me.

His face takes up the horizon ahead until all I can see is him.

Until all I *want* to see is him.

A breath shudders from me as his mouth finds mine. It's our second kiss today, but it's all the more powerful because of his admission. Because of where we are. Because of the creature I'm riding. *Because.*

The tremor that works through my body should agitate Jas, who's a very sensitive creature. But maybe she *is* my wingwoman. She plants—stays firm and holds fast—as Colt's hand slides around my nape and pins me in place as he teases my mouth. Dropping soft and reverent kisses here and there. Cherishing me with how gentle he is at first. Little pressure aside from how he's controlling the weight of my head.

I release a soft moan, unable to believe this is happening and how good it feels.

How right.

Then, *fuck*, both our phones issue an alert about my blood sugar.

Talk about the worst timing ever.

I shouldn't let him take responsibility, but I watch as he jumps into action—his phone's out, the reading comes next, and he clucks his tongue at Jasmine to bring her nearer.

The next thing I know, I'm shifting in the saddle and removing my feet from the stirrups as I turn to face him better while he hand-feeds me gummy bears from Jas's saddle bag.

I didn't want that to interrupt us, but being cared for by him keeps my arousal buzzing in the background. Enough that I don't argue when he hands me a granola bar and a bottle of water a short while later.

When he's happy with my blood sugar, he repacks the saddle bag and I pounce.

The moment our mouths collide, he hums—he's not turned off by the alert. "You taste like honey," he teases, his tongue exploring me like he's trying to get his own sugar high.

I'm more than willing to be his sweet treat.

I relax more, letting him control the pace because, God help me, that's all I've ever wanted.

His soft, teasing nips have me parting my lips and his tongue slides home.

As we connect, both of us groan. I cup his face too, holding him in place now, not letting him go. Not allowing him to leave me.

I don't think I could bear it if he did.

Everything in me feels both tight and hot as if this coiled spring has been charging for as long as I've known him.

He's right—he could never have seen me the way that I did him because I was a child and he wasn't a monster.

But I'm not a child anymore.

And the ten years' distance, the ten years of separation, if nothing else, has given him a glimpse of that—I'm a woman.

Someone he missed.

Someone he wants.

Someone he loves.

I grab his belt buckle and drag him toward me as he thrusts his tongue against mine, sending sensation charging through my veins. Then, I shriek when his hands somehow find my hips and he hoists me from Jas's saddle and onto Fen's back.

It's such a seamless move that I'm almost jealous at how easy that was for him, assuming there was practice—

"I used to bring Callan onto the saddle with me when he was younger and got scared," he rumbles. The words make the sensitive skin of my lips feel like they're vibrating. "Retract your claws, little cat."

That's when I realize I was digging my nails into his nape.

Rather than argue with him about being jealous, I slot my legs around his waist, moaning when I feel the pressure of his dick at the crotch of my jeans.

As he holds me close, his hands slide down to my ass, and that's when he gently nudges Fen with his knees.

A keening whine escapes me as the horse's gait has his hardness thrusting over my sensitive core.

It feels too good.

So raw and real and natural.

We're out here, under the sky, the prairie around us, our scents mingled with Fen's and Jas's permeating the air, nothing but us for miles and miles.

It's primal and it triggers something in me that I didn't know I was still capable of feeling after being 'civilized' by city living.

The urge for skin-on-skin contact takes over me like a craving.

I let him go so that I can unfasten the buttons on his plaid shirt. His fingers put a halt to my ministrations. "Whoa, Zee."

I can tell he wants to slow this down but I can't.

That's the last thing I want. If anything, I need to pick up where we left off this morning.

Ignoring him, I find a pocket of space and slip my fingers beneath the buttoned shirt.

Only to find a freakin' Henley.

My growl is explosive and feral and it epitomizes how I feel. How *he* makes me feel.

I grab his jaw and hold him in place as I push my forehead onto his. "I've wanted you since I knew what teenagers did together over in Pleasant Park, Colton. Touch me. *Please.* I feel like I'm going crazy!"

His expression heats up but I know it's the way my words wane into a broken whimper that has him angling backward so he can drag off his shirt, a couple flying buttons be damned. Then, he draws the Henley over his head, arching up to settle the fabric under his ass to keep it from flying away.

My tongue cleaves to the roof of my mouth at the sight of him.

He's so different than how he used to be. While the muscles from hard work were there before, he's matured. Like a fine whiskey.

My fingers spread over his chest, nails scoring red ravines over his abdomen as I explore what has always been forbidden to me.

I can't decide if this is a dream or some kind of delusion, but he feels *so* damn good to my touch that I never want to stop. And then my fingertips brush over scar tissue—burns—and while I'm thrown back in time to a night that changed our lives for the worse, I don't stop touching him.

Won't.

I *can't* let go of this connection. Not when I'm feeling his courage. His strength. These scars maketh the man. They're proof of who he is and what he is. Tangible evidence that he'd keep me safe if ever I were in danger too.

I release him only to find the hem of my sweater and to raise it and my undershirt overhead, leaving the fabric to puddle between us as my hat tumbles off and goes flying.

Neither of us gives a damn as he returns his mouth to mine. This time, his fingertips dig into my ass as he actively encourages me to ride him, his knees directing Fen into a swifter pace that amps up the friction between us.

Soft whimpers explode from me as I press my chest to his, bare skin finally touching bare skin.

I sob against his throat, head tucked underneath his chin as release cascades inside me.

It's rough and ready—just like this encounter.

Unexpected and all the hotter for it.

When I sag into him, the abrupt blast of pleasure taking the starch from my bones, he presses small kisses to the line of my jaw.

His tongue explores my mouth like he has all the time in the world. I know he doesn't. But the reverence is back, and it's not in his kiss anymore. It's in his touch. It makes it seem as if I'm his axis.

He's still hard between us. A solid band of heat that makes me crave a deeper connection.

I've dated a lot of guys, but in the past couple years, I've mostly stopped because Tee's right—the dating pool is grim.

And I've always had this man to compare against whatever loser I met on an app.

Yeah, he's always been the measure.

Always.

I can admit that now.

I kiss him back, surging into him, wanting him to find his release too, but he doesn't use his hold on my ass to jerk off.

No, he just tastes me.

Savors me.

Enjoys me.

I feel like a vintage bottle of red wine that needs to be opened to breathe. That's decanted into lead crystal. That's sampled like a delicacy.

Curling my fingers around two of his belt loops, in turn, I relish the act of being savored.

Of being enjoyed.

Of being tasted.

It's novel.

There's no rush.

No groping.

No quick sprint to the third act.

God, it sums him up all round.

My nails scrape through his hair, making him shudder, but

that's when a whip of wind lashes at us. We break off when I shiver and he untangles my sweater, obviously wanting to cover me up, but I twist away, finally noticing that we made it to one of the McAllister lakes.

One of *my* lakes, seeing as I'm the majority shareholder of the Bar 9.

That Fen took this path and that Jas followed tells me Colt's not as much of an upholder of the rules as I thought.

The water beckons me as soon as I set eyes on the glistening surface that sunlight bounds off of, the stillness revealing crystalline depths that remind me of the beauty of home.

I work fast to disentangle myself from his hold and jump from Fen to the lakeshore.

"Zee!" he calls as my abrupt move jostles the saddle blanket on the stallion, but I ignore him to wade to the waterline.

As he follows me, I get to work on my fly, and when he grabs my arm, panic in his gaze, it fades as he stares at my hands and what they're busy doing.

The slow smile decimates me, but it's when he rumbles, "Again, chaos?" that my heart skips *two* beats.

His fingers slot through my hair as he strokes that big paw of his over my head while his soft, teasing drawl sends ripples of warmth throughout me.

I missed him so damn much.

It's as if permitting myself to accept how large the chasm he left behind in my life rams it home harder than ever.

"You going skinny-dipping?"

"What else?" Then, pouting, I grumble, "You didn't think I was going to hurl myself into the water, did you? End it all after my first orgasm with you?"

He pulls a face. "You need to give a man time to register what's going on before you dash off a horse, then dart *half-naked* over to a lake."

"Were you going to jump in after me like last time?" I joke.

"Where my chaos goes, I follow."

How his gaze darkens makes me shiver and it has nothing to do with the wind chill.

I must be mad stripping off here, but it feels right.

Like how it's supposed to unfold.

With our eyes locked, my fingers unfasten my fly. Aside from that, I don't bother with my jeans yet. I toe out of my sneakers first then drag the denim and my panties down my legs. When I straighten, his jaw's like obsidian. There's a tick pinging the muscles there, straining under how hard he's gritting his teeth.

Deliciously satisfied by that reaction, I unfasten my bra, letting it tumble onto the lakeshore.

Still focused on him, I retreat a step.

And another.

And another.

Not stopping until the water collides with my feet.

I continue, letting myself wade deeper into the lake, grateful that this one is a natural mineral hot spring.

"Are you a chicken, Colt?" I tease.

I swipe my hand across the surface, letting fine droplets skim around me in an arc.

He doesn't answer my taunt.

At least, not with words.

He toes out of his boots.

I stop messing around.

Nothing's more interesting than him.

Than what he's doing.

Than his focus on me.

Than his actions.

My heart pounds like it wants to crack through my ribs as he unbuckles his belt.

There's nothing decorative about that buckle. Much like the rest of the man. You'd never know he was a Korhonen at first glance.

Then, his fingers are messing with his fly.

Off his jeans go.

Along with his boxer briefs.

My throat bobs as he stands there naked for a millisecond before wading into the water to join me.

Every step he takes brings him closer to me.

Finally, he's there.

417

One hand slides around my waist, and the other swoops in at my hip, drawing me into him so that my front slots against his.

There are probably a thousand words we should share, but I don't have it in me to utter them. Instead, I lean on tiptoe, the warm water slipping over my calves and knees like silk, spreading a chill throughout my extremities when the wind hits me, but it's easy enough to ignore as our mouths meet again.

At long last.

I sag into him the second his lips part and I let him take over me how I've always wanted him to. How I've needed him to. Forever.

This goes deeper than dominance and submission.

It's my soul knowing I'm safe with him. My body. My being. Maybe one day, my heart too.

I cross my wrists around his neck to hold myself as close to him as possible. My breasts rub over the hairs on his chest, stimulating delicate nerve endings in a way that another man's mouth wouldn't have.

This is Colton.

My Colt.

I can feel myself melting, all my barriers lowering because he's the only man I've ever truly wanted and he's here. In my arms. Wanting me back. No constraints. Just us.

I can feel *it* too.

His want. His need.

He's a thick brand at my stomach. Hot and hard and pulsing with life.

I think back to the last time we were in a lake together—I asked for IVF and a divorce.

Nothing could be further from my mind.

He thrusts his tongue against mine, making me feel like a banquet. Exploring and tasting and nipping and stroking. His hands don't roam. Just his lips and tongue and teeth and mouth. It's the most intense kiss I've ever experienced, which is impressive because he already takes up my top three kisses *ever*. This one makes me feel like it could last an eternity without either of us stopping for air.

I melt further into him. All soft lines to his hardness. Then finally, as he finishes dominating my mouth, his hands drop to the curve of my ass and he kneads one of my butt cheeks.

His knuckles dip deeper, rubbing the outer periphery of my folds, making me moan and jostle in his hold. I'm still sensitive from before and that single touch exposes how wet I am.

I part my legs—I have no choice.

I want nothing more than for him to touch me, and giving him full access is the smartest way to make that happen.

His knuckles move higher. Higher. Higher still.

"Eyes on me, Zee," he demands when my lashes flutter shut.

God help me.

I open them and nearly swoon at the hunger raging in his.

For me.

Breathing stilted, I grow tense, waiting for that connection of bare skin on bare skin, and I cry out, mouth falling from his as I turn lax in his arms.

It's so simple it's crazy that I'm this sensitive, but I can't explain it. Don't want to. This is Colt—that's the only explanation I need. I was born to melt for this man.

It was written into my DNA.

His nose rubs along mine before he presses kisses to my brows, temple, and forehead as he runs his knuckles over my clit.

My muscles jolt, limbs growing tense with the oddly impersonal touch. "Do it properly," I moan.

"You want my fingers on this little pussy? Where do you want them? Tell me. I'll put them right where *you* need them."

With a shudder, I whisper, "On my clit. I need you to rub my clit."

"Like this?" The tips brush over it. "Or like this?" They move from side to side. "Or like this?" He moves the flat of his hand in a circle.

"Second one," I mumble, arching up and against him. "Oh!" The sound spills from me as he gives me what I asked for.

Unbidden, I shift my leg, hitching it so that it hooks around his hip and digs into his ass. It opens me up, granting him more access.

That's when his other hand joins in and the soft kisses he dots all over my face cease as he reunites our mouths.

With my focus divided, I drown in his kiss and his touch while one set of fingers rubs my clit and the other slide into me —first one, then two.

"So fucking tight," he groans before returning to devouring me.

My pussy clenches around his digits as he pleasures me, gracing me with his whole attention, giving me what I've unconsciously craved for years.

He slowly steals the air from my lungs, and my heart stutters as the tingles in my center arc out in a wide spray that affects my whole nervous system.

I'm so close—too close.

Just as I gasp for air, desperately choking on it as my head tips back in wonder at what he's making me feel, he stops touching me.

Distressed, I cry out, "No, don't. I need you, Colt. Please!"

But the fear he'll abandon me fades as he hooks his hand around my knee and hoists me into his arms.

With my legs butterflied around him, I can feel his dick rubbing up against my clit. His strength torments us both as he hovers me there, his tip brushing my heat in time to his pulse that throbs through his shaft.

"Do you want me, Susanne?"

I'm not sure why, but that he chose to call me Susanne *matters*.

"Always," I rasp, not caring about how many vulnerabilities I'm exposing to him.

His forehead plants on mine as we stare at the space between us.

I help guide the tip home but he does the rest—as soon as he's inside me, he controls the pace as gravity impales me upon him.

Inch by glorious inch, he fills me.

It's everything I dreamed it'd be back in the days when I

was clueless about sex, but it's also *more*. Because I'm not in the dark about sex anymore. I know it can suck and nothing about this does.

The sun beams overhead, droplets of water trickle down my calves, around me there's *my* land where the horses, as free as us, frolic in the shore nearby, and this man, a man I've always wanted but never been allowed to have, is inside me.

"Fuck! You feel so goddamn good, Zee."

Back to Zee.

That also matters.

My arms cling to him as I dig my heels into his taut asscheeks and use that as a fulcrum to thrust onto him.

It's difficult; the muscles in my abs and thighs are screaming, but it's worth it for that downward thrust where every inch of him sinks into me.

"You fill me so good," I garble.

That heat that seared my belly before brands my insides with his name, and the only thing that'll soothe it is his seed.

"I need you to come inside me, Colton."

When I buck into him, tormenting us both, tears pricking my eyes with relief and joy as he grinds out, "What are you doing to me?"

When his hands bite into my hips hard enough to leave marks later, I shudder and up the pace.

Faster, faster.

Enjoying his grunts and curses and heavy exhalations as I pleasure him. As I take control in a position where we depend on the other for stability.

"So good, too good."

That's when one hand lets go of my hips, the other arm bands around my spine for support, and his fingers find my clit.

A couple brushes of the tips to the nub and I'm shuddering like they're set on vibrate mode. His fingers are *not*, however, a sex toy, but they might as well be.

"Colt!" I scream, head tipping back as my climax detonates inside me—against my will.

And he feels every part of it because that old pal gravity has me turning into a vise around him, every one of his inches surrounded by my release.

He groans my name, long and low, but it starts with a hiss and ends with heavy, panting breaths as he comes inside me.

Raw.

I can feel him throbbing and it's everything I dreamed of and so much more because his forehead rests on my shoulder and each exhalation he makes brushes the upper swell of my breasts.

The peak hits us hard and keeps us locked together for endless moments.

But nothing lasts forever.

Eventually, he leaves me. His arms don't, though.

He rocks back a couple steps. "Brace yourself."

Still lost in my daze, I shriek when he tumbles us into the lake. I should have known it was a controlled motion because we don't collide. We simply slip into the water.

"Jerk," I cry.

His chuckle is tired as he moves us closer to the shore so that he can plant his ass on terra firma.

When he does, I thought he'd untangle us, but he doesn't. If anything, he settles back, the warm lake water cosseting us while I act as an unofficial blanket.

I don't complain, simply tip my head to the side and rest it over his heart.

His pulse turns calm and steady, with only a slight lilt to it that tells me he exerted himself.

I don't know why but it makes me sad. That union was in the past. *Already.*

A part of me is scared everything's in the past with him. We've never had a future together, and one certainly isn't promised...

"I missed you," I rasp, "and I never even had you."

I shouldn't have said that. I know that as soon as I let the words fall from my lips, but he doesn't shove me away at the reminder of times gone. Doesn't grow tense.

Instead, he asks, "Will you miss me now that you've had me?"

I didn't expect that answer. "I don't want to. I want this to be a step in the right direction."

"I don't deserve for you to stay. Not after how I treated you."

"Isn't that for me to decide?"

"You should send me to hell and—"

"Why would I do that when it would take you away from me?"

My hands find his arms and, nails digging into his biceps, I cling to him. He's always been so steady. So solid. Like the Pando tree whose roots spread far and wide for dozens of acres, able to weather any storm.

Even the fire, he weathered.

Eyes warming from my words, he cups my head, only there's no pressure to it. Mostly, I feel like it's an extension of his hug.

"Would you like to know when I started missing you?"

I nod, nose rubbing against the hair on his chest.

"The day I flew us here. That was compounded by walking in on you and Callan playing games."

"You missed me so soon?" I rear back so he can see me gaping at him. "And with Callan... why?"

"It's a tangled web of reasons... Our stay at The Manchester was a massive reminder of the change in our relationship. I missed what we used to have together. The ease of conversation. How it'd flow between us.

"Then, that you were making the effort with my kid brother who hates people in general. That you made him laugh, that you played games with him. That you were able to laugh freely with him and couldn't or wouldn't with me when, in the past..." Before I can say a word, he rumbles, "For reasons that I deserve. I knew that. But it's what made me miss you more. I never thought I'd have that with you again and it was my fault."

Maybe it's because we're both here naked, flaws out in the open, that I can whisper, "Why was it so easy to believe that I did it?"

"Because in my family, when you love someone, they hurt you." A heavy sigh escapes him. "There's nothing I can do to make up for what I did aside from striving to be the man you deserve, Zee. If you'll give me the chance..."

His initial words had me growing tense in his arms but I soften. Resting my forehead on his chest, I murmur, "Your damn father has a lot to answer for."

He grunts.

Sensing his disappointment, I clutch at his arms. "Isn't this me giving you a chance, Colton? In my family, when you love someone, they cherish that love. Apart from *Grand-mère*. But she's Venusian."

I feel rather than hear his huff of laughter. "You know Clyde was convinced last year that Mum was having an affair with your father. That Callan was his son."

"That asshole," I spit, glowering at Colt. "How dare he? He was the cheater. God, *he's* the monster!"

"What aren't you telling me, Zee? What makes you so scared of him?"

"The fire wasn't enough?"

"Maybe, but... you've always been scared of him. That fear's only strengthened with time."

"How about seeing what he put you through?"

He shakes his head. "You don't trust me yet. That's fine. But when you do, will you tell me then?"

I'm not sure why but that has me squirming on top of him. His arms let me loose which, though I wanted that, fills me with sadness. I don't go far. Just roll into the water.

He watches me. I half think he expects me to get up and dress, but I don't.

I stare over the massive lake before us.

"I saw Clyde with Marcy here once."

That has him tensing.

"What?!"

I peer at him. "A week after the fire. I had nowhere else to go so I came here. I think they had the same idea."

His nostrils flare. "Did he murder her?"

"No. At least, I didn't stick around long enough to see him do that. You think that's why she went missing?"

He curls upward, legs bending at the knee so he can rest his arms on them. "I've thought he had something to do with it for a while."

"So did Lydia Armstrong."

His mouth tightens. "You know about the letters?"

"I didn't know I'd received one until I heard you talking with Cody today, but everyone knows she blamed the Korhonens."

"How much did you overhear?"

"Do I look like Arwen on Jas?"

My lips curve when his ears burn red. "Maybe. You weren't dressed for the part."

"I didn't know you were into cosplay, or do I mean roleplay?"

"You don't know what I like." Before I can be offended, his gaze fixes on mine. "Yet."

And with that one word, it's like all the tension in me evaporates. It's a miracle that I don't flop back into the water.

There'll be a next time.

Thank God.

Yet.

"They were in a relationship?"

I swear our conversational shifts give me whiplash. "Yeah. They were having sex when I caught them. Your father's a dog."

"They saw?"

"No. I ran off."

"It was..."

"It wasn't rape," is my flat retort.

"Do you think he had something to do with Marcy's disappearance?"

"I used to think the triplets were his."

"Excuse me?!"

I lift my legs and rest them against my chest. Looping my arms around my shins, I hold myself as tightly as I can before I whisper, "But then they turned into miniature Daddies. There was a point where I knew Mom found it hard to look at them after he died—they were so alike. Little mirror images."

A hand settles on my back. "They were having an affair?"

"I have the unfortunate habit of seeing things I'm not supposed to."

His whole body stiffens. "That time, it wasn't consensual?"

I can't utter a word. So I tip my head to the side.

"How old were you?"

"Too young to see that."

His palm strokes along my spine before seeking my nape. Clasping me there, he murmurs, "What do you need me to do?"

The question takes me aback. Enough that I face him with a frown. "What do you mean? What *can* you do?"

There's a flatness to his gaze as he rasps, "Whatever you need of me."

Sputtering when I realize his intent, I scuttle closer. "The last thing I need is for you to turn into a vigilante, Colton." If I sound chiding, so be it, but then I repeat, "He's a monster."

He strokes his thumb over my jaw. "I'll make him pay."

It's a simple promise, but it isn't what I need to hear from him.

"I don't need you to do anything," I counter.

"The whole town believes—"

"—whatever the rumor mill wants it to." I hitch a shoulder. "I don't care what they think of me."

"That's why you haven't left the ranch since you got here, huh?" he jeers.

My nose crinkles. "It's rude to point out someone's flaws when you've slept with them."

"No sleeping was done."

"That's neither here nor there."

His lips tug into a grin and his hand settles at the center of my back. "Have you heard from him recently?"

"I'd have told you if I had."

"It's not like him to be so quiet."

"You think he's up to something?"

"Knowing him, yes. The hit-and-run was definitely unexpected but who knows what else he's scheming."

"Business-wise, can he do much if you're the head of the Seven Cs?"

"I'm the head of the company that owns the ranch. He's still in charge of the rest because he built that himself. That should keep him plenty busy. He's capable of dumb decisions but he makes high-risk moves on the stock exchange and they have big payouts. I have to figure that's how he's been keeping things afloat for so long with the oil field acting as his collateral."

"Are you investigating how he got away with lying about your uncle's will?"

"Bet your fine ass I am." At my snort, he asks, "Do you want to get out of the water?"

"No. I like it. Reminds me of when I was younger."

He's quiet then... "Is that why you found refuge in the lake that first day?"

"Used to do it all the time with Walker."

"Chaos," he teases lightly.

"I was forged in half-frozen water. If I had balls, they'd be made of ice by this point. At least this lake is the hot springs. But... I didn't expect this," I whisper eventually, basking in him, in this pocket of time where everything feels surreal and yet hyperreal.

His hand strokes over my hair. "Me either."

I lick my lips. "I-I think we don't need to worry about IVF anymore."

I thought he'd laugh. Instead, he tenses up, snags me around the waist, plops me on his lap, and then cups my cheeks so I'm looking square at him.

"How about that's a conversation we have when we're in the right place for it, hmm?"

"But the contract?" I half squeak.

"Fuck the contract." He kisses me. "Fuck the Seven Cs. Fuck the Bar 9. Let's have *this*. Here. Now. Us."

Because I never wanted anything more in my life, I nod. "It might be too late."

His gaze never leaves mine. "I'll use protection in the future."

"What if—"

"We deal with what comes." His jaw firms. "No divorce,

Zee. Be here *freely*. I've already paid off the Bar 9's debts. Your *grand-mère* won't lose her home and neither will the triplets. Be with me of your own free will or don't be with me at all."

Swallowing, I start to answer but he shakes his head.

"Think about it. Think about what being my wife for real means. Because once we agree that this is *it*, you're mine."

His words make me melt, but I'm a modern freakin' woman. If I let him get away with murder this early on, there'll be no saving him down the line.

"You can't base this off of a hookup," I spout.

"I told you earlier—men are forever late to the party. We always clicked. It was the age gap that screwed things up for us. Rightfully so. But if you'd been in my class, I'd have had a ring on your finger—"

"I was a McAllister!"

"I want to say that I'd have dealt with the outcry, but I wouldn't have had the balls until I was eighteen. Still, that's what I'd have done. You'd have been mine then and there and we'd probably have three or four kids roaming the ranches by now." His large palms tip my head backward. "Think about it."

I am.

Three of *his* kids.

God, I've never wanted kids in my life. Not outside of duty. But the prospect of—

My throat bobs but he shakes his head. Again. "Tomorrow."

I scowl. "I can make up my own mind!"

"I'm not letting you think up ways to end this in the future. I'm giving you the time and space to decide because, baby, if you're not ready *or willing* for me to claim you as my wife, then this thing'll burn out before it's had a chance to begin.

"I meant it when I said that once I make you mine, there's no going back. Do you hear me?"

Oh, I heard him.

So did my heart.

Every part of me knows I should reject his Neanderthal-like stance, but mostly, I'm overwhelmed that Colton is saying these things to *me*.

About *us*.

And here's where I get my proof that, despite Tee's claims, masochism isn't my jam. Because maybe I *should* want to make him pay, make him earn my forgiveness, but why would I do that when it would shove distance between us?

Ten years was distance enough.

I just want him.

Forever, him.

Reaching between us where I can feel his cock twitching into hardness, his own words turning him on as much as they do me, I straddle him and bring our sexes together.

Gazes locked on one another, I rub the tip through my folds until I find my entrance. Pre-cum and his last release ease his path as I slide him home, neither of us bringing up protection, both of us more focused on how good it feels to reconnect and so swiftly too.

My eyelids flutter to half-mast, but his remain open. There's a ferocity in his expression that makes me melt. That the most feminine part of me wants to soothe.

I lift onto my knees and ride him.

All around me, the water laps and kisses my skin, making sensitive shivers work their way up and down my spine. Whenever I breach the surface, I can feel it whisper over my clit, adding a caress that makes this a million times hotter.

His hands find my ass and he pulls the cheeks apart, letting more water touch me, brushing where we're joined, the soft waves from my movements making me hyperaware of our union.

Quickening my pace, I chase release. I've no right to come so many times in one day, but apparently, the universe doesn't agree. His being a caveman shouldn't turn me on, yet those words of his are like magic to me.

My nails scrape over his back, leaving marks that'll be there until tomorrow. Deep score marks that are as much a claim as the one he wants to stake on me.

I can feel everything in me tighten before the implosion strikes.

It decimates me—in the best possible way.

His hoarse yell is music to my ears as both of us rise and fall together, bound by the water, forged by the land that bore us, united in a way that no laws made by mankind could ever reap...

And whether he wants me to tell him tomorrow or today, the truth was set in stone the first day I stumbled into his stables and he found me there.

I'm his.

Forever.

Chapter 40
Colt

Are You With Me - nilu

It's the motorbikes that wake me.

The second the heavy rumble of those damn crank-shafts rattle through the silent night air, I sit up in bed.

My empty bed.

I have a pissed-off wife next door who thinks I don't respect her judgment calls, but that's the least of my problems.

Swiftly, I roll out of bed, grateful that I was too tired yesterday to toss my stuff in the laundry basket because I drag my clothes from the floor and dress.

After we returned from our ride, the herd over on the northwest quadrant were displaying signs of distress. Theo called me in to help and we discovered a pregnant heifer whose leg was trapped in a fence. The shock had her giving birth early, but we showed up too damn late to save either of them.

The memory has me scrubbing a hand over my face as I stride out of my room and start down the hall, shoeless so as not to disturb Zee.

I can't imagine she'd hear the bikes, not after years of adapting to living in the city, but a man can try.

Yawning, I make it to the staircase when I hear a, "Colt? Is that you?"

Hearing trepidation in her voice, I immediately return to the end of the hallway where our suites are. "It's me. You should go back to sleep."

"Where are you going?" she asks drowsily, deciding to kill me by opening the door wider and letting me get a good look at her.

She's wearing an oversized sleep shirt with elephants on it.

It shouldn't be sexy.

It shouldn't.

And definitely not at a time like this.

But it is.

The only thing that could be sexier is her in my shirt. And I'm not sure if that'd win over her being naked.

Seeing her today out by the lake—

"Colt?" The fear's gone. Humor's replaced it. "Are you regretting sticking me in here?"

I huff. "I wanted you to—"

"I remember. You don't have to remind me." She rolls her eyes, her disdain for my request very clear.

"I need you to stay in your room."

"What?" Her brow puckers. "I'm not a child—"

"You heard those bikes?"

"Of course. The noise woke me. But—"

"I need you to get inside because they're going to approach the property and I don't want you anywhere near them."

"But—"

"No! No ifs, buts, or maybes. Keep your pretty ass in that bedroom or I'll tie you to the radiator. I'm not going to let anyone hurt you."

She blinks. "You're being serious, aren't you?"

"Deadly. So, do I have to lock you in the bathroom or...?"

"I'd prefer that option to being tied to the radiator. But I'll stay put." Her mouth works. "What's going on?"

"There was a weed farm on the Bar 9. MC owned and

operated." When a squeak escapes her, I tut. "It's fine. I handled it."

"Are you in danger?"

"No, chaos, I'm not." I cup her cheek. "*If* you stay here. I can't be thinking about shielding you at the same time."

She bobs her head. "Understood. B-Be safe."

"Of course." I press a quick, hard kiss to her lips then stride off, splitting my attention between the crankshafts that are getting ever closer and the sound of any footsteps behind me.

Once I make it to the end of the corridor, I take off for the office where our gun safe is.

Quickly retrieving a shotgun and a box of cartridges, I slip them into my pockets for easy access before loading the empty chambers.

That done, I head for the door and open it just in time to see four single headlights coming up my driveway.

I cock the gun, lift it so the front sight is at eye height, then I watch the bikes and once they're forty feet away, I pull the trigger.

The sound echoes around the homestead, as does the screeching of the bike as it brakes to a halt. The other three stop too and one of them growls, "What the fuck?"

"Plenty more where that came from," I shout into the distance. "If you think you can come onto my fucking property and not shed any blood, you heard wrong."

There's only silence in response to my warning.

Then, the security lights from one of the nearby outbuildings pop on as a single biker walks toward me.

Because he could be armed with only God knows what, I reload, cock the gun, lift it to eye height, and aim five paces away from his feet.

Many things can be said about me, but one of them is that I'm a damn good shot.

When he jumps up, I quickly reload and hit the ground to his right side. I do the same thing to his left.

"You want to keep dancing, I have all night," I jeer.

"Fuck you," the guy snaps. "We came here to deal—"

"No deals. No drugs. Nothing. You touch any part of my

property and I won't waste my breath talking to the RCMP. I'll blow your fucking heads off."

"You're making a mist—"

"No. *You* made a mistake by coming here tonight. *You* made a mistake by growing weed on my land. And *you* made a mistake by thinking I'd be afraid to stand my ground."

My words are punctuated by the sound of my shotgun cocking.

That's when I hear a booted footstep scraping on the gravel driveway.

It's closer than the asshole I'm talking to, so I turn toward the sound and shoot.

To the biker's screams, I holler, "I wasn't trying. Next time, I'll aim to kill."

"He got me, Razer. My fucking knee." The asshole cries out in pain. "Oh, my fucking—"

"You'll regret that," one of the guys snarls.

"No. You will. Come around here again and you'll pay."

I hear thudding this time, but it's quickly followed by a dragging sound.

Next thing I know, the bikes are roaring to life and they're driving off.

I don't put down my weapon until the sound of the crankshafts is a whisper in the distance, and only then do I turn on my heel.

Adrenaline's flooding my system but it's a high I'm not afraid of. This land is mine and there's no one alive who'll steal it from me.

Once I've locked the door, I turn and find Callan, Mum, and Mrs. Abelman standing in the vestibule, all of them in their pajamas.

"It's okay," I assure them. "They're gone." I stab a finger in the air at Callan. "We'll need to fix our gate if they gained access to our driveway."

He hisses. "I'll call Theo and we'll take care of it now."

Mum's mouth trembles. "You shouldn't have dealt with them alone."

"They won't be coming around anymore. Go back to bed."

"I can put pressure sensors on the driveway," Callan offers.

"No. Any more security features and this place is going to make us look like Bond villains. Go on. Bed. The lot of you."

Mrs. Abelman sniffs her disdain for my edict, but it's Mum who grumbles, "Who's the parent here?"

Still, they retreat to their respective rooms and I make my way to the gun safe, where I lock up the shotgun. Then, I head upstairs. Which is where I find her sitting on the top step.

It's oddly reminiscent of the day Lydia died—Zee watching and waiting for me, protecting me in her own way... Something nobody has ever done before.

As I climb the stairs, I ask, "You okay?"

"You were in danger!"

"From those punks?" I scoff, holding out my hand for her to take. "You didn't answer my question."

"I'm fine." She rubs her forehead with her free hand. "You're a Korhonen, yes, but you're not untouchable."

"You're scared for me." She lets me tug her against my chest. When I brush her forehead with a kiss, I murmur, "I know what I said about us spending the night apart..."

"Can we not do that?" is her choked answer.

Another kiss to her temple and I guide us both to our wing. I can feel the soft jitters rushing through her small frame and I know it's going to be one hell of a night. The prospect only has me tightening my arm around her as we step down the hall.

I bring us to a halt outside of her room. "Do you want a choice on what you eat or shall I pick?"

Her nose crinkles. "Do you hate it?"

"Hate what?"

"That I'm diabetic."

My brow furrows. "No. It's a part of who you are."

"I hate it," she rasps. "Sometimes I wish I were normal. Wish that my husband going off with a shotgun and facing a bunch of bikers just made me scared and didn't send my blood sugar spiraling. We're going to sleep together for the first time, and all night, we're going to get alerts because I'm—"

"Those alerts keep you alive." Turning her to face me, my

437

hands cup her shoulders. "They keep you *here*. With me. That's the only place I want you, Zee."

"It's the only place I want to be."

"Then why the long face?" I tease, even as my heart soars at her admission. "Part of being with me is dealing with a kid brother who never shuts the hell up, a mum who forces us to drink tea, and a housekeeper who's part poltergeist. We all have our crosses to bear."

Her snort has me grinning as I chuck her under the chin. "Shut up."

I wink. "Who's deciding on your food, hmm?"

With a soft huff, she disappears into her bedroom. Twice, she looks back as if she expects me to disappear, but I just hold out my hand for her to take.

Right on cue, an alert sounds.

Before she pops a dose of glucose gel, she passes me a few more as well as some granola bars.

With a tug on her hand, I lead her into my bedroom.

She doesn't cross the doorway, just hovers there. "It looks as if it's the same room your grandfather slept in."

"He did."

"The same furniture?"

"I changed the mattress," I tease.

"That's a relief." She detangles the clasp of our hands and drifts around the bedroom. "I didn't realize you were that much into baseball memorabilia."

"Recent thing. Comes with access to a trust fund and a reckless lack of care about how much I spend."

At my mocking tone, she hums and trails a finger along a glass box that houses a baseball while I head for the nightstand to check her blood sugar on my cell. Seeing it's approaching normal, I direct, "You can eat the granola bar."

She does but asks, "What's special about the ball?"

"Mark McGwire hit it for his 70th home run in the '98 season with the Cardinals."

"You're a Cardinals fan?"

I scoff. "No. But I'm a collector."

"Why?"

"You want to know?"

Her eyes big in her pale face, she turns to me. "Of course."

"If I hadn't been the eldest, I'd have tried my luck at going pro."

"Wow."

I nod. "Cole isn't the only one with skills."

"Huh." She points to a frame housing a ticket stub. "Why's this one important?"

"It's Jackie Robinson's debut ticket stub from '46. He was the first African American to appear in the MLB in his debut with the Montréal Royals."

She points to a baseball card. "Why do you have this one?"

"It's the first card I bought. It's Jackie Robinson's rookie card."

"I saw the one in the office."

"Cole bought me that." I point to a Babe Ruth 1946 American League baseball bat. "And that... for my birthday."

"He did?"

"Yeah, he knows I'm a collector." Noticing she's finished her snack, I hold out my hand for her. "Come on. You can check the rest tomorrow if you're still interested."

Her nose crinkles but she drifts over to my side. "I knew you liked baseball but didn't realize you were such a fan."

"Why would you? We never talked about sports," I comment, pulling back the cover on her side of the bed. Then, I pause. "I sleep on the left. Is that okay?"

"You willing to give it up for me?" she jokes.

I grin. "In exchange..."

"For?"

"I'm not sure yet."

Her matching grin has me chuckling. "You're in luck. I like sleeping on the right." As she clambers onto the large, heirloom bed, I watch her sleep shirt skate higher along her thighs before she tucks herself beneath the covers. "It's big in here."

"Yours is just as big," I point out, turning to the side so she doesn't see my erection. An erection that has everything to do with her being in here. In my bed. Fuck.

I shrug out of my jeans and Henley then climb in beside

439

her. The second I'm settled, she lifts my arm and burrows into me. I chuckle because she's cold to the touch and it makes me jump because I run a lot hotter. As her feet tangle with my legs, I drawl, "Am I going to be your personal hot water bottle?"

"Maybe," she mutters with a sigh, the tension draining from her as she wraps her arm over my stomach.

I should have known she'd be like this—an octopus in bed.

Not that I'm complaining.

As large as the mattress is, it could be a single for all the room we take up.

With her nose brushing my arm, she whispers, "I don't want to lose you, Colt."

"I'm not going anywhere."

"Do you promise?"

"I promise."

She shifts then leans on her hand and looms over me. Her hair tumbles forward in a tangle of caramel locks that tickle my shoulder. "It was kinda hot."

"What was?"

"I watched from my window... You going all Clint Eastwood on them. Pretty sexy, actually."

"It was, huh?"

"Yeah. Very. That guy you hit... wonder how he's faring on the highway."

I snicker. "I'd imagine he's in a world of pain."

"Serves him right," she grumbles. Her throat bobs as she gently swoops down and pecks my cheek. "Am I yours too?"

"I think you know the answer to that already."

I turn my head so our mouths can brush and when they do, she sags into me, immediately letting me in.

As my tongue drifts past her lips in a soft exploration, she sighs again, but this time there's less anxiety and more relief.

I get the feeling she's never wanted to be anywhere but here in her whole life.

And I know that feeling well because I'm experiencing it too.

I gently turn us over so that she's below me and the strain's on me. I don't want her pushing herself, but I need her to feel what she does to me. Need her to know how nothing has ever been more right to me than her presence here—with me.

Her soft moans drive me crazy, enough that I untangle our legs and settle between hers. I've never been more grateful that I'm going commando. Or that she is too beneath her sleep shirt.

She's wet already. Not like earlier, but her need is as raw as my own.

I draw back. "Do you want me, Zee?"

Her whimper has me biting back a growl. "Yes! Come inside me, Colt."

That triggers a memory. The last one I want to remember.

My lips return to hers and, as I explore, I hit up the night-stand for the condoms I put there this afternoon.

When her fingers seek mine, I know what she's doing. The crinkling of the wrapper gives it away. The next thing I know, she's delving between us, her hand shaping my dick and sheathing it with protection.

When I'm covered, she slots the tip to her entrance and digs her heels into my ass.

As her spine arches, I determine to keep it nice and slow. I need her to know how much I want her. How she's safe with me. How she's *it* for me.

When tears leak from her eyes and wet my cheeks, I don't pull back.

I give her my everything.

When she cries out, her body shattering around me, I let myself go. And a few minutes later, the crying baby alert blasting us, she deals with that while I throw away the condom.

This is life now. This is us.

As she takes another dose of glucose gel, I murmur, "You won't be sleeping in that other room again. Never hated a wall as much as I hate that one."

Her smile's small but there. "Bossy."

I tap her on the nose. "You love it."

She sighs.

And that's all the answer I need.

Text Chat

Zee: Did you feel it?

Tee: What?

Zee: The earth move?

Tee: NO WAY!!!!!

Tee: Tell. Me. Everything.

Zee: A lady doesn't tell.

Tee: You're not a lady. You're a cowgirl.

Zee: I'm both.

Tee: You're seriously not going to tell me anything?!

Zee: Seriously

Tee: You suck!!! But, okay. Fine. Just… he rocked your world?

Zee: Four times.

Tee: :O :O :O

Tee: I'm so jealous and so happy for you all at the same time!!!!

Tee: SQUEEEEE. My girl got laid and her husband knows how to jingle her dingle! WOOP.

Tee: How's that thing going in town?

Zee: What thing?

Tee: The hit-and-run thing

Tee: I swear Pigeon Creek went and got more interesting after we left.

Zee: It's too interesting.

Zee: Things are crazy

Tee: I'm glad you have Colt. He'll keep you safe.

Zee: Doubt I'm in any danger lol.

Tee: You never know. Psychos are everywhere.

Zee: Reassuring

Tee: Hey, I'm the one who should freak out. The only thing I have to protect me from a home invader is massive intellect.

Zee: I have faith in your brain.

Tee: I love you too. Go and hop on that husband for me, you hear?

Zee: That's not weird. At all.

Tee: :*

Chapter 11
Colt

I pin my wrists together and hold them out.

"Don't tempt me," Terry warns, holding the door to the interview room open.

Marc Robard, my attorney, takes a seat beside me as I settle in for whatever BS Terry's going to ask me about.

There's a reason I haven't been arrested, as much as there's a reason why he asked me to come in. A part of me thought it might have something to do with last night's fun and games, but I don't think Terry would have disturbed me so early in the morning if it was MC-related.

I woke up to Marc's call with the RCMP's request for another interview, then had to disentangle myself from Zee's arms.

This was *not* a part of my to-do list today and my patience is rapidly wearing thin with this imbecilic investigation.

"When was the last time you spoke with Clyde?"

"Around about the time I got married. I know he sneaked onto the ranch one day after the wedding. Mrs. Abelman's the only one who spoke to him.

"As I've already told you, Zee's talked to him more recently. He wants her to spy on me."

Terry blinks. Marc clears his throat.

"Your family, I swear."

"Tell me about it. He's ignoring me. Since I threw him off the ranch, he's not very happy with me, much as I'm not happy with him."

"For the obvious reason that he wants to spy on you?"

"That and he stole from me."

Terry rubs his jaw. "What did he steal?"

"The ranch."

"The ranch," the sergeant repeats blankly. "How did he do that?"

Marc interrupts, "We'll present our case to the appropriate channels once our investigation is complete."

Terry frowns. "Then why tell me?"

"Because I didn't want you to think I was colluding with him for any reason. The man made my childhood hell and nearly killed my mother. I put a protective order on him and you think I'm on his side?" I scoff. "You have to wonder if he's trying to frame me to stop the investigation into his dealings. He could lose everything if he can't stop me from digging deep."

Terry's eyes widen but it's Marc who demands, "Was there a reason for this interview?"

"For the record," Terry mutters, still looking shell-shocked by my comment. "I'm showing Mr. Korhonen Marcy Armstrong's journal."

My brows lift. "You found her journal?"

"Doug gave it to us."

I stare at him, then at it. "There's a new piece of evidence in there?"

"Until recently, it was hidden," is the only answer he'll give us. "'CK and I met at the lake tonight. I'm going to tell him about the baby,'" he quotes.

Tension fills me. "I had nothing to do with her. I didn't even talk to her, never mind get her pregnant. What I do know is that Clyde used to take girls up to the mineral springs on the Bar 9."

"How do you know this?"

I take Zee's truth and bend it: "I saw him there. In fact, I saw them together after the fire."

"Cole was a grade below Marcy."

"He wasn't here that year, was he? He was playing in Winnipeg. Callan was too young, I was in university, and Cody had graduated and was in Saskatoon after enlisting. None of us dated Marcy, dammit.

"You know I wasn't behind the hit-and-run. My prints weren't—"

"Prints can be wiped away and you *did* pay off the blackmail demand. Plus, Susanne could be lying on your behalf—"

Outraged, I snap, "I'd never get anyone to lie for me. Certainly not my wife. You're only doubting her word because she's a McAllister."

"My client has already explained to you, sergeant, that he paid the blackmail demand as an act of kindness for a neighbor in acute financial distress."

"And because she was threatening Susanne," Terry says pointedly. "If Marcy was pregnant and Clyde was the father then you'd have another child to split your inheritance with."

"You're clutching at straws. That's not how the Korhonen inheritance works. The eldest inherits the ranch. I wouldn't have to share anything with him or her."

"There'd be a trust fund—"

I scoff. "And? Not like we can't afford it. Anyway, why do you keep asking me where he is? You're the cops. Shouldn't you know better than me?"

"He's more slippery than an eel."

"That's doing a disservice to an eel." I grunt. "Are you finally bringing him in for questioning?"

"And to take his fingerprints. If you do hear from him, remember to keep in touch."

"Did you have to drag me out of bed for *this*?" I snipe once the recording's off.

He prods the diary. "She was pregnant, Colt. That puts a whole other slant on things. Especially when Lydia believed you were the baby's father."

"But I wasn't, dammit," I snarl.

"Why didn't you mention seeing Marcy with your father during the original investigation?"

"I didn't think it was pertinent."

"We decide that. Not you," Terry snaps. "You'd better not be withholding any information from me, Colton. I'm catching heat from all quarters here. Don't add to my burden or I'll bring you in with cuffs next time."

"I'm not withholding anything. I don't have anything *to* withhold. I came to you about the poison pen letters. I put the suspicion on me when I didn't have to do that. I had no reason to kill Lydia. I wasn't the father of Marcy's baby.

"That year, I was too busy on suicide watch with Callan and not failing my classes that fucking anything in a skirt was the least of my worries, dammit.

"Lydia was wrong to suspect me. The CK in that diary will be my father. You and I both know what he's like. She was just hoping that Marcy wasn't sleeping with someone thirty years her senior."

"I need to bring him in."

"I don't know what to tell you. He isn't answering my calls either."

Terry squints at me. "If he contacts—"

"Yeah, yeah. I'll let you know." Then, a thought occurs to me. "Cody said Clyde had been to visit him in the hospital."

"Which hospital?"

"Montfort in Ottawa. I doubt he's still there since Cody came home, but it could be worth a shot checking it out."

"I appreciate the intel, Colt."

When Marc and I leave the interview room and handcuffs *don't* decorate my wrist, I mutter my thanks to my attorney.

"You talked too much," he chides.

"It was an informal interview."

"Nothing's informal when it's being recorded. Keep your mouth shut next time, Colton. It'll serve you better if you do."

"I want to help. The sooner this is over the better. I didn't hurt anyone, Marc."

"Whether you did or not, the cops always look for an easy way out. Reilly is either dumb, on the take, or is trying to do your father a favor. He clearly wants to pin this on you so confer with me next time," he warns.

I scrub a hand through my hair. "Fine."

Chapter 12
Zee

THE FOLLOWING DAY

When Callan walks into the kitchen, he freezes in the doorway.

I study him then return to my task—frosting a cookie.

He steps toward me, his gaze contemplative. "What are you doing?"

"Use those IQ points to figure it out, Callan."

"Okay, let me rephrase. *Why* are you frosting a cookie?"

"Because I want to."

Directing a line of bright red frosting around the circumference of the sweet treat, I flood the perimeter when that's done and use a scribe to smooth it out toward the edges. Because the frosting is thinner than usual, I have to work quickly and carefully—I don't need my brother-in-law distracting me.

"Why though? Is it for a special event?"

"I like doing it."

And it's helping to lower my stress levels—I've been on edge since Colton was called in for questioning again yesterday.

I know Callan's been just as stressed. We're trying not to

show it though—Colton's the only one of us who's been relatively calm about this whole affair.

His brow furrows. "I'm confused."

"It's a hobby, Callan. Jesus."

"But you're diabetic!"

"And? Type 1. I could eat them if I wanted to. Anyway, I used gluten-free flour for you."

"For me?!"

No one could ever accuse him of having a massive ego.

"'Course. Figured you'd eat as many of them as Colton." I shove the plate of unfrosted cookies at him. "Have at it."

He picks one up like it could explode in his hand. "So, why do you want to decorate them?"

"It relaxes me. What is this—twenty questions?" I point at the stool. "Sit. It's rude to hover."

He does as I order and continues watching me, one elbow on the counter, his fist propping up his chin as he eats. "What are you doing?"

"I just told you."

"I mean, what's going on with the stuff in the bag? The frosting's wet?"

"Oh." *He's interested.* That I can handle. "This style is called wet on wet. See how the base isn't dry? When you apply the frosting from the piping bag this way, the two melt into each other and it dries flat."

"Why does it dry flat?"

"It's a miracle."

His nose crinkles. "That's not an answer."

"The flood," I explain, pointing to the base with my scribe, "has to be the same consistency as the piping detail or it can cause little craters. But I can use this tool on my piping lines and make pretty patterns."

For a few minutes, he's quiet, just watching me complete the design. Then, he asks, "Did you get Mrs. Abelman's permission to use her kitchen?"

I hum.

It had been less about getting permission and more about

reassuring her that I had no desire to take over the cooking in its entirety—no, thank you.

"She must like you. She wouldn't leave me in the kitchen when we had to bring in cakes for a bake sale. She did all the work and I got the credit for it."

"Does that seem fair?"

"No, but I didn't have to bake so that's something."

"Didn't think you were a cheater, Callan."

I look up quick enough to catch his scowl. "I didn't cheat."

"If you say so."

His tone is disgruntled as he asks, "Have you thought about who you're competing for at the Pigeonberry Festival?"

"Huh?"

"For the best pie. Mrs. Abelman always wins best jam," he boasts.

"Good for her," I reply, humor pricked.

"So?"

"So?"

"Who are you competing for?!"

I just smile at him. "I don't think I have a choice."

He scowls at me then grumbles, "What are you designing?"

"Shoes."

He points to my camera setup. "Why are you filming it?"

"Accountability."

"Huh."

"Huh?"

"Not to post online?"

"Oh, I post it, but that pushes me into doing it. I find it relaxing but I'm not great at scheduling downtime. Posting online pushes me into practicing my hobby."

"That's illogical."

"Who said I was logical?" I taunt, amused because he's scowling more now. "Did you find out how Fen got loose yet?"

His brow puckers. "Colt's been on me about that too."

"Because he wants an answer—"

"Are you pestering Susanne?"

I don't stiffen intentionally, but Lindsay *never* uses 'Zee' and it's pissing me off.

"I'm not pestering Z*ee*, Mum," Callan corrects with a sniff.

I knew I liked this kid.

Lindsay drifts toward the line of stools and lingers behind Callan. I'm used to Tee's eyes on me, but this is a whole different audience.

It's impossible to stop my cheeks turning pink over being the center of their attention.

The silence that settles among us is strange.

It's probably why we all hear Colton's voice from the front door as he slams it closed.

"You'll get your ass home, Cole, or I'll head to New York myself and drag you here... No. We made arrangements and we're going ahead with them. You'll— No. Cole. How many goddamn times do I have to tell you? I don't care if you're in the playoffs. Pretend to have the flu.

"Mum's expecting you too."

Lindsay clears her throat. "Cole's—"

"He thinks I started the fire." I settle a measured look on her. "I'm used to it."

"You're willing to disappoint the whole family because of this?" Colt argues, breaking into our conversation. "I arranged the BBQ and a birthday party for you around the playoffs. I've changed the date twice! This one fits in with Callan's graduation ceremony. You only have to be here twenty-four hours, dammit.

"You think it's fair to cancel? She's my wife. Whether you like it or not. Look, this is a big deal. It's important to me." He sighs. "It's not as if I ask a lot of you."

Callan mutters, "Cole'll get to know you, Zee, and he'll realize you didn't do anything wrong."

I hitch a shoulder. "He'll think what he wants, Callan. There's no changing someone's mind and he hung, drew, and quartered me a long time ago."

"It's not fair though. You didn't do it."

"In the name of family unity—" Lindsay tuts. "—Cole should make an effort to come home. I'll speak with him if Colt can't get him to."

"Thank you, Cole. I appreciate it. Honestly, once you get to know her, you'll realize you were wrong about her. I'll see you next week. Yeah. Great. Thanks."

His footsteps echo down the hall, but his head is bowed over his phone as he steps into the kitchen. He jerks back when he finally sees us watching him. His lips form an easy grin as he finds my gaze and then strolls my way.

When he curves an arm around my shoulder, in front of his mother and brother, I can feel my cheeks grow pink again. He busses my temple and I don't bother to hide how much I like that.

"Colton," Lindsay greets, her gaze flickering between us. More than aware of this new update. "You persuaded Cole, then?"

"You heard that?" The question's aimed at her, but I can feel his attention on me.

"We heard everything."

"It's fine, Callan. Leave it alone."

Callan cracks his knuckles. "He better not give you any crap. If he does, Zee, I'll handle him."

"You're gonna defend my wife's honor, huh? Don't you think you should let me do that?"

"Depends."

"On?"

"How low you're willing to go."

"Callan," Lindsay warns.

"What, Mum? Zee's cool. I don't think it's fair to blame her for something she didn't do."

"Grief isn't rational," I tell him simply. "I've been the bad guy for long enough that it's hard to shift the narrative in his head. Neither of you need to defend my honor. It'll be fine. I'll stay out—"

"No," Colton interrupts. "You won't. This is your home. You won't hide away. I'll handle him." To Callan, he orders, "Leave it with me."

Callan sniffs but the conversation shifts tracks when Lindsay asks him if he wants to watch a movie with her. I can sense Colt's surprise when he agrees, but it means that we're alone in the kitchen once they're gone.

"You know I won't let him be hard on you, right?"

"I know that you don't have to worry about it if he is."

He leans against the island, meaning that he can look at me more easily. "Would you let someone talk shit about me?"

"You know this is different—"

"No. It isn't. Anyway, I'm going to tell him about the will."

My hand cramps around the piping bag as I over-squeeze, and a blob of frosting floods the segment I'm working on. Turning off my camera, I decide it's wiser to give it a rest before I ruin the design I've been concentrating on for the last forty-five minutes.

Wiggling my fingers, I ask, "You think this is the best timing?"

"Doesn't matter if it isn't. Cody and Cole need to know."

"Callan doesn't? He's eighteen."

He rubs his eyes. "I keep forgetting."

"Easily done. He's been eighteen for two seconds and under eighteen for eighteen years."

My teasing has his lips quirking so when our gazes clash, I smile at him.

"You invite your family to the BBQ yet?"

My smile turns into a grimace. "I have."

"Your *grand-mère*'s not coming?"

"Carson said he's working on her and, to be honest, I don't want to know how."

Laughing, he chucks me under the chin. "It'll be fine."

"She has two choices." I peep at him. "Tee said she'll come."

"That'll be interesting."

"One way of putting it."

"I'm heading into town." He picks up a sugar cookie. I can't hide my delight when he hums in pleasure as he takes a bite. "Goddamn that's good. So much better than Mrs. Abelman's." Before I can glow bright red, he drawls, "Do you want to come with me?"

"God, that's the last thing I want to do."

"All the more reason to rip the Band-Aid off. I need to head into the General Store. We can grab you some boots then we could get something to eat at The Coffee Shop." He shuffles over to me. "Like a date."

"Really?"

His elbow nudges mine. "You like the idea of that?"

"Of course I do. It's what my teenage self dreamed of."

"Your teenage self was pretty innocent if that's how low you sank into depravity."

"For us, that *is* depraved. A McAllister and a Korhonen? In Pigeon Creek? On a date?"

"True. Positively risqué." He smirks. "How about it then? Let's be depraved together."

A tingle whispers through me. That smile... it's so good to be in the shadow of it. To be the reason for it.

"Okay then."

Chapter 43
Zee

Here With Me - d4vd

Heading into Pigeon Creek shouldn't be anyone's idea of hell, but it's mine.

That I'm here for a 'depraved date' says a lot about how much I used to dream of this.

A part of me wants to cling to Colt's arm when he opens the truck door for me. Cling and cling and cling. Never let go. Just hold on. But I don't. Exactly because I want to do nothing more.

Then, he takes the choice away from me by wrapping an arm over my shoulder and hooking me into him so that we're walking around in a surprisingly smooth tandem.

During the walk to the General Store, I see Tee's dad who greets me with a one-armed hug and Colton with a suspicious glower.

"I always knew Martin didn't like me," Colt drawls. "But it's only recently I've come to learn why.

"He was one of the few on Team Zee." I pat his chest in

461

mock sympathy, trying not to flush when he snatches a hold of my fingers and presses a kiss to the tips.

"I owe him a massive thank you then."

Heat blossoms on my cheeks, so I'm grateful when we reach our destination and focus shifts off the reason behind Martin's dislike of my husband.

The Glovers, owners of the General Store, stare at us like I've grown a second head. Mary watches me like I'm going to start pickpocketing, then sniffs at me when I try on a pair of boots. Meanwhile, both our husbands discuss the best chicken feed for Ida's new hen house and the new security cameras they've installed since Lydia's death.

Because Pigeon Creek has always been considered a safe place, few took any steps to secure their properties. That's all changing now that a murderer is walking around and Sergeant Reilly is in no way close to finding Clyde *or* making an arrest.

Satisfied with the simple, brown-leather, hand-tooled boots, I merely settle a cool look upon Mary that makes the distaste in her eyes grow as I lever them off my feet and hand them to her to box up.

The town's hatred is a visceral touch that never stops making me feel sixteen again. Colt's focus can't always be on me, but once I return to his side, and with his arm tucked around my waist, I feel so much better. Like I have stalwart support when I've never had it before.

Once Hilary Browne and Jessica Cardinal stride in, making up the devil's trifecta of the worst (still-living) bitches in town, I can hear them alternating between dissing me *and* tattling about the new celebrity who moved into the old Linnox place. A celeb who has yet to show his or her face in town.

Smart man/woman.

It's with relief that Colt approaches the counter to have the few items he's purchased bagged up.

When we're standing there, he stuns us all by rumbling to Andrew, "Everyone's entitled to their petty squabbles, Andy, and they're also entitled to a warning—if I see Mary look at my wife as if she's a piece of dog crap on her shoes again, I'll be taking my business elsewhere."

The chatter between the devil's trifecta immediately stops.

I didn't realize he'd noticed Mary's dirty looks, but that he did has my hand settling on his hip so that I can squeeze him there in thanks.

Andrew sputters, "I don't know what you mean, Colton."

Still, as happy as I am for his defense, the last thing I want is to feed the fire of their dislike of me. "This isn't necessary, Colt. We should go—"

"It's very necessary," he disregards, holding me closer. "I'm talking to a business owner about a member of staff—"

"She's his wife."

"She's an employee in his business," he corrects. "As a member of the town, I can't request a shift in her behavior, but as a patron of this establishment, I can make certain demands as, without my business, the store would likely fold..."

Andrew gulps. "I'll talk to Mary."

"See that you do," he rumbles as we walk past the stunned women.

That he even goes so far as to tip his hat to them is just the cherry on top of the sundae.

Still...

"You made that worse!" I muse as we're walking through the door and onto the street, the corners of the box containing my new boots digging into my calf with every step until he snags the bag in his fist.

"I'm not going to let this continue. I can't make them like you—"

"No, seeing as this isn't kindergarten and you're not my mom," I insert.

"No," he drawls. "But I could be your daddy."

When his brow arches, I shove his arm. "Shut up."

Smirking, Colt's fingers tighten around mine. "I can put weight behind my actions. I choose to stay local. I choose to support the town. But Saskatoon's ninety minutes away and I can have things delivered to the ranch. If they're going to treat you poorly, then I can do the same to them. Simple."

His defense of me feels *good* but it doesn't sit right with me and I'm not sure why.

I'd have done anything when I was sixteen to have his backing, but I'm no longer that girl. I don't care if the folks of Pigeon Creek dislike me. Their validation isn't something I need anymore.

My brain screeches to a halt as the decade of self-loathing that's part of being hated by the town drifts away like it weighed no more than a feather.

It means that as I walk with him, aware of the whispers that once would have brushed my skin like rain dosed with acid, I don't feel the pain.

Beside me, Colt gets angrier and angrier, but he's only been dealing with this for a couple hours.

This is normal for me.

Maybe accepting and rejecting it is something I can do because he's on my side?

Gah, I'll never understand how my brain works.

"Has that happened before?" Colt demands, tugging me to a halt before I can step toward The Coffee Shop.

"Every time. Why do you think I stopped coming into town?"

"I'm so goddamn sorry, Zee." He runs his free hand through his hair. "Let's go to Saskatoon?"

"For?"

"A real date."

I don't bother hiding my delight as I lean on tiptoe, my intent obvious. As his mouth presses to mine, I sigh into the kiss. One hand settles on his nape so I can hold him closer.

"*They* can hate me. *You* can't."

He cups my cheek. "Even when I thought you'd betrayed me, I didn't hate you."

"Don't lie."

"I'm not. You broke something in me. But you fixed it. Wanna know how?"

"How?"

"By." He kisses my forehead. "Being." He kisses the tip of my nose then, against my lips, he rumbles, "You."

Chapter 44
Colt

Freak Me - Another Level

Our depraved date in Pigeon Creek wasn't exactly a roaring success, so I take her to The Manchester again—it's one of four hotels we own in Saskatoon.

Mostly, it's my end destination because neither of us is dressed up enough for a swanky restaurant, and the perk of owning an establishment is you can use it however the hell you want.

She's not as quiet as I feared she'd be on the ride into the city.

If anything, she's chatty.

I have a feeling that this whole experience weighs more heavily on me than it does her, but it's undoubtedly guilt talking.

I perpetrated her treatment, something I've witnessed for myself several times by this point. Sure, I gave her an alibi. I didn't do anything else, though. Didn't tell the town to leave her alone.

"I heard Ida say you were driving to the border on Saturday," she says, breaking into my thoughts.

"Yeah. I go every now and then."

"Why?"

"Ever heard of Dove Bay Sanctuary?"

"I have actually. Some CATSA agent at the airport gave me the number when Tee had this meltdown at security."

"She thought you needed sanctuary from me?!"

"No. It was a misunderstanding," she assures me.

"Should hope so. Jesus."

"What about it?"

"I own it. The sanctuary, I mean." I clear my throat. "Mrs. Abelman runs it, but I help with some of the more sinister cases. This weekend, there'll be a drop-off. A politician's wife managed to get away earlier this week."

She sits taller in her seat. "Oh, my God! And you're going to bring her to the ranch?"

"To one of our bunkhouses," I correct. "You might have seen it. It's over in the southwest quadrant."

"It's in the middle of nowhere. Right?"

"Yeah. They both are, but only one is visible from the house."

"I wondered what was going on there." She twists to face me. "I'm coming with you."

"When?"

"This weekend. We can pick her up together."

"You don't have to—"

"Sure I do. She might be terrified of you. Another woman's presence might help her."

Her tone's somber but deadly serious so I shrug. "Fine. If you're sure."

"Of course I am. Holy crap, I knew you were perfect but this is *so* you. Just wait until I tell Tee—"

"Why are you telling Tee?"

"Because she was ready to canonize you before, but now you might just become her version of the pope."

"Thanks. I think."

"High compliment. Trust me."

"Oh, I do. Keep it on the down low though. We function best in secrecy."

"But you're telling me...?"

"Of course. You're my wife." I glance at her out of the corner of my eye and see her coy smile at my declaration. So I snag her hand and kiss her knuckles. "We're almost there."

"Where's there?"

"The Manchester."

"I loved that hotel! This depraved date is hitting all the right notes."

"Give me time and we'll make music together."

"Smooth, Colt, very smooth," she teases.

Laughing, I drive into the underground parking lot where we have some private spaces rather than wait for valet service when we reach the hotel.

"You might not have noticed before but they're going to be obsequious in here," I tell her as I slot my arm along the back of the passenger seat and use it to stare out the rearview window as I reverse into the space.

"They are?"

"It's a Korhonen property."

"You own The Manchester?!"

"Clyde's a moron in many ways, but he sometimes makes the right decisions. The hotel is a part of Seven Cs' investment portfolio."

"Or he takes good financial advice."

"Yeah, we'll go with that option."

"No compliments for him allowed," she agrees with a cackle. "I didn't realize it was your hotel when you brought us here for our wedding night."

"It wasn't relevant."

A smirk dances on lips I want to devour. "I can deal with being the owner's dirty little secret."

I rub my thumb over her rings. "How are you a dirty little secret?"

"The staff won't know I'm your wife, will they? Unless you have a newsletter that goes out with family announcements in it. They might think I'm your mistress—this *is* the second time you've brought me around..."

"Fair point," I mock as I lean in. "But I'll let you onto something that is a secret."

She leans in too. The faint scent of her musky perfume hits me and makes me want to bury my face in her throat. "What is it?"

"I'm going to introduce you as my wife." I tap her nose. "That way they'll know you're their boss as well."

"That's boring!"

"The truth often is."

She ignores my teasing. "We could have a whole moment, Colt!"

"You want to be Julia Roberts to my Richard Gere, huh?"

Her eyes close. "You've watched *Pretty Woman*?"

"My brothers are Cole and Callan, sweetheart. I've seen more rom-coms than I would like to admit to."

Those crazy long lashes of hers flutter. "Stop being perfect."

I hide a smile. "Wanna watch it together?"

"It's my favorite movie so, yes. But don't tell Tee. She's already jealous of Callan. If she thinks she has to share her favorite movie with you too, she'll end up moving in when she comes to visit for the BBQ."

"She can if she wants."

"Huh?"

"She can stay with us for a while if she wants. Not like we don't have plenty of room."

"Yeah, but..."

"But?"

She blinks. "Guys don't let BFFs move in with them."

"Have you seen the size of our house? And anyway, she makes you happy and I think, from what you've said, she isn't doing so well in New York. She reminds me of Callan, to be honest."

"She does?"

"Yeah. All big feelings with no vent. It's like their brains know too much so they feel too much and see too much.

Vicious circle. People like that have a person they can depend on. I'm that for Callan and you're that for Tee."

"She's not a burden," she argues.

"I never said she was." I settle a look at her. "Callan's not a burden either.

"Ask her. She can if she wants. If she doesn't, she can go back to New York."

"You're nuts."

"About you," I counter, pressing another kiss to her knuckles. "I want you to be happy here."

Her eyes grow round as she stares at me, then, in an explosive flash of movement, she's suddenly sitting on my lap in the truck, straddling me, hands clutching at my arms, mouth on a collision course with mine.

She tastes better than those cookies she makes—sweet and sinful. I could eat her up every day for the rest of my life and die a happy man.

My hands settle on her ass as she grinds into me, but it's how she thrusts her tongue against mine that has me rocking back because damn, I stoked a fire in her I didn't know I was building.

A whimper escapes her as she breaks off the kiss to pepper my face with smaller ones. She graces my nose, my cheeks, my chin, my brows, and my closed eyelids in the most tender experience of my life.

She showers me in gratitude, exuding it like that perfume of hers laces every breath I take, but gratitude wasn't why I offered to let Tee move in with us.

Pigeon Creek is enemy territory for her.

I don't want her to leave.

I'm being selfish.

But, I figure, a man's allowed to be selfish when it's centered on keeping the woman he loves happy.

Because I do—there's no way this mass of feeling in me is anything but love.

Not friendship love like when I was younger.

But the big passion the poets write about and the artists paint.

471

The love that's impossible to describe and define.

That is what I feel for her.

When my eyes drift open, I see tear tracks on her cheeks and frown at the sight. "Hey, what's this?" I ask, stroking my thumb through one of the glistening lines.

"You're being so kind and I—"

"I'm not being kind," I argue. "I'm being smart."

"You are?"

I slide my other hand to the center of her back and tug her into me. "Right here is where I want you, Zee. With me. A piece of your heart is in New York City. It's in my best interests that Tee moves back."

"Why?"

I tip her chin so I can press a kiss to it. "Because then you won't go, won't think about leaving. You'll be here. Where I need you."

Zee licks her lips as she stares into my eyes. "I don't want to go."

"Good." I nuzzle my nose along the line of her jaw. "I want you to be my wife, Zee."

"I thought I was?"

"You are. But I want you to be mine for real." She shivers when I nip her earlobe. "Do you want that too, baby?"

"You know I do." It's a keening cry that settles right in my dick. "I've always wanted you, Colton. Always." Her arms tighten around me. "I've been waiting for *you* to want *me*."

"You can feel that for yourself, can't you?"

"I can. God, I need you inside me, Colton. Now. Please."

"In the truck?"

"Right now." She growls the confirmation, her hands finding her fly as she unfastens the button.

The logistics are hard for my brain to figure out, but I push back my seat as far as it'll go then turn her on my lap so that she's facing the windshield.

She wriggles her hips, nudging my cock with every pass, then I realize she's yanking down her jeans to her knees. "Wear skirts next time, dumb, dumb, dumb Zee," she mutters to herself.

Before she can continue, my hand slides around her throat, my other arm banding at her waist as I drag her into me.

Letting the words tickle her ear, I rasp, "Why are you talking down about my wife?"

Her head wiggles beneath my grip, and I let go when I realize what I did, but her fingers slap over mine, holding firm as if she likes the pressure there.

A part of me's horrified by the aggressive act, flashbacks from my childhood only adding to the terror, but she whimpers. "God, that feels good."

I stare straight ahead, trying to get my brain in gear, but all I can rumble is, "Is that what I asked?"

"No. You asked about..." She moans. "I'm so wet."

The urge to feel how wet she is reigns supreme because I'm clearly the only one freaking out here.

"I asked why you were calling yourself dumb."

"Because if I was smart, you'd be able to feel how wet I am," she retorts with a sniff. "I don't talk smack to myself, Colton, not unless it's deserved, and in this instance, it is."

The bite in those words talks me away from the proverbial edge.

My fingers flex, allowing me to monitor her stuttering pulse. She'd only let me do this if she trusted me. I have to find comfort in that.

"Feel what you do to me, Colt."

I know exactly how she's feeling.

For a second, I close my eyes, but then she grabs the arm I banded around her waist and tugs at it. The demand is silent, but I comply nonetheless. Like a man being happily led to his doom, my fingers cup her mound where the soft hairs prickle my palm as I let them swoop down to cover her sex.

I can already feel her excitement and my dick pounds in glee.

It's probably the only part of me that wasn't disgusted by how I caught hold of her.

Her hips arch. "Colton! Please!"

My response to her plea is automatic—I tunnel a digit

between her folds, shifting until it's sliding directly over her clit.

Fuck, the sounds she makes should be criminal.

How my body responds is as inevitable as the passing of time.

"This little pussy's hungry for me, hmm?"

She chokes off a sigh. "God, yes. Please, Colt. Please." Pressing into me, she wriggles when I don't rub her clit. "That feels so good. More. Please, more."

I grit my teeth as her nails bite into the hand that's holding her close. "You want to come, baby?"

"I do. I so do."

A glance at the private parking area reassures me that no one will see into the cab, that no one will see what's mine.

Not her pleasure, but Zee.

Mine.

The two sides of my brain go to war.

Colton—reasonable, polite, apathetic.

Colt—the man. The leader. The husband.

The second is the one who grinds out, "Who does this pretty pussy belong to?"

A cry escapes her. "You. Always you."

And that's what I've needed to hear for years.

I just didn't know it until now.

She's always been mine.

Always.

Drenching my fingers in her, I retreat to her clit and give her what she begged for—me.

I want her pleasure. Now.

I want to hear her cries. Now.

I want to feel her response to me. Now.

It's deliciously immediate.

She grows tense on my lap, her limbs locking up as she jerkily rides my fingers, and when she releases a hoarse cry as she clamps her thighs around my hand, I know she got off.

The butt of my wrist finds the tender nub next as I thrust two thick digits into her. "You're so tight." I groan. "I can't wait to fill you up."

Her moan is guttural. "That's all I want."

"*All*?" I half-tease.

"Yes," she hisses, then she proves that even in this state, she knows me too well. "Don't tease me!"

I spread her wider, feeling the walls flutter around me. "Only my dick'll do?"

Her nails swipe at the fingers still holding her throat in place. "Yes." Another hiss. "Give it to me."

"You're bossy when you're riled up, huh?" I rumble in her ear, biting the lobe this time as I simultaneously fuck her with my hand.

Though she yelps, it doesn't stop her mumbling, "Your cock, Colt. I need it. Give it to me. God, your fingers... they don't... Deeper. Please. Jesus—"

Fired up, I release my hold on her. Entirely. Before she can so much as release a cry of complaint, I'm lifting her onto my lap.

When her head bumps the roof, I cringe, "Sorry, babe."

She rubs the point of collision but she's smiling which eases my guilt. "You wanna rub it better, cowboy?"

"I'll rub something better."

"Promises, promises." She winks. "You should have warned me this would be where we'd end up. I wouldn't have worn skinny jeans."

"But your ass looks so great in them."

"You feel like cutting them off me?"

"Not if you want to go into the hotel. I'm the owner, but you'd still face indecency charges."

"I thought I was *the* Mrs. Korhonen." She grunts as she rolls the tight denim down her calves, and her cry of, "A-ha!" tells me she liberated herself from the jeans. "Doesn't that mean I can do anything I want?"

I slide my hand over her stomach and drag her into me. "You think I'm going to let anyone see what's mine?"

"Fuck," she whispers, wriggling more but this time with the intent to twist around.

I yelp when she comes within an inch of kneeing me in the balls.

"Oops! Sorry."

"You're not sorry at all."

"I am. I have a use for the family jewels and squishing them isn't one of them."

"Good to know," I rasp.

With her sex spread, I rub my knuckles over it, making sure to pinch her clit between my fingers on my way to unfastening my fly where I draw out my cock.

Before I can tease her again, she's there—her hand around me, stroking me, jerking me off. The pressure's lighter, but it's better than anything I can do.

"Wait," I order when I sense her getting ready to put me in her.

"What now?" she whines.

"Condom."

I lift my hips to release my wallet from my back pocket, snagging the condom I tucked inside earlier, groaning as our sexes brush.

"Fuck," I bite off as I pass it to her and she rolls it on me. Then, wasting no time at all, she rocks forward, notching the tip to her sex, sliding it through her folds, getting me wet with her before I feel that emptiness that's begging to be filled.

Her eyes lock on mine as, slowly, her pussy swallows the head of my dick.

I grind my teeth when she whimpers.

Inch by inch, she cries out. Tensing and softening. Flowing and rippling all around me.

It's torment, but what a way to go.

I don't push her or rush her. Just let her take her time.

Mostly because I know she's not teasing me.

She might be slick, but she's tight. Even more so in this position. Her nails tell their own tale as they dig into my shoulders, scraping and scratching as she sinks onto me.

Finally, every inch is claimed of that incomparable, delicious wet heat.

I slide my arms around her bare waist, dragging her into me, not wanting an inch of space to separate us. "You feel so fucking good, Zee."

Her ass wiggles from side to side before she moves in a figure eight, which has both of us moaning.

One of her hands slides over my scalp, letting me feel her claws there too as she tips my head back and joins our mouths.

Perfection.

Heaven.

Nothing like it.

No one.

Just her.

She's all I can see, feel, hear, smell, and taste.

She's all I *want*.

Everything.

It's her.

All her.

She clings to me, seeming to sense the ground-shaking revelation that hit me, and through it, she rides me until both of us are crying out our mutual releases as we come.

Together.

Her pussy milks me dry with the ripples from a climax that has her clamping around me and shuddering with pleasure, but my brain's hardwired into thinking of what we could have cemented into place here today...

Something we didn't lock down when we were here for our wedding night:

A future.

A marriage.

An 'us.'

Text Chat

Callan: @Cole, you need to back off Zee

Cole: This has nothing to do with you

Callan: Sure it does. She's my sister-in-law and I like her.

Cody: Leave it alone, Callan. He'll figure out for himself that she's good people once he gets his ass here

Callan: Yeah, well, he wanted to worm his way out of coming!

Cody: You're such a baby, Cole.

Cole: Hey! I'm coming when I'm in the middle of this thing called the playoffs.

Cody: Should think so

Cole: It's a good thing I'm the GM's billet brother. You don't even want to know what she asked for in exchange!

Callan: When you arrive, don't be a jerk. It's crazy around here. We don't need you making stuff worse

Cody: He has a point

Cole: What is this? Gang up on Cole day?

Colton: No, that'll be your birthday. It was going to be this big surprise too.

Callan: *snorts* He always has to spoil things, doesn't he?

Text Chat

Rachel: I can't find the files for the O'Donnelly-Burroughs case. Help?

Zee: They're in the drive. Can't you see them?

Rachel: No. I looked there earlier.

Zee: Maybe the cloud needs to update? Restart your computer?

Rachel: You always tell me to do that

Zee: And aren't I always right?

Rachel: Goddamn computers.

Rachel: It's restarting

Rachel: Rex said it was good to see you this weekend.

Zee: Man, it was awesome to see them too! So unexpected. When Colton told me that he was going to pick up a woman who needed sanctuary at Dove Bay, I had no idea the Sinners were transporting her!

Rachel: You're one of the few who'd be happy to catch up with that bunch of reprobates lol.

Zee: Ah, well, I'm not in the inner circle, but I know they have good hearts.

Rachel: Only because you ARE in the inner circle :P

Zee: Haha, okay, maybe. Finally managed to get Link to call me Zee.

Rachel: The end of an era.

Zee: I'll take it.

Zee: How long have they been transporting DV victims?

Rachel: It's part of Nyx's rehabilitation

Zee: It is?

Rachel: Yes. You don't want to know the details. Trust me. But this is infinitely less illegal and runs fewer risks of us having to defend him in court.

Zee: Win-win lol.

Rachel: Okay, the file's in the folder. Sorry

Zee: No worries. It's why you pay me the big bucks ;)

Rachel: Everything okay with your husband? Parker tells me he's being harassed by an RCMP sergeant?

Zee: It's starting to feel that way. He's being questioned as we speak.

Rachel: If I were his attorney, I'd file a complaint.

Zee: I wish you were his counsel!

Rachel: Anything you need, Zee, I'm here.

Zee: Thank you, Rachel. I really appreciate that.

Chapter 15
Colt

"This is getting ridiculous," Marc Robard bites off at Terry as he holds open the door to the interview room that's becoming a second home for me. "You have no reason to keep pestering my client. It's beginning to look like harassment."

I raise a hand. "Relax, Marc. I'm sure Terry isn't wasting my time. Again."

Terry narrows his eyes. "We have reason to believe—"

"You have no reason, Terry. No logic. No brains. No smarts." The indictment comes from the doorway where Juliette's standing, leaning heavily on a cane. Her hair's scattered and her face is pinched and colorless. "I remembered what happened the day that bitch died."

"Mrs. McAllister!" Terry chides, but he's obviously acclimated to her abuse.

"What? You'd better write this down before I toddle off this mortal coil." She scowls at me. "What are you doing here, boy?"

"Terry wants to interrogate me."

She harrumphs. "Are you sure you don't need to go back for basic training, Terry?"

"That's *sergeant* to you, Mrs. McAllister." He's flustered though. Juliette certainly knows how to rattle him.

"Sergeant, would you stop bothering my grandson-in-law,

please? He has my ranch to save and you're wasting your time anyway. I remembered who killed that stupid woman."

Terry gapes at me, then at her. "Excuse me?"

"I'm the one with hearing problems, *sergeant*," she sneers. "Do you want me to write it myself?"

"You'd best step this way," he encourages, head whipping around, clearly on the hunt for any underlings who witnessed this humiliating takedown.

"There's no need to go anywhere," she declares, settling herself on one of the plastic chairs in the station's waiting area. She places her cane in front of her and leans her hands on the knob. "Clyde did it."

"Clyde? Korhonen?"

"Know another Clyde, idiot?"

"Juliette," I chide, but I have to hide a smile. "Are you sure my father—"

"Might be old, but my eyes still work."

"Why didn't you bring this up sooner?" Terry remarks.

"Because I get confused about my days."

Something in her expression has me...

I blink.

What was that?

"But I know it was him. Clear as day. He was wearing a hat. A trilby. Probably thought he looked like Frank Sinatra but all I saw was a cheap imitation." She guffaws. "Old fool. You were friends with him, weren't you, Terry? In school?

"That's probably why you didn't take much notice of a dying woman's words. Always thought you were useless, but this takes the cake. Why are you pestering my grandson-in-law when his father's guilty, Terry?"

"Mrs. McAllister, to kill her, Clyde would have to be in town and we don't have proof—"

Marc's brows lift. "A friendship in school is a conflict of interest, sergeant."

Juliette snaps her fingers. "More than that. Bet he takes bribes."

"Mrs. McAllister!" Terry protests.

I study him. "If I find out that's true, Terry, there'll be hell to pay with your inspector."

His gaze shifts to the left. "That's everything, Mr. Korhonen. I'll be in touch if we have any further issues. Mrs. McAllister, I'll take you home."

"Will we make it? That's the question. Or will you kill me to silence me?"

Marc coughs out a laugh. "You made your statement in front of several witnesses, ma'am. I can promise you that if anything does happen to you, I'll be the first to report it to the RCMP."

Juliette's nod is stouter than stout. "Pleased to hear someone around here has a lick of sense."

When Terry guides Juliette to his pickup truck, still on the receiving end of a tongue-lashing, Marc murmurs, "Why do I get the feeling she's not as batty as she tried to make out?"

Because he's correct, I just scratch my chin.

"Wonder why she waited so long to come forward."

"With Juliette, who the hell knows?"

Chapter 16
Colt

THE NEXT DAY

"**H**eard about that scene in town."

I pause halfway up onto the saddle. When Fen tosses his head in annoyance, I let my boots settle on the ground and turn to face Theo. "When?"

"With Mary and Andrew."

"Oh. That."

"What did you think I meant?"

"With our Dove Bay resident."

"What's going on with you? You've barely spoken to me since December, asshole. Are you still pissed about Maria?"

His sudden burst of temper has me frowning at him. "No."

"Liar. I had to tell you, man."

"I didn't blame you."

"Are you sure?" His expression is the epitome of dubious. "Because the fact we've barely talked outside of work issues speaks louder than words."

"You're reading too much into stuff. What's going on with you? Why are you bringing this stuff up?"

His nose crinkles. "Bea and I argued."

"Oh." I roll my eyes because *that* explains everything.

Theo's as good with feelings as I am. *Usually.* Unless Bea's accused him of being a robot. "When?"

"When I went to check on her last."

"She won't answer the door for me, so you're doing something right. She has no idea how head over heels you are for her, does she?"

"No." He grits his teeth. "She doesn't. But you *have* been acting secretive with me, Colt. Did you not want me to tell you that I saw Maria with another guy when I was in Saskatoon?"

I rub Fen's ear when it flicks away a fly. "We weren't official or anything."

"I don't understand where your head's at. Last thing I heard you're glum over losing Maria, next thing you're married to the woman who killed Loki—"

I grab him by the collar. "She. Did. Not. Kill. Loki."

His eyes widen as he tries to shrug off my hold on him. "I know you gave her that alibi to keep her ass out of jail. I never understood why you protected her after what she did."

"Theo," I interrupt. "I get it. We're friends. You can say shit to my face that other people wouldn't get away with, but don't push me too far. Zee is my wife. That's what matters.

"*This* is why we haven't talked much, isn't it? You think I'm the one who's been quiet, but when was the last time you came to the house for dinner? You're avoiding Zee."

He pulls a face. "I'm not breaking bread with a murderer. I saw what her actions did—"

I tighten my grip on his collar then let go of him in a smooth move that has him jerking back a couple steps. "She didn't hurt anyone. She didn't set fire to our stables. She didn't kill Loki. Hell, she's the only reason Terry hasn't put my ass in jail.

"You hear anyone in Pigeon Creek talking smack about her, I expect you to defend her as a courtesy to me. Understood?"

He rubs his neck, but I know that's for show. Jesus, we got tossed around more by bucking broncos in our day than what I put him through. "If she didn't, who did?"

I settle a measured look on him. "Clyde."

Theo lets loose a snort. "Yeah. Right."

"Yeah. *Right.*"

He gapes at me. "You're not joking?"

"I'm not. What about this conversation is funny? I haven't been talking to you because, to be frank, I don't have anything to say.

"It's not because of a woman, be that Maria or Zee. It's nothing to do with Bea or Marvin. I'm not *sulking* with you like a child. We're grown-ass men who've been friends long enough to know one another. I.e., if you think getting married turned me into a social butterfly, you're mistaken."

Turning away from him, I saddle myself on Fen's back in a smooth rolling jump that I've perfected over the years.

"If we've done gossiping like teenage girls, get on your damn horse so we can start working."

Though he frowns, he nods and I leave him to it, taking off for the northwest quadrant where we have four heifers still waiting to calf.

Five minutes later, once he's seated on Esmeralda, he joins me out in the pasture. "I guess I just don't know what's going on. You didn't tell me you were getting married and then you *emailed* to tell me you'd been detained."

"Time was short."

"What stopped you from talking to me afterward?"

"Theo, you were dealing with Bea." I shrug. "Plus, it was a nonstarter of a conversation. I didn't do it. Saw no need to bring it up. What did you argue about?"

"With Bea?" At my nod, he grumbles, "How Esmeralda has more capacity for feeling than me."

"That's no harsher than her calling you the Tin Man." When he tugs on his collar, I grimace. "So, this is you practicing how to be more emotionally available? Can't you do this with someone else?"

"Oh, yeah. Who? My brothers? My dad?" He narrows his eyes at me. "I was your wingman for four years in university and you can't do this for me?"

"*My* wingman? Ha! I was yours."

"Okay, so maybe you were," he grouses. "Not my fault all the women want you."

"They wanted you too." Grinning, I nudge Fen with my

knee to shift him a few paces away from Esmeralda when Horny Houdini looks too interested in her for my taste. "They wanted me and the Korhonen millions first."

"Those dang millions." Still, he smiles and the atmosphere feels lighter until: "How did you end up being married to a stranger, Colt?"

For a second, I don't answer.

I let a thousand memories tumble through my mind.

A thousand that I never shared with anyone.

"She isn't a stranger."

Huh.

That 'light' atmosphere feels like laughing gas has been pumped into it.

My grin widens at how freeing it feels to admit *that*.

"What do you mean?" Theo asks, no small amount of confusion lacing the words.

"I mean she's not a stranger."

"Are you being pedantic? Sure, we were raised in the same town and went to the same school and know all the same people but—"

I press my knees into Fen's sides to still him. Theo gently tugs on Esmeralda's reins until he's next to me. "Listen, bud. You want to be more emotionally available, open your ears. I knew her a long time ago. Before the fire. We used to hang out when she was a kid."

"That doesn't make any sense."

"No. It doesn't. Why do you think I never told anyone? They'd either think I was a creep *or* that I was plain weird. Never mind the crap that comes from her being a McAllister and me being—"

"You?"

"Exactly. She'd run away from home and hide in the stables. Figured that was the safest place from her grand-mother. Knew hell'd freeze over before Juliette would come knocking on our door to see if we'd found her wayward grand-child, and we struck up a friendship." I hitch a shoulder. "She'd lost her dad and I couldn't get rid of her. When she talked, I listened. She had a sweet soul..."

"But you never let on that you were friends. Is that why you said Clyde did it—"

I knew he didn't believe me. He'd have given me the third degree if he had.

"I can see why Bea got mad with you. Look, Clyde was pulling an insurance fraud. There. Simple. That's why he did it. I only just found out or I'd have reported him to the Mounties faster than Fen can hit thirty miles per hour."

"Who told you it was Clyde?" His lips tighten. "Susanne?"

"She was there. She saw him do it. And, rightfully so, she knew no one would believe her. So many things left unsaid and all because of her surname." If my gaze is pointed, so be it. He winces. "Before you ask *why* a man as rich as my father would defraud an insurance company, it's because he's been lying to us for years. When Uncle Clay died, he left the ranch under my guardianship. Not Clyde's—"

"That bastard," Theo grinds out, finally angry about the correct thing.

"Precisely. He must have needed the cash." I rub my cheek. "I've been looking into what happened ten years ago. Gathering evidence to—"

"You want to have him arrested?!"

"Damn straight. I've set a forensic accountant onto it and I'm having the board investigated too, as well as the trustees of the family trust fund because he must have gotten to them somehow."

"Blackmail?"

"I wouldn't put it past him. Either that or bribery. If he can burn a herd of innocent animals alive, why wouldn't he be capable of blackmailing an official or bribing them?" I grit my teeth. "I want him to rot in jail, Theo. If I never have to see him again, it'll be too soon."

"*This* is why you've been acting weird, isn't it?"

"I haven't been acting weird!"

"You have. You've dealt with all this stuff on your own." He punches me in the shoulder. "Dammit, don't you know that a problem shared is a problem halved?"

"What was I supposed to say?"

"What you literally just said, jackass. What the hell are friends for if not to help out when you need it?"

"I didn't need help. I need the people I've paid to dig up the dirt on my asshole of a father to come through for me." I sigh. "But thanks, man."

His gaze is perturbed. "Do you not trust me or something?"

"No one outside of the employees I've hired to do this task and my wife knows about anything I've shared with you, Theo." The tension in his shoulders lessens. "Not even Callan." His eyes bug. "Exactly. I've kept this close to my chest because..." I rub a hand over Fen's head. "...I have a feeling I've barely scratched the surface of Clyde's sins and only God knows when we'll strike the mother lode."

"I hope it's not a streak, huh? But a full-on gold rush."

"You and me both, man. The fact that he's gone missing, that he was the father of Marcy's baby before she disappeared, that he mowed Lydia down... The gold rush seems to be underway already. Now, can we do something manly after all this talk?"

Theo scratches his cheek. "Helping heifers give birth manly enough?"

I snicker. "It's good enough for me."

Chapter 17
Zee

After driving me over to the Bar 9 on his ATV, Callan hovers only as long as it takes for me to clamber off the back before departing for the Seven Cs.

We have a code—I text him and he'll pick me up. Later, I'll show him how I keep beating him at *Driveclub*.

Mostly, I went with the 'code' option because I knew if I drove myself over here, I'd end up leaving early and the day after tomorrow's the family BBQ that Colt insisted on hosting despite the situation with Lydia.

I want to make sure they're all coming. Even if I have to drag them there.

If Colton's kid brother will suffer through a family get-together on his birthday, then my *grand-mère* can attend too.

When I step into the house, I can hear arguing in the kitchen—my family does a lot of that. And Tee wasn't exactly *quiet*. It's why it's pleasant at the Korhonens. Silence isn't a rare commodity.

I head that way, past a mountain of crap in the hall, taking note of the state of the den which makes me think my brothers took over when *Grand-mère* fired our housekeeper to cut costs. Grimacing at the state of the place, I find the triplets all in different levels of undress in the kitchen.

Calder's wearing boxer briefs, Colby's in jeans, and Carson's—

"Carson, why aren't you wearing any clothes?"

My answer is probably on the floor—the pile of laundry makes the Rockies look small.

His head whips around. "Zee? What the hell are you doing here?"

Thankfully, he keeps his ass facing me.

"I'm going to wrestle *Grand-mère* into attending the BBQ."

Colby snickers. "Like she's a steer? I'm coming to watch the show. It'll be fun."

I stride over to him. "Walker and I weren't allowed to walk around in pj's after ten but you three get to be butt naked in the kitchen? What's that about?"

"We wore her down," Colby jokes.

"Exhausted her," Carson agrees.

Calder shrugs. "She doesn't leave her quarters that much anymore. We have free run of the house."

My brow puckers at that news. "Doesn't she go on the range?"

"She's ninety-two, Zee," Calder tells me like I'm an idiot.

"I mean, I know. But I thought she'd die on a horse is all."

"Oh, she rides. Just doesn't do any work on the property. She goes over to the hot springs sometimes on horseback. Says it helps the arthritis in her hips," Colby explains as he hauls me in for a hug. "About time you came home." He's already over six feet so I'm pretty much in his shadow. Annoying. Especially when he rubs his knuckles over my hair. "I thought you'd forgotten all about us." His bottom lip mock-quivers. "Our big sis doesn't care about us."

"I care enough to keep a roof over your heads," is my flat reply, despite the fact I know he's teasing.

They all wince at my words.

And I can't be sorry.

Not when they know *why* I'm home.

Not when they know how I'm treated here.

Just because I've processed that BS doesn't make it right.

"I figured you were assimilating to your new circumstances," Calder reasons.

"Barely left the ranch until the other week."

Colby's hold on me tightens. "Heard about that."

"I wish they'd let up on you," Carson agrees, but this time, he's grabbed a dish towel and he's using it to cover his junk as he side-walks to the kitchen table.

"Hell'll freeze over first. It's fine."

"It's not," Calder retorts. "I'm glad Colt stuck up for you. It's all anyone can talk about. Folks' noses have been out of joint so the kids at school are gossiping."

"Gossip. What Pigeon Creek was founded on. Just goes to show that they'll believe anything of the McAllisters."

Colby nods. "Everyone's crossing the street whenever we show up in town."

"Assholes." I huff. "Anyway, I'm glad you're here. I wanted to talk to you too. I need you three on your best behavior at the Seven Cs—"

"Duh," Colby grumbles.

"I mean with Callan."

Carson's nose crinkles. "Why? He's an asshole."

"He's sweet."

"Asshole," Calder confirms.

"He's not!"

"He thinks he's so much better than everyone." Colby yawns. "Plus, he's a real bore."

"I like him so don't give him any crap."

Carson frowns. "So, you've been spending time with Colton's little brother and not your own? Nice, sis. Nice."

"You could have come and seen me too," I say unrepentantly. "The road isn't blocked on either end."

Calder shakes his head. "Bet you'd have shifted your ass for Walker."

Colby grunts. "Don't go there, Cald. Jeez. Walker would never have let us get into this mess in the first place, so we don't need to be in a pissing competition with our dead brother."

I arch a brow at Colby. "When did you get so wise?"

"While you were in New York."

"Burn." I cringe. "But no denying it's the truth."

"Couldn't be helped. Can still sting though." Colby nudges me. "You think Callan is cool. Might be nice if you thought the same about your actual siblings..."

My gaze flicks between them and I notice that no one is arguing with him.

Because they've been straight up with me, I admit, "I hate this house. With every fiber of my being."

"Better than hating us, I suppose," Carson mumbles.

"Never hated you. If I did, I'd have lost your numbers while I was in New York. Just, this place has a lot of bad memories for me." I decide to go for broke. "And you guys remind me of Dad something fierce. It hurts—"

"We're like him?" Calder rasps, startled but *happy...*?

"Yes. Especially to look at. My grief's still raw but that isn't your fault." I bite my lip. "I'm sorry."

Carson asks, "How are we like him?"

"Your nature... It's all him. I wish you'd had the chance to know him." Awkwardly, I give Colby a one-armed hug. "I'm going to be sticking around though. That's kind of why I'd like you to get along with Callan."

Calder scowls. "What does he have to do with anything?"

"I figured you could come to the Seven Cs and we could hang out there." I clear my throat. "Colt already said that was fine, but I don't feel comfortable forcing you guys on Callan in his own home if you hate one another."

Calder snags his coffee cup and eyes me over it. "Sounds like you came here with ulterior motives."

"It hurts that you doubt the strength of my cynical nature, Calder."

"We'll be nice to the dweeb if it means we can go over there and hang out with you."

"My heart feels full." My tone's sarcastic but I mean it.

"It should. He's a real know-it-all," Carson drawls.

"It's the curse of being clever. I'm used to it with Tee."

"I'll tell her you said that," Calder warns.

"You can tell her at the BBQ. She arrives the day of. Has to perform at a wedding the night before. You know she'll agree with me." I grab the coffee cup Colby hands me and, as I sip it, take a second to appreciate that Colt knows how my coffee should taste.

A pounding sounds overhead.

"What's that?" I ask, peering at it and grimacing when dust motes dance into my cup.

"*Mamie.*"

I don't care that I spray out a mouthful of coffee or that Colby cries, "Eww!" when some of it drips onto him.

I gape at my brother. "*MAMIE*? She lets you call her that?"

Carson snorts. "Didn't have a choice. Calder wouldn't call her anything else. Then we all joined in."

With a mocking grin, Calder studies his nails. "It worked."

"What have you done to our grandmother?" I tease, though I can't deny, I dig it.

"Like Colby said—worn her down." Carson pulls a face. "Though age might have done that."

"And the cancer scare last year," Calder points out.

I stagger into the kitchen table. "Cancer scare?"

"You've been away." Colby pats my shoulder. "And she's proud. She's bound to keep stuff from you. We know because we drive her to the hospital appointments. She hid it from us when she had those polyps removed from her throat. We only found out when she couldn't yell at us for three months solid."

Carson coos, "Three months of silence. Bliss."

Yeah, she's a yeller.

Still, she's always been a force to be reckoned with. The notion of her being sick and not telling me doesn't sit right.

Distance leaches responsibility in a way I didn't anticipate. But it doesn't absolve me of it either.

Of course, there's barely any distance between us now and I still haven't shown my face around this place.

"Did you hear about her telling Reilly she saw Clyde in our truck the day Lydia died?"

"Yes. Colt was there when she showed up." My brow furrows. "Do you think she was lying?"

"Who knows with her?" Calder shrugs. "Either way, Clyde's in deep shinola which is exactly where *Mamie* likes him."

She's not the only one.

"I'd best go and see her."

"She's not that bad, Zee," Colby assures me. "Aside from the arranged marriage stuff."

"So reassuring, dude." I shove the coffee cup at him. "Let's get it over with."

"Tear off the Band-Aid," Calder agrees.

"Pour salt in the wound," Carson concurs.

"Sounds more like it." With one foot out of the kitchen door, I ask, "You will be nice to Callan, won't you?"

Carson sighs. "We will."

I turn to look over my shoulder. "They have a home theater room. You could come and hang out sometime this week if you want?"

"Will Callan be there?" he asks warily.

"Nah. He'll stay in his room. But I don't think it's fair to..."

"I get it. I'd probably pour a whole thing of sugar in your coffee if you brought him here."

"Wow, Calder. Thanks for the death threat."

He smirks behind his coffee cup. "You're welcome. And we'll text you when we have a free night."

"Our social calendar's pretty full," Colby declares. "But for you, we'll make some room."

"Now I do feel *loved*."

"So you should," Carson calls out as I head into the hall.

The second I'm gone, they bicker like they were when I came in.

I never got to hear Walker like that. It was him and me for a long while with the triplets too young to do little other than be annoying with such a big age gap between us.

And Walker was quiet.

More so than me.

We always got along well too. There was no back-and-forth like with the triplets. We could sit in the living room, him working on one of his projects, me reading or studying, not a word uttered but both of us quietly content.

God, I miss those moments.

When I shuffle past Walker's room, I press a hand to the door.

The grief never stops. The tears diminish. The anger fades. But the longing never goes away. It's a lingering ache that I know I'll feel until I die.

Because I don't want to make things worse, I don't open his door. But I do open Mom and Dad's. It's exactly how it was that last day...

Even the sheets are mussed because after Dad died, she stopped making the bed in the morning.

Gaze flickering from one picture frame to another, I feel emotions clog my throat. The air's musty. Dingy, to be honest. But I like it. It's a shrine. Just as Walker's room is. Though it's a lot less dusty in here than I imagined.

For the first time since she passed, I breach the entrance.

I pause at her vanity and lift the bottle of perfume on there. It smells faintly of her, but not. Less fruity somehow.

I spray some on my wrists, disappointed by the slightly alcoholic tint to it that's more prevalent once it's been exposed to the air.

Pulling open the drawers, I smile when I find the makeup I used to play dress-up with.

The gold tube of lipstick doesn't gleam thanks to the myriad fingerprints covering it and there's powder everywhere —Mom was many things, but not a great housekeeper.

I take a seat on the cushioned stool and stare at my face in the mirror.

I'd been a kid the last time I sat here. She'd stood behind me. Shaking her head as I managed to spread mauve eyeshadow over my face and spill my glass of orange juice everywhere.

My fingers trail over the gold ridge that edges the table. It was probably an heirloom. That it was spared from the cull that happens whenever we run out of cash and sell off our antiques tells me how important this shrine is to *Grand-mère*—it will never be touched.

Not as long as she lives.

My gaze turns distant until I find a slight ridge that doesn't fit in somehow. I peer at the table, applying pressure to it, thinking it needs to be moved back into place. But as I do, it depresses entirely and a soft clicking motion sounds.

My lips part as a drawer opens, a small one.

Inside, there's a book. Nothing more. Just that.

It's black. Thin. Like an old-fashioned address book.

Hesitantly, I reach for it.

A faint musty smell permeates the air as I crack a spine that hasn't been touched for years.

At first, I'm not entirely sure what I'm seeing aside from a bunch of numbers and letters... Then, when my mind shifts away from surprise and begins to function, I pick apart what I'm reading.

It's not a diary, more a ledger, one that tallies the household budget for weeks at a time. Each page is filled with months' worth of numbers as if she were conserving space, but it means the book is filled with years of records.

She notes the cost of groceries, the price of clothes—a 'W' for Walker, an 'S' for me, and 'Cs' for the triplets. At the side, Mom wrote a '+/-' sign to keep a running total and that number would have been bleak were it not for the four hundred dollars added to the budget every four days.

And I mean every four days.

For years.

It's the 'CK' that's at the side of it that has me slamming the book shut.

Because I'd prefer to argue with *Grand-mère* than think about what that means, I slip it into my pocket, head for her room, and knock when I finally make it there.

"*Entrez.*"

I roll my eyes at that and immediately, my mind shifts away from the ledger.

God, she's so pretentious.

"*C'est moi,*" I greet as I pop my head around the door.

What I'm faced with takes me aback. Her hair is worn loose around her shoulders and she's still in her nightgown. She isn't wearing any makeup either.

Not for the first time, I'm coming face-to-face with the realization that my indomitable *Grand-mère* is getting old.

And fragile.

She's the kind of woman who still wears a hat with a pin and gloves when she leaves the ranch so not once have I seen her nightwear. I haven't witnessed her hair out of a tight bun or her face without minimal makeup until now.

It's disconcerting and I don't like it.

"Are you just going to stare, child?" Her mouth pinches as if she smells something bad. I've always felt like I'm the perennial source of that stench. "You're letting in the cold air."

"It's warm out," I reason, but I step inside.

"I feel the cold more. What are you doing here, anyway? I thought the Bar 9 was beneath you."

I narrow my eyes at her. "Beneath me? No. Home? Also no."

She winces but doesn't argue with me.

So I don't perpetuate the argument.

"I came to ask a favor of you."

"A favor? I never did manage to teach diplomacy to you and Walker. I tried with the triplets though. They were better students."

Calder's antics downstairs are either proof of that or the direct opposite.

At least Colby and Carson appeared to have listened.

Aside from Carson being naked in the kitchen...

"I'm sure they were. *Mamie*."

She cringes again. "God, don't you start with that horrific diminutive. Do I look like a *Mamie*?"

From where I'm standing, perhaps.

I don't say that though. She's not so right about my diplomacy skills.

"What do you want?"

"The day after tomorrow, we're holding a family BBQ at the Seven Cs."

"I've already heard all about it."

"I know. The triplets implied you weren't coming."

"I don't eat food items that can be abbreviated."

Pressing my back to the door, I shove a hand into a pocket, fully aware that she hates it when I do that. "Chicken isn't an abbreviation. Anyway, I want you there."

"Why?"

"Because you're my family."

I can tell she wants to snipe at me.

I know it makes me petty, but I run a hand through my hair. Aware that my ring finger will glint in the light.

Her jaw clenches at the sight.

Zee - 1. *Grand-mère* - 0.

"What time does this atrocity start?"

"One PM."

"Will that hockey player be there?"

She says *hockey player* like she does *lawyer*.

"They all will."

"*Mon Dieu.*"

"Why do you think I want you to be there? If nothing else, the fact that it will make the right impression should encourage you to attend."

Sniffing, she retorts, "Is Calder making my coffee?"

"If he is, then I pity you. Would you like some that doesn't taste of pond water?"

"*S'il te plaît.*"

"You'll come?"

"If I must," she dismisses, turning her head to the side so she can look out onto the ranch.

If the words weren't a dismissal, then that is.

Sighing, I turn toward the door but I pause to ask, "Did you see Clyde in our truck?"

"Do you think I'm in the habit of lying to the authorities, child?"

A nonanswer if I ever heard one.

My marriage is the only time the matriarch of the Bar 9 and the patriarch of the Seven Cs have ever worked together as a team...

That makes her statement to the RCMP questionable.

Are they taking her seriously? Or filing it as a petty griev-ance between long-held enemies?

Pursing my lips, I return to the kitchen.

"That was fast," Colby remarks when he spies me.

Thankfully, Carson is still sitting at the table, shielding me from his junk.

"She wants me to make her a coffee."

"As payment for attending the BBQ?"

"No, Calder." I flash my ring at him. "This did the talking for me."

"Where can I get me one of those?"

"Did you come out and I missed that announcement? Anyway, as far as I know, the Korhonens are all straight."

His nose crinkles as he clicks his fingers. "My plans are foiled."

"They're certainly something."

An hour after I drop off *Grand-mère*'s coffee in the French press she likes and with some of the cookies I know she prefers, she makes an appearance downstairs.

That's when I'm shown another side entirely to my stalwart grandmother.

The triplets *rib* her. And she lets them.

Walker was grounded for talking back and I was never allowed to sit at the kitchen table with my elbows on it, but Carson's still embracing his naturist self and Calder never lets her get away with anything yet doesn't earn so much as a harrumph.

But, as I watch their interactions, their byplay, I can't help but be grateful that their relationship with her is different.

They didn't have Mom and Dad around like Walker and I did. They were our light in the shadows. It's only right that she softened that harsh exterior to let them in because if she hadn't, they'd have had no one.

For that and that alone, I can be thankful.

I can also feel guilty because clearly, I've sucked as a big sister more than I even realized.

So, when Callan comes and picks me up after receiving our

code, I kiss her on the cheek in silent gratitude because if it weren't for her, the boys would have been orphans for real. And if it weren't for her, I'd never have been able to escape Pigeon Creek to mature in NYC...

She might be a pain in the ass, but she's our pain in the ass.

I don't suppose I can ask for anything else.

Chapter 48
Colt

Run - Stephen Fretwell

"Hey, Colt!" Mia, Cole's fiancée, chirps in greeting. My younger brother, on the other hand, looks like someone died.

"Mia." I press a kiss to her cheek. "Good to see you."

She nudges Cole when he folds his arms in greeting and glowers at me. "Don't be a baby. He wanted you to spend your birthday with people who love you. That's not a crime, Cole."

He squints at her. "Whose side are you on?"

"The side of righteousness."

"You and your sci-fi books."

"What does sci-fi have to do with righteousness?"

"Duh. Isn't it obvious?"

After all these years of railroading three brothers, I'm a pro at spotting an argument in the making so I clear my throat.

His attention flickers to me, and so does his fist—he punches me in the shoulder. "You suck."

"I don't." I'm in no mood for his BS, birthday or not.

Ignoring the big baby masquerading as my little brother, I

go through the preflight checks and we're in the air not long after.

One smooth flight later, we disembark. Unsurprisingly, the whole family—aside from Zee—is waiting beside the runway.

Mrs. Abelman included.

"It's our resident poltergeist!" Cole greets, arms wide as he draws her in for a hug, laughing as she bats at his shoulders for him to let go of her.

Even Mum's laughing as she's chiding, "Cole, leave Ida alone."

"Why would I do that? How would she know I love her otherwise?"

Mrs. Abelman snorts as Cole hooks Mum in a hug too. "I can cope with less effusive declarations of love, Cole."

Mia grins as she holds out her hand for Mum. "So great to see you again, Lindsay."

Mum tuts and kisses her cheek. "Less of the formalities, dear."

The words rub me on the raw. "Somehow, I don't think you'd say that if Zee were the one visiting."

I'm not afraid of confrontation, but it's not something I seek either. So my words are the verbal equivalent of a first punch.

Aware that I'm the center of everyone's focus, I arch a brow at Mum who splutters, "I don't know what you mean, Colton!"

"I think you do," is my soft retort because I apparently woke up on the wrong side of the bed this morning.

Guess that's what happens when evidence rolls in, confirming that your father's a lying, conniving, devious piece of shit.

Cole flicks a look between us. "Everything okay?"

"Everything's fine," Mum quickly counters, her brow puckering with genuine confusion that irritates me more. "Colton can't expect me to grow attached to Susanne when his marriage has an expiration date. Unlike with you and Mia." She goes so far as to kiss Mia's cheek for a second time, which is like tossing a red rag in front of a bull.

"My marriage has as much of an expiration date as Cole and Mia's—it's up in the air. Only the fates will decide how long we're together for. What I *do* know is that Zee, her name is goddamn Zee and I've asked you a dozen times to call her by her chosen name, will be the mother of your grandchild. She deserves more respect than you're currently giving her."

Callan cackles. "Go, bro." When he holds out his fist for me to bump, I scowl at him until he huffs.

"This isn't a joke."

"I never thought it was. I've told Mum to call her Zee but she won't."

Noticing that Mia's cheeks are bright pink, I cup her shoulder. "This has nothing to do with you, honey. I'm making a point."

Her timid smile has Cole squinting at me with displeasure, but I'm not going to apologize. Mum needs to listen to me, and if shaming her in front of the whole damn family is the way forward, then that's on her.

"Cole, you're with me."

He harrumphs at my order but, after kissing Mia's cheek, trudges over to the truck while the rest of the family gets sorted with the ranch hands helping out.

As soon as I'm behind the wheel, I purse my lips. "You going to treat Zee with kindness or talk to her like she's dog shit?"

"I was thinking of pretending she doesn't exist."

"She didn't set the fire, Cole," I say with a sigh.

"If she didn't, then who did?" he snaps. "You're so certain that she's innocent, but that fire had nothing to do with faulty wiring."

His insistence has me studying him. "What are you talking about, Cole?"

"I've been thinking about that time a lot recently. Ever since Mia came into my life, I realized the wound's still gaping and hasn't been healing. We talked about it and... I remembered something." He scrapes a hand over his head. "I overheard Pops on the phone with someone. Looking back, I think it was the insurance adjuster. It sounded like he was paying him off."

It's one thing for me to come outright and say that I think

Clyde set fire to the stables, but Cole doesn't trust Zee and despite this new revelation, why would he take her word for it?

Pensive, I stare at the range, finding the comfort in it that I usually do, but there's nothing there that puts my mind at ease. Not with one of our sore spots being lanced like an infected boil, revealing decades' worth of unhealed trauma. Because this doesn't start and end with the fire—it's one big amalgamation of a childhood gone awry.

We're silent on the ride to the house. I didn't mean to be quiet and I'm definitely not mad at Cole for getting in his feelings, especially when he *did* come home like I requested and in the middle of the playoffs, but neither do I know how to get the words out that I need to.

It feels like Pandora's edging ever nearer toward her box and I'm supposed to brace for impact but no one gave me a seat belt.

"You okay, Colt?"

The question jerks me from my heavy thoughts. I turn to glance at my little brother who's studying me, concern lacing his expression.

"I'm better than I have been in a long while."

Reluctantly, he concedes, "Marriage is suiting you?"

"Yeah. It is. Could be that it's Zee who's suiting me more than marriage." My hands tighten on the wheel. "I knew her. Before the fire. She's no stranger to me."

"Huh?"

"After her dad's funeral, she'd sneak into the stables and I'd go sit with her." Having shared this with Theo, it's easier to talk about. "Got to know her over a real long time. Learned the measure of the girl. Didn't trust in that measure when I should have—"

"I don't understand."

I rub my jaw. "Who could blame you?"

He turns in his seat, demanding, "Colton, you *knew* her? Were you dating?"

"No, we damn well weren't. You know what the age gap is between us. Do you think I'm some sicko? I guess I was like an older brother. At least, on my side, that's how it was."

He's quiet for a second. "You mean she liked you differently than you did her?"

"The age gap was something I couldn't see past. Doesn't matter so much when one of you is approaching thirty and the other said farewell to it a couple years back."

"I guess not," he mumbles, tone stilted.

"I'm going to be honest with you, Cole, and you're not going to like what I have to say."

"I'm already not liking it."

"I figured as much." The wheel creaks under my palms. "Couldn't blame you. Figure you'll be angry at me for a long while and that's okay. But... I thought she did it too."

He doesn't explode. Doesn't punch me in the shoulder.

If anything, his silence is more unnerving.

Cole is *never* quiet.

Like a fool, I attempt to fill the vacuum. "I gave her an alibi because she was young and, to be frank, as messed up as we were. *Are*," I correct.

"Why?"

"Because she tried to kiss me that night and I rejected her. During the fire, she was trapped with Loki." My throat tightens as realization strikes. "She was depressed before her brother died. That day, the family received news he was presumed killed in action. I guess I thought she was fucked up enough to end it all and hurt me at the same time."

"And you still gave her an alibi?"

His wooden tone has me gritting my teeth. "She was a kid—"

"She was a killer!"

"She didn't do it."

"You expect me to believe that *now*?" he snarls.

"I don't expect you to believe anything without asking questions. But I want you to know something—"

"That you've been lying to me for years?"

"No. Well, yes. But, this time it's about Uncle Clay."

"What about him?"

"He left the ranch's stewardship to me."

"What?!"

"Yeah."

"But Pops—"

"He lied too," I tell him simply. "And I can't imagine how much he had to spend in bribes to keep the trustees from kicking up a fuss, but I have to reckon that the insurance payout on the fire would have kept things ticking along for a while. Franny alone must have reeled him in a couple million."

"Are you trying to tell me that you think Pops set the fire?"

"I'm not trying. I'm telling you."

"Proof?"

"Mrs. Abelman found Uncle Clay's will. We had no evidence of any bribes by that point—"

"Meaning you have them now?"

I nod. "Today. I only went looking because Zee told me what she saw that night. I listened to her side of the story for once. I treated her like shit for the past ten years, Cole. Cut her out as if she meant nothing to me, but she *wasn't* nothing.

"While my relationship with her was fraternal, her feelings were different. Though I did love her in my own way.

"Cutting her out was my self-imposed punishment for sparing her from the aftermath of what I thought she did." I rub my jaw. "I know it's a mess, but I never let her tell me anything. I stopped seeing her. Refused to talk to her. Avoided her and the ranch at all costs—"

"I remember Callan complaining that you weren't coming down on the weekends."

"I had to. As much as I didn't want her to go to jail, I hated myself for being so goddamn weak because she killed Loki and Betsy and the rest." Spying the house in the near distance, I brake and switch off the engine. All while bracing myself for the fallout. It's brewing. "Then, Callan tried to—"

"Yeah," he interrupts. Neither of us likes to bring up that time.

"There was no more avoiding the ranch. Once this whole marriage contract BS came about, she signed everything but she said she wouldn't marry me unless I answered a question."

"Which was?"

"Did I think she had it in her to kill Loki?"

"He was your horse. Why would she—"

"As much as he was mine, in a way, he was hers too. You don't share heart horses, I know that. But they were pretty damn close to it. He loved her and she loved him. She was always hiding in his stall. Always giving him attention and talking to him. It was like he was her only source of comfort in a time when she was having to face grief and loss every couple years.

"I know it makes no sense when she had her own mount, but she was different with Loki and he was the same with her. You know how he was—hated being tended to by anyone other than me. I spoiled him, but that was nothing to her." I grip the back of my neck. "She'd never have hurt him and I told her so... Here we are."

"You gaslit me," he growls.

"I did." I turn to him, wanting my brother to see that I take full accountability for this situation. "I'd already perjured myself for her, Cole. I couldn't let you fuck that up."

His stony gaze turns on me. "Did you kill Lydia Armstrong? Callan told me she was sending Zee poison pen letters too. Were you trying to protect *her*?"

"No, dammit. I didn't kill her. Clyde did."

He skims over my words like I never said them. "Callan said that she lied to the cops for you. That her alibi was fake."

"Callan talks too damn much."

How the hell did the little shit even know that?

"Only fitting. One fake alibi deserves another."

His nostrils flare and that serves as my first warning. When he punches me, I don't fight back. Just hiss as blood spurts from my nose. Then, he shoves open the door and jumps out, striding off to the house without another word.

I watch him go.

I don't stop him or call him back.

He's within his rights to be furious at me and I more than earned that punch.

Tenderly, I touch where his fist landed. Accepting that I probably earned the busted nose too.

Finding a less-than-clean rag in the glove compartment, I

stem the bleeding as best as I can, not willing to start the engine until Cole's made it inside.

When I see him disappear into the house, I set off once more, but instead of joining him and the rest of the family, I turn toward what was the border of Zee's land and mine and what's now ours, and I park up ten or so feet from one of the Bar 9's lakes.

Does it come as a surprise when, forty-five minutes later, I spy Jas in the rearview mirror, Zee atop her saddle?

Not particularly.

I have no idea how she knew where I'd be, but I'm not going to complain. I watch her amble to the driver's side of the truck, her movements silken as she and Jas work together like they've been partnered for a lifetime.

"Cole's pretty much his own weather front," is her greeting.

My lips quirk at the apt description. "Can bring a blizzard and a heatwave all in the same day."

"You told him about the fire?"

I shift a look at her, glancing away from the crystalline surface of the lake. "I did. Was he cruel to you?"

"No. You need ice on that."

I shrug. "Isn't the first time one of my brothers hit me. Probably the first time I deserved worse though."

"He didn't—"

"I lied to him. For a decade, Zee." I suck in a breath, regretting it when it makes my busted nose ache. "There were always going to be repercussions for that."

"You told him everything?"

"Sure did. He's a blabbermouth. He'll tell the others too. Saves me the job."

Whistling, she jumps off the saddle.

"Let her go. Jas won't run away."

"You sure?"

"100%."

As I thought, Jas doesn't chase liberty—she's too spoiled to want it. The Camarillo merely wanders to the shoreline.

"Have you changed your pump site today?"

She rolls her eyes. "I know you're the town's daddy, but you don't need to baby me."

"Not a crime to care," I murmur.

I get it.

The fatigue she must feel from being hypervigilant is something I can't imagine dealing with, and now, she has me, Tee, Callan, *and* Mrs. Abelman monitoring her blood sugar. It's only because we give a damn but it must be tiring.

"No," she mumbles. "Sorry. Callan came at me while you were out, about my cookies."

"What about them?"

"He says my blood sugar spikes when I decorate them."

My brows lift. "He wouldn't say that if it weren't true."

"I'm a perfectionist," she counters.

And that makes her blood sugar spike? How random.

"It doesn't matter. It's just why I'm grouchy."

Nodding my understanding, I turn to watch Jas as she prances in the water. Which is when I come to an admittedly abrupt decision, but today feels like a good day for that. "Things will be getting busier over the upcoming year."

She tilts her head to the side. "Why?"

"I'll be setting up the breeding program."

She rests her arms on the open window and pushes her face toward mine. "I know you mentioned it before, but are you shifting away from beef stock?"

"Not entirely, though we both know it isn't sustainable. Not in these numbers." I snag her fingers in mine. "I thought maybe you'd want to be a part of it."

"Me?"

The joy in her eyes only cements my belief that this is the right time. "Yeah. You were always great with the horses."

"Maybe with the care, but I'm no good with stuff like breeding. I always feel sorry for the mares." Her free hand toys with the medallion she always wears.

"You equine feminist, you."

"Don't you know it." She shivers. "I hate the noises they make. It creeps me out." It doesn't take much to figure out why that is and I gently squeeze her fingers in comfort. Instead of blanching or blushing though, she mutters, "You know when I went to see the triplets and *Grand-mère?*"

"Uh-huh."

"I found something in one of the drawers in Mom's vanity."

Her tone tells me it wasn't a 'good' something.

I stay silent, waiting for her to find her words.

"I think Clyde was paying Mom for sex."

That has me blinking.

And gaping at her like a fish.

"That's pretty much how I've felt ever since I found out," she mumbles.

"Why didn't you tell me sooner?" I chide, opening the door. Soft enough it doesn't jar her but enough that we have to untangle our fingers.

In a flurry of movement, I shove my seat back as soon as we're apart, then I open the door wider, grab her hand, and haul her onto my lap.

It takes some fiddling but we make it work without her banging her head.

"I was studying her ledger—"

"Ledger?" I ask, confused. "Like for accounts?"

"Yeah. That's what I found. Her little black book," she says grimly. "We were always in the red. Until 'CK' made a deposit." She shudders. "I think he wanted to make the same deal with me at the airport. The way he touched my cheek..."

Outrage fills me. "That asshole." I draw her tighter into my hold.

"That asshole singlehandedly propped up the Bar 9," she rasps. "The duration of their arrangement is insane to me."

"When your father was alive?"

"No. But this went on for *years.*"

"Shit."

Nodding, she mutters, "Maybe I'd be better with the breeding now that I know it wasn't... what I thought it was."

My mind's blank.

I have no idea what to say to her to make any of this right. I don't know if it's within my power to—

522

"We need to hire my family some staff to look after the house. They're not doing so great on their own."

Okay.

Change of topic coming right up.

Not healthy but damn if I have a better idea on how to improve this shitshow.

"Sure thing. I'll get Theo on it."

Relieved, she sighs. "Thank you. Your mom called me Zee."

I kiss her temple. "When?"

"When she introduced me to Mia. Who, by the way, is sweet."

"She is." I gesture to a smaller lake in the distance. "Cole proposed to her on that lake over there."

Her brows lift. "When it was *my* lake. Why, Mr. Korhonen, were you trespassing?"

I grin at her. "The whole setup was pretty neat if I do say so myself. The water was frozen and he'd hired this violinist to serenade them. Then, Callan, Cody, and I placed hundreds of candles on the ice. She's a figure-skating coach and he was her pupil, so, mid-routine, he proposed." I tap my nose and then point to a barely there rise on the horizon. "He doesn't know that we watched."

Amusement lights up her eyes. "Did he fall?"

"Once. But it was a controlled landing. When he went down, he proposed."

"That's sweet."

"He can be. When he tries not to be a pain in the ass." I clear my throat. "Once we get over this hurdle, he'll be a good brother-in-law."

"He doesn't have to like me, Colt," she reasons. "I don't need that from him."

"Maybe you don't, but I do. I didn't raise him to be a dick to women and certainly not to family."

"You didn't raise him."

"Not as much as Callan, but I did for a while. Clyde was no use and, toward the end of their marriage, Mum wasn't bearing up well. It's how he got the courts to agree to his petition for sole custody."

"To cut the ties between mother and sons like that—so cruel."

I crack my knuckles. "Sums him up."

She slots her fingers with mine. It takes me back to when we were in Loki's stall. Her silent support and comfort got me through some of those rough times.

I brush my lips over her knuckles, watching her small smile and finding a different kind of solace there than I ever did when we were younger because she's mine now.

That small smile is for me and it means so much more when it comes from Zee, my wife, than Zee, my sixteen-year-old friend.

"You never told me what this is." I gently tug on her necklace.

"You never asked."

"I'm asking now."

"Tee's nonna gave one to each of us. It's St. Christopher. He's the patron saint of travelers. Tee, of course, lost hers about three days into owning it, but I always wear mine."

"Didn't it remind you of home?"

"Sometimes." She cups my cheek. "I think I am a masochist."

I snort. "Then we're in the same boat. I also told Cole about the will."

"Figured as much. What did he say? Aside from causing this mess." Her thumb gently swipes along my busted nose.

I'm grateful I found some antibacterial wipes in the glove compartment or she'd have been greeted with blood too.

"They'll probably serve my ass on a plate at the BBQ for lying to them, but his big mouth will spare me from having to tell Callan and Cody everything."

"Will they forgive you?"

"Eventually." I scratch my jaw because the last thing I feel like doing is grilling hamburgers. "If you hear fighting, leave us to it."

"You're grown men!"

"We're brothers," I mutter. "It's how we deal with feelings. Fists and banter." She pulls a face then settles her forehead on mine, careful around the damage to my nose. "It'll be a fresh start. Of sorts. But if it means Cole will leave you alone, it'll be worth it."

"No, Colt, I—"

"Everything'll be fine. I have you."

Her throat bobs but she whispers, "You do."

"Then that's all I need."

And I seal it with a kiss.

Chapter 19
Zee

"**Z**EE! Butch Cassidy stopped writing to me!"

I'd recognize that voice anywhere—even if she's later than expected.

My head whips to the side as I find my BFF standing on the small step of the truck that helps short-asses like her climb aboard. In her hand, there's a white sheet of paper and she hollers, "WHAT. A. JERK!"

I'm too accustomed to her outbursts to be embarrassed that the whole Korhonen family as well as my own is lingering around the BBQ.

If anything, this is a break in the tension.

Ironically, that tension has nothing to do with the enmity that's simmered between the Korhonens and the McAllisters for centuries—nope, it's to do with the fact that Cole, as expected, ran his mouth, and Cody and Callan have joined the 'scowl at Colton' brigade.

A union that's only strengthened since Callan shared the news of the breeding program with Cole. He was *not* happy to hear that update.

"What did you do?" I holler back at Tee.

"Why am I the one to blame?" She disembarks the truck with a sassy jump, shouts a 'thank you' at the ranch hand Colt sent to pick her up at the airport, then stalks over to me. "Maybe he's the one, huh?"

"You know you say stuff to get a rise out of him," I remark, having heard too many of her first drafts to the guy.

Yes, *first drafts*.

She writes him essays.

"He likes it when I get in his face. The douchenozzle told me he was retiring and that he thought another soldier might benefit from hearing from me." She stomps her foot. "What does he think I am? Some letter-writing hooker?"

"I mean, I doubt it?"

"Then what?! Does he think I write letters for every soldier I come across?"

"You did join that program—"

She slaps the letter against my chest. "He dumped me!"

"You weren't dating," I soothe.

And fail.

"You're not making this any better."

I grimace. "No. I'm sorry, honey."

"Read it."

That's when Colton swoops in. "Everything okay?"

"Does it look like I'm okay, Colton?" Tee declares, arms flailing to her side. "My heart is broken."

"Who broke it?"

"Her pen pal," I mumble as I scan the letter.

Colt settles a hand on Tee's shoulder. "I'm sorry, Tee."

"He's much better at this comfort stuff than you," my best friend grouses, then has the audacity to drag my two-hundred-thirty-pound husband in for a hug. "Men suck, Colton."

He awkwardly pats her back. "I know."

"I mean, you're a man. Would you throw away YEARS of friendship?"

He casts me a look that's tinged with desperation when she doesn't let go of him. "Years?"

"Yes. *Years*. Then he dumps me. Who does that?"

"You were dating?"

"Why is everyone obsessing over that?" That means Parker

said the same thing. "You don't have to be dating someone to get dumped! If anyone knows that, it's you two."

Colton cringes but agrees, "No, fair point."

"Tee," I chide. "Was that necessary?"

Still embracing my husband, she squints at me. "Did it hurt when Colton ghosted you?"

"You know it did."

"Then you know how this feels." Her bottom lip wobbles. "I loved him, Zee. I did."

Heart hurting for her, I tuck her in a hug too. "I'm sorry, honey."

She sniffles. "Was that so hard?"

Man, I suck.

I nuzzle my nose against hers then kiss her cheek. "I got you All-dressed chips."

I know she's pouting. "What about Nanaimo bars?"

"Made those."

"What about a Coffee Crisp?"

"Yup."

She heaves a sigh. "You don't totally suck as a BFF. Who busted Colt's nose? It was prettier back in New York."

I snort. "Cole."

"Huh. Did you deserve it, Colt?"

Colton pats her back again. "I did. I need to deal with the grill, Tee."

Sniffling, she lets go of him because he mentioned the magic word 'grill,' but I quickly tug her into a proper hug.

As we collide, her cheek brushes mine and, this time, I feel the tear tracks there.

"I'm sorry I doubted you, sweetheart."

"You didn't doubt me. You know I'm difficult," she excuses soggily. "But he liked that. I know he did. You don't talk to someone for years and years if you hate their guts."

"You're right. Maybe he thought you wouldn't want to be a pen pal with someone who wasn't enlisted anymore?"

"More like he didn't want to tell me his address."

"What do you mean?"

Her cheeks flush with heat. "I mean he never told me. For security purposes."

"I'm confused. How did he ever receive a letter from you?"

"Via his service number. I guess he's more of a jerk than I realized. Clearly, he doesn't think he'll have time for me seeing as he's back here and can get laid instead of writing to me.

"But he could have gotten laid with me. What did I have to do? Send him a manual? Visit these coordinates, go to the fourth floor, knock on the door, kiss resident's mouth, spread legs, insert penis here?"

A laugh bursts from me but her woeful expression has me quickly containing it. "Did you tell him you'd have been amenable to a relationship with him?"

"No. I'm going to miss him. How can he just cut me off like that?"

The guilt that hits me at her words is blindsiding. I didn't cut her off, but I left. Now Butch Cassidy's disappearing on her too. God.

I clear my throat. "What about the coffee shop lady?"

"I told you that's over. I tried it with a girl who plays the viola too, but she sucked at oral."

"Is that a pun?"

"No. Maybe I can't orgasm with someone else. I should probably accept that."

"You can't accept that. Not at twenty-six."

For the first time, her gaze flickers at our audience. "I bet *he* was good at oral."

"Ignore them, Tee."

"My replacement's watching us."

"Callan's not your replacement," I chide.

"I should arm-wrestle him for the title of best friend."

"Not necessary."

"I-I think I'm the problem, Zee," she whispers.

"You're not the problem."

"I am. That's why you're dumping me for a teenager—"

"I'm not dumping you for a teenager!" I snag her hands and give her a hard shake. "You rock. If some douche soldier doesn't realize what he's missing by cutting you out then that's on him."

Dislodging my grip on her, she cups her elbows in a gesture that doesn't suit my ebullient friend.

A part of me could kill this soldier jackass for making her self-soothe, but instead, I draw her into another hug and decide to distract her. "I'm relying on you, babe."

"What for?"

"To break the ice. Thanks to your flight being delayed, it already got underway without you, so now, things are awkward."

"'Showdown at high noon' awkward?"

"Something like that. Except Colt's brothers are more pissed at him than at the prospect of sharing a meal with my family."

"What did he do?"

"He gave them proof that I didn't set the fire."

"You can give me the deets later." She props her chin on my shoulder. "Cole's still annoyingly hot."

I grin because I know she can't see. "Colt's hotter."

"Cody's the tastiest of them all."

"As tasty as Beaver Tails?"

"Looks like he has a stick up his ass, so no. He's a soldier too, isn't he?"

"Not anymore. He's back from Saskatoon. He's doing this basic training thing to be the town's new marshal."

"Once a soldier, always a soldier, but..." Whistling, she pulls back. "I wonder what the uniform will look like."

Because that's such a Tee thing to say, I burst out laughing.

Her lips quirk at my reaction but she muses, "Callan's eyeing up the triplets like they're going to throw water bombs at him."

"They promised to be on their best behavior."

"Ha! So, they'll only throw *water* balloons at him, then? Not ones filled with dog shit?"

"Ugh. I don't want to remember what happened the last time they did that."

She snickers. "Doesn't take much to remember. It was worth it. That bitch deserved to have her car covered in turds—"

"Lydia Armstrong died, Tee," I chide.

"I know, but she was still a bitch."

I whack her arm. "Be nice."

"Be nice about the woman who never let you walk past her without calling you horrible names? Ha. I don't think so."

"She didn't deserve to die like that," is my stout retort. I grab her hand and drag her over to the grill. "It's time to meet the rest of the family, kiddo."

Her fingers tighten around mine. "Parker said she contemplated making it up here then decided she'd rather stick pins in her eyes."

I snort. "How did I end up with two drama queens for best friends?"

Over burgers and potato salad, hot dogs with homemade relish, and a steak as thick as my fist, Tee eventually calms down. She mostly avoids *Grand-mère,* who deigns to speak with Lindsay and Ida, and sticks to hanging out with the triplets, Mia, and me.

Callan stays near the grill with Colton. I know he's pissed because I heard them arguing before Tee showed up, but I figure it's a comfort thing. Especially with the triplets on his home turf.

Cody and Cole are in cahoots, sitting and glowering at Colt while eating the food he prepares.

I try to be the butterfly—chatting with Mia, buttering up *Grand-mère,* making sure Tee and the triplets aren't getting up to mischief, hovering beside Callan and Colt in an attempt to smooth over troubled waters.

It's exhausting.

I hate hosting.

But... it's also nice.

Really nice.

These are my peeps, after all.

"You haven't eaten anything yet. Go and be with your family. I'll play hostess."

The words have me spinning on my heel because, not for the first time today, Lindsay is being pleasant...

"It's fine," I hasten to assure her.

But she shakes her head. "Christy is only out here for a short while and God knows if we'll ever get your grandmother over to the Seven Cs again." She pats my shoulder. "Anyway, I've never been the hostess at any family event where Clyde couldn't ruin it. It'll be a novel experience."

Though I grimace, it's not like I can refuse. Nodding, I thank her and then retreat to the grill.

Seeing that Callan drifted over to his other brothers and left Colt alone, I murmur, "Did you two finally stop arguing?"

"Is that even possible with Callan?"

I hitch a shoulder. "I'm not saying you'd win but sure."

"In this instance, I told him to go and spend some time with Cole and to stop with the passive-aggressive comments to me. He can do that anytime. Whereas he barely sees Cole." He shoots me a look. "You haven't eaten anything."

"I'm fine."

I *may* have left it longer than I should to eat because of how crazy the day's been, but I know my limits. Still, I appreciate his care as he hands me a cheeseburger in an oat bran bun.

"It's the special ketchup," he assures me, and that it's in my bread with my ketchup makes the burger better.

I know he cares, but this is like a food-shaped hug. And it tastes great.

As I eat, he asks, "Everything okay with Mum? I saw her come up to you."

"Sure. She's being nice."

"Glad to hear it," he says darkly.

I arch a brow at him. "You couldn't expect her to warm up to me. Not when she didn't know if I'd be sticking around."

The 'hiss' of beef grilling and the 'pop' of hot dogs roasting are louder than his next words: "And are you?"

My smile is wry. "You know you don't have to ask me that."

The warmth in his eyes would be enough to keep me toasty on a cold winter day.

"A husband likes to check in."

"Consider yourself checked in."

"For how long?"

"At my hotel? At least, say, forty years."

He clucks his tongue. "Fifty would be better."

"Every rancher nickels and dimes."

"It's in our blood," he agrees with a wink. The 'our' has me smiling at him. But he nudges me with his elbow. "Would you mind checking on Callan?"

"Why?"

"I don't want him to start an argument with Cody and Cole. They're bickering so one is incoming."

My man has eyes in the back of his head, I swear.

"He's on your side—" I raise a hand to stop him from arguing. "Of course he is. Don't answer that. He's mad. You broke his trust."

"I know, but I'd prefer him to air our dirty laundry later and not in front of your *grand-mère*," he says with a sad chuckle.

"I dunno. You'll make her a very happy woman if you do," I sing.

His mouth curves into a sheepish grin. "I wouldn't ask you to be their referee, not when Cole's so, well, *Cole*, but—"

"You don't have to say another word."

With a wink, I pop onto tiptoe and kiss his cheek. As I drift over to his brothers, I grow aware that mine hijack Colt because he immediately bursts out laughing. I'm glad—he deserves the break in tension.

His siblings, surprisingly, *aren't* talking about arson, insurance fraud, or anything related to Colt's fears.

"You need the practice, Callan," Cole tells him. "They're written by women for women. It's like a textbook—"

"I don't want to!" Callan declares, cheeks blazing.

Not in anger, but... embarrassment?

Cody snorts. "Leave him alone."

"No. We need to get him some action. You know half the girls in our year would have happily taken our V-cards."

"Maybe we're not all man-whores," Callan bites off.

"You have to pop your cherry eventually, Callan," is Cole's grumble.

Uncomfortable on Callan's behalf, I pat his back. "Everything okay here?"

Callan freezes for a second, then: "Everything's fine."

When he storms off toward the house, I heave a sigh. "We won't get him out of his room for a week."

"Sure we will," Cody says cheerfully, nudging his brother in the side with his elbow. "Once Cole heads back to the city. With his lady porn."

"It's good shit," is the middle brother's declaration. But he doesn't look at me and keeps his head bowed.

Because I don't exist or...?

"Callan's a nice kid," I insert softly. "He'll find his path without you pushing him."

"She's right, Cole."

"I'm worried about him."

"Why?" Cody asks. "I don't get it. He's safe—"

"He never leaves the ranch," Cole counters. "I tried to get him to agree to spend the summer with me in New York City but he refused."

Because I can sense genuine concern for Callan, I assure him, "He's happy here."

Cody nods. "He is, Cole."

"How can he be?" is Cole's retort. "He's eighteen and has seen nothing of the country. Never mind the continent. *Never mind* the world. He needs to spread his wings."

"Not everyone wants the same things." I stare at my burger rather than look at them. "It's not my place to say any of this, but I'd have been happy staying here. It was only circumstances that took me away from Pigeon Creek.

"I learned a lot, realized who I am and what I need, but not everyone has to do that. I actually brought this and attending university elsewhere up with him, but I think he's one of those people who truly is content with their corner of the world being the only part they see."

He wants to snap at me. I can see it in his eyes. He doesn't like me. Until recently, he thought I was an arsonist who killed his beloved horse. And despite Colt's admission, there's still a smidgen of doubt that tinges his expression.

But kudos to him, he holds his tongue.

Cody, apparently aware of his brother's dislike for me,

shoots me a gentle smile. "Your friend has three personalities rolled into one person."

The conversational shift comes as a relief.

"She has four on a bad day." I take a bite of my burger, chew, swallow, and then inform them both, "Colt's a good man. I'm sure he'd be the first to say that he deserves it if you give him a hard time, but... you should bear that in mind before you do."

"You stopped being a big baby yet?"

The interruption is welcome.

When Mia slips onto Cole's lap, she hooks an arm around his neck. "Don't mind this one, Zee. He's all bark and no bite."

"Hey!"

My lips form a quick smile. "I don't mind. He's sticking up for his brother."

"You're a better person than me for taking his BS." When Cole pulls a face, she taps his nose in a silent warning. "Be nice."

Cole huffs. "Is it true that you play games with Callan?"

I pause at the about-face. "Yes."

"Thank you."

"You don't have to thank me. I enjoy it."

"He's a little shit but he's lonely." Cole locks his eyes on me. "I appreciate you keeping him company."

"Honestly, he's fun."

Cody clears his throat. "We just need a woman his age to think that."

Cole argues, "I'm telling you he has to start reading smut."

Mia groans. "You still harping on about that? Not everyone's into it."

"Only a sadist isn't into happily-ever-afters."

"He likes first-person-shooter games," I point out. "I don't think romance fits in."

"But that's where you're wrong. There's romance for everyone. It's the genre that keeps on giving."

Cody sighs. "I thought once I left home, I wouldn't need to hear soliloquies on how awesome romance books are."

"That's because you don't understand their awesomeness. Romance makes the world go round."

Laughter echoes around the BBQ. Not from one of us, but Tee who's talking to Lindsay.

Is it my imagination or does Cody cut her a glance?

"Wouldn't have taken you for a gamer, Zee," Mia comments, her tone kind.

"I grew up with boys. One of whom became a soldier. Them's the cards that fall."

Cody's brow puckers. "I forgot Walker enlisted. Fuck."

"It was a long time ago," I say simply.

It's my cue to leave though.

As I go, Cole grates out, "What did you say that for, dipshit?"

I let my gaze drift to the sky.

Cole Korhonen being kind to me?

There have to be pigs flying over the Seven Cs...

But nope.

There isn't a single bewinged *porcus* in the sky.

Another bawdy laugh from Tee has me glancing around at the miracle that is this BBQ.

My family. His.

Enemies.

But we ended the rancor that our ancestors wrought and while they're rolling in their graves, we're chatting, listening to music, and eating great food.

It's probably the first time that a sense of belonging fills me.

Maybe it was Colt's declaration, his admission to Cole, the presence of our families, or maybe it's my own words to his brothers, but this is my place.

The acknowledgment flutters inside my chest, filling all the empty spaces. It sinks to my feet and grounds me.

I'm home.

And as that acceptance settles in for the long haul, of course something has to come along and take a massive dump on it.

A fancy sports car shoots down the driveway, and by the tension in Colt's shoulders, it doesn't take a genius to figure out who's behind the wheel or *how*—someone on staff took a bribe to give him access through the front gate.

Clyde parks the car diagonally across the lane.

If I needed a reminder on how much of an asshole he was, I got it.

"A family BBQ without the patriarch?" he booms, tone hearty like he's welcome here.

As if three of said family hadn't colluded to toss him off the ranch in the first place.

Dead silence falls at his words, but despite knowing the hatred my husband has for his father, what he does still takes me aback.

In response, he calmly places the fork and tongs in his hands onto the side, turns away from the grill, then walks over to Clyde who beams at his son as if he's the prodigal father, but his eyes widen as Colt's fist soars forward, colliding with the asshole's nose.

A shriek escapes Lindsay, but the triplets are soon cheering, "Get him, Colt! Do it! Do it! Do it!"

Before our eyes, Colt lights into his father, punctuating each hit with a curse or a warning.

"You tried to set me up, you asshole."

"Told you not to come here."

"You killed Loki."

"You got her pregnant?!"

"You wanted them to suspect me."

"You started the fire."

"How dare you show up like you're still fucking welcome."

"You stole the ranch from me."

"You lied about the will."

Each snarled word seems to alleviate his outrage until, finally, Cody and Cole are the ones who drag him off their father, holding him back when Clyde, hunched on the ground, slurs, "Always did hit like a girl."

My man roars his fury and fights his brothers' hold. He almost succeeds too. It's only Callan shouting, "The police are on their way, Colt!" that appears to stop him.

"Now that they've tied you to Lydia's death, I hope they

figure out how you killed Marcy as well. You sick fuck. Getting a sixteen-year-old pregnant—"

"What?!" Lindsay gasps.

Cole stares at his father. "I always knew you were a pile of horse manure, but you never fail to live up to my expectations."

"Dumping the truck on our land was a shitty thing to do," Cody growls.

"Did..." Clyde rolls onto his side and pukes. "...nothing."

"This is better than *General Hospital*."

Of course that comes from *Grand-mère*.

I move over to Colt and curve an arm around his heaving side.

The whole thing couldn't have taken more than three minutes. I feel like a whirlwind blew onto the Seven Cs—

"What's he even doing here?" Callan demands.

"Wanted. See. My. Boys," Clyde mumbles before he plunks back on the soil.

Colton tenses and I can read the disbelief in his expression. Acting on a hunch, I snag one of the thin plastic gloves I bought so *Grand-mère* could pick up chicken wings without getting her fingers dirty.

Not giving Colton a say in the matter, I slide them on and drop to Clyde's side.

"Don't sully yourself by touching him," my husband spits.

But I ignore him—Clyde came here for a reason and I want to know what that reason is.

"Why are you here?" I demand.

Head lolling from side to side, he pauses to blink at me. "Clarisse?"

I shut out the tender note to his voice as he utters my mom's name, but I can hear the triplets discussing that among themselves as I pat his pockets.

When I find a piece of paper, I pull it out and spot the same handwriting as I did on the poison pen letters.

Korhonens think they can get away with murder.

539

I won't let that happen.

You killed two people that day—my daughter and my grandchild.

You. Will. Pay.

The courts might never get any justice out of you, but I can.

I want a hundred thousand dollars before the month's out.

You know where to find me.

"Why are you here? Is it because of this?"

Clyde groans as I thrust the piece of paper in his face.

I use his chin to hold him in place. "Tell me why you came here, Clyde."

"Missed you, Clarisse."

Though I wince, this isn't about my mom and whatever weird relationship they had together. "Why did you come here?"

"Put letter. My. Office." His hand grabs mine. "Not kill. Her." He vomits. "Clarisse."

Before I can pick apart that minefield, Callan bites out, "He was going to plant it in Colt's office!"

I turn to my husband who has fire in his eyes. Glancing at the hold his brothers have on him again, I mumble my thanks to the universe. Left to his own devices, I don't think Colt would have stopped doling out the type of punishment Clyde served upon him for years.

A long time ago, I remember telling him how I'd like to witness when the abused turned on the abuser. I got my wish, but from his expression, there's no closure to be found here. None at all.

The cops arrive but they don't take him away. An ambulance does.

For the first time in centuries, two sets of enemies work together, united in the face of a shared nemesis, as they describe how Clyde stormed onto the scene and started a fight that Cole, Colt, and Cody were all involved in.

Self-defense... when it wasn't.

Everyone shares in the mutual lie to protect Colton.

The sergeant appears dubious but he declares, "I'll let this go seeing as you kept your word about contacting us as soon as he showed up." He stares at the letter I handed him upon his arrival then glowers at Cody. "I've heard all about this ridiculous new idea coming out of the provincial government... If this is how the head of the marshals will treat a suspect, we have some interesting times ahead."

The pissing contest matters more to him than the day's events because the sergeant makes a retreat before Cody can respond.

As quickly as the chaos commenced, it fades.

I stick to Colt's side while he methodically scrapes off the charred meat that burned onto the grill as Tee declares, "I was right. Pigeon Creek got way more interesting while we were in New York."

I wish I could argue with her... but I can't.

Text Chat

Parker: Just a heads-up, but Tee's Butch Cassidy is going no contact

Zee: You're about four hours too late with that warning

Parker: Sorry. It was nuts around here. My bad

Zee: I read his Dear John. It was weird.

Parker: I heard it. Four times. Then she took a picture for me and forced me to read it back to her

Zee: Your sacrifice is appreciated

Parker: SHE MADE ME ACT IT OUT, ZEE

Parker: Then all hell broke loose on the Sinners' compound

Parker: Samael went missing.

Zee: Nyx's kid?

Parker: Yup. Toddled off and fell asleep in the shop. Scared everyone shitless. Think Nyx lost three years of his life. Sammy's jealous of the new baby. Used to having all the attention.

Parker: But, hey, they're the ones who named him after a demon so they have to deal with the aftermath.

Parker: How's our girl doing?

Zee: She's all right. Got drunk. May have flirted with one of Colt's brothers. Will regret that in the morning, but she's safe.

Zee: Hey, I'm thinking of asking her to move back to Pigeon Creek.

Parker: 'Bout time

Parker: There's no Beavis without the Butthead, babe

Zee: Think she'll say yes? Her work is in the city.

Parker: She hates her work lol. You can't seriously think she won't come back. You have no idea what she's been like. I've gotten the whole magnum opus while you were away because she didn't want to stress you out

Parker: I'm thinking about taking Valium, Zee.

Parker: I only stayed up here for her benefit.

Parker: For MY mental health, please drag her back to Canada?

Zee: She's not that bad lol

Parker: I'd prefer to corral Nyx's mini demons in the future

Zee: LOL

Zee: Now who's being melodramatic?

Parker: It rubs off on a girl

Zee: Only because Sweet Lips is in Coshocton and he can't do it for you...

Zee: *smirks*

Parker: You think you're so clever

Zee: I do

Zee: Seriously though, I appreciate you sticking around for her. At least she hasn't been totally alone. <3

Parker: It's fine. We have that massive case going on so it's all hands on deck anyway. Plus, Sweet Lips is a massive distraction.

Zee: He is?

Parker: You've seen his face. How can I resist sitting on it? A girl has to work.

Zee: LMAO

Parker: I miss him though. Sigh. No one tells you that love can hurt in a good way.

Zee: No, they don't. <3

Parker: So hurry up and ask her lol. I'm ready to go home.

Zee: Will do!

Zee: Oops, I GTG

Zee: Chaos of our own, but ranch-style

Parker: You lost one of the sheep?

Zee: Sheep? You think we ranch sheep? LMAO

Parker: Someone has to

Zee: You're not wrong...

Parker: But you don't ranch sheep?

Zee: Cattle. And horses. One's going into labor. She's an old lady and Colt's stallion broke into her stall and managed to put a bun in her oven. He's scared she won't make it through and thinks it's his fault

Parker: So, what you're telling me is that Colt's horse is into non-con?

Zee: If you ever decide to leave your safe spaces and come visit us, I'll intro you to Cole. He's into romance too. In a big way.

Parker: You made him ten times hotter and I was already in love with his pink pants and skating skills.

Zee: *snorts* He didn't wear them today

Parker: I can't wait for tomorrow night's game. The Stars are going to bust some balls. I'm surprised he managed to take any time off

Zee: Think it's because he's friendly with his GM and he's cutting it close. He'll attend Callan and the triplets' graduation, then he and his fiancée are outta here.

Parker: You had a BBQ with Cole Korhonen…

Parker: *swoons*

Zee: ;)

Zee: We also had a showdown, got interrupted by the cops, and there was an arrest…

Parker: WHAT?

Zee: TTYL

Parker: You can't leave me hanging like this!!!!!!

Zee: Sure I can. ;)

Chapter 50
Colt

"I swear today's a punishment for the sins I committed in a past life," I grumble as I run my hand over my head, wishing I could do something for Harriet when there's nothing to be done during a healthy labor.

My fingers, knuckles, and wrists ache from the pounding I served Clyde earlier and my voice is nasal after my face met Cole's fist, but it's *all* worth it.

The sense of accomplishment in my chest is at odds with the gnawing anxiety for Harriet.

After the day we had, Callan can't lose Harriet too.

Having canceled Cole's birthday party, I forced Callan to go to bed because it's his graduation tomorrow and he knows she's in good hands. I don't want to wake him up with the news that his father was charged with trespassing and fabricating evidence (no vehicular manslaughter charge yet) and that his horse *and* her foal died during labor.

"I'm surrounded by melodramatic people," Zee grouches, but the arm she's slung around my waist tightens in a half hug.

"She's done this so many times, she's an old pro," Margot, our vet, chirps from my other side. "You need to take a chill pill, Colt."

"Is that your official diagnosis?"

"Yup!"

Barely an hour ago, Harriet's foal alert warned us she was going into labor and Margot bounded in fifteen minutes later. We were lucky she was at Theo's ranch.

Bea's sister Margot has been with us for years. Once the breeding program becomes more established, I intend to hire her full-time.

As used to this process as I am, it doesn't stop me from wincing when Harriet drops to her forelegs and tumbles onto her side.

"You're such a man," Margot jibes with a soft laugh at my reaction. "Do you need nitrous oxide?"

I shoot her a disgruntled look but flick my eyes over the mom-to-be as I inform Zee, "She made it to day 320. This whole thing has been cut too close to the wire."

"I told you she would," Margot inserts.

"You a seer?"

"Horse whisperer." She taps her nose. "That's me."

I'd call her out but she isn't lying. Margot's our local miracle worker.

"I wish this weren't coming so quickly. We'd have gotten the straw out for her but she wasn't showing any of the signs—"

"She'll be fine."

Harriet grunts as if to tell me Margot's lying. The whites of her eyes are showing as the muscles in her abdomen cramp and flow over her side like a wave. In between grunts, her legs jerk and spasm.

She rolls onto her forelegs and stands so she can pace. That's when I get a good view of her back end where her tail's erect and the milky-colored sac droops from her with two small hooves peeping through the opaque membrane.

"She's making progress but we're edging toward forty-five minutes," Margot murmurs in an aside.

Unbeknown to Harriet, who's unaware that nature needs to hurry the hell up, her abdomen heaves from exertion while her grunts echo around this half of the stables that's empty of other mares as we're out of foaling season.

When the exhausted dam plops down, this time, she does it

with her back end in plain view. Contractions expose a breach in the sac, revealing two skinny black legs.

The sight triggers activity from Margot and me.

"You wanna pitch in?" she asks.

Though it's her job, we both know there hasn't been a foal birthed on the Seven Cs without me around since I returned home from university. Even then, I'd travel back as soon as I could to be with the dam and her new foal.

A sharp neigh from the mare has Margot tossing me a towel. Cautiously, I approach Harriet, who lifts her head so she can huff angrily at me.

"It wasn't me," I protest. "And we'll keep Fen away from you in the future, I promise."

My reassurances are ignored once I've wrapped up the foal's hooves in the towel and, in time to her contractions, help her where I can. The ticking of the clock as we edge toward a birth that runs too long echoes in my head.

My relief when the foal's forelegs are fully out shifts as she rolls upright only to fall back down. Her exhaustion has me gritting my teeth.

"There's a good girl," Margot praises.

Zee chimes in, "You got this, honey."

For what feels like endless moments, Harriet lies there, building the strength for what needs to be done.

"Margot?"

"It's fine, Colt. Just a couple more minutes then I'll intervene. But I know she's got this."

Like she agrees, Harriet snorts and, with one big push and a soft tug from me, the foal's head finally pops out, the sac covering the whole of its face.

My relief is intense. As is my gratitude. The guilt I've been feeling since Fen's breakout—all three-hundred-and-twenty days of it—dissolves in a rush.

"Almost there, Harriet," I cheer as, shifting the towel under the shoulders, I bring the foal out into the warm summer night.

More comfortable with this part of labor, I quickly clear off the sac, rub the towel over the snout and eyes, and scrub away the amniotic fluid as gently as I can while checking they're breathing.

"Do you know what it is yet?"

I find Zee watching me with a soft smile lighting up her features and I can't help but be happy she was here.

With a grin, I answer, "We're about to find out."

I beckon her into the stall but she hesitates. "Will Harriet let me? She barely knows me. She won't recognize my scent."

"She needs some love after going through that, don't you, Harriet?" is Margot's cheery declaration as she bustles around in the background.

Still hesitant, Zee steps into the stall and moves away from the foal and over to Harriet's head. Crouching down and gently petting her, she croons soft words of praise to the mare who's been hard at work for the past fifty minutes.

I switch roles with Margot who exclaims, "And we have a colt, Colt."

"It wasn't funny the first time, Margot, and that was at least fourteen foals ago."

She cackles. "Got a name yet?"

The foal rocks his shoulders back and forth, flailing as he stretches his forelegs like he's ready to stand, which he definitely isn't, so I move beside Zee and run a hand over Harriet's still-heaving side.

Her exhausted whinnies have me grimacing with guilt. "I'll padlock his stall, Harriet. I swear."

She nickers as if that's precisely what she wanted to hear.

Zee chuckles. "I think she's pissed at Fen."

"He needs to watch his back. You got a name?"

Her eyes widen. "You can't give me that task!"

"Sure I can. Only right. The first foal of our marriage..."

"Some women get jewelry or flowers, Colt," Margot inserts.

"Some women would prefer that if they weren't born on a ranch," Zee defends hotly, making me chuckle as she glowers at the vet.

Which, of course, is when I remember they were both in school together.

Harriet breaks into the standoff by rearing upright, having decided it's time to investigate her baby.

As she sniffs him, we back off a few steps while a couple stablehands come in to clear up the birth.

It's only when Harriet stands and begins licking the foal that Zee tucks her arm around my waist. "Trever."

"Trever?"

She shrugs. "With two E's. He looks like a Trever with two E's."

"I didn't know they had characteristics."

A soft smile dances on her lips. "You have to be a special kind of person to recognize them."

Chuckling, I press a kiss to her temple. "Trever it is."

Chapter 51
Zee

"I hope you know I meant you no ill will, Zee."

Halfway down the corridor toward the kitchen on this interminable day, I pause outside the solarium that's Lindsay's territory.

The last thing I want is a showdown.

It took a while for Harriet to let Trever approach her for his first feed so we only went to bed after a rushed shower an hour ago. The call of nature woke me up, and then I got hungry.

This is what happens when I listen to my stomach at 5 AM instead of simply grazing on the multitude of snacks in my nightstand drawer.

Popping my head through the doorway, I ask, "I'm sorry, Lindsay, did you say something?"

I know exactly what she said, but *awkward*.

Especially as I'm wearing one of Colt's T-shirts.

It's not like I announced to the house that I'm sleeping in Colt's room, but my pajamas, or lack thereof, might give it away.

In fact, I can feel her eyes scanning me as I hover in the doorway. She doesn't comment on his tee though, just repeats, "I never meant to be rude."

"No, of course not," I mutter, more embarrassed than before.

To be honest, whether she did or didn't, I wasn't affected. She pissed Colt off. Not me.

"I mean it. Any of the boys will tell you that I've never been good at letting people in. You don't after being married to a man like Clyde." Her lips purse. "But now that I know you're sticking around, I'll be sure to make more of an effort."

"I appreciate that, Lindsay. I'll—"

She doesn't give me the chance to escape. "Ida called Terry while you two were dealing with Harriet."

Curious, I step deeper into the room. "The sergeant? What did he have to say?"

"Clyde's fingerprints were found in your brothers' truck."

"Really?"

"Which corroborates your grandmother's statement." Smug satisfaction leaches into her voice as she continues, "He also said Colt broke Clyde's nose and his orbital bone."

"What made Terry share any of this with Ida?"

"They've often conferred on cases for Dove Bay. It helped that Clyde wanted to call Colton and he refused to answer."

"I didn't know that."

She hums. "I didn't either. It appears Colt's washed his hands of his father."

"You don't sound like you approve."

Her shoulder hitches. "Hardly. Clyde made his bed a long time ago. It seems to me that he's dealing with the repercussions of that and he deserves to have the book thrown at him."

"He said he didn't kill her."

"Who's *her*?" she dismisses.

I know she's right, but I can't help but think something was off about that scene today.

Oh, I believe he was going to plant that letter in Colt's office. But how he looked at me... I assumed the relationship between Mom and him was entirely transactional. Then, he said Mom's name so my perception of that has shifted.

He genuinely thought he was talking to Mom and everything about his demeanor was different.

"The entire day's been one revelation after another."

I can't argue with that.

Not when *Grand-mère* was as strident as ever today, totally unlike the one I saw at the Bar 9.

I can't help but feel like something's changed and I missed the memo.

Because I'm at a loss, I ask, "What else did the sergeant say?"

She lifts the glass of wine in her hand to her mouth and takes a deep sip. "Doug received a letter from Lydia after she passed away. It detailed the location of a journal and advised him to send it to the police if anything happened to her—"

"The journal that Colt was questioned over!"

She nods.

"I wonder who sent the letter."

"According to Terry, Jessica Cardinal."

"Two women bound by their mutual hatred of the Korhonens."

"One Korhonen, in particular," Lindsay corrects. "Not that I can blame her. Anyway, Doug said that Lydia had been acting strangely ever since they put their house on the market. He put it down to the stress of moving, but this diary... he'd never heard about it before. He thinks she must have found it when Lydia was packing up Marcy's room." Lindsay stares at the arrangement of flowers she's installed in the empty hearth since the weather grew warmer.

"I wonder if the police came across any mentions of her having a relationship with Clyde in it... They must have or surely they'd have brought Colt in for more questions."

Her brows lift. "You knew about Marcy and Clyde?"

"I witnessed it."

"You've developed a habit of being a witness, haven't you?"

Blankly, I stare at her. "I never thought about it that way before. Tee always did say I was sneaky. I thought it was more about having the knack of being in the wrong place at the wrong time."

"Or the right, considering."

"Right?" I ask warily as I perch on the edge of the armchair opposite her.

557

It's the first time I've ever been welcomed in here, so despite her 'greeting,' I'm unsure of my place.

"You see things that no one else does. It's to your misfortune that you never had a voice before." As I grimace at how accurate that is, she clicks her fingers. "Not anymore. You're Colton Korhonen's wife. People will listen."

So, Colt looped her in about what I saw during the fire.

"Will they? They haven't so far."

"That's because you've been living like a hermit. It's half the reason I didn't think you and Colt were getting along.

"Somehow, under this roof we all share, you managed to move into his bedroom with none of us knowing."

"Not even Ida?"

"No." She studies me. "Are you going to talk to the police about the arson in the stables?"

Uncertainly, I shift on the seat. "I wasn't going to. I mean, if he's behind Lydia Armstrong's death then—"

She tuts. "He murdered our private herd of horses, Zee. The loss of which my sons still mourn to this day. Why shouldn't he be punished for that crime? Even if the only true punishment will come from him defrauding the insurance company.

"You're Mrs. Colton Korhonen," she repeats. "There are some perks to the name. If you have the strength to use them."

"Did you?"

Lindsay wiggles her hand from side to side. "I knew how to throw my weight around in town. It was under this roof that I never found my feet."

"I'd have thought this place held nothing but bad memories for you."

"The advantages outweigh the memories. They might linger in the shadows whenever I turn a corner, *but* I can see Callan and I've missed so much with him that I'd have taken any opportunity to make that right.

"Then, there's Colt. Initially, I wanted to make sure he was okay in this marriage that bastard forced upon him, but then it shifted when I knew there'd be a grandchild... I won't miss being a grandmother.

"Now Cody's home too, so I get to be with more of my boys and I've already wasted so much time with them.

"Plus, there was a delicious satisfaction in living under this roof when Clyde wasn't welcome. It'll be even better if he's in jail." She settles back in her armchair with relish. "I'll accept the title of petty bitch. I know that's what you're thinking."

"I wasn't, actually. I was thinking if anyone deserved to be petty, it's you."

"We'll need to host another BBQ with your family. This time, one he *can't* ruin." A curious light dances in her eyes when I snort. "So, will you report him to the police?"

This is why she wanted to talk to me.

Not to seal Clyde's fate. But to seal mine—Mrs. Colton Korhonen.

No one will believe me, though.

No one.

Apart from, of course, Tee.

Who always believed me.

And her parents and brother who never cut me off.

And Colt—who accepted the truth despite years of thinking I was guilty.

Callan never thought it was me, even if his theory was founded on lies.

Cody accepted my word the first day we met.

Then there's Lindsay. And probably Ida. The triplets too...

And Cole?

It might only be thirteen people, but it's more than I've had before.

"I-I suppose there'd be no harm in making a statement."

"The only harm would be to the man himself," she agrees softly.

Getting to my feet, I ask, "Do the police believe he killed Marcy?"

"There's no evidence. No body, no crime. Either way, Lydia knew there was something in that journal that was worthy enough of blackmail. Maybe the cops will pick up on that. Or, as you said, maybe they already have and that's why they've left my boy alone."

"Did Colt tell you she was sending him, *us*, poison pen letters?"

"No." Her eyes narrow. "He didn't. How strange."

Awkwardly, I mutter, "It's late, Lindsay. I need to get some more sleep. See you in the morning."

Though she nods, I can tell my small addition to the conversation has left her perplexed.

I don't blame her. None of this makes sense.

I forge a path to the kitchen as per my original plan and pour myself a glass of milk then stick a spoon in the jar of peanut butter and suck on the scoop as I make my return to Colton's bedroom.

Our bedroom.

It will be once I can redecorate. The furniture's old-fashioned enough that I quite like the pieces thanks to a childhood of growing up around this kind of stuff, but the walls are a dark navy that makes the space feel too hemmed-in for my tastes.

When I open the door, Colt's sitting up in bed, reading a book.

"What are you doing awake?"

He peers at me over the book. "You were gone a while."

"And it disturbed you?"

"I've grown used to you being there." There's a wry twist to his lips. "Trust me, it surprised me too."

I snort as I climb into bed, somehow satisfied that his mom knows where I sleep—as if that makes it, *us*, official. It wasn't that we were hiding it, but it's not something you advertise either.

"What are you eating?"

"Peanut butter." I wiggle the glass at him. "Milk."

"None for me?"

"You can have some milk."

"So kind."

"Trust me, I know." As he snatches the glass and takes a sip, I murmur, "I spoke with your mom."

"What's she doing awake?"

I ponder the scene I came across. "She looked like she was plotting."

560

"Clyde was the master of his own demise. She doesn't have to do anything."

"She wants me to reinforce it."

"How?" I don't have the chance to answer. He clucks his tongue. "She wants you to tell the police about the arson?" When I nod, he studies me. "Are you going to?"

Placing the now-empty spoon on the nightstand, I murmur, "Yes."

His hand settles on my thigh. "We can go tomorrow."

"You don't need to come with me. Tee will."

It's his turn to cluck his tongue. "Hey, that's my job."

"Don't tell her. She's already fighting with Callan for the position of my BFF," I tease.

His smirk is so delicious that I'd eat him up if I weren't exhausted. The day has been long and the mayhem varied. Honestly, I'd still be face down on the pillow if I hadn't needed the bathroom.

Curling onto my side so I can look at him, I drowsily share the little I learned from his mom. That's when I slip in, "She said you refused to take Clyde's call."

"That he thought I'd help him arrange for his lawyer to come to Pigeon Creek is crazy in itself." He tucks a lock of hair behind my ear. "The asshole was putting the suspicion onto me."

My tired brain's slower to function than I'd like, but... "Why do you think Lydia sent you poison pen letters?"

"And you."

"She only sent that after we got her fired."

"I think Lydia was spraying in the wind, sourcing cash wherever she could. They were on the brink of losing every-thing so she had to double her odds. Even Juliette was targeted."

"Seriously?"

"Yes. I don't know for certain what Lydia had on her, but Juliette paid it."

I gape at him. "No way."

"Yes way."

A hand curves around my waist and draws me against his

chest. Despite the shocking news, I snuggle into him, mumbling, "Your mom knows we sleep together."

"Do more than that."

"You know what I mean."

"What you're saying is that she knows this is your bedroom now."

Happily, I sigh. "Can I paint it?"

"Sure."

"What about my old bedroom?"

"Convert it into an office."

"You sure?"

"Never been more sure about anything in my whole life," he vows, smoothing a hand along my back until I drift off.

Suddenly, tomorrow's problems aren't much of a burden.

Because I have a new bedroom—and it's one I'll be sharing with my husband.

Permanently.

Chapter 52
Zee

"**Y**ou sure you want to do this?"

I flick a scowl at Tee. "Don't talk me out of it."

"We've been standing here for twenty minutes."

"Colt isn't complaining," I argue, though he brought out his phone ten minutes ago and has been sending emails with one hand as his other is currently being strangled by mine.

"Colt gets laid." Tee pauses. "*By* you? *With* you?"

"This isn't an English lesson," I hiss, growing tense as the clipping sound of heels echoes down the corridor behind me.

The police have been eyeing us oddly since we showed up.

At first, one of the officers approached us, thinking Colt was here to see his father. But when he refused, the guy behind the desk blinked, took his seat once more, and returned to work.

Sure, every couple minutes, he glances at us, but that's fine with me.

Tee huffs. "These chairs are uncomfortable."

"You didn't have to come."

"Duh. Of course, I did. But I didn't think we'd be waiting for you to get a move on. Not when we have to haul our asses to the triplets and Callan's graduation ceremony."

"Sorry to disappoint."

"You're not sorry. If you were, you'd have spoken to the

very nice man behind the desk." She beams a smile at him. "Gary, did anyone ever tell you you grew into that chin?"

'Gary,' aka Officer Yardley, snorts. "My mom. Every time she sees me."

"You married?"

He doesn't glance away from his computer but holds up his hand and flashes his decorated ring finger at her.

"You're not trying to pick up a guy, are you?" I groan.

"Gotta make it more exciting around here," she drawls. "This won't be a totally wasted trip if you decide to chicken out."

I glower at her, but before I can utter a word, Colt clucks his tongue. "Tee."

My best friend sniffs *and* shuts up.

As she studies her nails, I study the desk.

My throat grows thick with an emotion I can't describe. It's not sorrow or anger. It's like all the years of repressed sentiment is suddenly blocking it.

Not that it's stopping me from breathing, but it's there.

Making it hard to focus on anything else.

"I don't know why you're scared," Tee grouses a few minutes later. "He's already behind bars. What can he do to you?"

And there we have it.

In that uncanny ability of hers, she hits the nail on the head.

Colt, seemingly aware that my batty best friend has indeed picked up on something, zooms in on me. His cell phone gets shoved in his pocket and he turns to face me, blocking my view of the desk.

His free hand cups my chin, and his thumb swoops over my cheek as he tips my head back so we're looking square at one another. "Is that what has you so anxious?"

I swallow. And it's hard. Enough that my throat aches. "Maybe," I manage to croak.

"Baby, don't you know you're untouchable now?"

My eyes flare wide. "Huh?"

Those same half-grinning lips press against my forehead,

but Tee interrupts whatever he's about to say with, "You're a Korhonen, babe. I mean, come on."

"So's Clyde! There's no type of legal defense he can't afford. He'll end up serving two months on probation or something," I squeak. "Then he'll come for me—"

"You. Are. Safe," Colt assures me, his voice tender and calm in the face of my fears. "I will never let him hurt you. *Ever.* I've spent years watching that man hurt the people I love most. My hands were always tied. But he's the one who unknotted that tie—"

"He could run me over like he did Lydia," I burst out. "Retaliation. Revenge. You name it—he's capable of it."

"Yes, he is," Colt agrees, but his thumb brushes over my mouth. "If you think I'll let him get anywhere near you, you're seriously underestimating what I feel for you."

"What exactly do you feel for me?" I whisper.

His grin is confident but warm. Not cocky, just *happy*. "I love you."

"I love you too." Swiping at the tears that are suddenly pouring down my cheeks, I mumble, "I can't believe I said that for the first time in the RCMP detachment."

"Doesn't matter where it's said so long as we mean it."

As he wraps me in his arms, I close my eyes in the warmth of his embrace.

Anything can happen in this world and despite his words, I know there's no way to make me safe outside of putting me in an iron lung, but Lindsay was right.

I'm not nobody Zee McAllister anymore.

Neither am I my mother.

Or Marcy.

It sucks, but to a man like Clyde, position is everything and he's the one who took me from the bottom rung of the ladder and settled me close to the top.

"This is so sweet," Tee croons, a lot closer than she was before. Colt and I jump when her arms slide around both our waists and she joins us in a group hug. "How do you feel about being my sister wife?"

Despite my nerves, I huff out a laugh. "Wouldn't *you* be *my* sister wife?"

"I almost regret not being raised on the ranch next door to the Seven Cs." She pouts then smacks said pout on my cheek in a loud kiss. "You going to kick some creep's ass, Zee? I think you should. You got a whole new start waiting for you, babe. You need to close this part off. Reclaim it. That dick tried to ruin *both* your lives. Payback's a bitch when it's served cold."

Colt snorts. "Think you're mixing metaphors, Tee."

Snootily, she tells my husband, "If the mixed metaphors fit then isn't it a cocktail of awesomeness?"

I grace him with a pious look. "Well, Colt. Isn't it?"

"I guess it's a cocktail I'd be willing to try," he says wryly.

Tee cackles, smacks him on the cheek with a matching kiss, then shoves me. Because of my current position, it pushes me deeper into Colt's arms.

Because he's Colt, he doesn't falter at the sudden momentum.

He holds me.

Like he'll never let me go...

"I've got you, Zee Korhonen," he rumbles, the words loaded with meaning.

My voice is back to being croaky, but for a different reason this time as I whisper, "Thank you, Colt."

"*Everything* for you, baby. Are you ready to talk to the police?"

Anxiously, I nod.

Then, I reclaim my past. My present. And my future.

Chapter 53
Zee

God Only Knows - The Beach Boys

EIGHT MONTHS LATER

"**G**rand-mère?"

The distressed cry has her papery eyelids drifting open. When she sees me, though, a soft smile curves her lips. It's a smile I saw, more often than not, around Walker. Not me.

The notion has my throat bobbing.

"You came." Her fingers seek mine. The bones are more fragile than ever. The skin just as papery, revealing bluer than blue veins and bruises too from the IV the nurses put on the back of her hand.

"Of course I did. The boys are on their way. You need to hold on," I encourage.

Colt's hand settles on my shoulder, big and warm and just *everything*. He's safety and security and home. "How are you feeling, Juliette?"

"Like today's my last day on this miserable planet," she grumbles, scowling at him. "Don't be soft around me, boy. I'm dying, not having a personality transplant."

"*Grand-mère!*"

"*Mamie,*" she corrects.

Fear floods me. "They're going to fix you, *Mamie.* You're not dying. Remember? You said you'd die when you were good and ready."

"I think I'm good and ready now, child."

Colt's grip on my shoulder tightens. I know, in the months that we've been together, he's grown closer to my family. A strange form of respect has bridged the two.

I've been jittery since I got the call. Had to eat when that was the last thing I wanted after my blood sugar dropped, but I don't want to focus on that. *Mamie* needs me.

Mamie.

I never thought I'd see the day she'd let me call her that.

A sob catches in my throat.

"I need to tell you something, Susanne." Her nose crinkles as she corrects, "Zee."

God, she is *dying.*

My mouth trembles. "What, *Mamie?*"

"I have to share this with someone, but I need you to promise me that you won't tell a soul." Her eyes lock Colton in place. "You neither, boy."

"Your secret's our secret," Colton vows.

"I always liked you." She nods at his assurance. "Knew how that bastard treated you and that mother of yours. We all knew. None of us did anything though. Cowards. I tried to run him over once but it didn't work—"

"*Mamie!*" I chide, shocked by her admission.

"Child, I'm not a good person." She lets go of my hand to pat it. "I'm fine with that, but I need you to know this because I need him to suffer."

"Who, Juliette?"

"Your father, of course." Her sniff is 100% disdain and sounds so normal that it's hard to believe we're in the hospital. Surrounded by machines. That her lips are turning blue. That her breathing is raspy. That her words are slightly slurred. "I always hated him. Clayton was a good boy. Just like you. Never did trust Clyde. Thought he did Clay in but no one would listen to a McAllister. Never did. Never will. Until now.

"God, that day he came to the Bar 9 to see me, I was sure I was dying because happiness was that old bastard coming to *me* for *my* water. And I knew exactly what to do. The whole town'll listen to a McAllister now. You'll see to that, won't you, Colton?"

"You know I will."

"And you'll protect my grandchildren?"

"Damn straight," he rumbles. "And your great-grand-children."

"Knew it. I called it from the start when I saw you and her cozying up in the stables." She harrumphs. "As if I'd be too scared to enter Korhonen land. You little shits always tres-passed on our lakes so I did the same when Susanne, I mean Zee, went missing one too many times. Thought about blowing your head off with a shotgun. But then I saw you care for her. Help her after that useless father of hers died—"

"*Mamie!*"

She huffs. "Oh, child, he was. I know you love him but his head was in the clouds. No good for a ranch. None at all. But Colton is. He'll bring the Bar 9 back to how it should be. Biggest in the whole of Canada. Put us in the record books again." A satisfied expression settles on her weary features. "And no Clyde around to muck it up. I want him to rot in prison, child, do you understand?"

I blink at her. "I-I understand, *Mamie*."

"When I tell you that I'm not a good person, child, I say it only so you'll brace yourself." I protest but she shakes her head. "I'm not. I always knew I'd do anything for the Bar 9, but I didn't realize until I was older what I'd do for my daughter and her children.

"Lydia Armstrong, she—"

When she starts coughing and doesn't stop, a cacophony of alarms sets off. Nurses rush in and push us out but *Grand-mère* growls, "I'm dying, you fools. I need to speak with my—"

Colton drags me outside until they get her settled. He holds me against him, his hand cupping my head while *Mamie* barks cusswords at the nursing staff as they make her comfortable, but she doesn't stop grumbling until I'm back with her.

This time, when her hand grabs mine, it's fierce. She's clinging on. I can feel it. Whatever she has to share with me, she needs to impart before she dies.

We've never gotten along, but the prospect of being in a world without my strong-willed grandmother has soft sobs wracking my frame.

"Listen to me, child," she whispers, her tone feverish. "Lydia was blackmailing me. Said she had proof your mother was fooling around with *him*. Said she'd prove that Clarisse was a whore." Her eyes narrow. "No one casts aspersions on my family unless it's me.

"I paid because I couldn't let anyone tarnish Clarisse's name, then one day, I went into town and there she was, waiting to be served in that old fool's bakery. A smug smile on her face. I wanted to smack it off her. In my younger days, I would have. But I didn't.

"I knew the boys' truck was at the garage, but it was lunchtime and the damn thing's key is stuck in the ignition so I knew I could start the engine. And as luck would have it, she was walking down Main Street.

"When no one saw me, I just drove off. I don't know what I was thinking. Mostly, I wanted that smile to be gone." Her eyes flare. "One of the happiest moments of my life was when I ran her over."

I gape at her. "*Mamie*, you can't..."

"She was threatening your mother's reputation. Threatening yours too. Casting aspersions on her name cast aspersions on you all. I fought too long to let that happen. I didn't sell you to that bastard for your name to be raked through the mud after you were married.

"I'm sorry, Colton. I've hated your family for so long and I was acting on instinct when I dumped the boys' truck on your land. I saw that big stockhorse of yours roaming around. I've watched you on him. You let him loose and he always comes back. I stole him and rode off to the Bar 9, knowing he'd wander back.

"When I got home, that's when I realized how foolish I'd been." She taps her temple. "I knew this was going, but that was proof of it. The panic set in because I'd used the triplets' truck. Of course they were going to be blamed. I dumped it on your land! You'd be suspected. It was a nightmare.

"Then, Lydia did me a favor." She chuckles and it's cold and mean and cements all her words into reality. "She must have hated Clyde more than she ever hated me." Her gaze locks on mine. "I looked at her like I'm looking at you, child. She couldn't mistake me, but the whole town knows she was mumbling about Clyde when she died. That was when I realized everything would be alright."

Colt clears his throat. "Why are you telling us this?"

"So that you know and if he appeals and worms his way out of the sentence, you'll fix it so that this dying woman's wish comes true—I want him to rot. I want that prissy little bastard to suffer. I don't know what your mother was doing with him, but it can't have been any good.

"He's the reason you left, Sus—Zee. The second I heard about the fire, I knew Clyde had something to do with it. Never loved the land. Not like Clayton. Clayton would have died first rather than let his horses perish in a fire.

"When I heard Clyde just stood there, watching, I knew. Bet he killed that Marcy girl too." Her words slur even more. "Evil man. Evil. I'm no good. But he's evil. Want him to suffer. Want him to know what it's like for no one to believe you. To hurt—" She jerks awake and her hand tightens around mine to the point of pain. "Promise me, child. Promise me."

I think about the years of suffering Colt endured, of what Clyde put Lindsay through, of Callan's persistent fear. I think about Loki burning to death and Clyde stealing the ranch, of him framing his flesh and blood by dumping another blackmail demand in Colt's office.

Somehow, it's the easiest thing in the world to whisper, "I promise."

"And you, boy?"

Colt doesn't even have to think. "I want him to rot in a jail cell as much as you do, Juliette."

Righteously, she nods. "Knew I picked right. Only the best for my Susanne. Always loved her. She looked and acted like me too. Bossy little thing." Her milky eyes drift. "Do you know my Susanne, dear?"

I rear back at her question, but Colt's there to prop me up. "Yes, we know your Susanne, Mrs. McAllister."

"She's a fancy paralegal down in New York," she boasts, making my stinging eyes widen at the pride in her voice.

Pride she never once showed me before now.

The thudding of footsteps pounds outside the door and when my brothers come skidding in, somehow, I know it was just in the nick of time.

"Such a good girl. Not like my boys. Always naughty. Up to mischief. Oh, Walker, where are you? Where is he?" she cries, her hand turning into a vise. "My boys. My girl."

"*Mamie!*" Calder shouts, his hand gripping hers as Colby jostles the bed as he half-jumps on it in a panic.

Carson stands by the door, his face like ash as he watches on as Juliette McAllister, the old bitch of the Bar 9, drifts out of this world and into the next with her family surrounding her.

Chapter 54
Colt

The wind whips at Zee's skirt as she stands in front of two graves—one empty, one newly filled.

I stepped out of the Bar 9's family cemetery to deal with the guests who attended the burial, keeping a gimlet eye on my wife who looks frailer than I'd like.

All morning, I've been checking up on her, making sure she's been eating, knowing full well her blood sugar level is not a priority for her right now.

If it's a weight I can take off her shoulders, then I will. Gladly.

Returning to her side, I rest a hand on her waist. "It's time to go home, chaos."

Though she stiffens, she turns into me. "Do you believe her?"

It's the first time she's brought this up since Juliette passed so I've had a few days to think about it *and* to rationalize my response. "I think she believed it," is what I settle on.

She squints at me. "That's not an answer."

"Sure it is." My lips kick up at the corner when she scowls. "I can imagine no bigger *or* better serving of humble pie for Clyde than to get his ass thrown in jail for someone else's crime. Especially a McAllister's.

"You just know that our ancestors are rolling in their graves in delight. I think I saw some of the soil shift on your great-grandfather's..."

"Don't even joke about that." She snorts. "I thought you'd be mad."

"Why?"

"She put quite the burden on us."

I shrug. "The child in me that he terrified is quite satisfied with the outcome."

"A part of me thinks we should tell the cops."

"And break her heart?" I half-chide, hiding a smile when she glowers at me. "You know she'd come back to haunt us if we did."

"At least I'd get to see her again." Her mouth firms as she studies Walker's empty grave and Juliette's new resting place. "I'm tired of losing people, Colt."

My fingers tighten on her waist. "I can't promise you that we won't lose anyone else along the way, Zee, but we're on this road together. You'll never be alone—"

"You swear?" she pleads, blanketing my hand with hers.

I kiss her temple. "On my life."

As she turns into me, fully this time, I slide my arms around her and hold her close.

Since Juliette died, she hasn't cried, but her tears wet the front of my shirt as she finally lets go. I don't say anything. Just hold her through this storm.

It isn't the first and won't be the last, but we'll weather them together from now on.

Chapter 55
Colt

Turning Page - Laura Steiner

THIRTEEN MONTHS LATER

Sliding a towel around my waist once I've stepped out of the shower, I leave the bathroom and head into the living room of the presidential suite at The Manchester.

Settling by the window, I stare at Saskatoon and take a sip of wine.

Before Zee, getting married wasn't a priority. So, marrying twice sure as hell never made an appearance on my agenda.

The last six months of wedding organization torture were all worthwhile when I saw Zee walk down the aisle toward me in Pigeon Creek's church.

To be fair, Kennedy Van Der Mils sure knows how to perfect 'the big day.' This celebration was a thousand times more special than our first—and my wife deserved nothing less than to fulfill every aspect of her dream wedding.

When Zee winds her arms around my waist, my fingers automatically bridge hers, exposing her *Lord of the Ring-*themed nails. All for me. As was the white cloak that channeled Arwen while also being so uniquely *her* that the image will imprint itself on my mind for a lifetime.

I shift in her hold so I can see her face before taking my eyes on a downward trajectory.

A baseball jersey and lacy short shorts—I'm in heaven.

Like the smart man I am, I haul her up high, grabbing her thighs and notching myself between them.

Her core settles on my abs.

Her breath immediately hitches as she secures her arms around my neck.

When she shimmies against me, I ask, "You want this, baby?"

"I want this. *You.*" Her throat bobs as she reaches for my hand. "Let me show you."

She digs her heels into my ass and levers herself up then draws my fingers toward her center.

Hot.

The faint stirrings of slickness.

I slam my mouth onto hers, desire rushing through me as I chase what's permanent—here. Now. Tonight.

She's my wife.

Twice over.

Whatever she wants, whatever she needs, it's my goddamn duty to give it to her.

Especially if that includes *me.*

The thought has me shuddering as I pin her to the wall beside the window.

Biting her bottom lip, I tug it away from her teeth then spear my tongue into her mouth when she whimpers and opens for me.

I taste her, every inch, savoring and sampling because she's better than a Deep N' Delicious cake. Every stroke of my tongue over hers has minute shivers rushing along her spine, making her writhe into me, dragging me to the outer edges of my control with every millisecond that passes.

Who am I kidding?

My control's shot to hell.

I might as well have tossed it out the window the second she embraced me.

Her hands cup my head, nails digging into my scalp as she steers me, hungry for *me* in a way I've grown to anticipate.

As she thrusts her tongue against mine, she wiggles her hips from side to side then, when the friction isn't enough, rocks her pussy over my abdomen. The notion drives me crazy because there's fabric separating us and I could feel that delicious heat on my bare skin if she were naked.

I lever her legs from around my waist and lower her to the floor. She moans a complaint, but I don't wait for her to voice her concerns. I snag the waistband of her short shorts and tug them down her hips.

"I need you naked," I rasp.

Sagging into the wall once she realizes my intent, she watches as I drop to my knees in front of her and help her strip out of them.

She stares at me.

I stare at her.

"Are you wet for me, Zee?"

A broken whimper and her tossing the jersey overhead is my answer.

Did I—

"Was that a Korhonen jersey?" I rumble.

My jaw aches with how hard I clench it when she nods.

I can't stop myself from snagging it and shoving it at her.

The flash of my name has me seeing red as she drags it back on.

One set of fingers slides between her knees, encouraging her to part her thighs.

She obeys. "Oh, God."

"Tell me, Zee. Tell me what I'll find when I touch you."

"You can feel it for yourself."

"No." They slide higher, skipping her pussy, settling on her sit spot. "Tell me."

"I ache," she groans.

My other hand mimics its twin's hold.

I lift her a few inches.

"Where, baby?"

"My p-pussy."

"You need to come, or do you need me to fill you?"

That broken whimper morphs into a cry as her head tips back.

"Zee," I warn.

Her throat bobs. "Both. Can't I have both?"

Satisfied with that answer, I rub my lips over her inner knee, enjoying how she shivers at my touch. Her responsiveness will always light a fire in my veins.

Each caress has her reacting like I sucked on her clit. My tongue darts out and I find the tender skin behind the joint. Her hips buck and she moans long and low.

"God, what are you doing to me?" The words are thick. Heavy with want. Need.

"Do you want to feel my tongue on your clit?"

"Yes, fuck. Yes."

"Do you want to come on my mouth?"

Her broken moan isn't enough of an answer.

I tilt her ass forward and hover my lips above her clit.

Then I wait.

"You bastard."

"Son of a bastard, maybe," I correct, watching her eyes narrow at me. "Do you want to come on my mouth, *wife*?"

"Yes," she growls. "*Husband.*"

The immediacy of her answer has me sliding my tongue through her folds, her pleasure the only goal in mind.

Her slit is wet.

So wet.

God, my wife wants me.

It's a miracle I'll never get used to.

I feast. Sucking on her clit hard and fast, sliding my tongue over her until I thrust in as deep as I can. She cries out, nails back to digging in my hair, scraping over my scalp as she rolls her hips, chasing her pleasure.

There's nothing I want more than to give it to her.

Jesus, I don't think there's anything I've *ever* wanted more.

Like I haven't done this a thousand times, I investigate

every inch of her, hunting the parts that are the most sensitive. I seek each one, desperate to hear her cry out my name.

I savor her unique taste, her scent, revel in it as her responsiveness makes this a 4D experience—the thought makes me grin.

When she finally cries out my name, I double down. Now that I've heard it once, I want to hear it again. And again. I suck harder. Flick faster. Bite instead of nip. No longer teasing in answer to her cries.

She freezes against the wall, a still tableau as she finds her crest. It ripples through her and chokes off her air until she lets it loose in a scream.

But I don't stop.

I can't.

"COLTON!" she shrieks as I continue to eat her out. "No more, no more, no more!"

When she shudders, muscles twitching as she fights my hold on her hips, that's when I relent.

I pull back.

Settle her feet on the floor.

Catch her when she collapses.

In a smooth movement, I surge high, snagging her and dragging her to the bed, only pausing to appreciate her in a jersey with my name on it.

Then, I drop the towel and snag a condom from the nightstand. Once I'm naked and I've covered myself, I clamber on top of her, parting her thighs and letting my cock rest on her slit.

I give her my weight for a second until I press most of it on the forearms I settle on either side of her face.

The heat of her is an aching torment.

"Zee," I rumble.

When her eyes flutter open, I see the moment she recognizes what's happening.

Her chin dips a quarter-inch.

And I thrust home.

She cries out, pussy clenching around me as that one thrust triggers another tinier orgasm. Her knees dig into my hips, nails

G. A. Mazurke & Serena Akeroyd

clawing at my back as hers arches, sharp enough to toss me off if I were a lighter guy.

My wife has the heart of a wild horse. The trappings of society, of her situation, might have formed her, but in her soul, she was born for the range, and I can feel mine clamoring for hers.

But that's not what this is about.

"God, move, *Colt!* Please!"

Since she asked so prettily, I thrust into her.

Slow and long. Making her feel every inch. Not pounding into her. If I do, this'll be over and that's the last thing I want.

I take her to another pinnacle with my thumb on her clit, aware I shocked her as she squeaks out my name. Her pussy tightens around me, clutching and clinging and clamping down. Doing its level best to get my cum.

It doesn't work.

I want another one.

I won't stop until she gives it to me.

Then, when she's so hypersensitive she starts crying, I tease a final one out of her. This time, she's wrung dry. Sobbing. Sweating. Our skin cleaves together where it touches.

A single swirl of my tongue to her nipple has her shrieking as if I stung her. Then she cries, "Please, Colt. Please. I can't again. I can't. Come for me. Let me feel you. Please? Please. Please. Please!"

The urge to find my own release is so ridiculously prevalent it's a miracle I can see straight, yet I can't help but think this is one way of making a memory that'll last a lifetime. One that'll supplant our original wedding night with ease.

So, like the dumbass I am, I withdraw from her.

Entirely.

She lets loose a sob at the sudden emptiness.

Then, my hands push on her knees as I butterfly her to the bed and I'm back where I was earlier.

"You sure you can't come once more for me?" I demand, not touching her at all aside from her knees. "Not one more?"

"I can't. I can't!"

"Are you lying to me? I bet this pretty little pussy has one more in it."

She shudders.

"Show me that gorgeous slit."

Her eyes are wide at my words. "H-How?"

"Spread it with your fingers."

Her brow puckers. If she doesn't do it, then I'll relent, but I know she's—

Her fingers part the lips, showing me the soft gape from where she took me.

I tell her as much: "You took me so beautifully, baby."

"Then why did you leave?" she keens.

Because I never want you to forget this night—what I can make you feel...

"I wanted to taste us. Don't you want that too?"

Her tits bob, the nipples taut buds that beckon me nearer.

"I can't come again."

"I think you can."

"No, no, no," she moans.

"Touch your clit."

She shudders but her fingers slide higher.

"There's my girl," I whisper, enjoying how her eyes flare at the words. "Tell me what you want."

Her bottom lip pops out as she circles her clit. "I'm empty."

"I'll fill you soon," I promise.

Her other hand tests her slit. "What will make you come back to me?"

My cock bobs with need. "Another orgasm."

A soft whine escapes her though she nods. Hesitantly. But she gives me permission...

The second my tongue finds the hypersensitive nub, her whimper makes my dick throb.

She fights my hold and nearly suffocates me as she squeezes her knees together and rocks from side to side as I flutter my tongue on her clit. Focusing there because I need her to get off again.

It's a point of pride.

Her sharp shriek tells me I'm close. How she jerks her hips is another clue.

Just before she hits it, I stop and maneuver out of her chokehold on me.

"I hate you," she screams, body straining until I blanket her.

My dick settles on her weeping pussy.

The scream bites off.

Her feral eyes find mine.

Her nails drag along the breadth of my back, scoring lines into the skin in a way I'll check out in the morning.

I kinda like the idea of setting off on our honeymoon in the States with her claw marks etched into me.

Seems fitting.

And everyone'll know I'm hers and, from the hickeys I intend to leave on her neck, that she's mine. If any of those goddamn baseball players catch a glimpse of her—yeah, baseball players—they'll see she's hands off.

Zee picked the honeymoon so we're going around the US, touring all thirty MLB baseball stadiums. The prospect must be hell for a hater of baseball, but when I complained that it wouldn't be fun for her, she kissed me quiet. Now, she'll tour each and every one of the stadiums in this jersey.

Talk about a gift that keeps on giving.

Before I can sink home, she rasps, "Wait."

Her fingers, once gripping my shoulders to hold me close, shove me away.

Floored, I back off.

Then, she slides her fingertips over my shaft, finding the end of the condom. As she rolls it up, I catch ahold of her wrist and still her.

"Zee?" I caution, panting because her touch is not only driving me crazy, but the promise of what she's doing makes me want to blow my load.

Her eyes lock on mine. "I'm ready, Colt. And I know you are too."

She's not wrong.

The past couple years have been hectic but great.

Clyde's sentence for first-degree murder and insurance

fraud was thirty years. If he only serves twenty-five of them, I'll be pissed, but some of my vengeance for the shitty father we got will be appeased, even if it doesn't come close to righting the wrong that was losing Loki, Betsy, and our other horses. I know Zee feels the same because getting him behind bars at all was worse than a dogfight.

After his arrest, Lydia's victims came forward. Turns out Marcy's diary housed a lot of secrets—those were what pinned Clyde down. His big drunken mouth was the source and they fed Lydia's blackmail operation. And it *was* an operation because she extorted enough people to cover the debts on her house and more.

Clyde threw Terry under the bus and a welter of other officials in an effort to reach a plea deal too. At least we're down one corrupt cop in town.

The breeding program is up and running, and my brothers are doing... well, they're *doing*.

Mom's practicing as a vet again after she went through the process of renewing her license, and she and Mrs. Abelman finally stopped hiding what they mean to one another.

After Juliette's passing, the triplets moved in with us, bringing their brand of mischief along as I attempt to teach them how to ranch—they declared a ceasefire with Callan, though they exist at opposite ends of the house.

The Bar 9 and the Seven Cs no longer exist—we merged in more ways than just our marriage, and now we live on the Bar 7.

But we still haven't fulfilled the contract because neither of us needed to.

Our marriage may have started by uniting two ranches, but it became about us.

Holding off on having a baby was our way of reclaiming our relationship.

Today's wedding was about Zee's reintegration into Pigeon Creek—she would never have gotten married in the church there before.

But this isn't *before* anymore.

It's now.

Now, Pigeon Creek is her home.

By choice.

And on our second anniversary, it seemed only right to renew our vows in the town where our ancestors were enemies and where our descendants will be family.

"You sure?" There's no withholding my grin.

It's loaded with my joy.

Sure, this is a topic worthy of discussion, but hell, I love her more than I did yesterday, and raising a family with her is all I've ever wanted, without knowing that's what I needed.

Her grin is as wildly joyous as mine. "I'm beyond sure."

I remove my grip from her wrist and let her fingers draw off the condom.

As she drops it on the floor beside the bed, I find her and slot the tip into her pussy.

Sinking back in, skin on skin, something we haven't done since that day at the lake, a shudder wracks through me at how damn good she feels.

"Oh, Colt," she cries, her hands at my shoulders, nails clawing at me again.

That small pause forgotten as we get back to where we were.

Her.

I.

Us.

Forever.

That we could make a kid tonight exhilarates me.

I never asked to be a father. Certainly never expected this. But there's nothing I want more than to be the daddy of a mini Zee.

Rocking my hips, I bite her bottom lip. "God, you take me so well, baby. Every fucking inch." I bottom out. "You feel so fucking right. So perfect."

She whimpers, spine arching as her head tips back on the pillow. Then, heels digging into my ass, she growls, "I want you to fill me."

From whimpering to growling in less than one minute?

I'd be a fool not to obey.

I give her what she wants—my hands grab her upper thighs and I use that grip to sink my cock into her.

"Colt," she moans.

"Zee," I rumble.

She sobs through it, heavy and thick with fulfilled need as we both reach a peak that has us seeing stars.

And as I fill her with my seed, I thrust. Gently. Slowing down. Savoring the moment as I claim her.

Without my brain registering that it's the only claim I've ever wanted to stake.

As both of us implode and explode, each of us picking up the other's pieces, I rasp, "You are *mine*, Zee Korhonen."

Her eyes drift open. One of her hands shifts higher, the tips rubbing along my jaw. "Are you mine, Colton Korhonen?"

I nip one of her fingers. "Since I was seventeen years old."

Chapter 56
Cody

Arcade - Duncan Laurence

PAST A WEEK AFTER THE BBQ...

The second I heard the words 'Butch Cassidy' being screeched across the ranch, I knew who was doing the shouting.

Except...

There's no way that the Tee I've been writing to for years and the Tee who's friends with Colt's wife are one and the same.

That's just *impossible*.

Improbable.

Im-damn-*plausible*.

Like being killed by a shark in the middle of the Canadian tundra.

Or winning the lottery without a ticket.

Right?

But then I kept an eye on her. I listened. Okay, eavesdropped. And I watched her with Zee. Who has to be the friend 'Z' she always talks about.

"This isn't happening," I mumble to myself, watching Tee beat Callan in some sort of battle scene in *The Witcher*.

Yet the impossible, improbable, and implausible is happening.

She's here.

In my kid brother's gaming room.

Eating popcorn.

Literally *keeping up* with Callan, the know-it-all.

In fact, she's whupping his ass.

And God, is she pretty.

I cut ties with her because I thought she lived in New York and I was making my home in Saskatchewan.

Now, I find out she's moving *into my house*.

"Cody! You going to play with us? I have another controller," Callan calls out.

I shoot him a tight smile that grows tighter when Tee flashes me a look.

Her gaze is piercing.

Direct.

Just like the woman I came to know.

Just like the woman who got me through that fucking mess in Vladivostok without even knowing it.

Just like the woman I didn't want to say goodbye to but who I wanted to protect.

Regardless of this revelation, nothing's changed. Not really.

My goodbye will have to stand.

Even if she's sitting so close to me, I could tangle my fingers in her hair and kiss her like I've wanted to for years.

Even though she smells like popcorn and I want to taste it on her tongue.

So many words I left unwritten...

...and I regret each and every one of them.

* * *

Cody's story is next!
You can preorder here:
http://books2read.com/pigeoncreektwogamazurke

Afterword

In early May, I lost an integral part of my team - Cynthia Mejia. May her gentle soul rest in peace.

We're left behind to remember her and to cherish her memory.

Much love, Cynthia.

You are missed.

xo

Extended Epilogue, Bonus Scene, & Author Note

Thank you so much for reading *Things Left Unsaid*!

I hope you're excited for Cody's story!

Long-term readers will have recognized the name 'Trever.' I named Harriet's foal after my gorgeous fur baby who I lost in 2022. Expect to see more of his brand of mischief on the page. :)

You can enjoy an extended epilogue here!

https://dl.bookfunnel.com/u97lcrhenz

Don't forget - the moment *Things Left Unsaid* hits 500 reviews, I'll be dropping a bonus scene in my Tea & Spoilers Room!

You can join here:

www.facebook.com/groups/SerenaAkeroydsTeaAndSpoilersRoom

Much love and thanks for reading,

Gem

Xo

Connect with G. A. Mazurke

For the latest updates, be sure to check out my website!
But if you'd like to hang out with me and get to know me better,
then I'd love to see you in my Diva reader's group where you
can find out all the gossip on new releases as and when they
happen. You can join here: www.facebook.com/groups/Sere-
naAkeroydsDivas. Or you can always PM or email me. I love to
hear from you guys: gamazurke@gmail.com.

Notes

1. Zee

1. Presumed Killed In Action

About the Author

G. A. Mazurke is the crazy lady behind Serena Akeroyd, crafter of smexy heroes you just wanna lick. While Serena has us expecting dark romance with lots of twists and turns ... G. A. is her more mainstream/contemporary personality.

She explores her sweeter side while keeping the sexy we love, where the women fall hard but the men fall harder.

Some of G. A.'s books will cross over into Serena's universes... so expect a cameo or two from beloved characters, while discovering new bands of brothers, with the banter, the laughs and the tears you are used to.

Triggers

Please be aware that *Things Left Unsaid* does deal with themes of child abuse and domestic violence, though never between our hero and heroine.

The characters in this story have experienced loss. From parents to siblings to pets.

A decade ago, there was an arson attack on a stables on the Seven Cs.

And our hero has experienced physical abuse as a child at the hands of his father.

There's also misinterpretation of self-harm.

Though these don't take place on the page, they are events that contribute to the people they've become.

Made in the USA
Las Vegas, NV
05 April 2025

20594751R00341